'So this is sex we're talking about.'

'Yes and no. Sex, yes, but it was more than that.' Sloane lowered her eyes and bit her bottom lip. 'Layla,' she said softly, 'I've always had this fantasy that someday I'd meet someone so exotic, so romantic that I would be overwhelmed to the point of abandonment.'

'And you found it.'

'I thought I had, but it all turned so ugly.'

Layla reached across the plush seat to pat the back of her friend's hand. 'Perhaps you should rethink your fantasies, cookie.'

Sloane made a weary effort to smile through trembling lips. 'I suppose,' she sighed. 'Right now it all hurts so badly.'

Layla took a deep breath. 'I know, darling. Trust me. I know.'

Beverly Sassoon

FANTASIES

ARROW BOOKS

Arrow Books Limited
20 Vauxhall Bridge Road, London SW1V 2SA

An imprint of the Random Century Group

London Melbourne Sydney Auckland Johannesburg
and agencies throughout the world

First published in Great Britain by Century 1990
Arrow edition 1990
Reprinted 1991

Typeset by Deltatype Ltd, Ellesmere Port
Printed and bound in Great Britain by
Courier International Ltd, Tiptree, Essex

ISBN 0 09 978190 5

I would like to dedicate this book to Catya, Elan, David, and Eden Sassoon. My love for each of you is pure and uncomplicated. It comes from deep within my soul and has no conditions.

And to all those who have ever had a fantasy.

ACKNOWLEDGEMENTS

I want to thank the following people for touching my life at exactly the right moment, in exactly the right way. Each one of you has made a special contribution that has made it possible for me to be the best me I can be.

Tillie and Wayne Adams, my mother and father, whose love I appreciate today more than ever.

Sharon Martin for her timing.

Bill Young for his devotion, laughter, and brotherly love.

Irene and Dr. Michael Pines for their ability to listen and understand.

Carol Connors for being the sister I never had and filling my life with music.

Rita Vale for being there at all times in a new beginning.

Carmen Parra for her years of caring.

George Shaw for knowing where it was all along and letting me find it myself.

Vidal for helping me to chart my course.

Maile Glover for helping me to navigate. Her years of loyalty as a friend and dedicated professional have helped to bring it all together.

Eden Sassoon for her serenity, endurance, and understanding.

David Sassoon for his compassion and communication.

Elan Sassoon for his insight and the courage to do it his way.

Catya Sassoon for her strength, willingness, acceptance, and belief in her mom.

Elaine and Jacques de Spoelberch; Ernie Del and George Savitsky; Lucianne Goldberg, Claire Zion, and Bill Grose for their special attention, talents and confidence.

I am especially grateful to have discovered the Higher Power that was by my side when I didn't know it.

Prologue

Sloane stood at the corner of Park and Fifty-Second Street waiting for the light to change, savouring the touch of spring in the air and the feeling of being in the city again. The day of her wedding, so many lifetimes ago, it had taken over five minutes to get from her limousine to the door of the Carlyle. She had been only eighteen then; she couldn't believe she was just nineteen now. She felt as if she were a hundred years old. Today there were no pushing, shouting photographers, no television crews elbowing and shoving, no microphones thrust into her face. Today, no one recognized her.

She pulled down the wide brim of her black straw hat until it touched the edge of her wraparound sunglasses.

On this kind of day New York seemed like the centre of the universe. The air that she remembered as fetid and thick as syrup was crystal clear and almost odourless.

She filled her lungs. The breath caught in her rib cage, producing a surge of dull pain. She exhaled slowly and closed her eyes for an instant in remembrance.

How, she thought, had it ever come to this?

Under her crisp grey linen dress and silk raincoat she wore only panty hose. The thought of anything else's constricting her made her cringe. As she'd dressed that morning, she'd barely been able to stand the weight of the thin dress fabric on her shoulders.

Then, on the New York-bound flight, she had carried the split of dreadful airline champagne that was her breakfast to the front of the first-class lounge. The electronic magic of telephoning from thirty thousand feet in the air still amazed her. When Layla's smoky voice came on the line, it had been as clear as if she were sitting in the next seat.

'Layla. It's me!' She spoke as loudly as she dared. There were only three other passengers in the lounge, but her paranoia told her they were not only listening but interested in what she had to say.

'Sloane! Darling! Where are you?' Layla asked in her familiar, expansive way.

'I . . .' Sloane glanced around the lounge. The man across the aisle had his head back. His eyes were closed. The earphones of the small tape cassette in his lap were firmly set on each side of his head. 'I'm on the plane. I'll be in around noon.' She closed her eyes against new tears. 'I'm sorry to do this to you on such short notice,' Sloane apologized.

'Don't be ridiculous. You come straight here to the office as soon as you land.'

'Layla, I know this sounds crazy, but could we go to lunch?'

'Ah . . . sure. If that's what you want,' she answered. 'Anything you want.'

'It's just that I'm starved for my old world. I thought lunch out would be cheerful.'

'Of course, darling. If you feel up to it. Are you all right? You want to tell me about it?'

'It's a long, ugly story. I'll tell you at lunch.' Sloane didn't want to talk. Not this way. She was so tired. So bone tired. She couldn't even cry anymore. She didn't have the strength.

'Sloane, darling,' Layla shouted over the crackle that was developing on the line. 'That man who called me from Acapulco last night. Was that the bullfighter?'

'No . . . no,' Sloane said. 'He was a friend. He helped me after . . .' She couldn't continue.

8

'Sloane, now listen to me,' Layla shouted. 'Are you hurt? He said there'd been an accident.'

'Well, not quite. I can't explain it over the phone like this.'

'I'll send the Rolls out for you. I have your flight number. Yitzak will meet you at the gate.'

Sloane sighed with relief. 'Thank you, Layla. That would be nice. I promise, I'll tell you all the awful details at lunch.'

'I'll be waiting.'

'Fine,' Sloane said, her spirits lifting for the first time in days. 'Still the Four Seasons?'

'They've installed a plaque over my table,' Layla said, laughing. 'Would you rather someplace less public?'

Sloane paused, then answered, 'No. The Four Seasons is fine. No one is going to recognize me anyway.'

The vast grill room of The Four Seasons had always depressed Sloane. Whatever season the management was trying to evoke with various flowers or potted plants, it always seemed like perpetual winter to her. The two-story-high plate glass windows were draped with curtains made of thousands of tiny chains that produced the gloom of a January rain. She preferred dining in cozier surroundings, Le Cirque or the Quilted Giraffe. But lunching with Layla Bronz meant The Four Seasons, where she held court at one of the banquettes against the west wall. The restaurant table had been Layla's lunch-time office since Sloane had known her. Here she brought the movers and shakers of her world. Here she dazzled and gossiped with the most amazing variety of people. Sloane knew she had dual goals: to fill up the glossy pages of *Realto* with lavish advertising for expensive objects, and to gain information. Information was Layla Bronz's coin. From information came money, but more importantly – Layla's grail – power.

9

Realto magazine was Layla's life, and she used its pages and their contents the way a Latin American dictator used his army.

Sloane stood at the reception desk at the top of the stairs. The maître d' instantly stepped from behind the reservation desk and bowed slightly, inclined his head, and lowered his eyes. 'How nice to see you again, Miss Taylor. Miss Bronz is expecting you,' he said in a hushed and reverent tone she knew had nothing to do with her and everything to do with Layla.

In the gloomy light made even dimmer by her dark glasses, she could see Layla seated at her table. Two nattily dressed men stood in front of her listening rapturously as she gestured and chattered. Layla hadn't changed her slicked-back ballerina-style hairdo in all the time Sloane had known her. She had tail-fin cheekbones and cossack's teeth. Her wide-set, dark eyes never left any face she addressed. One could almost see her brain working, driven by an unflagging energy that could tire a weaker being rapidly. Sloane felt better just watching her. Layla had been her enemy, then her friend despite the difference in their ages, and then had been a major force in Sloane's career. Just seeing her again filled Sloane with a sense of longing, a sense of wanting things to be the way they had been when Layla's influence had changed her life. Maybe Layla could help her figure out what had gone so terribly wrong.

The men stepped back as the maître approached the table, Sloane following a few steps behind.

'Sloane, darling!' Layla called, throwing her hands in the air. Each finger was tipped by a perfectly shaped long orange oval. The two men bowed, nodded, and moved on to their table against the far wall as Sloane slid onto the seat next to her friend.

Her arrival produced a flurry of service to the table. A captain, a waiter, and a busboy materialized from somewhere in the gloom and began circling the table,

10

hands fluttering. Sloane whispered her order to the captain as he deftly placed a fresh bourbon on the rocks in front of Layla. When they had all disappeared, Layla turned to face her. 'I almost didn't recognize you,' she whispered. 'You're done up like Liz after a lift. Are you in hiding?'

'In a way,' Sloane offered lamely, staring down at the snowy tablecloth.

Layla looked around. No one was paying them the slightest bit of attention. 'All right, lamb, tell,' she commanded in a low, conspiratorial voice. 'What the hell happened down there?'

'I don't know.'

'Is it over?'

'Worse.'

'What happened?' Layla watched as the waiter placed a flute of champagne in front of Sloane and disappeared.

Sloane took a long sip of the powder-dry wine. She felt it slide down her throat like an icicle. The difference in taste from the swill she had been drinking all morning sent a shiver down her spine. 'I think he tried to kill me,' she said without inflection.

'He *what*?' Layla shrieked, staring at her. Two heads at the table to their right leaned imperceptibly forward.

'Shhhh . . .' Sloane frowned, glancing around.

'Sloane, darling,' Layla said, leaning closer, a grave urgency in her voice. 'You're terrifying me.'

Sloane turned so that the brim of her large hat shielded her from view. She removed her dark glasses and looked straight at her friend.

Layla's bejewelled hand flew to the throat of her high-necked couture blouse. The bangles on her wrist slid down her arms, making a tiny eighteen-carat crash. 'Sloane!' she gasped through a sharp intake of air.

Sloane hadn't looked into a mirror since she left the plane, but she was sure nothing had changed.

Layla Bronz had never seen anything quite like it. The

11

famous face, one of the most beautiful she had ever known, looked like raw, purple hamburger from the bridge of the nose to above the eyebrows. The face of Sloane Taylor could change from wide-eyed ingenue to dark goddess of evil, depending on how the photographer caught it. But always, behind the wide-set, grey-green eyes and translucent skin, there glowed the presence of an incorruptible soul. Now, staring in horror at Sloane's face, Layla felt her stomach lurch.

Layla had once been in an auto accident with Long-Gone Tony. Taking a sharp curve on the Amalfi coast, they hit an oncoming truck. The windshield of the truck was shattered by the head of an Italian busboy from the Hotel Luna Convento. She had visited him the next day in a tiny hospital in the hills above Positano. That was the only other time she could remember ever seeing a pair of eyes quite like Sloane's at this moment. 'Good God, Sloane,' she said, her voice shaking. 'How awful.'

Sloane quickly replaced her dark glasses and took another sip of wine as Layla lifted a finger from the side of her glass of bourbon. A waiter appeared instantly. 'Please, Carlos,' she said, smiling, 'another champagne.' She turned to Sloane. 'Is that okay? I mean, you can drink.'

Sloane nodded slowly. 'Yeah, I can drink. I've been drinking for some time, quite steadily.'

'Is that a good idea? You're so swollen up.' Layla grimaced. Bad enough to look like that, without someone's commenting on it. 'You must be in terrible pain,' she continued, careful now that her voice was sympathetic.

'I don't know. I'm numb. My eyes don't hurt as much as this.' As she spoke, she quickly moved her hand to her cleavage and pulled aside the fabric.

Layla gasped.

Sloane's chest was the same purple-red as her eyes. Two crescents marked the top of her right breast. They looked like teeth marks.

'Sloane! Stop. I can't stand this.' Layla was angry now. 'This is an outrage! We'll have the bastard thrown in one of those charming Mexican jails for this. I'll call the editor of every newspaper in Mexico. He'll never work again!'

Sloane looked stricken. 'No, Layla, please. Don't do anything. Don't tell anyone. No one must know. Please! I'm so ashamed.'

Layla seemed afraid Sloane was going to cry. She signaled for the waiter to move the table so they could get up.

'What are you doing?' We haven't even ordered yet – '

Layla quickly gathered the crocodile bag and briefcase lying beside her. 'We're getting the hell out of here. Carlos . . .' She smiled stiffly at the waiter. 'Put the drinks on the bill, please.'

'Yes, Ms Bronz. Of course, Ms Bronz. You're not staying for lunch?'

Sloane should have known not to ask. Layla never answered rhetorical questions.

Sloane hurriedly followed her to the top of the stairs. When they reached the landing of the wide staircase leading to the East Fifty-second Street entrance, she asked, 'But where are we going?'

'You're coming with me. We're going back to my place and we're going to get you into bed.'

Sloane said nothing until they were safely inside the back of Layla's Silver Cloud. She leaned back against the plush of the seat and looked at Layla. 'Please, I mean it. No one can know.'

'No one is going to know, damn it,' Layla snapped.

Layla was furious. Furious at herself for not having done something earlier. All the signs of something crazy had been there. Everyone knew about how the world's most famous model, married to one of the world's richest men, had run off with Mexico's most famous bullfighter. It had all been fun and games, but Layla had thrown any editor or writer who wanted to do a story on the pair for her magazine out on their ear. Layla was no stranger to what loving a man could do to a woman's mind.

Layla had thought it had all just been a sudden freedom fling. It would soon be over and forgotten and Sloane would be back to work. Warner, somehow, would forgive her this. She would once again be the Bromley Woman, as Warner had promoted her to be all over the world, and everything would be forgiven and forgotten. All this business with the bullfighter would be yesterday's news, yellowing clippings in the media's great desk drawer.

But Sloane hadn't come back. She had disappeared into an exotic netherworld where no phone could reach her, where no one could find her. 'Sloane,' Layla now said softly, 'did you love him that much?'

Sloane stared straight ahead through the window that separated them from Yitzak. Slowly she said, 'It wasn't love, Layla. Not as you would understand it.'

'Try me.'

'I can't explain. Something bigger. Darker. Something almost evil. I couldn't leave. Forget it,' she said with a sigh. 'I just can't talk about it rationally. Not yet.'

Layla nodded. 'It's not drugs, is it, Sloane?'

'No, of course not. Drugs would be easy. There's help for that all over the place. There's help for booze and dope, for all kinds of addictions. Except this kind.'

'So this is sex we're talking about.'

'Yes and no. Sex, yes, but it was more than that.' Sloane lowered her eyes and bit her bottom lip. 'Layla,' she said softly, 'I've always had this fantasy that someday I'd meet someone so exotic, so romantic that I would be overwhelmed to the point of abandonment.'

'And you found it.'

'I thought I had, but it all turned so ugly.'

14

Layla reached across the plush seat to pat the back of her friend's hand. 'Perhaps you should rethink your fantasies, cookie.'

Sloane made a weary effort to smile through trembling lips. 'I suppose,' she sighed. 'Right now it all hurts so badly.'

Layla took a deep breath. 'I know, darling. Trust me. I know.'

Sloane lay back against a snowdrift of lace-edged Porthault pillows. Layla had called Nina from the car and told her to make up the guest room at the top of the house on Seventy-seventh Street.

Sloane loved the room. It was like a doll's, with a high-canopied bed. Being here, tucked in, pampered and fussed over, made her feel like a child again.

Nina had drawn her a perfumed bath and clucked disapprovingly as Sloane undressed. The bruises on her breasts and shoulders remained an angry, raw red in the centre. The edges were turning greenish. Nina's silence told her the maid had been warned to say nothing about Sloane's condition.

Nina was waiting when she returned to the bedroom enveloped in one of Layla's billowing satin nightgowns. She helped Sloane into bed and gently pulled the shoulders of her gown down to apply a cooling salve. When she was through, she replaced the gown on her shoulders, eased Sloane back against the pillows, and dimmed the bedside lamp two clicks.

'You are an angel, Nina.' Sloane squeezed her thin mahogany hand.

'Um. Angel,' Nina grumped. 'You've got a huge house full of angels out there in California. How come you're not there, Miss Taylor – or should I say, Mrs Bromley?'

'That's gone, Nina. It's just a name now. Everything is gone.'

'Some people don't know good when they have it,' she sniffed. 'What are you doing to yourself, girl?'

'It's a long, awful story, Nina.'

Nina shook her head in mute disapproval. She placed her hand on Sloane's forehead. 'You've got a fever, honey. You're burning up.' Her voice rose in alarm. 'I'm gonna call Dr Winship.'

Sloane tried to sit up, but the pain was too great and she fell back into the pillows. 'Please don't. It's probably just the flu.' But Nina had already left the room.

By the time the doctor arrived, Sloane's fever stood at 102°. He examined her, noting her bruises with silent concern. He administered a dose of antibiotics and she finally slept. As Layla walked him to the door, she said, 'Thank you for coming over, Roger. You are a darling.'

'Only for you, my dear,' the silver-haired man said with a smile. 'You were wise to call. She's a pretty sick girl. What happened? She looks as though she's been badly beaten.'

They were standing in the foyer. Yitzak stood at silent attention waiting to drive the doctor home. 'You know something, Roger? I think that girl is in terrible trouble.'

The doctor nodded. 'She's got some mild virus, Layla, but more importantly, she's been badly abused. She may even have a cracked rib.'

Layla stared down at the Tabriz runner and traced the pattern with the toe of her pump. 'Those marks on her breasts, Roger. Those are bite marks.' Layla's gaze drifted. 'I think she's gotten herself in way, way over her head.'

The next morning Layla awoke at six, worried about Sloane. She went to check on her, but upon entering the guest room she saw the rumpled bed. The bathroom was empty.

Layla found a note scrawled on a piece of the Tiffany stationery she left for guests in the little French writing desk between the windows.

I've gone back, Layla dear, it said in Sloane's familiar tiny hand. *Thank you for trying. I can't live without him.*

Sloane Taylor Bromley, raging with fever, covered with bruises and abrasions, was gone. Drawn away by a force she had said was stronger than love.

Layla slowly folded Sloane's note and stood tapping it against her chin.

They were all to blame. They saw what was happening and did nothing, thinking the situation was temporary. An affair that burned with such white-hot obsession surely had no staying power. Her secretary, loyal, level-headed Kayzie, had made an attempt to stop it when it had started. But Sloane would not, could not listen. Her husband, Warner, for all his power and money, could do nothing to rescue her. Not even Cole, Layla's faithful associate at the magazine, nor Alan, Sloane's friend since childhood, could stop her from her inevitable journey toward this destructive liaison.

Layla crumbled the note and returned to her office to call Warner at his estate in Bel Air. Even though it was three o'clock L. A. time she knew Warner would not want to wait for news like this.

He picked up the call himself on the first ring.

'Darling?' he said expectantly.

'Hello, Warner,' she said softly, lighting a cigarette. 'Don't be angry, please, there was nothing I could do.'

'Layla, what is it?' he asked with alarm.

'She was here. I got a call yesterday from some friend of hers in Acapulco. He told me she was on her way, but I had no idea what shape she was in until I saw her. Miguel Vellis had beaten her to a pulp.'

There was a long silence on the line. Layla knew Warner was taking the news badly. Finally when he spoke, he had to clear his throat hard. 'Where did you see her?' he asked.

'She wanted to have lunch. She had covered herself up pretty effectively, but under all the hat and dark glasses, well, she was a mess. I brought her back here and put her to bed. Poor darling. I don't think she's had proper sleep for days. I left her alone until now. I knew I should have checked, but I didn't. Now she's gone. My guess is that the bastard called her and talked her into coming back.'

'Layla, I don't know how much more of this I can stand.'

'What do you want to do, Warner?'

There was a long pause on the line. Layla drummed her nails on the desk.

'I think we've waited long enough, don't you, Layla?' he said, his voice tight with emotion. 'I say damn the publicity. We've got to go ahead with the story.'

'You're sure that's what you want to do, Warner? It will be a terrible scandal.'

'Do it!' he commanded. 'Get a hold of your reporter down there now. Let's put this animal out of business.'

'Melon Tuft can be pretty brutal. When she does a story like this, she uses everything.'

'Is there any way you can get her to go easy on Sloane?' he asked. Layla thought he sounded near tears.

'I'll try, darling. But once she goes ahead it's out of our hands. We can't control her. She'll write it her way or not at all and we need the story. It's your only hope of getting her back,' Layla said. She stopped short of adding . . . 'alive.'

Exhausted, Sloane found a seat in the waiting area for Aeromexico's Flight 704 for Mexico City, closed her eyes, and said the Lord's Prayer. She was impatient for the nine A.M. flight to board and leave, but even now she dreaded the takeoff. Warner once told her, back when she believed everything he said, that this was the one time a plane was totally vulnerable. If the giant engines failed, the plane couldn't turn back and land. It would freeze in the air, shudder, and plunge. Maybe she should wish the plane would crash. She could die somewhere deep in the Atlantic and nothing would matter anymore. Her torment would be over. Someone else could pick up the pieces, clean up the mess, and make the awful decisions that now confronted her.

She opened her eyes and looked around the crowded waiting area. The air smelled of cigarette smoke and sweat. The annoying businessman who had been staring at her since she arrived at the gate was still sitting across from her. By the look in his eyes, she knew he wanted to start a conversation with her. They always did. Men. Everywhere she went. Every plane, or restaurant, even on the street. Men always tried to find some excuse to talk to her and would go to almost comical lengths to make it look casual and nonchalant. They would drop things, ask her if she wasn't somebody they knew. Strangers helped her, unasked, with her coat or packages she carried. Men had been behaving like that for as long as she could remember. Even before she had the famous face. Sometimes she liked it, craved the attention. Other times she hated it. Right now it was the last thing she wanted. Now she wanted to be invisible.

Warner had liked her to get attention, even promoted it in subtle ways, as long as no one touched. That was a million light-years ago. A million drinks ago, a million sleepless, demon-filled nights ago. Alan, her oldest friend, now fed up with the mess she had made of her life, had compared her to a pony express rider who stumbles and falls but keeps on going. 'You just change ponies, Sloane.'

I'm fresh out of ponies. This last one damn near killed me.

Miguel.

The thought of him filled her with an overwhelming

sadness. She closed her eyes and massaged her throbbing temples.

'Miguel,' she whispered softly. 'How could this have happened?'

' 'Scuse me?' The man across from her leaned closer. 'Were you speaking to me?'

She opened her eyes. He wasn't bad looking, thirtyish, well-cut hair, a smooth brow, and good skin. He wore an expensive navy blazer with several overlapping brass buttons on the cuffs. Beautifully manicured hands protruded from the shimmering white of his shirtsleeves.

She smiled slightly and started to speak. The look on his face said it all. He stared at her with the alert, eager eyes she had seen so many times. Eyes that told her that this man, whoever he was, wanted to speak to the person he saw, the face, the body. He didn't want to speak to her – Sloane Taylor Bromley. He didn't care about her at all. But even if he had been able to see beyond the mask of perfect makeup that had always been her protection, even if he asked her to talk about herself, she couldn't. There wasn't anyone left inside to describe. Everyone she had tried to please had stolen a piece of her real self. Where was the Sloane behind the pleasing mask? Somewhere along the way she had lost the most important part of herself, her self-esteem. Perhaps she had never had it.

She felt her smile fade. 'No,' she said softly. 'No. I wasn't speaking to you.'

1

In the hot summer of 1966, Noreen Sloane Taylor lay sprawled on her couch watching Natalie Wood kiss James Dean on the flickering black-and-white television.

The tiny tract house in Bakersfield, California, sweltered in the hot winds that blew off the desert and swirled red construction dust through the treeless development.

Noreen's only relief came from a creaking hassock fan on which she rested her swollen feet. In the last two weeks she had left the worn Naugahyde chair only for a few hours of restless sleep and to go to the bathroom to see if anything was happening.

The baby *had* to come this week.

She was two weeks overdue and dreading the ordeal of labour. Noreen was tiny. She stood just shy of five feet and even pregnant had never weighed over a hundred pounds. She was terrified how her size might affect a normal delivery. Jack told her not to worry. He would be with her. That was all well and good, but he could walk away, have a cigarette, talk to people in the waiting room. She was the one who would have to take the pain.

She took another swig of her ever-present Coke. The ice had long ago melted. It tasted tepid, and sickeningly sweet.

She studied Natalie's face. Maybe, if she wished hard enough, she would have a girl who would look like Natalie. It could happen.

Please, God, let me have a girl, she prayed to the distant Baptist God she had abandoned to marry Jack Taylor, a fallen Mormon. She squeezed her eyes tight. *Dear Lord, I couldn't cope with a boy.*

To Noreen, boys meant sports and dogs and things rough and unpretty. They grew up to be men and a man's life was hard. Look at Jack — tall, handsome, jet-black hair, and a remarkable athlete. When she met him he was an all-California halfback. In college no one doubted Jack Taylor would be a first-round draft choice for the pros. Noreen had pictured her future as the wife of a famous sports celebrity, the travel, the clothes, the money, the lifestyle. She had been sure it was going to be like being married to a movie star.

They had married at the beginning of his senior year. When she became pregnant right away, the spectre of his having to go to Vietnam disappeared. But a month later their fabulous future came crashing down.

On a warm November afternoon Noreen sat in the stands and watched Jack get tackled. Her concern grew into terror as he remained on the ground, not moving, his legs jackknifed under him like a broken doll's.

The doctors said he would certainly walk again, even be able to dance with her in time. But the injury to his spinal column would keep him out of active sports for at least two years.

The job offers were not exciting. Selling cars, running a camping-goods store, managing a moving-company franchise. It was all sedentary work and unrelated to football, which, after Noreen, was Jack Taylor's true love.

He accepted the job to coach a high school team in Bakersfield before he told Noreen.

His taking that job had caused their first real fight. She was terrified he would reinjure his back and be a cripple. It took Jack's doctors and many nights of angry tears finally to convince her that he would be all right.

22

Noreen had relented, but something had gone out of her life. She knew she would have to invent another dream. Something to make the future worth working for.

Natalie Wood was speaking now. Her huge dark eyes were looking up at the camera, glistening with tears. Natalie had been making movies since she could walk.

The baby had to be a girl. The baby had to have Jack's black eyes and lashes and Noreen's high cheekbones and lithe figure. *Please God. So much has been taken away, please let me have* something *back*.

The contractions started just before midnight. She woke Jack. The old '60 Ford got them to the hospital with only moments to spare.

Noreen screamed when the doctor held up the baby. The shadow of the umbilical cord made her think it was a boy. A few seconds later, when the nurse placed it in her arms, she burst into happy tears. She had her baby girl! Now she had a chance.

And Noreen's prayers had, indeed, been answered. Mary Sloane Taylor was born beautiful. By the time she was six months old and sitting up in her stroller, she stopped people in their tracks. Shoppers at the supermarket, people on the street and neighbours alike, paused to remark on the beauty of the child. Her thick black curls, the double row of black eyelashes that swept down her pink cheeks, and the tiny budlike mouth enchanted everyone who saw her.

Jack begrudgingly resigned himself to his wife's near obsession with the child. It wasn't easy. He adored his wife and had been desperately afraid Noreen would leave him when it had become apparent that he would never be able to provide the life he had promised her. She had not left him physically, but that part of her that he craved, her tenderness, her caring about his welfare, was directed at their child like a bright, relentless sun that left him standing, untended, in the weeds of his failure.

He made the only accommodation available. He gave

23

in to Noreen and her as-yet-unfocused dreams for their beautiful baby girl.

When Noreen read an article in *McCall's* about sudden infant death syndrome, she left Jack's bed and took to sleeping on the pull-out couch in the baby's room. When the baby started to crawl, Jack, at Noreen's request, dutifully lined the underside of the coffee table with foam rubber in case she hit her head. When the fussing and concern over her every whimper and cough, every meal and bowel movement, got to be too much, he quietly slipped away to the local bar, where he would drown his sorrows in a few beers.

One night he arrived home later than usual. As he pulled the car into the driveway, he could see the kitchen light was still on and knew Noreen would be sewing at the kitchen table. She made all of the baby's little dresses, intricate creations, shirred and beribboned, each with a matching sunbonnet to protect her porcelain skin against the relentless California sun.

As he reached the screen door, he stopped short. Noreen was seated at the kitchen table as he expected. Mary Sloane, up well after her bedtime, was in her high chair opposite her mother. Something was strange about her face. The little girl looked oddly beautiful, like a painted doll. The table in front of Noreen was covered with makeup, blushers, creams, brushes, and tiny pots of colour. Propped against the tray of the high chair was a magazine open to a full-page photograph of Elizabeth Taylor.

Bewildered, he watched as Noreen raised a brush and applied another layer of colour to the little girl's cheek.

He pushed the door open. 'What's all this?' he asked, sweeping his arm around to encompass the scene.

'Doesn't she look fabulous?' Noreen beamed up at him, her hand pausing in midair. Seeing Jack, the baby squirmed in her chair and squealed with delight.

'Honey, is that a good idea?' he asked tentatively. 'I mean, won't that stuff do something bad to her skin?'

Noreen rose, wiped her hands on the pockets of her chenille wrapper, and started straightening up the mess on the table. 'I just wanted to see how she's going to look,' she said tersely.

'What are you talking about, "going to look"?' he said. He walked to the refrigerator and bent to look for a beer.

'That's what I wanted to tell you,' she said, returning to her chair. 'The most exciting thing happened today.' She placed both hands flat on the table, straightening her back against the hard chair.

He popped the top off the last bottle of beer. 'What?' he mumbled around the neck of the bottle.

'Well,' she said, starting slowly, savouring sharing her exciting news. 'We were at the supermarket today. I had Mary Sloane in that little seat in the shopping cart, you know. Anyway, this man comes up to us by the vegetable counter. I couldn't remember if we had any carrots, so I was just standing there thinking for a minute.'

'Noreen, honey, get to the point. What man came up to you?'

She reached for her purse on the opposite chair and extracted a card. 'This man,' she said, handing the card to Jack. 'His name is Sam Malloy and he's with a big model agency in Los Angeles. He said he'd never seen such a beautiful child. He really made quite a fuss. He wants Mary Sloane to model.'

Jack studied the card skeptically. 'Model? She just learned how to walk, for Christ's sake. What kind of modelling does a baby do?'

'Oh,' she said uncertainly, 'catalogues, television commercials, all kinds of stuff. You see babies in the magazines all the time.'

Jack took another swig of beer. 'Not my baby you don't.'

'I think it would be fun. It would mean going into L.A. a couple of times a week. We could —'

Noreen was cut short by the sharp sound of Jack's

slamming his beer bottle down on the countertop. 'I said no, Noreen! And I mean *no*!'

'But Jack . . .' Noreen could feel the hot tears welling up. She tried to fight them back but it was no use.

Jack pulled out the chair on the other side of the makeup-strewn table. He was dog tired. The team had lost the first game of the playoffs that afternoon by the humiliating score of 28–0. His back had been bothering him again and he feared for his job. The last thing he wanted to do was have to talk Noreen out of some harebrained scheme that even if it did work – which he doubted – would have the effect of putting his kid to work. He knew they needed money and it pained him. He also knew Noreen was interested in more than the money. She had always been movie-star crazy, reading those magazines, watching movies on TV until near dawn. A part of her had never grown out of her teenage crush on Hollywood. While it was her fantasy world it was harmless, but now it was spilling over into his life and he didn't like it one goddamn bit. What would people think of him, putting his *baby* to work?

He took Noreen's hand. He would try another tack. 'Look, hon. That kind of thing really isn't healthy for a kid. You never know who she's going to be around. She could come home with all kinds of colds and crud. You know how infections go around.' That should do it, he thought. Just the mention of germs made Noreen hysterical.

'Jack, if you don't let me do this, I will leave you.' Noreen spoke firmly, in a voice he had never heard her use. It was free of hysteria or anger, almost frighteningly calm.

Jack sat stunned. Noreen's big blue eyes were even with his and he could see a tiny nerve jerking at her right temple.

She rose and lifted Mary Sloane out of the high chair, hitching her up onto her arm. 'I mean it, Jack. Don't test me.'

26

He knew she meant it. He felt at that moment she was capable of walking right out of the kitchen with the baby, getting in the car in her bathrobe, and driving to Los Angeles with nothing more than the change from the grocery money.

He pushed himself away from the table. Every muscle ached with fatigue. His back and shoulders throbbed. 'Better wipe that crap off her face before you put her to bed,' he said.

Mary Sloane's career was never discussed again.

Before the year was out, Mary Sloane Taylor was earning more than her father. The little family moved to Santa Monica to be closer to her work. Jack was able to find a high school coaching position, albeit for less than he was making in Bakersfield, but his take-home pay was no longer the point. The down payment on the house in a middle-class neighbourhood was advanced by the ad agency with whom Noreen had signed a two-year contract for Mary Sloane. The camera loved the bright-eyed baby and she loved the camera back. She moved quickly in the business. Her first television jobs were doing commercial spots for local stores. She was four.

She was spotted by account executives for the Happy Snappy fruit juice company, who signed her to do her first national ad. Then came the calendar in which Mary Sloane represented each of the twelve months with a different breed of puppy. A very lucrative contract with a toilet paper company was her first speaking role on television.

At six, like every other little girl, she lost her two front teeth and her services were no longer required.

As far as Noreen was concerned, the situation was merely temporary. Mary Sloane's permanent teeth would grow in soon enough. She had to start school in the fall anyway. Noreen did not see this as a setback, merely a

pause in her career that would give her time for school
and lessons – in dance, piano, voice, and both singing and
diction.

Noreen had more plans for her daughter during the
hiatus that she did not share with Jack. A little plastic
surgery on what Noreen felt were her slightly protruding
ears was first. Next, Noreen arranged legally to drop the
name 'Mary' to the simple and more elegant 'Sloane.'

She was only seven.

She bounced into the house and flung her leotard and
ballet slipper bag onto the chair in the front hall. She knew
her mother would yell at her about leaving it there. She
didn't care. Mummy was driving out to Tarzana to visit her
ailing mother and that meant Sloane had the entire evening
to be alone with her daddy. She loved their time together.
Sometimes they stayed home and made a mess in the
kitchen, frying hamburgers and making homemade
brownies from a mix. Sometimes she dressed up and he
took her to a little Italian restaurant down by the Santa
Monica pier. These rare evenings were the most precious
hours in Sloane's life – just her and her daddy on a 'date.'

She was halfway up the stairs to her room to change
from her school clothes before she realized something
was different. There were low voices in the living room
and she could hear someone, a man, telling her mother to
pull herself together 'before Mary Sloane gets home.'

She whirled around and ran back down the stairs and
through the open arch of the living room. She recognized
Dr Williams and Eddie Worshovski, her father's assistant
coach, who picked him up every morning for work. Her
aunt Jean was there, and Mrs Marmelson from next
door. It wasn't a party. No one was drinking smelly
liquor from fancy glasses. There were coffee cups around
and an ashtray full of cigarettes. No one seemed to know
she was there.

'Hullo,' she said shyly.

Everyone stood and started talking at once. Noreen ran from the other side of the room, knelt down, and scooped Sloane up in her arms. She was crying. Her mother didn't cry unless something was terribly wrong, like the time Grandma Sloane had to go to the hospital in an ambulance with a plastic thing over her face.

'Mummy, what's the matter?' Sloane asked. She could feel her own tears starting in reaction to her mother's. 'Why are all these people here? Where's Daddy? Tonight's our date night. We are going to –'

'I know, darling, I know,' her mother said, still holding her. She pulled back and brushed a strand of hair from Sloane's forehead. 'Daddy's been hurt. He's at the hospital. Eddie and Dr Williams and I are going there now. Mrs Marmelson will stay with you and fix you a nice dinner.'

'But Daddy and I are going to make hamburgers. He promised,' Sloane said, her small brow wrinkled in confusion.

Dr Williams stepped forward and reached for her. She pulled away angrily. 'I want to see Daddy. What hurt him? Why?' Then the tears started in earnest. Great wet, rolling streams poured down her face with each gasping sob.

What had hurt Jack Taylor were the 224 cement-hard pounds of a high school junior Jack had suited up for a little practice scrimmage after class that day. The boys on the team hooted and cheered when they saw their coach in full team regalia trotting onto the field. The boy hadn't meant to hit Coach Taylor so hard, or from behind. It just happened. Jack Taylor crashed to the ground and once again, didn't get up.

Jack Taylor lingered on life support for less than a week. Then he was gone. 'Massive trauma to the spinal column' were the words Sloane remembered hearing. He was almost thirty years old when he died.

He left his tiny daughter with a lifetime's worth of love and no one to give it to.

In the year that followed Jack Taylor's untimely death, Sloane began to notice her mother change.

She got thinner, not a sick-thin born of heartache, but a trim, glamorous thin from strenuous dieting and tennis. Her clothes got brighter, her hair lighter until it was a beige-white, high and fluffy and immaculately tended.

Sloane would hear her on the phone in the downstairs hall referring to herself as 'Sloane Taylor's manager,' booking appointments for Sloane to audition or compete for everything from TV sitcom roles to Little Miss Whatever beauty pageants.

As Sloane grew more beautiful, her mother grew more ambitious for her, more aggressive in promoting her career and more relentlessly focused on Sloane's appearance. She blatantly maneuvered to get invited to charity functions to which she dragged Sloane, manipulating her daughter into charming important guests.

But Sloane never questioned her mother's judgment, nor refused to cooperate. She had been doing whatever her mother wanted for so long it just seemed natural, even when it made her uncomfortable to be nice to people she didn't even know.

And then Noreen started to go out on dates.

Steve, a friend of Sloane's agent, was the first. He came to pick Noreen up in a big white convertible with tail fins. Sloane came skipping down the stairs from her room, where she had been struggling with freshman algebra, happy for the distraction. She was wearing very short shorts and a skimpy halter top. From the middle of the stairs she could see a frown clouding Noreen's face. Sloane thought it was because she had taken a break from her homework. She would soon learn differently.

*

It was spring of 1984, Sloane's senior year in high school, and she was in her bedroom making her daily check to see what had been moved or changed.

'Daarrr-ling,' Noreen called from the bottom of the stairs.

Sloane quickly shut the drawer of her dressing table. The eyeliner she had wedged upright against the inside edge had been dislodged. Noreen had been snooping again.

She waited for her mother to call a second time. She could tell from Noreen's tone of voice that she was displeased about something. It couldn't be anything she had found in her room. There wasn't anything to find. Sloane had no secrets. Secrets would be impossible with Noreen around.

'Daaar-ling.' Noreen's voice grew more insistent.

'Yes, Mother?' She glanced around the tidy room and noticed the library copy of *Jane Eyre* lying on top of her schoolbooks. Well, she did have one secret after all. Quickly she slipped it into the storage space in the window seat. It wouldn't do for Noreen to think she had been reading. She was supposed to be lying on her slant board letting the blood rush to her head. Noreen insisted that it did something great for the skin, but Sloane never saw any difference.

'Darling!'

Sloane jumped. Her mother was standing in the bedroom doorway. She was wearing a blue silk shirtwaist dress that emphasized her China-blue eyes and tiny figure. Her hair was gleaming blonde-white and freshly coifed. Wispy bangs mingled with her false eyelashes.

Noreen was holding a sheaf of official-looking papers. 'Sloane, dear, I left these applications for you on the kitchen table. You didn't see them?'

'I saw them, Mother. I just haven't had time.'

Noreen eased herself onto the foot of the bed. Her feet did not reach the floor. She looked disappointed. A look Sloane knew all too well as the prelude to criticism.

'Dear,' Noreen said, arranging the applications neatly in her lap. 'You know the deadline for the Miss California is on the fifteenth.' She paused, her eyes falling on Sloane's school jacket. 'I thought you were going to send that blazer to have the sleeves fixed. They don't hang right.'

Sloane nodded.

Noreen pulled a sheet of paper from the pile. 'And they insist on a double set of photos. Did you pick them up?'

'Well . . .' Sloane began, 'I did, but the color was funny. That taffeta dress wasn't a real red red. It was kind of orangy. The lab said they would redo them.' She slipped out of her pleated school skirt and reached for a hanger.

Noreen's lips tightened. 'The color was funny,' she said, her voice flat. 'Don't you think I'm a better judge of that, dear? I would like to have seen them. Sloane, don't loop that skirt over the hanger that way. Use the one with the clips.'

'I'm sorry,' Sloane said softly. 'The pictures will be ready tomorrow. I'll pick them up right after school. Everything will be in the mail by tomorrow night.'

Sloane stepped to her closet and pulled out a white linen suit with blue piping on the jacket. She held it in front of her and faced her mother. 'Is this all right for dinner?' she asked hopefully.

Noreen glanced at the dress. 'Umm. Nice. I like you in that dress. But the last time you wore it you used too much blue eye shadow. Grey would be better, and wear your strap sandals. The heels make your legs look better.'

'So who's coming to dinner?'

'Oh . . . the Rigbys,' Noreen said to the ceiling. 'The Dennisons and a lovely man named Fletcher Walker.'

Sloane *knew* it. Whenever her mother put on that fake casual voice, she was up to something. This Fletcher Walker had to be yet another one of her 'must meet' people as she always called them.

She hung the dress on the back of the closet door and sat down on the chintz-covered stool in front of the dressing table. 'Okay.' She knew she was supposed to ask. 'Who is Fletcher Walker and why do I need to know him?'

Noreen carefully placed the applications on the night table, giving them a little pat. 'He owns Global-Walker Industries. He has a fabulous house out in Portuguese Bend and owns his own plane. But best of all, he's interested in sponsoring a girl for the state contest.' She leaned back, looking pleased with herself.

So that was it. Sloane knew she was supposed to be pleased. She wasn't. She had let the situation go unprotested long enough. 'Mom,' she said, 'you know if I enter the preliminaries I won't be able to be in the senior play. I already have the lead if I want it. I'd really like to do that.'

'The senior play?' Noreen said. Her tone held an edge of ridicule that made Sloane's palms grow moist. 'But you know, darling, the state contest leads automatically to Miss America. You can always do a little high school play.'

'I'm going to be a senior for only three more months, Mother,' Sloane muttered. Once again she was making her arguments too late. She should have started objecting to yet another beauty contest from the very start.

'Well,' Noreen said, pushing herself up off the bed, 'we shall see. Now hurry along, dear. People will be here at seven.'

Sloane knew what her mother would say next. She would bet her life on it.

Look your best, dear,' Noreen called through the door.

Look your best. How she hated that phrase. As though her life weren't a constant effort to do just that.

She sat at the dressing table staring at but not really seeing her reflection in the huge bulb-surrounded mirror. At the moment she wasn't wearing what she had come to think of as The Mask. The Look Your Best Mask consisted of a carefully made-up face, perfectly set hair, and the proper clothes. She refocused her eyes on her schoolgirl face which had only a hint of blusher, a precisely made-up mouth designed to look as though she hadn't spent fifteen minutes with lipliner, and thick dark hair, casually combed back behind ears. Now her hair would have to be washed, hot-combed for body, and smoothed into perfect shape before she could leave her room.

Everything good that had ever happened to her had happened when she wore The Mask. What would happen to her life, she wondered, if she did the unthinkable and refused to put it on anymore? If she refused to wear the makeup at all, even the little she used for school? Would she become invisible? She shuddered at the risk of it and obediently began to prepare for the evening's ordeal.

She liked the Rigbys well enough. Ed Rigby was her lawyer, or rather, the lawyer for Norsloane Productions, the company Noreen had formed to market her daughter. He and his wife, Carol, had been family friends since they first moved to Santa Monica, and Irv Dennison was her modeling agent.

The part she hated was having to be sweet to a stranger because he had the money and the clout to get her into more beauty contests.

They were all waiting for her, having drinks in the sun room. Noreen was flitting around with a tray of little sausages stuck with toothpicks and giving orders to a maid hired for the evening. Noreen was talking to her as though she had worked for the family for years.

Sloane kissed the Rigbys, hugged and kissed Irv Dennison and his wife, then turned and walked directly toward Fletcher Walker with her biggest runway smile. She was aware that Noreeen was watching her every move.

Fletcher Walker had to have been over forty. He was

tall and thin with thick, wavy grey hair. The crest of each wave glistened with hair goop. He wore heavy, square tortoiseshell glasses. His suit was as shiny as his hair and the same colour. His silk shirt and tie were pink and matched so precisely they looked like they came from a kit. He wore a huge gold Rolex over his too wide shirt cuff.

He was pleasant enough during drinks, and at dinner he mentioned that he was single. Sloane felt Noreen's foot bump against the side of her sandal under the table. That had been happening a lot in the last year, in restaurants, at other people's homes, in meetings at the agency. Even though Sloane had not worked nearly as much in the last three years, preferring to concentrate on her classes at Dearfield Academy, Noreen insisted that she do part-time modeling and fashion shows on weekends. Entering the contests, she insisted, had to do with publicity, not prizes. Publicity for what? Sloane often fumed. So I can be famous for being famous? She wanted to act. She wanted to be taken seriously for once, and being in the senior play was important. If only she knew how to fight for it.

She always had the same reaction to Noreen's bumping foot or the annoying humming sound she made when an attractive man entered the room. It didn't take Sloane long to realize that attractive to Noreen meant 'powerful' – a big agent, a producer, a well-known casting director or celebrity.

Listening to Fletcher chatting during dinner convinced her that she didn't particularly like him. She didn't dislike him either. Her feelings were of total indifference.

Because of her looks and celebrity she had been dating since she was fourteen with Noreen's wholehearted encouragement. Sloane enjoyed being popular; she liked the parties and dances and going to restaurants. But she might as well have been dating robots. Noreen never ceased in reminding her that 'men' – as she referred to anyone male and older than thirteen – wanted to be seen with her pehaps more than they wanted to have sex. It never occurred to Sloane that she could have a real friendship with any of them, much less fall in love. They were just dates. Like a new dress, they were something to wear when she went out. As far as she was concerned, Fletcher was simply another one, only older and duller.

She had just finished the tasteless chocolate mousse her mother bought from the supermarket freezer and scooped into fancy crystal glasses when she realized Fletcher was speaking to her. She looked up to see him from across the table through his swim-goggle glasses. From the quizzical look on his face she perceived that whatever he had said to her was a question.

'I'm sorry?' she said brightly.

'I said,' he told her, 'that I'd love to have you come to Long Beach for dinner tomorrow night. If you're free, of course.'

Before Sloane could make a sound she heard her mother piping up from the end of the table, 'Of course she's free!' She said it with such glee. Sloane stared into her dessert dish in mortification. 'You're free, right, Sloane, darling?'

'I'm delighted!' Fletcher cooed. 'Just delighted. I'll send my car. Say, sevenish?' He directed his words to the air in the middle of the table.

Sloane looked down the table at her mother, her lips together to form the word 'but.' No sound emerged. She closed her eyes for an instant and then said quietly. 'That would be very nice, Fletcher. Of course I'm free.'

The only thing she wanted more than to push herself away from the table and race to her room was to avoid a scene with her mother. She was trapped. A feeling she was all too familiar with.

The following day Sloane arrived home later than usual because of play practice. She would have to hurry to be ready for Fletcher Walker's car at seven. She knew there was no hope of getting dressed alone. Her mother always came to her room to supervise her appearance for any important occasion.

Noreen sat on the edge of her daughter's bed and frowned at the peach linen dress Sloane was holding. 'I think your black Oscar de la Renta. The one with the nice neckline and the puffed sleeves.'

Sloane was all too familiar with the dress. Noreen had wheedled it out of a boutique owner when Sloane did his show last winter. The dress was too old for her. The 'nice' neckline was cut nearly to the waist. 'You really think so, Mom?' she said. 'It's kinda low.'

Noreen ignored her protest and held out her hand. 'Let me see your nails.' Noreen grabbed her wrists. 'Umm. I think a brighter polish, don't you?' It was not a question. 'You go shower. I'll come up and do them as soon as I put dinner in the warmer.'

Sloane shook free and stuffed her hands in her pockets. 'I can do them, Mother,' she said in a small voice.

Sloane walked toward the bathroom, relieved that she would at least be alone in the shower. She turned on the cold-water tap and let it run until it was icy. Stepping into the frigid spray, she let it pound on her body, enduring yet welcoming the pain until she could stand it no longer. Maybe the shock would give her a heart attack and she wouldn't have to spend the evening with rich, boring Fletcher Walker and his rich, boring friends, whoever they might be.

The car arrived promptly at seven, but Sloane knew to linger getting dressed. Her mother would want to make sure the neighbours saw the white stretch limousine idling at the curb. The most exciting thing that happened on their street was Sloane's occasionally dramatic departures in fancy cars.

She settled back in the sleek, silent car. It had a bar, a television, and a stereo. Maybe the neighbours and her mother were impressed, but she wasn't. It never mattered how fancy a car was if it was taking her somewhere she didn't want to go. She hated getting things out of people. That had never bothered her mother. If she wanted something, she just asked for it. Sloane had seen people so shocked by Noreen's effrontery that they simply gave her what she wanted. Noreen had never been that way before her husband died, but then, she seemed to think it was her right. Asking for anything hence mortified Sloane, and as she grew older, her sensitivity about it just increased.

If this Fletcher person sponsored her for the Miss California pageant, she would be parading around in a bathing suit while her friends were packing to go to college. Everyone except her best friend, Alan Wade. All he ever talked about was getting out of L.A., where he felt no one understood him but Sloane. Since eighth grade they had shared a fantasy of running off together. Not as lovers. Everyone at school knew Alan was gay or at least sensed that he was different. Noreen felt their friendship was a complete waste of time.

'What can he do for you?' she had sneered.

'He's my friend,' Sloane would say softly, and change the subject.

Alan was becoming the catalyst for their escalating bickering.

He was at Dearfield on a gymnastic scholarship. He was also deceptively strong. Anyone who mistakenly thought he could be teased found out differently fast.

Alan became Sloane's ally in her running battle with her mother's attempts to control her life. Sloane reciprocated by listening to the continuing soap opera of his affair with a divorced Hollywood agent. The man alternately ignored Alan and showered him with gifts.

Alan's lifestyle and outrageous personality gave him a celebrity status within the closed world of the private school that matched Sloane's own – although hers was a result not of flamboyance, but of her enviable career and stunning good looks.

In the darkest, most depressing moments of her constant fight to endure her mother's domination, it was Alan who instilled in her an ability to detach herself from her feelings of being smothered by manipulation.

'This isn't all there is, honey-buns,' he would say during their long hours on the phone. 'There's a world for us out there, just you wait.'

The world he promised was New York. A fantasy place where they would both be free. They would have their own apartments and fridges full of Rocky Road.

New York.

It was only a dream but it was theirs and it kept them both sane. Just thinking about it sometimes made her wistful and sad.

That day in history class when she told Alan where she was going for dinner he said, 'Sounds like another "pleasing Noreen" project to me.' And he was right. She knew if he were with her now, he would answer her complaints by pointing out, 'You're the one riding in the car, babe. You're the one who got all tricked out with five miles of eyelashes and cleavage to Cleveland. When are you going to learn to say enough?'

'Stop it!' she said aloud. 'You know I can't.' She clapped her hand to her mouth and cringed, afraid the driver had heard her. He would think she was crazy, but the glass between them was firmly closed and she sighed with relief.

Without warning, the car suddenly turned off the main road and headed away from the ocean. The area Fletcher lived in was one of vast estates. She had been to promotion parties in the palatial homes here but never by herself. The car was moving along a private road.

On either side of the car stretched graceful white fences. Beyond the fences lay rolling fields that looked more like a vast manicured lawn. She knew there must be horses somewhere.

The house at the end of the road was an imposing

Italian villa with a circular driveway of cobblestones that made ominous rumbling sounds under the wheels. An elaborately tiled fountain splashed in front of the double door. Peacocks strutted at the edge of the driveway, cocking suspicious one-eyed looks at her as the driver helped her out of the car.

A uniformed butler stood in the doorway. He greeted her by name and ushered her into an enormous foyer off of which radiated several even larger rooms. She followed him into one of them, a library with shelves that rose two stories high, filled with thousands of leather-bound books. She stood in the middle of the room not knowing what to do or say.

The butler disappeared without a word and in less than a minute returned with a silver tray bearing a single chilled cocktail glass. He held the tray directly in front of her and bowed slightly. There was no way she could refuse the drink, even though it was the last thing in the world she wanted. Her drinking consisted of an occasional beer and a sip of champagne on her birthday.

She accepted the drink with a tentative smile and stood staring at it well after the butler disappeared. She recognized it as a martini. She took a sip. To her surprise it tasted interesting. She felt it sliding and tingling all the way down her throat. She sat down on the long leather couch in front of the walk-in fireplace and took a larger sip, liking the pleasant floating feeling it was giving her.

Uneasy, she looked through the double doors to the hall beyond. Where were the other guests? Where was Fletcher? The thought occurred to her that she might be the only guest and she took another sip.

Sloane studied the ceiling. It was a spectacular thing, a work of art. A wooden grid with insets of painted tiles, a different animal scene on each. As she searched the ceiling for some sort of repeated pattern, she heard a voice from the hall.

'Ah, there you are, my dear,' the voice boomed.

She turned to see Fletcher, no more attractive than he had been the night before, striding into the room.

'How wonderful you look!' he said extending his hand.

He was wearing a beige silk shirt open at the neck, beige silk trousers, and soft beige leather loafers with no socks. The clothing was almost the exact shade of his skin.

The drink was affecting her in an odd way. *Of course I look wonderful,* she thought. *I've got on my mask, Fletcher, and my mask will make you want to sponsor me for the Miss California pageant.* What she said aloud was, 'Hello, Fletcher. You have rabbits on your ceiling.'

He smiled and stared at her chest as they shook hands. She was overdressed. How could Noreen have let her wear this dress? It was too much for the occasion and she didn't like the way Fletcher focused on the neckline.

'I'm so glad you like it. It took forever to build. I brought the panels from Italy. Come, let me give you a tour.' There were little sweat beads on his sideburns making little white tracks in his bottled tan. 'Bring your drink,' he said, glancing towards her glass. 'Ah, you need another.'

Why not? she thought. That one tasted terrific and it made him bearable. Another one might make him almost interesting.

The butler was summoned, and once they were armed with fresh drinks they strolled through the ground-floor rooms.

Fletcher's lecture on Italian Renaissance art and European antiques was lost on her, but it didn't seem to matter. He droned on, in love with the sound of his own voice as he pointed out how he had spent his money. Sloane was distracted by the realization that she was indeed the only guest. Her rage at her mother was beginning to make her head pound by the time the butler announced dinner.

When they entered the vast dining room she was

confronted with a table large enough to seat fifty people. There were two place settings. His and hers.

The butler helped her into her chair. She thanked him and gazed around the table in panic. In front of her was a plate with an array of silver fanning out from either side – spoons and knives of different sizes and shapes to the right of each place setting, forks, several of them, to the left. There was more silverware across the top of the plates and four wineglasses.

A woman Fletcher introduced as the butler's wife served the first course as wine was poured. Sloane didn't know how to refuse politely and her glass was filled and filled again.

By the time a tiny glass of what Fletcher described as 'palate-cleansing sorbet' was set in front of her, the meal was a blur.

The only way she knew which implement to use was to watch what Fletcher did and try to copy him. Mercifully, he was a travel nut and talked on and on about places she had never been. She was able to ask him questions that would elicit long, rambling discourses on the beauty of central Turkey and the history of the development of Punta del Este.

Through the haze of wine she watched as the butler placed a glass bowl of some kind of clear liquid in front of her. At the bottom floated something that in the dim candlelight looked like cloves or raisins. She looked for the appropriate spoon. There was a dessert spoon remaining, and as she reached for it, she saw Fletcher nimbly dip his fingertips into the liquid and dry his hands on his huge linen napkin. Her body went limp at what she had almost done. She studied the spoon, trying to make it look as though she was interested in the monogram, then laid it aside and imitated Fletcher.

O Lord, how long? she thought in a silent prayer. *How long is this meal going to last? Which makes you pass out first, wine or boredom?*

As if by divine deliverance Fletcher pushed back his chair. In her relief and gratitude she vaguely heard him telling the butler to serve coffee and brandy on the terrace.

They sat opposite each other in high-backed garden chairs on the flagstone terrace. The night air smelled of jasmine. The view across the rolling lawn took in a man-made waterfall cascading down the hills that climbed away from the property. The waterfall was illuminated by hidden floodlights in the underbrush. It would have been a scene of utter calm and tranquility had she not been so drunk. Maybe she wasn't drunk. Could you be drunk if you were aware that you were? She laughed too loudly. Apparently it was the correct response to something Fletcher had said. He looked pleased and continued talking about the wonderful films he had of the rain forests on Saba – wherever in the world that was.

He was describing some sort of beast that hangs upside down in the rain forest and spits on camera lenses when she noticed the butler whisking away her empty brandy glass and replacing it with a fresh one.

'Come,' he said excitedly, 'let me show you my slides.' He reached for her hand, and before she could think of some way to protest, they were sitting on a low couch in a small screening room. Fletcher held a slide changer. Somewhere on the far wall she could distinguish a fuzzy square of light, changing stills of trees, small animals, and sky.

All she wanted was for Fletcher to bring up the Miss California contest so she could go home, tell Noreen she had done the job, and get out of the push-up bra that was crushing her rib cage and making breathing painful.

Now pictures of an airplane popped on the screen. He was saying something about flying it to a house he owned on Catalina Island.

'I'd love it if you would. I'm planning to fly over one weekend next month,' she heard him say.

'I'm sorry?' she apologized, desperately trying to clear her head. 'I was distracted. Your slides are so interesting. You would love it if I would what?'

'Come with me.'

'Where, Fletcher?' she asked, embarrassed for not having paid attention.

'To the house on Catalina. It's an extraordinary place. I had it built as the exact duplicate of my ski lodge in Aspen. We could take the Cessna and be there in no time. You could bring your portfolio and we could have a whole weekend to talk about the pageant. You know I'm interested in sponsoring a girl this year. What do you say?'

Sloane cleared her throat. This wasn't the first time a man had asked her to go someplace, do something she didn't want to do. She had the perfect answer. One that always worked. 'Oh,' she said, a lovely smile on her face. 'How sweet of you to invite me, I'm sure it's great there, but you would have to ask my mother. I couldn't possibly go without her permission.'

During the ride home, Sloane almost wept with relief. She really had to congratulate herself. Even drunk she had made it through the evening. She had looked wonderful and behaved perfectly. She had been patient enough to let him be the one to bring up the pageant – but no way would she go away with him. She had skillfully gotten out of it by making it Noreen's decision. And Noreen, of course, would never agree to such a plan.

Once again she had succeeded. She had been a good girl.

She had pleased Noreen.

She had also pleased herself. Tonight had been the first time she had been treated like an adult, a grown woman. From the very first burning sensation of the martini, something wonderful started happening to her. She felt more free, more alive, in control of herself. There was a release of tension in being drunk. Even in the presence of a bore like Fletcher Walker the evening seemed painless and easy. She hated being bored. Now she knew there was a solution. Just take a little drink or two!

The next morning she discovered there was a price to be paid. Before she even opened her eyes she could feel her head pounding. A dull, throbbing pain wrapped around her forehead and temples and down the back of her neck.

She sat on the edge of the bed, dizzy with nausea. She lurched to the bathroom and gasped. Looking back from the mirror was her own face all right, but bloated and yellow. Her always perfect skin was blotched, and the whites and rims of her eyes were rabbit-pink.

Before, if she had awakened feeling like this, she would have known immediately that she had the flu. She would have crawled back into bed, put her head under the pillow, and slept away the day. But she didn't have the flu. She had a hangover, and in a funny way it was a badge of maturity to show herself she could function with it. Somehow she'd get through classes. By after-school cheerleading practice it would probably be gone.

She took a hot shower and brushed her teeth and hair. She felt better but not perfect. It seemed a small price, really, she thought, remembering how the gin had eased her through a difficult evening. It was as though she had discovered a marvellous and easily accessible new friend.

But even by that afternoon she wasn't feeling much better. She was exhausted from dragging herself through the day. By the time she rounded the side of the field house on her way to cheerleading practice, she thought she was going to die. She could see the other girls on the squad milling around the cinder running track that encircled the football field. She knew they were waiting for her. She had one arm in her sweater, the empty sleeve was entangled in the strap of her bookbag, she was wearing the wrong socks, and she didn't have her notebook with the new cheers she was supposed to have memorized.

Alan, who was head cheerleader, was impatiently pacing in front of the stands. He looked wonderful, as usual, his taut gymnast's body encased in immaculate white jeans and a letter sweater. His preppy white bucks clashed marvellously with the thick blond ponytail he had been carefully cultivating since he was a freshman.

The Dearfield football team was scrimmaging out on the field. This would be their last practice before Saturday's championship playoff with St Stefan's.

'Anytime you're ready, Taylor,' Alan called as Sloane stumbled toward him. She knew he wasn't mad at her. He was just putting on a show for the others. She'd seen him earlier and he knew her condition was fragile.

She trotted up to him, close enough not to be overheard. 'Sorry, Alan,' she whispered. 'I think I'm going to die.'

'You look like you already have, sweets.' He smiled.

'That bad, huh?'

'It's the first hangover I've seen that throws its own shadow.'

'Don't,' she moaned.

'I think this is the first time I've ever seen you without makeup. You must be really sick.'

'I tried,' she said, touching her cheek. 'My hands were shaking so badly I stuck a mascara wand in my eye and gave up.'

He raised his arm to signal the squad to take their positions. 'How's your voice?'

'Not too great.'

'Well, fake it, sweetheart. This won't take long.' He turned away and shouted to the assembled girls. 'Okay, gang. Let's start with the locomotive. And really sing out. One! Two! . . .'

For the next twenty minutees the girls jumped and screamed in unison. Sloane wanted to collapse after the first two cheers. Sweat was running in a steady stream between her shoulder blades. Her hair stuck to the back

46

of her neck in wet tendrils that itched and tickled simultaneously.

As Alan started to windmill his arms and shout another cheer, she caught his eye and pointed to the empty stands. He kept on shouting but nodded at her. She climbed up into the stands and dropped onto a bench. She hung her head between her knees and took two deep breaths to keep from passing out. She sat quietly like that for a few minutes before she heard a soft sound.

Startled, she turned to see a young man, sitting two rows above her in the bleachers. He was young, but older than she. She had been so deep in thought she hadn't even seen him arrive.

He was sitting with one ankle resting on his knee, and leaning on his arms, which were stretched out to his sides, exposing his muscles. He was wearing a black T-shirt, white jeans, and a simple gold crucifix. His sleek, black, collar-length hair was combed back from a high, smooth forehead. Most of his face was obscured by mirrored sunglasses. He was smiling down at her. It was a half-smile really, barely revealing a line of blazing white teeth that contrasted with his sensuous lips. He certainly wasn't a Dearfield boy.

Slowly he pulled off his sunglasses. 'Are you okay?' he asked, still smiling.

She shuddered, then sat up straight and pushed her damp hair away from her face. Now she recognized him. His name was Fernando Cruz. He was the subject of great myth and sinister gossip around school. She knew he must be waiting for Selena Grant, another cheerleader and one of the wilder girls in her class. Selena took perverse pride in dating this good-looking Latino with a reputation of being everything from a drug dealer to a gang leader in south L.A. Selena had given the other girls fair warning. If anyone so much as looked sideways at him, they were dead meat.

This is all I need, she sighed to herself. *Being seen*

talking to Fernando Cruz! I might as well kill myself right now and save Selena the effort.

He was still staring at her, waiting for her to answer. She couldn't be rude. 'Yeah,' she managed, 'thank you, I'll be all right.'

'I'm Fernando,' he said pleasantly.

'Yes . . . yes, I know,' she said, standing up and smoothing her skirt. 'I guess you're waiting for Selena.'

'Just taking her to the dentist. Her car's in the shop.' His gaze had not left her face. 'How did you know who I was waiting for?'

Sloane shrugged. She had to get away, but she didn't want him to think she was putting him down. 'Everyone knows you and Selena . . .'

'Me and Selena are history,' he said. 'We broke up. We're still friends. But she goes with a buddy of mine now.'

Under different circumstances this would be considered hot news around school. But at the moment all Sloane wanted to do was to get away. The way he was looking at her made her feel strange. He had a beautiful face, but there was something about him that was disturbing. The way he was looking at her made her feel as though he was saying one thing aloud and another with his eyes.

'Aren't you Sloane Taylor?' he asked. 'I saw your picture in *California Life* magazine. You were on a horse. You looked like some kinda fairy princess coming out of a fog bank.'

Sloane felt the blood rising up her neck and onto her cheeks. The ad was for a local fabric shop. She was supposed to be Lady Godiva on a horse draped in yards of see-through chiffon. The ads she did had all seemed completely impersonal until now, with this person staring at her clearly thinking about what she looked like naked. She nodded nervously. 'Yes, I'm Sloane Taylor. Look, I really gotta go . . .'

Maybe he hadn't broken up with Selena. Maybe that was just a line. Maybe he was hitting on her and Selena was watching every minute of it. She glanced out toward the field and saw the football team had gone. The other girls on the cheerleading squad were milling around, looking over at her and whispering behind their hands.

Desperate, she finally decided that, rude or not, she was just going to turn and walk away. As she stood, she looked back at him. Their eyes held for an instant. She felt light-headed, blushed, and looked away. It wasn't until she reached the cinder track that she realized her hands were damp. As she headed toward the field house, she could feel his eyes against her back, burning a hot circle between her shoulder blades.

'Well!' said a familiar voice in back of her.

She turned to see Alan trotting toward her, his arms full of pom-poms. He had a disapproving look on his face. 'What was that all about?'

'What?' she said, pretending nonchalance.

'You actually spoke to that Fernado Cruz! I saw you.'

They were walking abreast now. 'Why not, for heaven's sake. He's human,' she said defensively.

'Barely.' Alan sniffed.

'Don't be such a snob.'

'I'm not being a snob. I'm trying to save your life. Selena Grant will rip your throat out.'

'They broke up,' Sloane said matter-of-factly.

'My! Didn't we have a real heart-to-heart. Did he tell you his hopes and dreams? His burning desire to be a rocket scientist?'

Sloane stopped walking and turned to face him, her hands on her hips. 'Alan Wade. What's the matter with you?' she demanded. 'He said hello to me. I said hello back.'

'I saw him watching you, Sloane. He was standing down by the track. When you sat down, he moved right in. Fernando Cruz is trouble and you know it. I heard he's into voodoo, and Jerry Russell told me he —'

Sloane started walking toward the field house again. 'I don't want to hear it, Alan. All that stuff is just vicious gossip. Nobody really knows anything about him except what big-mouth Selena spreads around.'

Alan, silenced for a moment by her vigorous defense, walked quietly beside her. As they reached the field house door, he finally spoke. 'He is hot looking, I'll say that. I wouldn't mind a whack at him myself.'

'You're shameless.' Sloane laughed as he held the door for her.

'I don't stand a chance. I think he's hot for you.'

'Big deal.' She shrugged but her heart was still pounding.

'Wait until word gets around,' he said, grinning. 'You'll see how big a deal it is.'

As they moved down the corridor toward the locker rooms, June Fenwick, one of the cheerleaders, pushed her way past them. She was a tiny redhead with enormous breasts and a Valley Girl accent. 'Saw you talking to Fernando Cruz,' she said to Sloane over her shoulder. 'You going out with him?'

'No!' Sloane snapped.

'Better not.'

'What's it to you?' Alan barked without looking at her.

'Like, he's some bad dude,' said June.

Alan spun around and pushed his face into June's. 'Buzz off, Junebug.'

June pinched her face into a hard little knot and flounced down the long tunnel toward the locker room.

'She's so jealous I can smell it,' Alan said, looping his arm through Sloane's protectively. 'But you see how quickly it starts.'

On their usual ride home from school in Alan's car, they said nothing more about Fernado Cruz. But Sloane couldn't get him out of her mind.

The following day after class she was waiting, as usual, for Alan in the parking lot. She looked up to see a sleek, black pickup truck move on slowly toward her and pull to a stop only inches from where she stood. Fernando Cruz was at the wheel. He was wearing his mirrored shades. 'Get in,' he said, smiling his crooked one-sided smile.

'Sorry?' she said, not believing what she had heard.

'Get in,' he repeated, leaning across the seat and pushing open the passenger door.

She glanced around the parking lot hoping to see Alan. 'I'm waiting for my ride,' she said lamely.

'It's here,' he said patting the seat next to him.

She hesitated. The force of his words and the expression on his face made refusing seem more embarrassing than saying yes. What harm would it do to let him drive her home? Smiling shyly, she got in the car.

2

'Bad girl! Bad, Bad, Bad!' Alan teased when she tried to explain her feelings that night on the phone.

'I know, I know,' Sloane said, rolling over and burrowing into the coolness of her satin bedspread. 'I just couldn't help myself. He's so . . .'

'So sexy,' Alan said helpfully.

'Oh, all right. Sexy. So sexy he makes my knees weak.'

'And dangerous.' Alan lowered his voice ominously.

'He's really not,' she said, again defending Fernando. 'He's quite sweet. He took me straight home.'

'How did you get in the house without Noreen seeing you?'

'She was at her tennis lesson.'

'Phew! Thank God.'

'Alan?' she said, whispering into the phone. 'Will you cover for me tomorrow?'

There was a pause on the line before Alan reacted. 'You're not going to go out with him,' he said apprehensively. 'Tell me you're not.'

'Alan, I want to. I really do,' she said. 'He excites me. I don't believe all those stories, the voodoo and drugs and gangs. But he's from a different world. When I saw Mother wasn't home, we drove down to the end of the street and talked for nearly an hour. He's the first guy I've ever met who let me finish a sentence.'

'You're sure it isn't because he's a forbidden fruit?'

'Maybe,' she answered, laughing.

52

'I can't change your mind?'

'Absolutely not,' she said. 'He wants me to come out to his house in Venice tomorrow. I'll need some reason to be late getting home. Will you cover for me?' She knew Alan could no more resist intrigue than she could resist her powerful attraction to Fernando Cruz.

'Yeah, I suppose I will,' he said. 'How are we going to do it?'

'What if I say we have extra cheerleading practice? That way she'll think I'm with you. Okay?'

'Umm.' Alan hesitated. 'I dunno. She'd kill me if she ever found out.'

'Alan, please.'

'Oh, all right. On one condition.'

'What?'

'If you do it with him – you know, I mean, really *do* it – I want all the details.'

'Alan!'

'Okay, okay, just be careful, pumpkin. This guy really is bad news.

Fernando Cruz drove with purpose, gliding in and out of the lanes of the freeway well above the speed limit. The hypnotic beat of the salsa music he had slapped into the tape deck vibrated from a large speaker directly under Sloane's seat, pounding against the calves of her legs.

She felt light-headed, slightly dizzy at what she was doing. The sheer defiance of it all excited her in a way nothing ever had before. From time to time Fernando turned to her, his eyes invisible behind his mirrored sunglasses. It was as though he sensed how she was feeling. The exhilaration of being free of any restraints overwhelmed her. She rested her head on the headrest and closed her eyes. The thrill of being with him almost, but not quite, overcame the slight feeling of apprehension.

He took the exit ramp marked Venice without slowing down. Within minutes they were pulling up in front of a run-down bungalow along a narrow man-made canal. It was several blocks from the ocean and sat in the middle of a block of small houses all sadly in need of repair.

Fernando turned off the ignition and the music from the tape deck stopped abruptly. But he made no move to get out of the car. It was so quiet she could hear herself breathing.

He took off his dark glasses and looked directly at her. She half-hoped he didn't want to talk. What if he said something that broke the spell. It was more mysterious, more exciting for him to remain silent. He leaned against the door and put one arm over the back of the seat as though waiting for her to say something.

'Is this where you live?' she asked, not knowing what else to say.

'Um-hum.'

'It's nice.'

'I thought we'd go in and have a beer.'

'Oh . . . okay,' she said agreeably.

'You drink beer?'

'Yeah . . . sure. A beer would be nice. It's warm out.'

Suddenly he threw back his head and laughed, a deep, throaty, sexy laugh. 'You know we aren't talking about whether or not you want a beer, don't you?'

'Huh?' She frowned.

'We're talking about whether or not you want me to make love to you.' He leaned closer, brushing his lips against hers. It wasn't a kiss. It was a teasing gesture that inflamed her. She reached for the back of his neck to pull him closer. He pulled away, returning to his position against the door. 'Because if you go into the house with me, that's what we are going to do. I'm going to make love to you like no one has ever done.'

She looked down at her lap, her face burning. If he only knew no one had ever done more than tongue-kiss her or fondle her breasts . . . She knew all about sex. All her girlfriends had been sleeping with boys since they were thirteen; most of the movies she had seen had some kind of sex in them; and endless discussions with her peers supplied her with all the information she felt she needed. It just had never happened to her, to her mind, body, and heart. She knew one day she would feel right about it and it would happen. At the moment, however, she was embarrassed to be a virgin.

He leaned forward again. This time he kissed her hard, his tongue searching the inside of her mouth. He kissed her mouth and cheeks, her eyes and neck and throat.

'Please . . .' she whimpered. She wanted him to stop so she could catch her breath. She was trembling.

He pressed his lips into her hair and whispered into her ear. 'You've never done it, have you?' he said softly.

She pulled back and looked up into his big black eyes. 'No,' she said. 'Not really.'

'Come,' he said, pushing open the door.

The house was little more than one big room. While the outside needed attention, the inside was another story. Someone had taken great care with the floor. It was bare and gleaming with layers of lacquer and wax. The windows were spotlessly clean and hung with crisp curtains made from white cotton sheets. Along one wall was a king-sized mattress and box spring covered with a worn but clean quilt and several pillows. Against the opposite wall was an enormous state-of-the-art television stereo system flanked by speakers nearly as tall as she was. The air smelled cool and clean with a hint of Clorox and pine soap. It occurred to her that he must have worked very hard at making the place presentable. She was touched.

Off to one side in an alcove was a tiny kitchen, also spotless and uncluttered. Fernando left her standing in the middle of the room and walked to the refrigerator. He extracted two bottles of beer and snapped off the tops under an opener mounted by the sink. He returned to the main room, handed her a beer, and took a deep pull on his own. He swallowed and looked at her. 'You,' he said slowly, 'are the most beautiful girl I have ever seen.'

Sloane could feel herself blushing. 'Thanks,' she said quietly.

'You've been told that before. A lot.'

'Well . . . yes.' She smiled. 'But no one has ever said it quite the way you just did.' She wanted him to know she appreciated the compliment.

'But everyone you've ever met has said it, right? I'll bet everywhere you go, the world tells you that.'

'I never thought of it that way. I suppose you're right.' Now she wasn't sure what he was driving at.

'And do you believe it?' he asked, taking another swig of beer.

Sloane was surprised by his question and took a minute to think about it. 'Sort of. I guess what I believe is that I'm not ugly.'

He laughed again, the same low, sexy laugh as before, and extended his hand to her. 'No, baby,' he said, shaking his head, 'you're not ugly.'

He relieved her of her untouched beer bottle, set it on the floor, and rested his hands on her shouders. With one sweep he lifted her up and carried her to the bed. He undressed her slowly and sensuously, kissing her intimately as each article of clothing was removed to reveal bare flesh. After freeing her breasts from her brassiere, he kissed her pink nipples, sucking gently until each hardened. Then he bit her, softly yet firmly, and she felt her body convulse with desire.

'Don't move,' he said hoarsely. 'No matter what I do.'

She stared up at him, half-afraid, half-delirious with excitement as he removed the last of her clothing. He moved onto his side and began to kiss her neck and throat, then moved to her breasts again. This time he bit each nipple and her hands sank into the thickness of his jet-black hair. She pressed herself against him and was surprised at how the steel hardness of his erection excited rather than frightened her.

She moaned with pleasure, and he eased himself in between her legs. When she realized what he was about to do, she gasped and tried to close them. He grasped her thighs with his powerful hands and parted them again. His movements were rough and demanding; the desire in them made her feel wild with a surge of lust.

For an instant, his eyes locked with hers. He smiled, then drove himself into her with one quick, hard thrust. She cried out in pain, but he didn't move. He just stayed buried deeply in her, his lips sucking at her throat, until she began to feel him throbbing inside her body. The sensation drove her over the edge and she began unconsciously moving her hips in a desperate plea for him to take her further. When she began to whimper, he started to move, pulling almost completely out of her and hovering until she cried out, and then thrusting fully and harshly into her again, and again, until all that existed in the world was Fernando and the feeling of him inside her. She found herself squirming with pleasure, then melting into the rhythm of his movements. She'd never felt so free, so fully unselfconscious, as if she were soaring on a cresting wave of singular intent, of pure pleasure.

Just when she thought she would die from the ecstasy of what he was doing, he grasped her legs and wrenched them up over her head. His thrusts became faster and deeper, and she cried out from a strange mixture of pain and raw pleasure. She looked up at him and saw that his eyes were wild, and a tiny stream of perspiration trickled down his forehead. He thrust harder and harder. As she began to feel shivering contractions, she called out his name. Together, they rode an overwhelming wave of shuddering rapture.

She went limp. Her entire body felt like some sort of soft, pliable clay. She seemed to float, flooded with an excruciating happiness and simple amazement at what he had just made her feel.

Slowly he rolled to one side, keeping one arm flung over her stomach. 'That was too fast,' he said. 'Next time, I'll take it slow and easy.'

Without warning she was seized by choking sobs. Tears streamed down her face. She rolled free of his arm and buried her face in a pillow, her shoulders jerking convulsively.

'Hey . . . hey . . . baby!' Fernando said with alarm. 'Don't cry. What's the matter? Did I do something wrong?' He leaned on one elbow and stroked her shoulder.

'No,' she moaned. She couldn't explain it. She wasn't sad, really. How could she tell him that until this moment she had spent her life trying to please everyone – Noreen, her friends, her employers, the great faceless public she was supposed to look pretty for. Now someone had not only tried to please her, but had succeeded beyond her wildest dreams.

She turned toward Fernando and threw herself across his chest. 'Oh, God, I love you, Fernando,' she sobbed.

'Yeah, baby. You're hot. Real hot.'

She didn't want to be 'hot.' Is that all he could say in response to what she was feeling? She pushed his remark out of her mind. She didn't want anything to mar the moment, the happiest in her life.

'You act like you're angry at me, Alan,' Sloane said, pouting.

They were sitting opposite each other at the coffee shop on Pico where he picked her up after her afternoon with Fernando.

'I'm not angry, Sloane. I'm scared.'

'What have you got to be scared about?'

'I'm scared you're going to get caught. People are beginning to talk.'

'Talk? About what?' Sloane asked hotly. 'What could they be saying?'

'Oh, come on, Sloane,' Alan said, pushing a half-eaten BLT with extra mayo toward the centre of the table. 'I don't know why I ordered this. I don't want it.'

'Alan?'

He sighed, a long, tired swoosh of air that seemed to deflate his whole body. 'Look, baby-cakes, I've been covering for you for nearly three weeks now. Somehow Noreen is going to find out about you and Fernando. Everyone at school knows about you two already. I mean, every afternoon? What do you two do anyway?'

Sloane stared into her iced tea for a long moment. It had been quite a juggling act for poor Alan. Desperate to explain her absences, they had invented an after-school theatre workshop that Noreen seemed to buy. Alan knew, of course, that Sloane and Fernando were going to the house in Venice to make love. What he didn't know was how wild, how erotic, how almost obsessive their lovemaking had become. She would do anything Fernando asked her to, anything, even if it hurt. For two, three, and sometimes four hours they would make love until they lay soaked in their comingled body fluids, spent, exhausted, and blind to everything in the world except the wonder of what they could do to each other's body.

Fernando wasn't a boy. He was a man. A man who had taken total control of her senses. On the third afternoon she'd spent with him, he went to a drawer in the kitchen and returned to the crumpled bed with some dirty magazines. Sloane had never seen anything quite like them. Ordinarily she would have been repulsed. Now, with every nerve ending turned into a sexual conduit, she leafed through them with growing excitement. Fernando wanted to try every position on every page. With each orgasm he unlocked yet another door within her mind, liberating a part of her she hadn't known existed.

This afternoon they had been able to spend only an hour together. He'd said he had someplace to go. He didn't say where or why and she found herself consumed with jealousy.

When he had told her, she had flown to the bed, undressing as she walked – hoping, wondering if she had the sexual power to make him stay.

He stared down at her naked body as he unbuttoned his black silk shirt. 'Put your hand on yourself,' he commanded her.

She looked up at him for a moment, not fully understanding. He leaned over, took her hand, and placed it between her legs. 'Now, use your fingers. Do yourself like I do you.'

For an instant she felt a wave of embarrassment. He wanted her to masturbate. 'Do it, baby,' he demanded. As she tentatively started to stroke herself, he stepped out of his jeans. He wasn't wearing underwear and his erection stood hard and glistening, bobbing slightly. 'This should help.'

He stood over her watching for a full five minutes until she could stand it no longer. 'Fernando, please. Now?'

'Stand up.'

Obediently she stood. Her legs felt like jelly.

'Stand up against the wall and turn around.'

She cried out as he entered her, thrusting higher and higher, half-holding her up. 'How does that feel? Huh, baby? Feels good? Huh?'

It felt so good that thinking about it now made her shiver. She crossed her legs in the booth and cleared her throat, trying to push the thoughts out of her head lest they show like some dirty movie across her forehead.

'Sloane? Are you with me?' Alan asked.

'Huh? Oh . . . yeah . . . sorry.'

'Have you ever asked him about all the stories?'

'What stories?'

'The drug dealing, the gangs. Where he gets the money to just lounge around all day waiting to pick you up. I mean, who is this guy anyway?'

Sloane suddenly felt a flash of defensive fury. 'This *guy* is the most beautiful man I've ever known. And he doesn't do drugs. If he did, wouldn't I know about it by now?'

'Sloane, wake up and smell the coffee. They say he's done time.'

'They say! They say! Who the hell are *they*? It's all just vicious gossip because he's different.'

'Different!' Alan said, throwing up his hands. 'He's that all right. Sloane, let me ask you something. Has he ever taken you to a restaurant or a movie? Have you met any of his friends? Have you two done anything together but go out to that house and screw each other's brains out?'

Sloane grabbed her handbag from the seat next to her. 'Alan Wade! You can't talk to me like that. How dare you?' She slid out of the booth and raced toward the coffee shop door.

'Sloane, wait!'

She turned to see him throw a handful of crumpled bills onto the table. He caught her as she opened the door and grabbed her arm. 'Sloane, honey, don't get mad. I'm just trying to make you see he's using you.'

'What do you know about it?' she asked, her voice cold.

'I know a lot about it, believe it or not. I love you and I care what happens to you and I'm saying this isn't good for you. What are you doing about not getting pregnant?'

Sloane stared at him. 'I went to a doctor and got the pill,' she said softly.

'Jesus, what if Noreen finds out?'

'She won't,' Sloane said. 'But you know what, Alan? I don't care if she does. Not anymore.'

'Don't be ridiculous, Sloane. Of course you care.'

'Not if it means losing Fernando.'

Alan shook his head. 'Oh, God, girl. What am I going to do with you?'

'I'm sorry, Alan,' she said, lightly brushing his cheek with a kiss. 'It's just that I love him so.'

'You love him,' Alan said dully. 'Sloane, pussycat, does he love you?'

She couldn't answer. She didn't know.

'Come on, love,' Alan said, 'I'm working tonight at the salon, I'll drive you home.'

When they pulled up in front of her house, Sloane quickly said good-night to Alan, thanked him for caring so much, and promised to call him the next day. On the bathroom mirror she found a note in her mother's looping hand.

Having dinner with Mark Reynolds. When you get home, don't leave the house. I must talk to you. DO NOT LEAVE THE HOUSE! It was signed 'Noreen.'

She sat down on the edge of the bed and studied the note. What in the world could all this be about, she puzzled. The signature 'Noreen' and not 'Mother' was a bad sign. She did that when she was annoyed with Sloane.

And Mark Reynolds! She wondered if she'd ever get up the nerve to tell Noreen how the studio executive her mother thought was such a 'dreamboat' had tried to slide his hand down the back of Sloane's shorts one evening when they were alone in the kitchen.

Don't leave the house! That would be easy. She had no intentions of leaving even her bed. All she wanted to do was crawl under the covers and relive her incredible afternoon with Fernando. Short as their time had been together, she had reached a new level of abandon. She could still smell him on her skin.

She undressed and slipped into bed without her nightgown. She would never sleep in one again. She drew back the top sheet and pulled the extra pillow under the covers with her, hugging it to her body, pretending it was Fernando. Her life now was totally focused on the moment she would meet him each afternoon. She had nearly forgotten her need to please Noreen. But now, with the note, the old worries began to nag her. So what if Noreen found out about Fernando?

She rolled over and buried her face in the pillow. No, she couldn't do it. Her mother was all she really had in the world. She would be so hurt, so disappointed. What would she think of her being with a man like Fernando? She knew her mother would make her stop seeing him. She wanted her to be with someone like Fletcher, someone respectable, powerful, rich.

The instant she thought about Fletcher her head began to throb. He had called repeatedly in the weeks since their dinner date asking when they were going to have their weekend in Catalina. The imaginary play workshop she and Alan had dreamed up served more than one purpose, and she had been able to make a convincing case for being too busy.

Last week Noreen had walked into the room while she was on the phone with Fletcher and heard her repeating her excuses. When she hung up, her mother said, 'Why don't you go, dear? You can't stay a virgin forever.'

For a moment, Sloane had been stunned. Then she began to laugh. Not two hours before, she had reached her third orgasm of the day with Fernando, her legs locked around his neck, thighs pressed against either side of his head as he did that wonderful thing to her with his tongue. It had taken every bit of restraint she could muster not to make a remark about her vanished virginity. 'You're right Mom' was all she had managed.

She burrowed deeper under the covers, squeezing the pillow between her legs, blotting out everything and anything in the world that didn't have to do with Fernando. Awash with the feel of him, the smell of him, the incredible things he did to her, she fell into an exhausted sleep.

The first thing she was aware of was a smashing sound followed by a blinding light. Not a warm light like the sun, but a cold, shadowless light.

'Sloane!'

Her eyes flew open. Her mother was framed in the open bedroom doorway. She must have kicked the door open. It was still vibrating. The knob had made a slight indentation in the wall behind the door. The blazing light was coming from the overhead fixture that was used only when the cleaning lady vacuumed. Sloane realized it had to be almost midnight.

'Get up!'

Sloane pushed herself up from under the covers, remembered that she had gone to bed naked, and pulled the sheet up to her neck. 'Huh?' she said, squinting into the harsh light. Her heart was pounding at having been so violently awakened.

'You don't have anyone in there with you, do you?' Noreen said sarcastically.

'What?' she said, shocked – and then frightened – at the suggestion. 'Mother? What is all this?'

Noreen did not move from the doorway. 'How was your workshop, darling?' she said. The way she said 'darling' sounded more like a sneer than an endearment.

'Fine . . . fine, Mom,' she said, on her guard. 'Is that why you left me a note and woke me up? You were concerned about my workshop?' Sloane was fully awake now and aware that her mother knew something, but what? She felt her best course was to play innocent.

'Don't you lie to me, Mary Sloane Taylor!' Noreen exploded. 'I know what you've been up to. And to add to the humiliation so does someone else.'

'Mom . . .' she said weakly, her mind racing to figure out how her mother could have found out.

Noreen stepped to the side of the bed and ripped the top sheet from the bed. Sloane cowered and pulled a pillow over her nakedness. 'Mom, don't,' she whimpered.

'What in the name of God are you doing without your nightgown?'

'I was hot. I didn't want to . . .'

Her mother turned and grabbed a robe from the chair beside the bed and threw it at her. 'Here, put this on. You disgust me.'

Sloane stood and slipped into the robe. Her hands were trembling. She wasn't going to say another word until her mother told her more about what she knew.

'What were you doing in Venice? You might as well admit it now, Sloane. I can prove it.'

Sloane pulled the cord of the robe so tight she had to swallow hard. 'All right,' she said, 'I was in Venice.'

'With a man,' Noreen said tightly.

Sloane's head snapped up in shock, 'Mother! For God's sake, where did you get that?'

'Fletcher Walker saw you,' Noreen said.

Sloane couldn't believe what she was hearing. 'Fletcher? He called you!'

'He most certainly did,' Noreen said. 'He was out there looking at some beach-front land. He pulled right up next to the two of you at a red light. He said you were with a Hispanic man and you were kissing him!'

'Fernando's a friend,' Sloane said softly. 'I met him at school.'

'Dear Lord,' Noreen said with an exaggerated sigh. 'Dearfield is letting in that sort of student?'

'He's not a student. He . . . he . . .'

'He what, Sloane? You better tell me everything.'

'He was waiting for Selena Grant during squad practice and —'

'Selena Grant!' Noreen nearly screamed.

Sloane felt a thump of fear deep in her stomach.

'I play tennis with Judy Grant. The Grants were worried sick about that guy! They did everything they could to break that up. They told me terrible things about him.'

'Those are just rumours, Mom,' Sloane said, heartsick at hearing Fernando criticized. 'I think Selena started them all. He doesn't do drugs or belong to a gang or anything like that.'

'Whatever. He's a dropout and a bum and I'm ashamed that you would have anything to do with such a person.' Sloane watched as her mother's face took on an expression of having smelled something bad. 'Fletcher was very upset.'

'Mom,' Sloane said pleadingly, 'what difference does it make *what* Fletcher thinks? It's none of his business.'

Noreen's face crumbled. She sat down on the foot of the bed and began to cry. 'Sloane, he's not going to sponsor you for the pageant. He wanted to take you on that lovely trip and you put him off and put him off. Then he sees you with this . . . this . . . person. What do you expect?' Noreen reached for a tissue on the end table and sat down again. 'After all my work and worry and planning.'

Sloane sat frozen and mute. Her hurt and anger hammered against the inside of her head. She did not have the vocabulary or the nerve to express it. No one had ever given her permission to show anger and stand up for herself. Noreen had always done everything. Now her defender was attacking her. And why was her mother more concerned about Fletcher's opinion than she was about Fernando?

Noreen wiped her eyes, smearing her mascara into big raccoon circles. She pushed up off the bed. 'Well, that's that,' she sighed. 'You're not to see that man again. You are grounded, young lady.' Noreen stepped toward the door. 'I want you in this house a half-hour after class.'

'Mom . . .' Sloane was desperate to summon one weapon, strike one blow.

'What is it?'

'Mark Reynolds shoved his hands down the back of my shorts,' she said striking blindly.

Her mother's face tightened with rage. 'What?'

'He came into the kitchen one time while you were getting dressed. I was making a sandwich and —'

'I don't believe you,' Noreen snapped. 'Mark Reynolds is one of the most respected men in the entertainment business. He would never!'

'Well, he did.'

Noreen walked to the side of the bed, her eyes burning. Momentarily emboldened, Sloane looked up at her mother. 'And so did that guy Brice . . . Brick . . . whatever. That B actor you went to the Academy Awards with. Only after I pushed his hands off me he tried to put his tongue —'

Noreen raised her arm. She smashed it, palm open, across Sloane's face.

Sloane's hand flew to her cheek. For a split second she felt as though she were going to throw up. She swallowed and closed her eyes against the sudden, hot tears. When she opened them a moment later, her mother was walking out of the room.

Sloane sprang up to slam and lock the bedroom door. She leaned against it shaking. *I've got to get out of here*, she thought. *I can't stand being around her anymore.* 'Fernando,' she whispered aloud. She didn't even know how to reach him. Their entire relationship had been confined to his picking her up after school and leaving her at the coffee shop to wait for Alan. Alan! He worked until midnight. He might still be there. If she could reach him, he would come get her.

Her mother had never raised a hand to her in her life. What had just happened had probably been inevitable. She sat down on the bed and punched the number for the

67

beauty shop into the phone. While she waited for the receptionist to page Alan, her eyes fell on the picture in a silver frame next to the phone. A tall young man with dark hair smiled into the sun. A tiny girl with a cap of the same dark hair sat on his shoulders, laughing. She remembered that day. He had been tickling her feet to make her giggle.

'Oh Daddy,' she said. 'Things would be so different if you were still here.'

Salon Salon occupied nearly half a block of street-level space in West Hollywood. It looked more like a seventies disco than a beauty parlor. The walls were lacquered a high-gloss black. Baby spots bathed each hot-pink chair at the dozens of work stations in a pool of light, leaving the rest of the cavernous room in nearly total darkness. Soft rock seeped from hidden speakers in the ceiling.

Salon Salon was more than a place to rescue roots and steam away dead skin cells. It was open twenty-four hours a day to accommodate its varied clientele. To its customers Salon Salon was a chic place to see and be seen, have one's hair done, catch up on the latest news, and in the tiny massage cubicles, if one so desired, score cocaine.

For Alan Wade, Salon Salon was the center of the universe.

Every Saturday and after gym class during the week he worked there. If he had worked at the epicentre of some imaginary universal FBI, CIA, and Interpol with taps on a worldwide phone system, he would not have considered himself closer to the heartbeat of what mattered in life.

Salon Salon had permitted him to meet and know the famous and the fabulous on a level that would otherwise have been unavailable to the teenage son of a waitress mother and an absent father. He would have worked there for free, but his scholarship at Dearfield barely covered tuition and he and his mother needed the money.

For Alan, Salon Salon was *People* magazine come to life. But the best part, the part that thrilled him the most, were the women. Wealthy women, working women, women who fucked for money, prestige, and career advancement, and women who earned it the hard way – by marrying the most powerful, richest, and to hear them tell it, meanest sons-of-bitches in the world.

He had started at the men's salon next door as a gofer, shampoo boy, and cuttings sweeper. It was there that he met Brad Rampart. Brad was an agent at Rampart, Wells and Steen, a personal management agency that represented film people when they fired William Morris or ICM.

Brad was divorced with two teenage children, and the minute he clapped eyes on little Alan's gymnast's body and long blond ponytail he fell madly in love. Alan, who had been aware that he was gay since he was ten, reciprocated. While their meetings were furtive and hurried, all Alan knew was that when he was with Brad, he was happy.

Alan was a quick study and by watching he learned how to cut hair. By the time he was a senior at Dearfield his Saturdays were booked until nearly midnight with his own clients. He only cut hair, nothing else, no colour, no blow dries, no body perms or facials. 'Strong chemicals might damage my hands,' he would say with a twinkle. 'My hands are my instruments.' And while he cut, he listened to his ladies.

Alan's ladies adored him. They told him everything.

His last appointment was to cut television star Crystal Kincaid. Usually she never shut up but tonight she was moody. She said little beyond explaining that she was upset because she had just learned that her agent was moving to the New York office.

Brad Rampart was her agent.

Alan finished cutting Crystal's powder-soft, overbleached hair with trembling hands. When he heard the receptionist paging him, he gave Crystal one more snip and excused himself. That had to be Brad telling him he was leaving. He steeled himself to be cool, even though his heart was pounding.

He took a deep breath to calm his jangling nerves as he picked up the phone on the receptionist's desk. 'This is Alan Wade,' he cooed in his sweetest Salon Salon voice.

'Alan?' It was Sloane and she was crying.

'Honey, where are you? Are you all right?'

'Can you come and get me, Alan?'

'Of course,' he said, glancing at his watch. 'Where?'

'I'm home but I can't stay here for long. Something terrible has happened. Please come now. I'll tell you all about it when you get here.'

'I'm just finishing up. Don't move. I'm coming right over. You're not hurt or anything, are you?'

'Not physically, no. I can't talk right now,' she said. 'Please hurry.'

Alan tore off his black satin smock, grabbed his knapsack from the coatroom, and bolted through the door to the parking lot.

He raced up Wilshire in a frenzy. If that damn Fernando bastard had done something awful to Sloane, he didn't know what he would do. Kill him, probably. Since they'd been kids, Sloane had been his sweet, unquestioning, truest friend. They could tell each other anything; Sloane was the first straight person to whom he had ever confessed his homosexuality. He could tell that she knew little of what that meant and she never asked, preferring instead to accept him at face value and never question his activities in what they referred to as his 'other world.' That suited him fine. There were two places in the outside world where he could be himself, at work and with Sloane. He treasured her. If someone had hurt her, they would answer to him.

She was waiting for him on the sidewalk outside her house. She had a small suitcase at her feet. On the drive to his apartment she would say only that Fernando had done nothing. It was Noreen.

He got her calmed down in the little apartment he shared with his mother. The living room smelled musty and airless. He searched through the breakfront in the dining area, where his mother hid the vodka she kept for rare company. Finding it, he poured Sloane a straight shot in a jelly glass, then joined her on the pillow-strewn couch.

Alan sat open-mouthed as she told him what had happened.

When she finally paused to take a gulp of vodka, she said, 'Can I stay here for a few days, Alan?'

'Dearest love, of course!'

Sloane stood up and walked to the window. 'I just can't face her. Not for a while. She's been telling me what to do for so long, I know I'd fall right back into her trap again.'

'I'm glad you see it that way, hon. I've been wanting to say something for a long time about the way Noreen manipulates you. Maybe tonight was just as well.'

'You're sure your mom won't mind me being here?'

'Are you kidding? She adores you,' Alan said. 'Look, I'll flop out here and you can have my room. But are you sure about all this?'

'I've never been so sure of anything.'

The next afternoon Sloane waited anxiously in the school parking lot. She couldn't wait to pour her heart out to Fernando about what had happened. Now they wouldn't have to hide. She had slept little the night before, imagining him coming to Alan's house to be with her. Perhaps now they could have a normal relationship. As exciting as the constant sex was, she longed to expand their time together so they could do ordinary things.

When he finally arrived, he was more than an hour late. As soon as his car stopped in front of her, she pulled open the door and climbed in. He turned and gave her a half-smile. Usually he kissed her.

'Aren't you going to kiss me?' she asked with a mock pout.

'Later, babe,' he said curtly. He hit the gas pedal hard. The truck shot out of the lot. He took the turn into the main street on two wheels.

Something was wrong. He was staring straight ahead silently and was driving too fast.

They had travelled less than a mile when he made a sharp left into the parking area beside a carefully groomed little park. He cut the engine and flopped back against the seat with a grunt.

'Fernando?' she asked. 'What's the matter?'

'Shit,' he said, slamming his fist against the steering wheel.

A wave of panic swept over her. She had never seen him so angry. It frightened her. Could she have done something wrong?

'Your old lady is something else,' he said slowly, still not facing her.

'My old lady? You mean my mother? Oh, my God, what has she done?' Sloane felt as though someone had dropped a huge rock on her chest.

'She got me fired.'

'From what, Fernando? I didn't know you even had a job.'

'Well, I do, damn it. At least I did.'

'Where?'

'In the kitchen at the Beau Rivage hotel. I worked the seven-to-three shift. While I was getting cleaned up this afternoon, my boss calls me in and cans me. What a kick in the ass.'

Sloane began to cry. 'Why do you think my mother had something to do with it?' she said through her sobs, knowing it was somehow true.

He turned and looked at her, his face hard with anger. 'Because he told me. She called the manager with some bullshit about you being underage and me having a record.'

72

'Do you have a record, Fernando?'

'That's another piece of bull, too. A dumb weapons charge from three years ago. I got pulled over on the freeway. I was keeping a pistol for a friend. He'd used it to stick up a liquor store. I had nothing to do with it but they busted me anyway. Your mother found out about it somehow.'

Judy Grant. Sloane knew it. Her mother must have called Selena's mother and pumped her. Probably right after she left the house last night.

'Look, babe, I think we should cool it for a while.'

'You mean not to see each other?' she said, her heart pounding so loudly she could hear it in her ears. 'No . . . please . . . I –'

'I gotta look for another job and hope my getting fired hasn't screwed me for good.' He sighed. 'What the hell happened with you two anyway?'

'We had a fight,' Sloane said, pulling herself together. 'She slapped me. I'm staying over at my friend Alan's.' She didn't want to talk about her mother. Her mind was fixated on his terrible words about not seeing her. She couldn't bear not being with him. Without Fernando in her life she had nothing. 'You don't mean what you said, do you, Fernando? Please say you don't mean it.'

He turned the key and gunned the engine. 'I meant it,' he said curtly, slamming the car into reverse. He backed out of the parking area so fast the tires spun and squealed.

'But I love you,' she said softly. She started to tremble and tried to hold back more tears.

'Look, babe. We had a real good time, right? We had a few laughs, okay? I don't need a hassle like this. I mean, man, when the assistant manager called me in and gave me all that shit, I almost croaked on the spot. Today she got me fired. Who knows, tomorrow she'll have me arrested. Who the fuck needs it?'

Sloane's mind reeled as they manoevered through the late-afternoon traffic. She stared straight ahead, leaning close to the window so that the rush of air would somehow drown out the memory of Fernando's words. She felt dirty and used and cheap, but worse, she felt completely betrayed and helpless. Twice in twenty-four hours she had felt more rage than she had experienced in her entire lifetime.

'Where do you want me to drop you?' Fernando asked matter-of-factly.

Into a big black hole, she wanted to answer, into the middle of the ocean, onto the middle of the freeway at ninety miles an hour. Instead she gave him Alan's address in as steady a voice as she could muster. In the silence between them, under the pain and rage that made her skin tingle and the back of her neck sweat with humiliation, she felt oddly calm, as though the world were spinning around her.

Something had gone 'click' when Fernando asked, 'Who the fuck needs it?' Was that all she had been to him? She felt something freeze and go hard as glass inside; she felt as if a door had slammed shut in her soul and someone had locked it and thrown away the key. *I'll never be rejected again. I'll never let someone else control my life again*, she silently promised herself. She still had her pride. She would not plead with him to change his mind. It would be too mortifying to beg him – or Noreen! – to love her.

The truck had not come to a full stop at the curb in front of Alan's apartment building when she opened the door and turned for one last look at him.

He was leaning toward her across the seat. 'Hey, babe.' He was smiling the crooked smile that had made her fall in love with him. His huge black eyes crinkled at the edges. 'This doesn't have to be forever, you know. I'll call ya. Why don't you give me this guy's number?'

'I won't be here,' she said, turning away.

'You goin' back home?'

She paused for an instant considering her future. It

seemed to stretch in front of her blank and empty. 'No,' she said. 'I'm going to New York.'

She slammed the door and started up the flagstone walkway to the apartment building. Her words had surprised her, but maybe now was the time to make her fantasy come true. She would discuss it with Alan as soon as he got home.

For the first month after she left home, Sloane communicated with her mother only through Alan. She didn't want to talk to Noreen and Noreen refused to talk to her. Finally, it was Alan who put an end to the stalemate between them.

One Saturday morning when Sloane returned from doing Mrs Wade's grocery shopping (a chore she had volunteered to do to assuage her guilt at overstaying her welcome), she found Noreen sitting on the couch.

'Hello, Mom,' she said, trying very hard to be casual. 'What are you doing here?'

'Alan gave me the key,' she said without rancour.

Sloane put the grocery bags on the table in the dining area. Should she sit down as if nothing had happened? Should she stand and make her mother more uncomfortable. She could almost taste the tension in the air.

She chose to sit on the edge of one of the dining room chairs and wait for her mother to state her position.

'We can't go on like this, Sloane. We're all either of us has.'

Sloane stared at her hands. She would have liked to hear her mother say she was sorry. The anger and bitterness had subsided a bit since that awful night but not completely. 'Why did you hit me, Mother?' she asked quietly. 'I can't think of anything you could have done that could have hurt me more.'

Noreen pursed her lips and inhaled deeply before she spoke. 'I've thought of nothing but that since you left,

Sloane,' she said. 'I was angry. Angry at you for losing Fletcher's sponsorship, angry because you were running around with that Fernando person, and I guess I was afraid.'

'Afraid?' Sloane asked. 'Of what, for heaven's sake?'

'Of losing you. Honey, you're everything I've lived for, even before your father died. And I saw it all slipping away.'

'It's already slipped away, Mom,' Sloane said.

'Why do you say that?' Noreen frowned.

'I've been doing a lot of thinking, too, Mom. And I've made up my mind. I'm going to New York to study acting. It's all planned.'

Sloane waited for what she was sure would be her mother's furious reaction.

'Do you have a date for the prom?'

Sloane looked at her mother in disbelief. Hadn't she heard what she had just said? 'Excuse me?' she said.

'I just wondered if you'd be going to the prom. It's next week, right?'

'Yeah . . . Saturday night.'

'And . . .'

'And?'

'Surely you aren't going alone.'

'Of course not, Mother, I'm going with David Grey.'

'Well,' Noreen said, fluffing her freshly done hair. 'Ask David if he would take a picture. I'd like to see how you look.'

So that was the way it was going to be. She was going to play the offended, pouting, hurt mother. 'Mother,' Sloane said, exasperated with the exchange. 'I could come home to dress, you know. Then you could take your own picture.'

Noreen stood and gathered her jacket and bag. 'That won't be possible, Sloane. I won't be there. That's what I came over to tell you. I'm marrying Mark Reynolds. We'll be in Hawaii on our honeymoon.'

*

Even now, after all this time, the pain of that moment still hurt. The memory of her mother's announcement still hit like the dirty punch of a professional boxer, hot and fast and under the heart. For days afterward it left her overcome with a sense of betrayal. Is that all she had meant to her mother? Something to devote herself to until she got a better offer? Alan had been a comfort during the first terrible days of adjusting, telling her she couldn't dwell on it – that she had to get on with her new life. New York glittered on the other side of the country. If she physically removed herself from the scene of her un-happiness, she would be free. Little had they known that the first things that hop into your suitcase are unresolved problems.

The excitement of actually leaving and the hectic planning for exams and graduation kept her mind off her own unhappiness.

Prom night was beautiful and balmy. A slight breeze moved the Japanese lanterns on the hotel terrace and cooled the skin after each dance. David Grey was the class president and habitual politician. He spent most of the evening table-hopping and asking teachers and chaperones to dance.

Bored and feeling as though all the pains she'd taken to look her best had been wasted, Sloane strolled out onto the lawn that bordered the parking lot. Leaning against the fender of someone's father's snappy Porsche was one of the best-looking men she'd seen in a long time. He was wearing the white cotton jeans, white polo shirt, and visored cap that was the uniform of the hotel parking attendant. As she made her way down the path, she could see he was staring straight at her. Their eyes met and held. There was a half-smile on his face as though he was daring her to speak to him. The look in his eye reminded her of Fernando. He couldn't have been much older than any of the boys inside gyrating around the dance floor in their rented tuxes, their pockets bulging with money their parents had given them to go get silly drunk and end up out at the beach at dawn.

As she approached him, he didn't move except to lower his eyes to the hem of her dress and slowly raise them back again to her face.

She felt a surge of heat run through her, a sensation that reminded her even more sharply of Fernando. And yet the feeling was different. With Fernando, he had led the way. He had decided when they met . . . and when they broke up. Now, letting this man undress her with his eyes, Sloane felt sexy. She liked the sensation of risk. But it was *her* risk. She could move closer and urge this boy on, or she could simply turn and walk back up the path and disappear. There would be nothing he could do about it. She was in control.

She slowed her pace but kept moving toward him, savouring the helplessly eager light in his eyes.

Before she could think what she was doing she was standing in front of him, so close she could see his tight shirt rise and fall with each breath. Neither of them said a word. He reached out and slipped his hand around her waist, pulling her to him and kissing her hard, his mouth open, his tongue darting.

They kissed passionately for a full minute. Sloane was swept with a wave of physical desire, an almost blinding rush of lust. Just as it had been with Fernando, this was liberating, even more exhilarating than alcohol.

When the boy finally pulled away, he wordlessly took her hand and led her to a nearby Rolls-Royce. It had a huge backseat.

She looked back toward the hotel. The band was rocking away, vibrating the night air, not quite obliterating the sound of laughter and voices.

She looked back at him, straight into his daring eyes. And then she smiled and opened the car door.

The whole thing couldn't have taken five minutes. As soon as he pulled the door of the Rolls closed, he was upon her, thrashing around in the yards of fabric of her dress, tearing at her panty hose with one hand and unzipping his jeans with the other.

It was all so fast and violent and thrilling she nearly passed out for a moment. Before she realized it she was back standing on the pavement straightening her clothes and trying to catch her breath.

She looked up to see him standing next to her tucking in his shirt.

'I have to go, someone will be looking for me,' she told him. These were the first words either of them had spoken. She smiled, then, radiantly and without a backward glance, she walked away.

She turned back up the walkway, almost skipping with pure glee. She felt high, free, her own woman. She felt, for the first time in her life, completely in control.

When she returned to the dance, the entire atmosphere of the evening seemed changed. She smiled at anyone she passed and accepted every invitation to dance. Her date was nowhere in sight and she assumed he was off with a group of other boys drinking. She didn't care. She was having a wonderful time. She was the belle of the ball who never wanted the music to stop.

The following day she couldn't resist telling Alan. She felt only a tiny whisper of guilt and wondered if that was an appropriate reaction.

For a moment he was mildly shocked. Then he started to laugh. 'Sloane Taylor,' he said in a mock scold, 'you are a bad, bad girl.'

'Maybe,' she had acknowledged. 'It doesn't matter, Alan. It's only a game.'

During those last weeks in California the game continued, two times, sometimes even three times a week. It felt so good! It was always fast, anonymous, and thrilling. She stopped telling Alan about it. It was her game, her secret, her source of power.

In the back of her mind she felt it would all stop once she got to New York. Playing the game was a part of her life in Los Angeles. In New York she wouldn't need to play. There she would be someone else.

3

Kayzie Markham arrived in New York city in the summer of 1984 on the nineteen-dollar People's Express Airlines flight.

The first breath she drew when she stepped off the plane was like a shot of pure adrenaline. Riding into the city on the Carey bus, she knew if she went north of Ninety-sixth Street ever again she would be gasping for intellectual oxygen.

Her parents tried very hard not to show their disappointment at her not going to law school. She smiled to herself picturing their brave faces pressed against the big windows at the airport as she made her way to the gate. They knew she was doing something she had to do. Since grade school she had loved the written word. In high school and college she aimed at an eventual job that had anything to do with writing. She didn't care if it was newspapers, magazines, advertising, or book publishing. If there was a job to be had, no matter how menial, she'd take it. She could have found such a job in Boston, but to her anyone who entered publishing in Boston was simply biding time until they could get to New York. Her dad kept ticking off the wonderful opportunities right there at home. Kayzie wasn't listening. He had been right about one thing, she thought. There weren't many jobs for people who didn't have an MBA. Her liberal arts degree meant about as much as her mother's high school diploma had thirty years before. Only now prospective

81

employers didn't dare ask, 'Can you type?' Now they asked, 'Are you familiar with a word processor?'

Well, she was damn fit. She could run any office machine anyone could point to. Three summers working in Washington for a senator who had been her father's law partner, plus a part-time job on the Mt Holyoke literary magazine, should count for something.

But noooo. Her experience meant nothing to *Rolling Stone, The New Yorker, The New York Times,* or *Forbes*, or even the little weekly on the West Side run by a guy who looked like a bean stalk with ears. He wouldn't hire her, either. He called her the day after her failed interview and asked her out. He said he liked athletic blondes who wore glasses and swore.

She was so lonely she agreed to a couple of beers at an outdoor cafe on Columbus and a showing of a grainy print of *Mr Skeffington* at the Regency.

He wasn't very interesting or fun, but the only other human she had had a real conversation with since she arrived was the wacky woman who lived in the studio across the hall. They met while Kayzie was waiting for the only working drier in the basement washroom to complete the wash-and-wear cycle. The woman had hair that looked like an exploding dandelion and talked a blue streak. She said she was a free-lance writer currently looking for work. At least they had something in common.

By the time winter set in, when the Chase Manhattan cash machine spit out a little slip with a low two-figure balance, Kayzie was ready to take a job working as an office temp.

This morning she realized she would have to apply wearing jeans and socks. She was down to no panty hose – zip . . . nothing . . . nada. Once more she reached into the bottom of her handbag and checked for the last truly valuable thing she had in her possession: her mother's charge card at Bloomingdale's.

She sat longer than the visit to the ladies' room required. She glanced up from the seat just in time to see the hand reaching over the top of the locked door of the booth. She stared in disbelief as a finger hooked under the strap of her shoulder bag, lifted it off the hook, over the door, and out of sight.

'Hey!' she yelled. 'Hey! Don't do that!'

Standing, she struggled to step free of the door that pulled inward against her. She called again, 'My bag, damn it! Someone just stole my bag! Son of a bitch!'

A woman standing in front of the long row of mirrors over the long row of sinks stopped primping and gave her a blank New York stare.

Kayzie raced out of the Bloomingdale's ladies' room, past a row of pay phones, down one of the shopping aisles that led to the shoe department, and skidded into a display of Maud Frizon shoes.

Too late.

She collapsed into a chair. Two anorexically chic young female salesclerks rushed up to her, their kohl-rimmed eyes round, their purple mouths pursed in concern; clearly, they were delighted by the distraction.

Kayzie spent the next hour in a daze, filling out forms in the manager's office, describing the split-second incident over and over to various members of the security staff. It was nearly closing time before she was through. Chutching a token generously proffered by the manager's secretary, she moved toward the Lexington Avenue IRT in the basement.

She squeezed aboard an uptown train before she realized she would need another token to get across town.

As the train rumbled out of the station, she felt someone pressing his crotch against her hip. He rubbed himself back and forth with the motion of the train. Panic and humiliation kept her from grinding the heel of her boot into his instep. By the time the train lurched into the East Eighty-sixth Street station, frustration and rage had produced a sour little trickle in the back of her throat.

The long, cold walk through Central Park filled her with conflicting emotions. For the first time since she had arrived she cursed the city, its dirt, its danger and cost, and its ability to crush the spirit of even the most hardened citizen. Then she looked out toward the skyscrapers that rimmed the park, jewels beckoning and full of promise, and a tiny gasp of awe escaped her freezing lips. This marvellous, maddening city was truly the centre of the universe – the final landing place of her soaring childhood dreams.

A saucer-eyed man wearing three suits of clothes and speaking Esperanto careened by. She stepped into the street that traversed the park to avoid him. She affected the New York night-walk that Melon, the woman across the hall, had shown her: shoulders hunched, head down, invisible.

Melon had been in New York only two months longer than Kayzie had and yet she acted like a native. When she had moved into the apartment across the hall, she had spent a fortune on fixing it up with money she said was from a trust fund from her mother's estate. Before they became friends Kayzie would pass Melon in the hall, her arms laden with shopping bags from the smart stores. Melon's door was always covered with messages from stores trying to deliver things. By the time the two of them actually got to know each other, Melon had run through all the money but at least she had a fully furnished apartment and closets full of happening New York clothes. That was something Kayzie envied more than a little bit whenever she opened yet another Care package from home of brownies or little puff-sleeve dresses she would never wear.

Kayzie had never met anyone quite like her new

neighbor. Melon was a free-lance magazine writer and supported herself between assignments doing something she vaguely referred to as 'telephone sales.' Through her contacts at all the magazines she always knew where the press parties were. Unless some guy took her to dinner, she ate at a movable feast of freeloads around town. Melon's entire diet seemed to consist of canapés from buffet tables either gobbled on site or secreted home in plastic Baggies she kept in her purse.

But that thought just reminded Kayzie of her own purse. *Shit:* particularly in such humiliating circumstances, it was a body blow, a tiny rape, that filled her with impotent rage.

She left the park at Central Park West and Eighty-sixth Street just as it started to drizzle. Suddenly a sharp, cutting wind swirled up Eighty-sixth Street from the river, sending the rain at a slant no umbrella would have deflected.

Keyless, she leaned on the super's bell in the hallway of her building, which had not too long ago been an eight-storey parking garage. When the yuppification of the West Side began, it too had been converted. Her apartment was a shoe box.

'Jaiss?' The super's voice rasped through the speaker box.

'Sancho, would you buzz me in, please? I lost my bag . . . my keys . . .' Her voice broke. She bit her lower lip feeling sorry for herself again.

'Who eezzz?'

'It's me,' she sighed, pressing her lips against the speaker box. 'Katherine Markham? Four B!' She was annoyed that after three months and the constant drizzle of small tips, not to mention the big fat 'fixture fee' bribe she had handed over, he still didn't recognize her voice. Back home people recognized your voice if you called across the lake in the middle of the night.

'Ho-kay, ho-kay. I bus you,' he slurred. As usual, the

super was drunk, but he managed to find the master key and accompany her to her apartment, which was on the top floor.

Her studio consisted of one large room with an incongruous structural column running directly up the middle of it. Others in the building who had the same column had tried everything from stick-on mirrors to trained ivy to disguise the thing. Kayzie's solution was to screw hooks on it and use it as a giant coatrack. She had done the best she could to furnish the box. She'd bought a Conran's pullout couch, two lamps from the Salvation Army Thrift Shop, and she'd found a coffee table on the street. Her mother shipped her an overstuffed easy chair, paying twice its original cost to get it to New York along with some framed posters left over from college.

She tossed her raincoat at the pillar. It missed and fell to the sisal rug from Woolworth's, where she let it remain. Her legs felt like lead stilts and her head throbbed with anger.

She went to the tiny counter that served as a kitchen and poured herself a very dark scotch. The light on the answering machine beckoned. Her mother, probably, wanting a report on the job search. She didn't really want to talk about it.

She rewound the tape, pushed the replay button, and sat down in the big chair.

Beep. 'Hi, Kayzie. It's Jerry from *West Side Life*. Thought you might like to go to the Third Avenue Fair on Sunday. Call me at the office.'

The bean stalk, she thought. Big deal. A burrito and a Tab at a block party.

Beep. 'Kayz! It's me, Melon. I left a whole side of salmon from a lunch at the Waldorf in your fridge. Mine's full. I'll be by to help you eat it. Bye-de-bye.'

Kayzie turned off the machine and took a deep swallow of her drink, making a face at its strength. For the first time she was glad she'd given her neighbor an emergency set of keys to her apartment. At least it wouldn't be too hard to replace her own set. She sat back and mentally poured the contents of her stolen handbag onto a blank sheet of paper. She pictured her keys, her mother's Bloomingdale's card, makeup, a brand-new blusher with a terrific sable brush, eight dollars in cash, and her prescription sunglasses. No way could she afford to replace those until she got a job.

The lobby buzzer jolted her out of her misery.

'Hi, you home?' Melon's disembodied voice chirped through the intercom next to the sink. 'I stopped by a thing at Tavern-on-the-Green on the way home. I've got a hunk of Brie to go with the fish. Can I come up?'

Kayzie was exhausted and didn't particularly want company. But she needed to borrow some money until she could get to the bank. 'Sure, come on up,' she answered, mimicking Melon's giddy tone.

Upon arriving in Kayzie's apartment, Melon unwrapped a piece of Brie the size of half a phonograph record and tore off a chunk. 'This wasn't easy,' she said around a mouthful. 'Some guy saw me take it, but I just kept on going,' she said, flopping onto the couch. Good manners prevented Kayzie from commenting on the deliberately provocative way Melon dressed. It was her business, but Kayzie often wondered how long before some pervert would bop her over the head and drag her into the park. She was wearing black satin pants, so tight there couldn't be room for underwear, and six-inch heels. The V neck of her hot-pink top revealed about six inches of cleavage. Her taxi-yellow hair was pulled back on one side and anchored with a cluster of black plastic grapes.

Kayzie eyed the cheese and shook her head. 'One of these days you're going to get arrested for swiping all this food, Mel.'

'Who cares? Pretty soon I won't have to steal to eat,' she said, slicing off a dripping wedge of cheese and offering it to Kayzie. 'I'll be rolling in dough.'

Kayzie was getting used to Melon's schemes. Every day there was something new. Some fabulous story she was going to write, some unreachable person she was going to waylay and interview. 'What now?' Kayzie asked between bites of cheese.

'I'm going to get an interview with Warner Bromley.'

'Impossible.'

'Don't you dare say impossible,' Melon snapped. 'Nothing is impossible.'

'I've read that he's never granted an interview. What makes you think you can do it?'

'Oh, he'll talk to me. I told his London office I was with *Realto* magazine.'

'You called London?'

'Sure, at this jerky job I have I can make all the calls I want.'

'Melon! You're going to get yourself in a pile of trouble doing something like that. You don't have an assignment from *Realto* – do you?'

Melon jumped up from the couch and flounced across the room toward Kayzie's refrigerator. She opened it and pulled out a foot-long package. 'Yawan some of this fish?'

Kayzie sighed. 'I better eat while I can. Your liberated food may be all that's left between me and starvation.'

Melon slapped the salmon onto a bread board and carried it to the coffee table, the head and tail protruding forlornly over either end. She forked up a chunk of flesh and popped it between her Frosted Burnt Sienna lips. 'Let me tell you about me and the great *Realto* magazine. I lied to you a bit.'

'About what?'

'About myself. You see, the reason I came to New York was to sell a story I had, ah, well, stumbled on in California. I didn't know where to go, and the first magazine I picked up on the plane was *Realto*. I looked at the page that lists who runs the place and called up the publisher. Anyway, I sold them my story and made a lot of money. I didn't buy all that stuff in my apartment with my mother's estate. I don't have a mother, and if I did, she sure as hell wouldn't have an estate.'

'Melon!'

'Are you mad at me?'

'No, I'm not mad at you. It's just that lying about a dead mother is a bit much.'

'I guess, but they told me it was better if no one knew where the story came from. I was pissed because I wanted my name on the story. Anyway, part of my deal with them was that if I could come up with something really hot, they'd run another story for the same kind of money and I'd get my name on it. I didn't realize at the time that I was sort of being set up. They're real sharp over there. In a way what they did was say here's half of what this story is worth, now go out and hustle something else and we'll pay you the other half.'

'So now you're going after someone they can't ignore?'

'You got it.' Melon took one more piece and began to wrap up the fish. 'You want me to leave this? There's plenty left.'

'Maybe you better. You saw what's in the fridge. I don't even have milk for coffee in the morning.'

'No luck with a job, huh?'

'No job, plus I got robbed today.'

Melon's mouth flew open. 'Robbed! My God. Where?'

'The ladies' room at Bloomingdale's.'

'In the john?'

'No. *On* the john.'

'While you were inside one of those tiny booths? Why didn't you let her go first?'

'Cute,' Kayzie said without smiling. 'Anyway, I was sitting there minding my own business when I see this hand reaching over the top of the door.'

'What colour hand?'

'What difference does it make, Melon?' Kayzie said, exasperated. 'I was too terrified to notice.'

'I just like to get the details so I can file them away. You never know where you can use something like that.'

'Damn, Melon, talking to you is like putting it all on a tape recorder.'

'So what did you have in the bag?'

'Everything – keys, cards, glasses, money, my life.'

'Do you need a loan? I got paid today. I could let you have something.'

Kayzie rose and walked to the windowsill. She began to pick the dead leaves off a nearly terminal philodendron. 'Just for groceries tomorrow until I can get to the bank,' she said gratefully. 'What I really need is a job. I've been to every publication in town. I'm willing to take any entry-level job and starve. I just want to be around writing and journalism.'

Melon rose, teetering on her high pumps. 'Look, I'm going over to the magazine tomorrow to pitch my Bromley story. Let me ask this guy if he knows of anything.'

'Would you? That would be great!'

Melon moved toward the door. 'You type?'

Kayzie drew a long breath and exhaled. 'Yes, Melon, I type.' Suddenly she felt an overwhelming fatigue. 'Thanks for the picnic, pal.' She closed her eyes. When she heard the door click shut, she opened them.

Melon was gone, and as she had expected, so was the fish.

Kayzie spent the following day cleaning the studio, a compulsive habit she indulged whenever she had to wait for something to happen that was beyond her control. At noon she ran to the corner deli, restocking the refrigerator with the money Melon had loaned her. By five the place gleamed and the bathroom sparkled. Now she could reward herself with a hot meal, a long bath, and whatever movie was on TV.

While she waited for the pasta water to boil, she walked to the single window. It had been snowing since sunset and inky water was beginning to leak through the cheaply constructed casement windows and spread onto the sill she had just finished scrubbing.

The rooftops below were dusted with a confectioners' sugar coating. The West Side was all earth tones during the day. When it snowed, it looked like a black-and-white photo of a nineteenth-century cityscape.

All day the thought of Melon's actually being able to find a job had filtered through the loud rock music she played when she cleaned. Melon was the most singularly self-absorbed human being she had ever met. She must really be desperate if she'd come to count on her. Often, just to hold your attention, Melon promised things she then promptly forgot.

When the downstairs buzzer sounded, she jumped. That would be Melon, perhaps with good news. Eagerly she pushed the button on the intercom. 'Yes!' she answered.

' 'S me,' Melon called. 'You're there?'

'I'm here. Come on up.' Kayzie stood by the door and said a little prayer to whichever saint was in charge of gainful employment while she was waiting.

Melon swept into the apartment looking like a polyester Sasquatch man. She wore a huge fake-fur coat that reached to her ankles and a high fake-fur hat that nearly buried her tiny face.

She threw a matching fake-fur muff onto the couch and flopped beside it. 'I got good news for you – that is, if you're serious about an entry-level job in journalism,' she said, picking through a bowl of stale Goldfish on the coffee table. Kayzie knew Melon was looking for a pizza flavoured one. She stared at her. Her trust in what Melon considered good news was not too firm.

'Don't tell me. You met someone from the *Times* and they're going to get me my own route.'

'Seriously, you're going to flip,' Melon said around a mouthful of crackers. 'There's a job opening at *Realto*.'

Something in Melon's tone told Kayzie she meant it.

Kayzie jumped to her feet. 'Melon! You mean it? I'll take it unless it involves prostitution. I couldn't take the small talk.'

'Sit,' Melon commanded in her best dog-trainer voice. 'I'll tell you all I know about it. Then you decide what you want to do.'

'Anything. Oh, God, Melon, I'm so broke.'

'Now, the publisher, a woman named Layla Bronz, just fired her assistant. She seems to have trouble keeping them. This guy I know there says you should come in about taking the job.'

'Why did they fire her?'

'Get this. Because she forgot to make dinner reservations and Bronz got a bad table at Lutèce.'

'That's important?'

'To these people. You bet.'

'She sounds like a dragon lady,' Kayzie groaned. She remembered that she was out of panty hose. She couldn't be picky.

Melon shrugged. 'I don't want to talk you into anything, but *Realto* is a very fancy place. You'd meet a lot of fabulous people, and who knows, you could end up a writer after that.'

'A secretary doesn't get much of a chance to write, Melon.'

'You never know. I think that's how Clare Booth Luce started. Anyway, what have you got to lose? Here.' She pushed a piece of paper across the coffee table. 'Call this guy Cole Latimer. Tell him you're a friend of mine and go see him about it.'

As Melon rose to go, she poured the rest of the Goldfish into her bag.

'Okay. I'll do it,' Kayzie decided with a smile. 'How can I thank you, Melon? This was very sweet of you.'

'Just get the job. I'm getting tired of having two mouths to feed.'

Kayzie spent all Saturday afternoon in the periodical library on Fifth Avenue. In the second-floor research room she typed Layla Bronz into the computer. It took well over three minutes for it to print out the list of articles about the woman. She pulled some of the references – and couldn't believe what she read. But what really got her were the pictures. Bronz arriving at the Opera Ball with Kirk Douglas; Bronz alighting from Donald Trump's limousine. Bronz arriving at Mortimer's for a private dinner in her honour hosted by the Kissingers, Henry looking jet-jagged and Nancy almost invisible in a cloud of cigarette smoke. There was Bronz testifying before a Senate subcommittee, Bronz receiving a citation for her contribution to some charity, and finally, Bronz, the King of Yugoslavia, and a small dog aloft in one of Malcolm Forbes's balloons over France.

By five o'clock she had read several magazine profiles and back issues of the *Times*. She knew a great deal about Layla Bronz, the powerful magazine publisher, but very little about Layla Bronz the woman. None of the articles seemed to know where she came from nor how she got to where she was. Obviously, the woman herself wouldn't say.

Kayzie awoke the morning of the interview with such an anxiety attack that she had to take a long, soaking bath. Before leaving the apartment she neatly folded her least-fictitious resume into her handbag in case the one she mailed to Mr Latimer had gone astray.

Dressed in her best and only suit, the same grey flannel number she wore to dinner the last time her father was in town for a Bar Association meeting, she checked herself in the mirror by the door. She saw a nice, plain face, made striking by the big, soft, grey-blue eyes framed by incongruously dark eyebrows. She adjusted the thin headband across the crown of her dark blonde hair, took one last look, and shrugged. 'Be grateful for inner resources, kid. Veronica Hamill in the next life, maybe.'

When she confirmed the appointment, she had been told to present herself at the Bronz private town house on East Seventy-seventh Street. The magazine's editorial offices were in a small office building next door.

As she turned the corner of Seventy-seventh, she could see the imposing house midway down the block. The real gaslights in brass sconces on either side of the front door cast a warm glow in the chill, grey morning air. There were large windows on each floor softened by lowered Austrian shades, opaque enough to let in light but hide any sign of life within.

She stood at the top of the high stoop, trying to control her nerves. Beneath the oval glass of the huge oak door was a small brass plaque stating RING BELL.

'Who is it?'

Kayzie jumped. The voice was coming from a small speaker mounted at the side of the door. 'Uh, Katherine Markham. I have an appointment to see Ms Bronz.' She made it sound like a question. 'I'm a friend of Melon Tuft.'

'Oh, yes, yes,' the voice said impatiently, 'Come in.'

The voice sounded male but she couldn't be sure. Slowly she turned the heavy brass knob and leaned into the door. 'Hullo?' she called down the long, dark hall. The walls were lacquered a shiny gardenia-leaf green. More brass sconces high on the walls defused the light and made the walls look wet.

To her left was a curved staircase. From the second-floor landing a pale head of hair peeped over the railing. In the dim light Layzie couldn't be sure of its gender. As she reached the foot of the stairs, she saw him. He was average height and wearing a navy blazer, and grey flannel trousers. As he made his way down the carpeted stairs, he reminded her of Gig Young in an old Doris Day movie. When he got closer, she could smell his cologne.

'Hi, there,' he said with an engaging grin. 'I'm Cole Latimer. So, you're Melon's friend.' He extended a hand bearing a heavy crest ring on the little finger.

She shook his hand briefly. 'Well, actually she's my next-door neighbor.'

'Ummm,' he said, moving his eyes in a V, sizing up the dull grey suit, the plain black pumps, and schoolgirl white blouse. 'I don't know what I expected,' he said brightly, 'but it wasn't you.'

'Thank you, I guess.' She smiled.

'Now,' he chirped, 'Ms Bronz left word that she would see you in her office here in the house. Most of the magazine is put together in that dirty yellow building next door. You'd be working for Ms Bronz personally so she wanted to see you here.' He turned and started down the hall. 'Come, she's on the phone right now. You can wait in here.' He gestured toward the massive double doors halfway down the hall on the right.

She stepped past him and entered a room that made her breath catch.

'I understand Ms Tuft thinks she can get an interview with Warner Bromley,' Latimer said from the door.

Kayzie attempted to listen and take in the room simultaneously. 'Ummm,' she responded blankly, her eyes moving slowly from the walls to the tabletops laden with a most remarkable assortment of objects.

'Forgive me,' he said. 'Where are my manners? Please do sit down. Let me tell Ms Bronz you're here.' He disappeared through another set of double doors at the end of the room.

Kayzie hadn't seen a room like this since she toured the furniture collection at the Metropolitan Museum. Tufted and fringed velvet sofas and armchairs in deep tones of red and gold sat at angles throughout the room. The massive carved fireplace mantel was flanked by eight-foot-high tapestries. The floor was covered with Persian carpets placed on top of dark red wall-to-wall carpeting.

Next to the couches and chairs were round tables of various sizes. Each was covered with gold watered silk, the glass tops aclutter with photographs framed in silver or tortoiseshell. There were engraved boxes, framed citations and medallions, and odd English antique-silver bits and pieces.

She ran her hand over a burnished wooden box bearing a tiny silver plaque that read, 'To Layla Bronz with deep appreciation — Ronald and Nancy — Inauguration Day, 1981.' There was a formal, signed picture of Prince Charles dressed in his Duke-of-Cornwall uniform, another of the late Shah of Iran wearing ski gear and smiling into a blazing sun; a pensive Mikhail Baryshnikov in leotards; Truman Capote staring into the camera with a stuffed python curled at his shoulder. Frank Sinatra smiled up at her over folded arms, and Gloria Vanderbilt looked cool and rich. Each photograph was signed with some personal salutation.

Two objects dominated the room: an overwhelming crystal chandelier that even turned low snapped rainbow points of light against the dark-panelled walls, and over the mantel, a larger-than-life oil portrait done in a Boldini style, dark-hued and romantic, of a beautiful woman mounted sidesaddle on a rearing stallion. The hooves attacked a stormy sky. The woman sat regally in a full black split skirt and a tall silk hat. A tiny black veil played across her high forehead and dramatically dark eyes. Kayzie plunked down into a velvet couch. All the room needed was a pair of borzois arching and drooping around the fire.

'Ms Bronz will see you now,' she heard Latimer's voice say from the door at the end of the room. He said it in an exaggerated way that implied that he and Kayzie shared some kind of joke.

Layla Bronz's office was only slightly less grand than

the room Kayzie had just left. The outer room had smelled of lemon furniture polish and cinnamon pot-pourri. This room smelled of an exotic perfume and cigarette smoke. The office faced the street, and the filtered light from the gauzy Austrian shades over the two large windows silhouetted the woman standing behind a Regency desk.

The top of the desk was completely covered with books, manuscripts, newspapers, and file folders stuffed with photographs. A brimming alabaster ashtray tee-tered precariously atop the mass of newspapers.

'Good morning,' said the silhouette. 'I'm Layla Bronz.'

Kayzie had to squint to make out her face. 'Good morning, Ms Bronz.'

'Here, let me turn on the lamp,' the woman said softly. 'I don't take the morning light too well. Forgive me.'

Her voice was several registers lower than Kayzie expected. She seemed to have a trace of an English accent although nothing Kayzie had read about her suggested she was anything but American born and bred.

With the lamp on, Kayzie could see that the woman was, indeed, the equestrienne in the drawing-room portrait, only more striking. She had poreless skin and was perfectly, if somewhat heavily, made up for the early hour. Her blue-black hair was parted in the centre and pulled into a chignon at the back of her neck. It sat low and full as if waiting for Gregory Peck to pull a hairpin and send it tumbling down her back.

'I'm Katherine Markham,' she said from a seated position. *God. How dumb,* she thought, cringing inwardly. *I'm already sitting down. Why didn't I say that when I was standing up?* She felt her armpits beginning to grow moist, threatening her one good blouse. *If I don't get this job, I won't be able to afford to have it cleaned.*

'So,' Ms Bronz said, pushing a cigarette into a long ivory holder. 'What exactly is a Katherine Markham?'

Kayzie shoved her hand farther under her thigh and

97

tried to square her shoulders. 'Well, ah,' she began, 'she's a BA in liberal arts, Mt Holyoke. Here, I have my resume.' She made a feeble attempt to reach her bag, but the strap was caught on the small gold crescent pin on her lapel.

Layla waved her unlighted cigarette dismissively. 'So do I. Cole gave it to me, but I'd rather hear it from you. Go on.'

'Ah . . . okay. My father's a lawyer in Boston. My mother teaches high school English. I worked three summers for Senator Stratton during college and edited the –'

'Donny Stratton?' Layla's voice rose. She exhaled a long blue stream of smoke and snapped shut the top of a lighter that looked like a jewel-encrusted Fabergé egg. 'Now, there is one gorgeous hunk of a man. Donny Stratton has the most beautiful legs God ever gave a man. Great buns, too. Lousy tennis player, but he makes up for it by giving you the chance to watch the buns at work. How is he?'

Kayzie jumped imperceptibly. Senator Donald Dunsmore Stratton was vice chairman of the Senate Foreign Relations Committee, a Boston Brahmin married to a fifth-generation socialite. He had three beautiful blonde children and the dignity of a prince of the church. It had never occurred to Kayzie that he had beautiful legs. Buns either, for that matter. 'Ah . . well . . . ah . . . fine, I guess,' she stammered. 'I just wrote his monthly news-letter for constituents back home. I –'

Layla's bracelets clattered as she responded to a tiny light blinking on the desk phone. It had not yet rung. 'Yes, Cole. Tell me the problem.' She spoke quickly, a slight irritation in her voice.

Kayzie studied her as she listened. Lordy, she thought, this was one imposing lady! Look at that suit! If it wasn't a real Chanel, it was one of those two-thousand-dollar Adolfos all the Nancy ladies wore.

Layla replaced the receiver and turned back to Kayzie. 'Do you think Don Johnson is sexy?'

Kayzie stared at her. 'Don Johnson? You mean the actor from *Miami Vice*?'

'That one.'

'I guess so.'

'Well, I don't. His press agent thinks he'd make a good profile. I think he's too down-market. Would you sleep with him?'

Kayzie blanched and then started to laugh. 'Can I make up my mind when he asks?'

Layla threw back her head and laughed, too. It was more of a cough, a singular sound. 'Now, back to Katherine Markham. It is Katherine, right?'

'Well, everyone calls me Kayzie. It's short for Katherine Zelda. My mother had a thing about Zelda Fitzgerald when I was born.'

'I hope she outgrew it. Zelda was completely bats.' Layla smiled, revealing for the first time a flash of even, white teeth. Immediately the teeth disappeared behind the crimson lips. She leaned forward and placed both elbows flat on the edge of the desk, interlacing her long, jewelled fingers. 'You know anything about the magazine business?'

'I read them,' Kayzie said lamely.

'Well, that's something. You type?'

Somehow the question was easier to take coming from her. She wiggled all ten fingers. The five she had been sitting on were sound asleep.

'Spell?'

'Not too bad. Embarrass with two *r*'s, harass with one, commas inside the quotes, semicolons out.'

'Well, that's a breakthrough these days. How about dealing with celebrities? I mean egos the size of Brazil. Movie stars, models, socialites, captains of industry, people who are famous for being famous. Bloodsuckers and leeches.'

'That would depend on what I had to do for them.'

'Nothing without your clothes on.'

'I see.' Kayzie nodded, trying to be as blasé as possible. 'I don't have a problem with celebrities. I've never known any. Ah . . . Melon Tuft said —'

'Christ! I forgot. You're the girl she sent around.' Layla frowned. 'How well do you know Melon Tuft?'

'Not well, we're neighbors. She's working. I'm not.'

'Did she tell you that the last few people who had this job didn't work out? If she didn't tell you, that's dirty pool, so I'm letting you know right up front.'

'She did mention that but it wouldn't have made any difference.'

'Straight answer, I like that.' Layla smiled. 'Tell me, Katherine Zelda, where do you want to be five years from now?'

Kayzie had to think for a moment. No one had ever asked her that. 'What do I want to be or where do I think I *will* be?'

'If you want to complicate it, be my guest.'

'I think I *will* be a writer five years from now. What I *want* to be is a writer and loved.' She felt slightly embarrassed at having said something so personal.

Layla nodded slowly, absorbing Kayzie's answer. 'And you think you'll find what you want here?'

'I don't expect to find someone to love me here, but I have a lot to learn about life and I could learn it here. That would make me a better writer. When I heard about this job, I thought it would be interesting, and frankly, I wanted to meet you. I figured that if I didn't get the job, at least I would have accomplished that.'

'My! That's very flattering. Most of the flattery I get is pure horse manure, but that sounded nice. Do you know why I have such trouble keeping someone in this job?'

'I have no idea.'

'The rules,' Layla said, lighting another cigarette. Kayzie was beginning to see that the woman used cigarette-lighting the way men use a pipe; it was a stop-action device. 'Are you ready for the rules?'

Kayzie nodded and tried to sit as straight as the angle of the couch would permit.

Layla exhaled. 'People who work for me are an extension of me. Everyone has a kink of some kind. I expect it. You can do drugs, drink, screw swans – I don't care as long as you do it on your own time. Here in the office or in public where people know you work for me, it's straight-arrow all the way.'

So far, so good, Kayzie thought. She didn't do any of those things. Maybe a glass of wine at lunch on Fridays, but no drugs surely, and forget swans.

'Do you get cramps?'

'Pardon?' Kayzie started. She seemed to recall hearing that some federal regulation prohibited that sort of question when hiring. 'Ah . . . sometimes.'

'Ever have them so bad you couldn't get to work?'

'No,' Kayzie answered, baffled.

'Here's why I ask. If you had cramps, if you have a hangover, if you meet some guy who keeps you up all night, what would you do?'

'I'd take a cold shower and two aspirin and come to work.'

'Good. You see, the point I'm trying to make is that I understand life's little dislocations. I can deal with any of them. But grandmothers dying, apartments getting burglarized, nonspecific ailments . . . those are excuses, often lies. We are far too busy getting a top-notch magazine out every month to figure whether or not we're being conned by our own people. We are workaholics and we like to hire workaholics.'

'I understand.'

'There's more.' Layla held up a forefinger. 'Anyone who works for me personally, as you would be, comes to know a lot about my private life. You'd have to deal with my masseuse, my lawyer, my broker, even the woman who comes to do my nails and eyelashes.' She closed her eyes and extended her head toward Kayzie. 'These are fakes and require a lot of upkeep.' She held out her hand displaying her long nails. 'And so are these. Now. Cole is my second-in-command. Buck Hayes is my editor in chief. He handles the day-to-day editorial work. All our reporters are free-lance. Also over in the other building is the art department, advertising, sales, marketing, et cetera, et cetera. I handle everything and you handle me. Then there is the press. Day or night, the press.'

'Night? What are the hours?' Kayzie ventured.

'Don't ask,' Layla said, fanning the air. 'By the press I mean anyone from *The New York Times* to Mike Wallace. *L'Osservatore Romano* to the *National Enquirer*. If I'm not in, find me. I always leave a trail. There are four hours of the day when I won't talk to the press and that's because I'm asleep. There is one exception.' She looked straight at Kayzie, who was hanging on her every word. 'I am always available to Warner Bromley.'

'Warner Bromley?' Kayzie caught her breath. '*The* Warner Bromley?'

'Right.'

She thought of Melon and how hard she was working to get an interview with him. She knew she wouldn't be sitting here if it hadn't been for Melon. She owed her one. But how to go about it. 'He's very famous,' she ventured. 'And yet I've never read a story about him. I mean, like a real interview.'

'He doesn't give interviews.'

'What if he did. Wouldn't that be worth a lot of money?' The expression on Layla Bronz's face made her wish she hadn't asked.

'If it happens,' Layla snapped.

'I see,' Kayzie said weakly.

'Now. When can you start?' Layla said without warning.

Good Lord, Kayzie thought, *I'm being offered the job!*
'Ah, well, right away . . . ah, is tomorrow too soon?'

Layla rose and extended her hand. Her index finger
drooped slightly with the weight of a huge amethyst
encircled with smaller diamonds. Kayzie took her hand.
It felt cool and strong. 'I like you, Katherine Zelda.'

'Thank you.' Kayzie laughed nervously. In the light she
could see Layla's long lashes and smoky-grey lids. She
was astonished. Her eyes were as dramatic and exaggerated as the ring she wore. And exactly the same
colour.

Layla withdrew her hand and held Kayzie's gaze. 'You
scared?' She smiled.

'A little.'

'Grand. Stay that way. We'll get along fine.'

It was snowing again as Kayzie made her way down the
steep front steps. She hadn't brought a scarf or umbrella.
She knew her thin raincoat would be soaked through
before she made it to Madison Avenue. She didn't care.
She had a job! Probably one of the most intriguing in
New York City. She didn't know how much she would be
paid, what she would be asked to do, or even if she would
know how to do it. She felt giddy. When she saw the taxi
rounding the corner, she decided to celebrate and hailed
it.

She couldn't wait to tell Melon. If it weren't for her,
none of this would be happening. Perhaps now she would
be in a position to do Melon a favour in return.

4

When she left L.A. for New York city in the summer of 1984, Sloane had anticipated Oz. She found Calcutta.

Alan had preceded her by a month to find an apartment and work out his threatened love affair with Brad Rampart. Armed with celebrity-client recommendations from Salon Salon, Alan found a job right away at Bergdorf's and gleefully phoned Sloane to hurry up and join him.

The day before she left, Noreen returned from her honeymoon. They endured a tearful lunch. Sloane promised all the things she knew she had to – to write, to phone, to 'be good,' to eat right, and of course, take care of her nails.

Sloane left feeling better about their relationship but glad that it would now be a long-distance one. She was free to be her own woman.

Alan got her a package deal at an East Side hotel for two weeks while his lover, Brad, worked on finding her a sublet. The day she was to check out of the hotel she called Noreen with the news. Alan's 'contacts', as she referred to them (actually it was Brad), had been able to get her a contract with Snap, a top model agency. Noreen said that was nice but explained she had to run because she was late for her manicure.

The sublet loft on Warren Street Brad found for her wasn't what one would call cozy. It had an eighteen-foot ceiling and an industrial elevator, but the rent was manageable and it was hers for a full year.

None of Alan's warnings about the city prepared her for the squalor, the mountains of garbage, and the filthy subway full of homeless people who moved in slow motion like great mounds of dirty clothing. It was a city of rudeness and rejection and yet with the energy and style that excited her.

There was a man who lived in a supermarket wagon on the corner of her block, she had roaches in her sink, and a kid smoked crack in the doorway of the restaurant across the street.

She had never been happier.

During her first few months in the city she learned several useful things. Pigeon droppings from higher than the second story permanently stained silk, heels higher than two inches required good medical coverage for the wearer, and twice a day a casual pass across the forehead and cheeks revealed enough dirt to warrant a facial. Strangers fell into two categories: pathologically kind or gruntingly rude.

Worse than the esthetic chaos was the competition. Without her California contacts, Sloane was just another pretty face. Her figure, her face, her portfolio, were no better or worse than those of the hundreds of other girls pursuing the same dream. She wondered whether being Miss California would have given her an advantage until she met Miss Iowa, Miss August, Miss Teen U.S.A., and Miss Sweden all passing time in the same agency waiting rooms she frequented.

She dated when someone insisted. There were coked-up Wall Street yuppies, cuff-shooting agents, and greying garmentos in silver suits. None of them really interested her and she dreaded the end of an evening when she would invariably say no. She had gone almost six months without playing the game and attributed that to the fact that she, at least, now had a modicum of control over her life.

The most enjoyable part of her social life was dinner

out with Alan and Brad or one of the friends Alan had made through his work. AIDS was clearing the great disco floor that was gay life in New York. The party, at least the reckless one being played before the Plague, was tragically winding down. Although Alan chose not to discuss the situation most of the time, she soon came to recognize his expression of utter defeat when someone at work began to lose weight and complain of physical problems that could no longer be dismissed as 'the flu' or a sore throat, when lesions once hidden by long sleeves or trouser legs began appearing on friends' faces and hands. She made a couple of hospital calls with him, laden with goodies that were never eaten and books that were never read. The visits filled her with an all-consuming sadness. In the back of her mind there was also fear for Alan and what might have happened in his past. She could not bear the thought of losing him.

Her most exciting hours were spent at her twice-a-week acting class. She loved everything about it, the atmosphere of dedication to a craft, the chance to stretch her mind and be someone else: an old woman one night, a whining child the next. It motivated her to read more than an occasional best-selling paperback or the morning paper. She was never happier than she was in the dusty walk-up apartment on Grove Street where the class met. Only there did she feel she was growing, learning more about herself and her reactions to life, things hardly provided in her work for Snap. Her bookings were routine but they paid the rent and the acting class fees. She knew now without a doubt that she wanted acting more than anything else. Unfortunately, so did every other model or waiter or clerk at Bloomingdale's. She read the theatrical trades every day and when her modeling schedule permitted, showed up for one frustrating and fruitless audition after another.

By the time she had been in New York six months, her disappointment had mounted into frustration, then desperation, and finally despair. Things just didn't seem to be working. It was hard enough to endure the arrogance of agents who promised you the moon but couldn't deliver, but dealing with the condescension of would-be producers who were more interested in seeing you cross your legs than act was more bitter.

She had talent, she knew she did. Why wouldn't just one of them take a chance on her?

She had made her way through the lobby of the casting director's midtown building feeling sick with disappointment and confused about her future. She hated the men who seemed to have gained control of her career and destiny. Her carefully cultivated mask and flirtatious manner seemed to have lost their magic for bending men to her will. In California, she'd worked with people who had known her — or at least known of her — as a professional since she was a toddler. She had worked in a business community where her name meant something. But none of that had translated to New York. Gone was the assumed recognition she had enjoyed back home. While her resume spoke of her experience, stacked up against the competition in New York, it wasn't all that exceptional, and alone it wasn't enough to open doors for her. Compounding the dreary state of her career was the emptiness of her personal life. It had been a long, lonely time since she had been held and loved by anyone whom she could love back.

Lost in thoughts and self-pity, she headed west across town oblivious to the noise and bustle of the streets. Unconsciously, she looked beyond the people she passed, never making eye contact. She angled her shoulders to avoid touching anyone.

She didn't know where she was going and she didn't care. She let the flow of humanity around her carry her. At Fiftieth Street the crowd slowed its pace as many turned into the side entrance of Saks. Before she knew it she was being pushed through the door. Why not? she thought listlessly, maybe she'd buy herself a tiny feel-good present. Even a new lipstick at this point would help.

Getting to the cosmetic area meant passing through the men's department. She passed a display of collarless shirts Alan loved so much and paused to check the price and sizes. As she lifted a pile of striped ones, she briefly looked up to find herself staring directly into a pair of almost hooded black eyes. A dark-skinned young man standing a few feet away was staring at her in open admiration. Tall, slender, and well-built, he looked as if he had stepped out of a fashion layout promoting an elegant casual look. He was wearing a soft grey leather jacket over a pale blue shirt like the ones on sale. His tight Jordache jeans followed contours of his muscular thighs. She could see from the angle at which he was standing that he had a dancer's buttocks. His sleek black hair was pulled back into a low ponytail that accentuated a vaguely Latin and very handsome face. As their eyes remained locked, she noticed the reason his seemed hooded was the shadow cast by his thick, dark lashes. Slowly, he smiled.

Disarmed, she smiled back, wondering if he had read her thoughts, sensed her loneliness and need. Thinking of it made her dizzy, almost as if she were falling. She immediately broke eye contact and sauntered away, heading for the escalator.

Since losing Fernando, she had an unbearable fear that if she loved someone with all her being, she would lose control of her emotional being and leave herself vulnerable to certain heartbreak. Even now, so many months later, she still felt the pain of loss. If she didn't care about a man, it was easy to control him, keeping him at a distance that tantalized him and kept her safe. But if she was attracted to someone, she became frightened; such men were too great a threat. For protection, she made herself unattainable. It protected her heart, which she now knew was too fragile to withstand deep love.

As she neared the top of the escalator, she glanced over her shoulder. The man with the thick eyelashes was a half-dozen steps below her. He was still staring at her. She smiled to herself. She had no intention of playing the game today. She hadn't played since coming to New York, and it was the furthest thing from her mind. Until she saw he was following her, that gleaming look in his eye. Her heart began to pound in a familiar rhythm that signaled every nerve ending that the bait had been taken.

Before she knew it, the chase had begun.

Deliberately, she rode the elevator up to the lingerie department and started strolling among the displays, pretending she was unaware that he was a few yards behind her. She stopped at a rack of sheer nightgowns and pulled one off its hanger. She held it to her body and stepped to the full-length mirror. There she could keep track of the man and safely tease him. She held the delicate black nightgown over her clothes, looking down at herself and then back into the mirror to see him standing only feet in back of her, smiling.

He said something in a language she didn't understand. It sounded vaguely Portuguese. He was holding another nightgown, gently fingering the texture of the fabric. With his other hand he stroked the soft material as lovingly as imaginary thighs. His eyes glowed with the promise of the real caresses he was offering.

In a pattern she was now quite familiar with, the bad Sloane that controlled her body began to argue with the sane Sloane who ordered her mind. She knew she should quit before it went too far, but the temptation was too much for her.

He was enraptured, following her every move with his eyes like a worshipful slave. And no one will know, she assured herself. It would make her feel better, even better than a new lipstick.

She turned and grabbed the nightgown out of his hands, letting him feel that she was offended by his behavior, and walked straight toward the dressing rooms. Her pulse was racing.

Once inside the cubicle she firmly closed the door and leaned against it to catch her breath. She glanced at her face in the three-sided mirror. It was flushed with the excitement of knowing that she had not lost the skill for delicious torment.

Ready for the next round of the game she arranged her mask, checking the makeup around her eyes. She pulled a lip pencil from her bag. As she finished redefining the line of her mouth, the dressing room door opened. With one swift motion he grabbed her wrists and forced them to her sides. He bent and covered her mouth with his lips. He raised one foot and pushed the door shut.

She struggled against him, knowing that initial protest was an integral step in the game. Her verbal objections were muted and then silenced by the warm wetness of his open mouth. He didn't stop until she was gasping for air. Now she had entered the most exhilarating phase of the game. He meant business, and the fact that they were in a relatively public, unlatched dressing room – and he obviously didn't care – just thrilled her all the more. She wrapped her arms around him, surrendering to his mouth, his hands, his muscular thighs pressing against hers. His hands disappeared under her sweater, fumbling for the catch of her bra. She closed her eyes in mute joy as he pulled her bra free, cupped her breasts, and teased them with his tongue. His hands roamed below her skirt, caressing her thighs, seeking out the valley between her hips. Her body arched and swayed, silently pleading . . . more! . . . more. He pinched her nipples as his kisses descended down her half-naked body. His mounting excitement drove her too near frenzy as he fumbled blindly for the zipper of his jeans.

This was the moment she craved with each game. That split second when a man could stand it no longer. When she was the total focus of all his senses. When his need to enter her was proof of her limitless power over him.

Sloane's entire being was transported into a dreamlike state. It had been so long since her body felt this good. The utter joy of sexual abandonment that had lain dormant deep inside her was now explosively alive. A man she didn't even know had totally succumbed to the power of her beauty. Though wildly aroused, part of her mind remained as calm as the eye of a devastating storm, at ease with the situation and blissfully accepting his silent, sensual tribute.

She glanced down and saw that he had released himself from the confines of his jeans. His proud erection was oddly framed in denim.

The dim voice of the sane Sloane danced through her mind in one last recriminating effort. *What am I doing? Am I out of my mind?* The voice fell silent in a wave of desire as he pulled her to him, wrapping his arms more tightly around her, his erection battling with the fabric of her skirt. His hands wrenched her skirt aside as his thighs pushed her against the wall. He reached behind her and cupped her buttocks in a steellike grip as he entered her. With a half-dozen driving strokes she reached orgasm and twisted her body away from him. His head, which had been locked between her neck and shoulder, suddenly sprang back. The expression on his face was a mixture of bewildered shock and disbelief at what she had just done. She yanked down her skirt, straightened her sweater and snatched her bag from the floor. Within a heartbeat she fled from the tiny room. She moved through the lingerie department as fast as she dared without attracting attention. As she reached the end of the aisle, she glanced back to see if he could possibly be following her. He was nowhere in sight.

As she descended the escalator, she smiled. She had a vivid picture in her mind of his standing in the ladies' dressing room, his painfully erect penis protruding from his jeans, his mind frozen in shock at what she had done to him.

She pushed her way through the Fifth Avenue entrance feeling almost weightless. She could feel a glow on her cheeks and a tingling in her limbs. Her mind clung to the moment. She knew it would not last for long.

She successfully hailed a cab at the corner of East Fiftieth Street in a dead heat with a woman laden with packages and a tote bag emblazoned with the motto: WHEN THE GOING GETS TOUGH, THE TOUGH GO SHOPPING. She wondered if she should tell the woman what she could get in Saks for free as she slammed the door and gave the driver her address.

That was the last frivolous thought she had. As soon as she leaned back, the voices started up in full cry.

What in God's name got into you?

But it felt so good!

It was cheap and degrading. Don't you have any self-respect?

Her euphoria drained away as she relived the experience through the eyes of the sane Sloane. Her mind reeled with internal disapproval and self-disgust, robbing her of the delight she had just felt. Suddenly her stomach turned against her, too. She felt sick, repulsed, ashamed, and confused. She prayed she wouldn't throw up in the man's cab.

'Driver,' she called feebly through the open partition. 'Could you please hurry. I think I'm going to be sick.'

'Do and you'll clean it up, lady,' he shouted back at her without turning his head.

His rude response was fitting. She deserved to be treated badly. She felt dirty inside and out. All she wanted was to get home and take a stiff drink into the tub, where she could wash away the slime she could feel growing on her skin and creeping through her spirit.

Through sheer willpower and fear of humiliation she controlled her nausea. She took one more deep breath

112

and felt the last wave subsiding. *Why?* she thought. *Why do I do that to myself? When I start it, I want it more than anything in the world. I want even more. It's the afterward that's so unbearable. It's just not worth it. I'm never, ever, ever going to do it again.*

'Am I doing something wrong?' She asked Alan when he called that night. She had taken the telephone to bed and was speaking from under an eiderdown quilt she'd bought to help her get through the unfamiliar cold of a New York winter.

'What happened, sweets?' Alan asked.

'Everything. I spent the morning in a bathing suit freezing my tush off standing next to a sixty-foot fishing smack at the boat show. I rushed to a runway gig at some cancer luncheon at the Waldorf where the clothes were two sizes too big. Then I went to that open call where some jerk who calls himself a casting director asked if I could juggle.' She wasn't about to tell Alan about her afternoon in the lingerie department.

'Juggle? I thought the play was set in nineteenth-century Russia?'

'It is, but evidently there is some village scene where the girl has to juggle.'

'Well, can you?'

'No,' she moaned, burrowing deeper under the covers. 'But I can act. You'd think they could accommodate me.'

'Pumpkin mine. Haven't you learned yet that this town doesn't accommodate? It sucks.'

'Oh, Alan. I'm so weary of it all. My only job for the rest of the month is dressing up like a Mountie and handing out maple leaves at Grand Central. I bet you didn't even know Canada Week is coming up.'

'God. What will I wear?' He laughed. 'So, what did they say at the audition?'

'They said to come back when I learned to juggle.'

'Wonderful,' Alan said flatly. 'You're not going to do that. Are you?'

'I could. I would learn to twirl on one finger if it would change anything. I've been here six months and my life hasn't changed.'

'Well, buck up, sweet-cakes. We have Friday night to look forward to.'

'Friday? What's Friday?'

'How soon the beautiful and gifted forget.'

'Alan, come on. I'm beat. What's Friday?'

'The big bash at Area,' he said, exasperated.

'Oh, that,' she sighed. The agency expected all the girls to attend client parties. To Sloane it was just another evening on the meat rack.

'What do you mean, "Oh, that"! It's the party of the month. And one never knows. You might meet Mr Right.'

Sloane poked a bare foot out from under the bed clothes, tested the temperature, and quickly pulled it back. 'I don't want to meet Mr Right. I want to meet Mr Producer. Mr Director. Mr Agent. All those people I used to resent Mother for forcing on me.'

'Yeah, but now you're doing it for yourself. There's a big difference.'

'Somehow I thought things would be easier,' she said.

'Come on, babe, lighten up. You're going to make something wonderful happen.'

'Oh, yeah? How does that work?'

'You force it.'

By two A.M. Caramia Dell'Aqua's feet had gone completely numb. She had been standing outside Area in a ten-below windchill since midnight. In all that time she had managed two pictures of the back of Molly Ringwald's head and one picture of the front page of the *Daily News*. The fact that it was covering Mick Jagger's

114

face would reduce its worth to photo editors to near zero.

Her Con Ed bill was a month overdue. If they cut her off, she would have no darkroom. Her ability to develop her own photos in her Tudor City apartment was her lifeline.

She stomped her high-topped Nikes against the frozen pavement and pulled the industrial zipper of her fake-fur jumpsuit high on her neck.

Caramia wasn't the only female paparazzo in the city. She was, without question, the toughest. She had legs like Navratilova and a backhand to match, which, when weighted with a two-pound Nikon zoom lens, was positively lethal. She had flattened many a competing photographer blocking a good shot.

When she wasn't celebrity-hunting, she augmented her meager income by taking fuzzy-focus pictures of romantic scenes for Touch Me Softly greeting cards. The people at Touch Me Softly airbrushed the couples in her pictures into anonymous silhouettes. Lovers walked hand in hand through Caramia's misty river walkways and Central Park's Great Lawn in the moonlight. Invariably she got a few wild, sexy shots that the card company couldn't use. Those she tossed into a file against the day she would do a book of 'arty' photos.

By two-thirty it had begun to snow lightly. The cold and the lateness of the hour had now reduced the line outside of New York's hottest club to two shivering couples. They were drunk or stoned or both and getting angry at the wait enforced upon them by Jocko, the two-hundred-pound doorman. Caramia knew they would never get in. The women had too much hair, badly coiffed. Their furs were skimpy and the men wore too many chains. Bridge-and-tunnel people did not dress a dance floor.

From time to time the door swung open, disgorging apparently satisfied customers in groups of twos and threes.

'Anybody in there?' she would ask each departing group.

'Mick Jagger,' someone shouted, his breath coming in great white plumes.

'Molly Ringwald,' another called over her shoulder.

'Shit,' Caramia hissed, and went back to stomping her feet. She wouldn't make a dime tonight.

Just then the door swung open. A young woman flanked by two beautiful young men, one in a white velvet cape and the other all in black with a blond ponytail and an angel's face, tumbled gaily onto the street. The young woman was laughing. Her head was flung back, exposing the translucent skin of her throat and chest beneath a full-length black mink coat. Her pale skin shone like milk ice under the dark fur and formed a perfect V that plunged from a tilted chin to her deep cleavage. Caramia's motor-driven Nikon slammed reflexively against her cheekbone. She aimed her flash at the thousand coats of paint on the door to bounce the light and backlight the woman's hair. Before she'd taken a full breath, she'd squeezed off three perfectly balanced frames. Then the woman walked past her and Caramia realized she wasn't anybody. Just beautiful.

'Just beautiful,' sighed David Inwood, the picture editor of the *Post* as he stared at the print Caramia handed him. It was late and he was bored and tired. The picture snapped him awake. Light reflected off a door behind the girl produced a glow around her dark hair. Tiny snowflakes were caught in her thick lashes and the fur of her collar. 'Just bloody goddamn beautiful,' he said in a broad Australian drawl. 'Who is she? I want her to have my baby.'

'Nobody.' Caramia shrugged and pulled her gaze away from the tiny lights of a boat moving slowly down the East River over the editor's shoulder. She reached across the pile of prints and tapped one of the pictures of Mick Jagger's covered face. 'Whaddaya think of these, Dave? Good, huh?'

116

Inwood glanced down at the Jagger prints. 'What is this supposed to be?' He scowled.

'It's Jagger.'

'Jagger? *You* say it's Jagger. 'E's got the friggin' *Daily News* over 'is 'ead! You crazy?'

'Still . . .' Caramia muttered, knowing Con Ed would not be getting their payment.

Inwood returned to studying the picture of the woman. 'How long you been in this dodge?' he asked.

'Something wrong?'

'Didn't anyone teach you to get people's names, huh? I mean, bloody hell. We'd run this if you knew who she was.'

Caramia's heart skipped. 'Oh! I got her name. Jeez. Lemme see.' She rummaged around in the scuffed leather camera bag that was her third arm. She found a small spiral notebook in the side pocket and flipped it open. She wet her thumb and scuffed the dog-eared pages back and forth. She hesitated. 'Dierdre Cummings. No. That was the girl coming out of Le Club.' She started flipping again.

David sat tapping the erasure end of a gnawed pencil on the desktop.

'Ah! Here it is! Here it is! I wrote it down. The two guys she was with said she was a model. Sloane Taylor . . . that's it!'

Cole Latimer drank a coke.

Then he drank a glass of tomato juice. Then he swallowed three aspirin, a yellow Valium, and a glass of Alka-Seltzer. He stood in front of the bathroom mirror dripping from a cold shower and burped a long, satisfying explosion of air that tasted faintly of the sour mint of last night's stingers.

He was forty, gay, and celibate. Recreational drugs had to go in the late seventies. He gave up sex not so much from lack of interest but from fear. He now devoted

117

himself completely to his job at *Realto* magazine. His devotion to Layla Bronz, its publisher, had been constant for more than fifteen years. Now Layla and her magazine were his entire life.

He rubbed his forearm and checked the clock. He'd better move. The first order of business this morning would be finding the perfect face, a woman who could, by looking into the camera and expressing a new, fresh image, turn around the sagging fortunes of Bromley Cosmetics. The company, which had been in business for years, was formally known as Glamour Girl. In a staggeringly swift and brutal $1.2-billion takeover by Layla's longtime lover and friend, Warner Bromley, the dated company faced a complete revamping. Six-figure executives were let go; a multimillion-dollar advertising account was yanked from the agency that had handled the account for decades and handed over to a brash new firm that Warner Bromley felt could move with the times. Warner's single-minded goal was to restore not only sagging sales but revamp a reputation in the marketplace of its being a company that made only stodgy, old-fashioned products that girls born in the sixties borrowed from their mothers.

Layla insisted that Warner was taking such a personal interest in the company because he was bored with his other holdings and found restoring it to its former glory an irresistible challenge. Cole felt that a cosmetics company with the implied atmosphere of countless beautiful women neatly meshed with what Cole saw as Warner's midlife crisis. Whatever the reason for his hands-on approach, it didn't change the fact that Cole had a job to do and the perception was that he wasn't getting it done fast enough.

Warner and Layla had made the decision to let *Realto* launch the new Bromley Woman – whoever she was – in a startling new ad campaign. She would be featured on the cover, an attention-getting first for a magazine that

118

used only known celebrities as cover art: Princess Diana, Elizabeth Taylor, Joan Collins, and Crystal Kincaid had been on the most recent copies. Whoever this girl was out there, she was about to become an instant celebrity.

Cole was told to find someone completely new, untainted by any known commercial organization, fresh, and God help them all, virginal. She had to have 'the look of tomorrow.'

Every time he thought of the phrase he groaned inwardly. What the hell did tomorrow look like? he asked himself repeatedly as he searched through portfolios and brochures from the top agencies. Now with a deadline facing him he had taken to staring into the faces of women on the street and in restaurants hoping to see something that looked like 'tomorrow.' He felt this was a ridiculous mission. Bromley clearly had some fantasy woman in mind. His only guidance to Cole had been, 'You'll know it when you see it.'

He hadn't seen 'it' in the selection process that had taken weeks. Now time was running out. With Bromley returning from Europe that day, the final selection had to be made before noon. He couldn't wait any longer. He would choose her from the dozen models who had made the cut.

'Virginal,' Cole snorted at his reflection in the bathroom mirror. If he didn't know what tomorrow looked like, he sure as hell wouldn't recognize 'virginal' either.

Bad enough she had to be the most beautiful woman in the world; she had to look as if she had never had sex. In New York City? *Realto* hadn't had a virgin on the cover since Roxanne Pulitzer's twins were featured, and they had been a month old. Why couldn't they have asked him to find a unicorn? He could have done that faster.

He hated the idea of interviewing the women; each one would be more beautiful and vapid than the next. Interchangeable airheads, all.

He knew each girl would be two people: the artfully

made-up and exquisitely groomed real human being, and the face that was metamorphosed through the camera lens onto paper. The plainest girl, if she had the right bones, could come to life once the camera transformed her. Great beauty often faded and flattened if there wasn't something going on behind the eyes.

He dried himself off and walked to the bedroom phone. His assistant picked up after the sixth ring.

'Drag you out of the loo, did we, Randy?'

'Oh, Mr Latimer. Sorry,' Randy cooed, 'I was on the other line with Ms Bronz's office. You're supposed to interview those models in the drawing room. Ms Bronz thought it would be cozier.'

Cole sighed. 'How many are coming?'

'I think it's down to seven, eight maybe. Wait. I have the file right here.' Randy paused. Cole could hear him counting in a whisper. 'Eight. Four can't make it.'

'Any of them look like a virgin?'

'A what?' Randy laughed.

'You heard,' Cole said impatiently.

'Is that a look or something medical?'

'Don't ask, my head is splitting. I'll be there in twenty minutes. Ask Susan to go through that file. Maybe she'll have some ideas. I'll take all the help I can get today.'

'Susan's gone. One Ms Markham is sitting in her chair. She's been here precisely fourteen minutes. I'm soooo glad no one told me. I'm crazy about surprises,' he said in a syrupy-sweet voice.

'Good Lord. I completely forgot. Would you apologize for me for not being there on her first day. I'm losing my mind. Poor girl. I think I even told her this would be a glamorous job. Wait until she finds out her first project is selecting a perfect cut of meat.'

Warner Bromley settled his lanky frame into the seat reserved for him on the Concorde's London-to-New

York 'takeover run.' His month abroad had seen the completion of a stunning turnaround in his European operations, and while his personal life could be less unsettled, he felt generally in control. His entourage of managers, financial advisors, and his French and German translators had departed London a day earlier to see that everything would be in order when he arrived in New York. The week ahead would be hectic with a series of meetings involving his U.S. holdings. His base of operations would be the penthouse suite he owned at the Carlyle Hotel. While Warner Bromley 'lived' nowhere because he was constantly on the move, he always thought of New York City as home base.

He rearranged the large down pillow his secretary always carried aboard in a specially made case and began a second reading of his most recent unauthorized profile in *Forbes* magazine. 'Flat of stomach, lean of loin and sleek as a seal, Warner Leonard Bromley, with a series of consistently dazzling moves, has become the undisputed Takeover King. . . .'

He couldn't have written a better lead himself. In the past few years Warner Bromley had stalked the world buying up overweight, sleepy companies. He then set to work slashing, trimming, firing, and selling to buy more in a ruthless war that won him the name 'Neutron' Bromley, after the bomb that kills people but leaves buildings intact. The *nom de guerre* did not displease him. He had been called worse. As a matter of fact, he rather liked it. It had just the right unsentimental ring.

He folded the magazine and slipped it into his brief-case. In another hour they would be over Nova Scotia and his cellular phone would be within calling range of the States.

Directly across the aisle sat his secretary, Rose Motherwell. Her silver pageboy curled along her chin line as she bent over a lap-top computer revising his schedule. From time to time during the three-hour glide

121

across the Atlantic she would step into the aisle, lean over the toes of his wing tips, and inquire as to his needs.

For close to two decades, Rose Motherwell had seen to Warner Bromley's every need except the one fate denied her. She was by his side everywhere but in bed. There were times when the longing for him became almost more than she could bear. Only her fierce puritan pride prevented her from revealing her feelings in any way save efficient devotion and dogged loyalty. Over the years her despair had knotted into a hard little fist of hope deep inside her chest. It was the clenching of that little fist that prompted a firm 'no' when dessert orders were taken or bonbons passed. The little fist propelled her toward the hairdresser, her masseuse and manicurist, and on her vacation, the couture shows in Paris, for on the salary and perks provided by her employer she had more disposable income than most wives.

In great measure due to Rose's vigilance, Warner had never married. There were other women, of course, dozens of them. She could not isolate him completely. But when a relationship started to burgeon beyond her control there were ways, subtle, quiet ways, to manufacture roadblocks. The sudden meeting in a distant place, the misremembered phone message, his general 'unavailability,' were all within her control. Years ago she had convinced him that personal publicity was something to be avoided at all costs. It would permit a life uncomplicated by the demands of celebrity, she told him. The real reason was to keep clever, fortune-hunting women away. Despite her efforts some did sneak through her protection, but they were disposed of with dispatch.

She recalled the most recent threat with satisfaction, the pads under her long pink nails clicking softly on the keyboard on her lap-top. Hilary Ronson, the grasping, adulterous wife of a tennis ace, had become quite bold in recent weeks. She telephoned him at the London office during the day and at hotels all over Europe. She paged him at dinner in Maxim's. She left cloying and increasingly desperate messages with his staff. A simple unsigned note to the woman's husband written on anonymous drugstore notepaper did the trick. Mrs Ronson's secretary phoned the London office and left a message. Mrs Ronson would 'be unable to join Mr Bromley for dinner in New York.'

There was one relationship in his life Rose had never been able to stage-manage. She had finally, if begrudgingly, given up even trying. Rose had never been told the origins of Warner's friendship with magazine publisher Layla Bronz. They had been friends, and she felt sure, lovers sometime before Rose came to work for Warner. Layla's calls were always to be put through and her mail to him delivered unopened. He never passed through New York without seeing her, and she remained an honoured guest at any of his homes around the world.

Rose accepted a flute of champagne from the steward and folded down her computer screen. She glanced at the printout of their New York schedule, reviewing the list of executives from the Bromley empire who had been summoned to his suite at the Carlyle. There would be managers from his vineyards in California, his television stations, scientists from the chemical labs that produced fragrances and creams for Bromley Cosmetics, even the managers of his crab-canning plant on the Delmarva Peninsula, the processing plants in Haiti, as well as the managing director of his oil company and hotel chain. And always the inevitable phalanx of lawyers. Of all his vast holdings, the one that currently held his interest was the newly named Bromley Cosmetics. He was determined to get it up to speed with the big competitors like Revlon and Estée Lauder. And who knew, the scheme he and Layla had cooked up to launch an unknown as the Bromley Woman might just work. It might also be an embarrassing and expensive disappointment. Although the prospect of Warner's surrounding himself with beautiful young women made Rose uneasy, it was something she could handle.

After one final check, Rose handed the schedule across the aisle to her employer. He looked over the three pages of meetings, breakfasts, luncheons, and dinners, checking each carefully to be sure he knew the name, family, and background of everyone attending. A change caught his eye. The evening hours for the following day, left free because of the sudden change of plans on Hilary Ronson's part, had been filled. He would be dining with Layla at her town house. *WB: Perhaps you will want to confirm the time personally*, read a notation in Rose's firm, crisp hand.

She knew his meeting with Layla would be the high point of his trip.

Kayzie Markham sat at her new desk, on her new job on this the first day of the rest of her life, feeling completely disoriented. Her boss wasn't even in town. Upon her arrival that morning she found a five-page, single-spaced memo from Ms Bronz spelling out what was expected.

She studied the memo.

Her first assignment was to order engraved invitations to the publisher's annual spring dinner dance, called The Realto Ball. The guests each year were those who had been mentioned in the magazine during the previous year, which meant anyone from royalty to convicted felons. Few did not clear their agenda to attend. The ball was one of the most exciting social events of the year.

Layla's memo cautioned her to stand by to help Cole Latimer. He would be interviewing a dozen or so models later in the morning.

Mr Latimer's assistant, Randy, swung into the room and dumped a folder full of pictures on her desk.

'He wants you to look at these and give him your opinion,' he said.

'Opinion of what?' she asked Randy's back as he skittered out the door without an answer.

The town house was empty at this early hour and the sound of the phone made her jump.

'Ms Bronz's office,' she answered brightly. The crackling of static instantly alerted her that it was an overseas call.

'Darling?' a man's voice boomed through the interference on the line.

'Ms Bronz's office,' Kayzie repeated, raising her voice.

'Let me speak to her,' the voice demanded.

'I'm sorry. Ms Bronz is out of town this morning.' There was an icy edge to her voice. Whoever this person was, he was quite rude . . . but he was calling on her private line. She had to be careful.

'Where is she?'

Kayzie frowned. She repositioned her tortoiseshell headband. It was a nervous habit that permitted her time to think in a tight spot. 'Who is calling Ms Bronz, please?'

'This is Warner Bromley. Sorry about the line. I'm on the Concorde. Where can I reach her?'

Kayzie snapped to attention and softened her voice. 'I'm afraid she's not reachable, Mr Bromley,' she said, her tone warming. 'She's in Washington.'

'Well, where in Washington, damn it? What hotel's she in?'

'Well, ah . . . she's not. I'm afraid she's at a White House prayer breakfast as we speak.'

Bromley responded with a whoop. 'Layla at a *prayer* breakfast! You must be joking!'

'It's the National Association of Magazine Publishers,' Kayzie said defensively. 'I don't think they are actually, well, you know . . . *praying*.'

'Well, patch me through to the White House.'

Patch me through to the White House? she mouthed soundlessly. She wasn't even sure she knew what that meant. 'I'm sorry, I can't do that, Mr Bromley.' She pictured Layla mumbling. 'Excuse me, excuse me,' as she pushed by the chairs of President and Mrs Reagan and half the cabinet as they sat, praying or not, over their loaves and fishes and fried communal wafers, or whatever the hell they ate for a breakfast with prayer as a theme. If Layla heard Kayzie's voice on the line, she wouldn't wait to hear who she was putting on the phone. Concorde or not. It would be goody-bye job, so long the crown work she needed, the contacts she hadn't paid for, and a promising new life in the publishing industry. She took a deep breath. 'I'm sorry, Mr Bromley. That won't be possible. But I will get her a message as soon as I can.'

'What's your name?' he barked.

'My name, Mr Bromley, is Katherine Markham. I am Ms Bromley's personal assistant and –'

'Where's Susan?' he demanded, cutting her off in midsentence.

'If you mean Ms Bronz's former assistant, I'm afraid she is no longer here.'

'Well, that's a good piece of news. Never could stand that woman,' Kayzie heard him chuckle.

Kayzie relaxed, as she always did when she spoke up for herself and got results. 'I'm sure Ms Bronz will be sorry she missed your call. What message may I give her?'

'Just tell her I'm on my way. I'll call her from the Carlyle.'

Twenty minutes later, four long white boxes arrived by messenger. They contained the most unusual roses Kayzie had ever seen. Nina, the maid, said they were called sterling silver roses, but they were actually a kind of lavender. Kayzie had read that these were the kind of roses Elizabeth Taylor was supposed to lie on when she threw her back out. Kayzie helped Nina get them all into vases and place them around the drawing room in time for Cole's meeting.

As she was walking back to her desk, Randy elbowed his way ahead of her. His arms were full of newspaper.

'Paaay-purse,' he sang as he dropped them onto her desk.

She leapt to keep the whole mass from sliding onto the rug. 'What's all this?'

'For you. Read and clip,' he said, making scissors with two fingers as he walked out the door.

'Clip what, Randy?' she asked.

He leaned back through the door. 'Anything you think Madame might be interested in.'

Kayzie stared at him. He had straight black hair cut at a geometric angle. It fell sideways across his closely set black eyes, making him look like a rat peering out of a hedge.

'How am I supposed to know what she wants?' she said, trying to control her irritation. It wouldn't do to make an enemy the first day on the job. Besides, he acted as though he knew where all the bodies were buried.

He put his hands on his hips. 'You got the job, didn't you?' he snapped, and disappeared.

So that was it. The little rat was jealous. He probably thought he should be sitting in Susan's chair. 'Tough darts, Randy-poo,' she said to the empty room.

She started to sort through the pile of papers. There was the *Times*, the *Daily News*, the *New York Post*, *The Wall Street Journal*, *The Washington Post*, the *Boston Globe*, and the *L.A. Times*. No *Pravda*, she thought. Must be late.

She had gotten as far as the Home section of the *Times* when Cole strode through the door.

'Good morning, my dear, I see you're in the media bath already.'

'Good morning, Mr Latimer. Maybe you could help me. What do you think I should clip?'

'Clip?'

'Yes. From all these papers.'

'Why, nothing. Layla would have a fit. She likes those kept absolutely pristine. Once she heard that Queen Elizabeth had her butler iron the morning newspaper if

127

someone read it before she did. It took us ten minutes to talk her out of it.'

Randy Rat, Kayzie seethed. She said nothing.

'Did Randy leave a folder with you?' Cole asked, his eyes sweeping the surface of her desk.

'Right here.' Kayzie handed him the file with the black-and-white glossies.

'Did you look at them?' Cole said, flipping through the folder.

'Very quickly. They're all so gorgeous. Are you supposed to pick just one?'

'Ummm. I'm afraid so. Here.' He handed back the file. 'What do you think?'

Kayzie studied the pictures as Cole tried to explain what they were looking for. She picked out two, a blonde and a brunette. 'I don't know,' she said. 'None of them really looks, well, virginal. I mean, they're all so sexy-pouty. Maybe these two?'

Cole studied the pictures and slowly shook his head. 'No,' he said. 'That's Peach Malloy. She's too well-known. The agency shouldn't even have suggested her. We want fresh.' He frisbeed Peach's picture onto the desk. 'And the brunette, she's Serena Novakoski. They used to have a poster of her at the agency. Someone pasted two straws to her nostrils. She won't do either. Now I'm afraid to look at the others.' He sank down into the couch that ran perpendicular to Kayzie's desk. 'Damn. What are we going to do now? We're supposed to have someone by the time Bromley arrives tonight.'

'Umm. He's already called. From the Concorde no less. The great man approacheth.' Kayzie began to rearrange the paper pile. The front page of the *New York Post* caught her eye. There was a full spread of a beautiful girl laughing with snow in her hair. 'Too bad we can't get this girl,' she said wistfully.

'What girl?' Cole asked without looking up. He was staring straight ahead as if in a trance.

128

Kayzie held up the front page of the *Post*. 'Isn't she great looking? Look at those bones.'

Cole leaned forward and frowned at the paper. 'Who is she, some singer?'

'It says here, "Model Sloane Taylor Laughs at —" '

'Gimme that.' Cole snatched the paper out of her hand. 'You're right. She's a knockout. Ever seen her before?'

'Well, I'm no expert, but I don't think so.'

Cole rested the paper on his knees and studied the picture, nodding slowly. 'Look, Kayzie, this is a long shot but what the hell. Call David Inwood, he's the picture editor over at the *Post*. See if he knows where we can find this girl. If she models, she has to be with an agency. Find out which one and get ahold of her. Maybe we can pull off a little coup here.'

'That's all I have to go on?'

'That's it, hon.' Cole pushed himself up off the couch and started for the door. 'And call me when you find her. We don't have much time.'

'Call me when you find her,' Kayzie whispered, blowing out her cheeks. 'Ooookay. Here goes nothing.'

5

Sloane swept her foot cautiously across the bottom sheet. She located the freezing-cold hot-water bottle and groaned. She had spent a terrible night trying to stay warm. Finally the bleak winter sun was beginning to filter through the high, dirty windows of the loft when she awakened. She didn't want to get out of bed and face the frozen water in the toilet. She lay, bundled like a mummy, trying to think of a way to get to the bathroom without her feet freezing to the floor.

The muffled sound of the ringing phone jolted her fully awake. She pawed through the bed clothes and found it at the foot of the bed.

'Ummmm,' she answered.

'Wake up, baby-cakes!'

'Hi, Alan. What's up?'

'You're famous!'

'I wasn't when I went to sleep.'

'That was four hours ago. You are now. Get your beautiful butt up and go buy the *Post*.'

'The *Post*? What's in it?' She was utterly mystified.

'You! You're on the front page and gorgeous.'

'You're kidding!' Sloane felt her heart skip. 'How in the world —'

'Remember when we were coming out of Area . . . that Amazon photographer with the fake-fur jumpsuit and the Day-Glo hair?'

130

'But I was just walking out the door. Why would they run a picture of that?'

'Well, it's kind of a nothing weather picture. There's snow in your hair and you've got your head thrown back. The caption says, "Let It Snow! Model Sloane Taylor Laughs at Sub-Zero Temps." It's not exactly "World Hunger Ends," but for you, sweetness, it's the story of a lifetime.'

'I don't believe this! Hold on, hold on,' she said as she heard the sound of her call-waiting. 'I'm beeping. Don't go away.'

She depressed the receiver button. 'Hello?'

'Sloane Taylor?'

'This is Sloane Taylor.' It was Rochelle, her booker at the agency.

'Sweetheart! It's Rosch. Have you seen the *Post*?' The woman Sloane had to repeat her name to when she dropped by the agency was now shouting 'sweetheart' at her.

'Hi, Rochelle. No, I haven't. I just found out about it.'

'It's fabulous! We already have a call for you. *Realto* magazine is on the other line. They want to see you right away.'

'Oh, my God . . . ah . . . Rochelle, could you hold on? I'm just getting off the other line.'

'Look, Sloane, this can't wait. Can you get over to *Realto* by eleven? Two twenty-five East Seventy-seventh. Ask for Mr Latimer.'

Sloane thought for a split second. Her hair was okay. She'd just have to do her makeup. Clothes were no problem. 'Yeah. Yeah, sure. What's it for?'

'To tell you the truth, I'm not sure. They're in some kind of sweat over something. The girl who called said something about needing someone for a cover.'

'A cover? On *Realto*. They only do megastars. I'm looking at the latest issue right now. It's got Debra Winger on it. Are you sure?'

'That's the only thing I'm sure of. She distinctly said "cover".'

Sloane was too excited to be annoyed. Under any other circumstances she would have wanted to know more about a booking, but this sounded too big to argue about. She assured Rochelle she would be there and hung up. She made a dash for the relative warmth of the tiny bathroom and turned the hot water in the shower on full blast. She was pulling off her sweatpants when she remembered. She pulled her pants back up and raced back to the phone. 'Alan!'

'Isn't Paris delicious this time of year?'

'God. I'm sorry. That was the agency. Someone at *Realto* magazine called because of the *Post*. They want to see me at eleven. They say they want someone for a cover!'

'May the gods of mammon and fame be praised!' he shouted. 'Who are you seeing there? The publisher is a private client of mine.'

'I'm supposed to see someone named Latimer.'

'Cole Latimer? La-dee-da.'

'You know him? Who is he?'

'He's the associate publisher. Quite grand. He's in Liz Smith and Page Six all the time. Dines with the ladies who lunch at Mortimer's. He's sort of King of the walkers but with clout because of the magazine.'

'Oh, Alan. I'm so excited. What do you suppose they want?'

'Well, I'd say it has something to do with the way you look. I mean, you are a model, right?'

'Okay, okay. I'm just curious. I mean, should I be elegant, or girlish, or do they want someone exotic?'

'Darling, will you stop trying to please everyone. Just be yourself,' he scolded. 'Want me to hop down and fluff you up?'

'Alan, would you? I need someone to hold my hand. Come quick.'

It wasn't until Sloane lifted her portfolio over the turnstile on the uptown platform that she realized how terribly nervous she was. She hated situations over which she had no control. This could be just the break she had been working for. Now perhaps all the maintenance of her skin, her hair, her teeth and nails, all those painful hours in the gym and dance class, were about to pay off. What if she had competition this morning? It could be staggering. The agencies would send only their youngest, prettiest models. She had to have something special, something that would make her different somehow from the rest.

She deliberately ignored the middle car, the one that lowered the odds of molestation, and boarded the last car on the train.

It was time for the Bad Girl Game. The game she could count on to make her eyes sparkle, her skin glow, her breath come in an even, self-confident flow.

Playing the game in New York was risky. The environment was too volatile, too hostile, too unpredictable. But she needed the extra edge. It was time.

She chose her position carefully and surveyed the other passengers. Dismissing several men as unsuitable partners, her eyes fixed on a dark young man leaning nonchalantly against a pole in front of the door. He had to be dark. Preferably as tall as Fernando. Latin would do but he had to have a good body. That was a must. And tight clothes. The face was never terribly important as long as he was clean shaven and had a decent haircut. A certain set of jaw and shift of eye would complete the profile.

She chose a seat directly opposite him. There was never any trouble getting their attention; she got attention no matter where she went. The trick was, without any overt movements or body language, to get the eyes and hold them. Once this was accomplished she would begin to run her own obscene movie right behind her eyes. On those rare occasions when her target became distracted, she would slowly cross her legs or almost imperceptibly move her shoulders back and slightly arch her back. It was all subtle, tightly controlled, and deliciously exciting. The rules were immutable. No movement, no words, and always in a very public place.

She established contact before the train pulled away from the platform. In the few minutes it took to reach the Sheridan Square station, her target was trapped. His right arm was wrapped around the pole, his left was bent slightly, a thumb hooked into a side pocket of his jeans. She made the eye lock and could see the beads of perspiration beginning to form on his forehead. More people crowded onto the train but he held his ground. She controlled her breathing and felt the beginning of the exciting flutter building in her stomach. When he realized she wasn't going to stop staring, he shifted his weight and leaned against the pole. He did not look away as a woman laden with shopping bags pushed by, blocking their sight line for a moment. The warmth in Sloane's stomach flowed through the muscles of her inner thighs and her throat began to close. As the train approached Times Square, where she would change for the crosstown shuttle, she tensed for her escape. The train slowed and she quickly moved her gaze downward toward his crotch. She could see an erection fighting the confines of his tight jeans. As he stepped toward her, his lips parted in a half-smile as if to speak, she slid her fingers through the handle of her portfolio and with one upward motion rose and stepped through the door. She hit the platform and kept moving. He wouldn't dare follow her, and if he did, she could lose him in the crowd in the tunnel that led to the shuttle. Would he follow? She would not look back to see. That was the best part of the game.

She miscalculated. The shuttle tunnel was not crowded

after the morning rush hour. She looked over her shoulder.

He was there. Not ten paces behind her, moving faster than she was and not making a sound on the thick soles of his running shoes.

She felt his hand on her elbow.

'Wait.' He spoke softly, matching her stride now and pressing his upper thigh against hers as she walked. She felt no fear. She knew he wouldn't hurt her. They never had. Swiftly, inevitably, he eased her toward the wall as others passed, ignoring them. They approached an indentation in the wall – a doorway? An exit? She couldn't tell in the gloom. He reached for her and spun her into the open space. He was as strong as he looked. She made no attempt to resist as he pulled her to him. He placed his hands on her hips and roughly pulled her to his chest, grinding his groin into hers. Neither of them moved from the waist up. She held her hips perfectly still as he ground the erection under his jeans into her with determined thrusts that had them both breathless. It lasted for a moment or two. She heard him gasp as he climaxed and felt a shudder run through his body.

Grasping her shoulders with both hands, he tried to look into her face and say something. She didn't want to talk to him. She had used as much of him as she needed. She turned her head so that her hair fell over her face and stood very still. When she pushed the hair away, he was gone.

She still held her portfolio in her right hand, her handbag was looped over her shoulder. It took her only a moment to regain her brisk pace. She could see the shuttle waiting on Track One and stepped aboard.

By the time she boarded the IRT and headed uptown on the East Side, she took her first deep breath.

She felt wonderful. She always did afterward. Until the guilt and shame set in. But for an hour or so after she

135

played her secret Bad Girl Game, it was the best cosmetic in the world.

'I'm very impressed,' Cole Latimer said, flipping through the pictures of Sloane's portfolio. He was beyond impressed. He was bowled over. Not only had this stunningly beautiful girl dropped into his life like an answered prayer, but she had that something extra that made it hard to stop looking at her. 'But I don't think they do you justice.'

'Oh, dear,' Sloane smiled. 'I spent a lot of time and money having them put together.'

As Cole finished going through her portfolio, she filled him in on her background, trying to take in the opulence of the room. Somehow she had pictured the meeting differently. She thought she would be lined up with dozens of other girls in a humiliating show-and-tell. But this was very pleasant. She liked Cole Latimer. He wasn't the least bit intimidating and she liked the twinkle in his eye that set her at ease immediately.

He closed the portfolio and drummed his fingers on the Leatherette cover. Finally he spoke. 'Miss Taylor, I've seen several girls this morning and none of them has what we are looking for. We want a certain indefinable *je ne sais quoi*. An innocence, a look of sophisticated naïveté if that makes any sense. The Bromley Cosmetic company wants to project a whole new image, and that image will be conveyed by more than clever photography. The person we pick has to have that something extra that a camera can't fake.'

Sloane had been sitting very still, her knees pressed together, her hands folded in her lap. She couldn't stand it anymore. 'Excuse me, Mr Latimer. But what exactly is the quality you are looking for?'

'Beats the shit out of me,' he said with a broad grin.

Sloane burst out laughing and Cole joined her. 'I'm so glad you said that. Thank you. I was scared to death.'

'I hope you're not anymore,' Cole said.

'No. No, I'm not. And I'm glad you like my pictures.'

'It's more than that. I like you. I think you'd be perfect for this Bromley project. It would mean a lot of work, a lot of travel, TV appearances and in-store promotions. I wonder if you have any idea of what being turned into a celebrity means. It can be a terrible thing. Does the prospect bother you?'

'To be honest?'

'I hope you'd be nothing but.'

'I really want to do this. The prospect thrills me to the marrow of my bones. I hope you choose me.'

'Miss Sloane,' he said, pushing himself up from the low-slung couch, 'you are not only a beautiful young woman but one smart cookie.'

Feeling a bit like a dutiful schoolgirl being dismissed, she rose as well. Cole stretched his arm toward her and lightly rested it around her shoulders. 'I'd like to speak to Ms Bronz about you as soon as possible. May I keep your portfolio for a day or so?'

'Of course,' she said as they walked side by side down the long hall toward the front door. 'Then what?'

'Then we would want you to meet Warner Bromley. He has the final say on this project.'

'Now I'm the one to be impressed.'

'If they both approve, I think you're about to change your life.'

'I don't know what to say. Everything is happening so fast.'

'You don't have to say a thing. Not even "taxi." I'll have the driver drop you wherever you're going.'

They had reached the double door of the mansion. He pressed a button on an intercom in the foyer and said, 'Yitzak, would you bring the car around, please. For a Miss Taylor.' He released the button and turned back to face her. 'Where are you going now?'

137

Sloane thought for a moment. 'Perhaps I should stop by the agency?'

'Ah, I wouldn't. Not just yet. Let me speak to Ms Bronz first. I don't want to give them a chance to raise your price.' He grinned.

'I'll be anxious to hear from you.'

Cole put his hand under her elbow and gently guided her down the steps. Just as they reached the sidewalk, a huge silver Rolls purred to the curb and stopped. Cole reached around her and opened the door before the driver could get out of the car.

Sloane stood and gaped at the car. She didn't want her surprise to show but knew it did. 'A Rolls. This is what I'm going off in?'

'If I have my way, Miss Taylor . . . Sloane, this ride will be the first of many.'

Sloane let him help her into the luxurious backseat. There was a chinchilla throw rug folded on the far seat.

Cole leaned through the window. 'And one more thing. Thank you.'

'You're thanking me? I don't understand.'

'Now I don't have to interview any of those totally unqualified women.'

She watched the window glide up into place. The driver turned and said, 'Where to, ma'am?'

Please, please, please let this be happening, she thought as the luxurious car moved down Fifth Avenue. *I know I don't deserve it, but I want it so badly.*

When the circulation of *Realto* magazine hit three million, Layla celebrated by redecorating her old brownstone. Cole had supervised the installation of a tiny two-passenger elevator hidden in the panelling of her office. It was designed to look like a part of a tall bookcase to one side of the fireplace. It was invisible until a latch released by pressure on the second shelf slid aside. Then the entire

138

shelf swung silently into the room to reveal the brass cage. It was all too Agatha Christie for words. They had giggled through several murder scenarios while four separate contractors and engineers tried to make the thing work. Finally completed, it was a masterpiece. The narrow, closetlike box moved silently and directly to the top floor of the house, opening into Layla's bedroom.

The foyer, bedroom, and adjoining dressing room were filled with antiques. The centrepiece of the bedroom was a king-sized elevated bed covered with pale pink satin and heaped with lace pillows. The room was done in shades of grey and the palest apricot, including the priceless Chinese rug. Grouped around the fireplace were several grey-velvet-covered bergère chairs and an out-sized lounge in pale apricot quilted satin.

Cole had waited all day to tell Layla the good news. As he stepped into the tiny foyer, he could see through to the dressing room. Alan, Layla's hairdresser, was standing behind her as she sat before a freestanding looking glass. Catching Cole behind her in the mirror, she wordlessly wiggled her fingers at him.

Cole stepped to the bedroom drinks tray set with crystal decanters and mixed himself a vodka Gibson, straight up.

'Darling, can I fix you something?' he called to Layla as he dropped three tiny pearl onions into his glass. She lifted a half-finished drink from a small table beside the chair and shook her head.

He walked casually to the open dressing-room door and leaned against the frame as Alan pushed the final black hairpin into Layla's intricately coiled hair. 'Hello, Alan,' he said. 'Don't forget the frangipani blossom behind the ear.'

Intent on his work, Alan ignored him. He cupped his hands under Layla's ears, framing her face. 'Spray?' he asked.

Layla nodded and put her hand over her eyes.

Cole sipped his drink, studying her reflection in the shadowless light of the dressing room. He took quiet comfort in the fact that in all the years he had known her she had never changed. The hair, the makeup, her style, and most remarkably, her energy, were the same in midlife as they had been in her midtwenties. 'How was your prayer breakfast, darling?'

Layla looked at him in the mirror as she patted her temples. 'That's fine, Alan. I'm too nudgy to sit here any longer.'

He gave the top of her hair one final burst of spray. 'No massage tonight?' he said, dropping the spray can into his bag.

'I cancelled. I have an early dinner date. Besides, I need to talk to Mr Latimer and I refuse to do so facedown and buck naked.'

'Was our president there?' Cole persisted.

Layla slowly swivelled her chair to face him. 'Of course he was there. You think I'd schlepp the seven-o'clock shuttle if he weren't? I even spoke to him.'

'Really. And what did you say to the leader of the free world?'

'I said, "Hi-ya handsome. How're ya hangin"?'

'You asked the President of the United States how he was hanging?'

'Sure. I've known him for twenty years,' she said, bristling.

'Still . . . ' Cole gave a sidelong glance at Alan, who was lingering over the packing of his grooming equipment.

She pulled up the top of the silver satin dressing gown that had fallen over her shoulders and slipped her feet into a pair of ridiculous feathered mules. As she brushed by Cole, she whispered. 'Can't wait to read that in Liz Smith's column.' She jerked her head imperceptibly toward Alan and headed into the bedroom.

Cole smiled and followed her. He should have known

Layla knew the remark would be all over town by morning. It would never be published, but it would become part of the fabric of her carefully created image.

Cole made fresh drinks while Layla stretched out on the chaise. He took one of the bergères opposite her. 'Well,' he said, 'what I thought was going to be a rat's ass of a day has turned out pretty spectacularly.'

'Oh? I leave town and you have a spectacular day?'

'I found the Bromley girl,' he said with a note of triumph in his voice.

'That was fast.'

'Wait till you meet her. Perfection.'

Layla narrowed her eyes at him. 'Shouldn't you interview a few more girls?' she asked, tapping her nails on the stem of her glass. 'How can you be so sure this one is right? We're talking about a six-, seven-million-dollar campaign here.'

'Trust me.'

'What's her name?'

'Sloane. Sloane Taylor.'

'And you like her?'

'Very much.' Cole smiled. 'She has a manner about her, a sort of unspoiled sweetness. Very much a lady. Warner is going to flip.'

'I hope not,' Layla said. 'I have a hard enough time keeping track of him as it is.'

'I hear he called from the Concorde,' Cole said, leaning across her legs to flick his gold Dunhill under the cigarette she was holding.

She exhaled a long stream of smoke. 'Yes. He's already here. I'm seeing him tonight.'

'Is Rose with him?'

'Ah, Rose. My own personal lion at the gate. What a prize she is, and worth every penny.'

'Poor Warner. Between the two of you it's a wonder he gets to take a leak alone.'

Something dropped to the floor in the dressing room.

Cole leaned to one side to get a better view and saw Alan fiddling with the zipper of his soiled backpack. 'Alan? Are we finished up?' he asked, louder than necessary.

Startled, the hairdresser reddened. 'Ah . . . just wanted to wash up,' he answered. 'Good night.'

'Good night, Alan,' Cole called. A second later he heard the elevator door close. 'You trust that guy? I'd hate to read in the columns what you just said about Rose.'

'Alan?' Layla frowned. 'I trust him implicitly. But so what? None of this means anything to him.'

'You are a kind and trusting person,' Cole said sarcastically.

'Feh!' she said, staring down into her glass.

Cole noticed her right foot had not stopped tapping against the side of the chaise since she sat down. He leaned his elbows on his knees and looked into her face. 'How many greenies did we take today, my love?'

'Just a couple,' she said, avoiding his eyes.

'How many is a couple?'

'Okay. Three. Four. I forget.'

'You really should lay off. They're losing their clout. What're you going to do when you really need to get up for a crisis?'

'Life is a crisis,' she snapped, looking at him with purple eyes several shades darker than usual.

'My, my, my, my. Aren't we feeling sorry for ourselves. What's the matter, darling? You should be delirious with Warner in town.'

'It's just that I haven't seen him for a month. You know how I get.'

'Any news from Rose?'

'Her mood brightened. 'Yes. The tennis pro's wife was sent packing.'

'Let me sing a chorus of "Another One Bites the Dust."'

At last, Layla laughed. Cole could hear the outlaw he loved lurking in the sound. 'That's better.' He smiled.

'I have the whole evening planned.'

'Tell.'

'Champagne here.'

'And dinner?'

'Nina's fixing lamb. His favourite.'

'I take it you won't be going out,' he said.

'No.' She smiled a lecherous grin. 'And neither will Warner. Not till tomorrow morning.'

The instant Alan hit the street he started looking for a pay phone.

He found one on the corner of Second Avenue and Seventy-sixth Street. He dropped a quarter and listened to five rings before Sloane picked up. He couldn't wait to tell her she definitely had the job.

'Ooo, baby-baby-baby. I'm so hot. Put it in, come on, sweetheart, come on. Oh! Oh! Yes, yes, yes. Deeper! Harder!'

Melon began to pant in short, controlled breaths. She was beginning to get a bad crick in her neck. She had finished the top coat of the last two nails on her left hand. An hour of cradling the phone between her shoulder and cheek had become uncomfortable. She heard a soft, guttural moan, reached over, and disconnected the phone.

She double-checked the billing sheet. In the last three hours she had provided twenty-two faceless callers with orgasms. She received twenty cents of every dollar-billed-minute whether the caller got off or not. Men, women, kids, gimps, perverts, anyone who would dial a phone was a customer. She didn't care. The longer they stayed on the line the more money she made. The job had taught her that on the phone, as in life, most men came too fast.

Chantilly Communications billed thousands of calls a

143

day around the clock. Melon and the other girls worked in tiny soundproof cubicles whenever they showed up. That was the beauty of the job. The work was flexible and the pay was as good as schlepping cocktails and half the hassle. It might have been boring as hell, but it paid the rent while she worked toward her next windfall from *Realto*.

She glanced at the stopwatch hanging from the desk lamp. The watch was standard equipment in this kind of work. Now she could call Randy and check in.

When she had told Kayzie about her deal with *Realto*, something had kept her from mentioning her arrangement with Randy and how he provided her with information on what was happening at the magazine. It was a matter of pride to her that Kayzie see her as more connected than she really was. Kayzie was everything Melon wasn't and she had never had a friend like her. Kayzie had been to a fancy eastern college, and she came from a proper family where people actually wished each other well and cared about how you were doing in life. Kayzie also had beautiful manners. She didn't swear, much, or screw around with guys, and she did nice things for Melon for no reason except that that's what nice people do. Ordinarily Melon suspected people's motives when they were kind to her, but she trusted Kayzie. Melon wasn't used to people like her. While she was flattered, it also left her confused and extremely insecure. For all of that she wanted deeply to impress Kayzie. It would kill her if Kayzie really knew about her. She had confessed too much to her already.

Melon had been buttering up Cole's ratty little assistant for weeks and it was paying off.

She punched in the number of Cole Latimer's private line and waited impatiently.

'Mr Latimer's line, Randolph speaking.'

'My, aren't we being formal today,' Melon said, imitating the English accent he affected whenever he answered the phone.

'Melon!' he whispered conspiratorially. 'Have I got some dish.'

'Oh, good, good, good. What?' Melon could hardly contain her excitement. Whenever Randy said he had dish, he meant it.

'Warner Bromley called from the Concorde. Are you ready? He'll be at the Carlyle late this afternoon.'

Melon let out a whoop. 'You angel! How do you know that?'

'He called the Dragon Lady's office this morning. She's in Washington but your pal, Miss Priss, took the call.'

'And you listened in on the line.'

'How else am I going to keep up?' he sniffed. 'It's not like she would tell me anything.'

'Hey. Go easy on Kayzie, Randy. She's a good kid. Remember, if you hadn't told me there was an opening, she wouldn't be there.'

'Yeah, I know,' he agreed. 'But I thought anyone you knew would be like you. Who knew your best friend was the Flying Nun.'

'Never mind. Who's with Bromley? Am I gonna have to wade through bodyguards to get to him?'

'His secretary always stays in the suite. You'll never get past her.'

'So how am I gonna do this, for shit sake?' Melon asked angrily.

'Look, Melon. I'm just the messenger. You figure it out. If I were you, though, I'd hang out in the lobby and jump him. He's got to come down sometime.'

'So that's what I'm gonna do,' she said, scooping her belongings from the desktop into her bag. 'Thanks, Randy. I'm outta here.'

'Oh, Melon.'

'What?'

'Take money. The Carlyle staff is tough.'

145

6

Rose Motherwell reached for the extension phone in the guest bedroom in Warner's Carlyle suite. With practiced stealth, she placed her hand over the mouthpiece and slowed her breathing.

That woman in the lobby had somehow gotten through.

In the two hours since they arrived at the hotel, the desk had called several times to ask if Mr Bromley would take a call from a woman in the lobby. Each time Rose refused the call. No sooner had she gone in for a nap than Warner, being thoughtful, had picked up the phone. Now he was trapped.

'I'm sorry, Miss,' Rose heard him say. 'I don't give interviews.' He was not amused.

'But Mr Bromley, you don't understand. This is for *Realto* magazine,' the woman insisted. She spoke in a breathless, almost childlike voice. 'It would be a major story. Possibly a cover.'

'Miss . . . ah . . .'

'Tuft, Mr Bromley, Melon Tuft.' Her voice hardened as she continued. 'I'm an investigative reporter. Perhaps you've seen my work. I've already researched a great deal of my story on you. Your friends wouldn't talk to me without your permission so I've spoken only to your enemies. I'd very much appreciate giving you the opportunity to answer your critics.'

'Miss Tuft, I'm sorry,' he said, recognizing a reporter's

trick appeal. 'I really couldn't consider it. Thank you. Thank you for your interest. Good-bye.'

Rose waited the heartbeat interval she knew it would take before he rapped on her bedroom door.

'Rose,' he said, his voice muffled and urgent. 'Are you awake?'

Quickly she swung her legs over the side of the bed, slipped into her suit jacket, and smoothed her hair.

When she entered the living room, he was standing in front of the picture window that overlooked Madison Avenue. 'Yes, Mr Bromley?'

'Call the desk, will you. They're putting through nut calls. I won't have it.'

Rose widened her eyes. 'Oh my, what happened?'

Warner waved his hands dismissively. 'Some woman in the lobby wants an interview. I shouldn't have touched the phone but I thought you were indisposed.'

Rose feigned horror. 'I better run down and speak to the desk personally. This is outrageous!'

Downstairs, Melon leaned against the narrow shelf of house phones just off the lobby and added up her losses so far. Ten dollars to the doorman just on principle; ten to the concierge in the event that she would have to stake out the lobby, and twenty to the deskman who eventually allowed the call to go through.

'Shit on a stick!' she hissed, and kicked at a sand-filled brass pot with the pointed toe of her sling-back pumps. Now she'd be stuck in the damn lobby until he went out for dinner.

She flounced toward a hard-backed settee between the elevators and sat down to wait. She glanced around, daring anyone she had bribed to say anything.

As she was arranging herself, she saw the elevator door directly across from her glide open. A trim, stylishly dressed woman with a silver pageboy and an angry expression rushed past her and headed toward the front desk. Melon made note that she wasn't carrying a purse. She couldn't be leaving the hotel, and her determined stride said something was on her mind. Whatever was upsetting her was going to be directed at the management.

As the woman reached the desk, Melon heard the name Bromley and stiffened. She rose and walked on the balls of her feet to muffle the sound of her heels. As she approached the desk, she could see the clerk she had bribed squinting his eyes at her. He was angry to have been caught and blamed it on Melon. 'I'm terribly sorry, Miss Motherwell. It's a complete misunderstanding. It won't happen again.'

Melon squinted back at him, her lips pressed into a thin line, and drew her finger across her throat. The throat registered on the clerk's face and he looked away.

The woman seemed placated, turned on her heel, and brushed by Melon as though she were a potted plant.

Motherwell. She was Bromley's guard dog. She tilted her head coquettishly and smiled at the deskman. This was going to cost her another twenty.

So be it.

If it took twenty or fifty or a hundred, if it took sitting on the hard-backed seat next to the elevators in the Carlyle lobby for as long as Warner Bromley was in residence, she would do it.

Melon Tuft had a theory. If you wanted something badly enough, long enough, and thought of nothing else twenty-four hours a day, you could get it.

In 1972, Mary Elizabeth O'Flanahan's mother and her boyfriend, a man named Slim Hartnell, ran a games concession stand on the Santa Monica pier. Until her mother ran off with the guy who sold stuffed pandas and counterfeit Cartier watches, Mary Elizabeth's life was relatively carefree. When her mother left, Slim packed up the adorably blonde eight-year-old Mary Elizabeth, who had always been called Melon, and her six-year-old little sister, Gracie. Gracie had never been quite right in the head due to either prenatal drinking on her mother's part or a high-forceps delivery. Or both.

Slim put the girls and everything else he couldn't sell or barter into the back of a beat-up 1965 Chevy station wagon and headed for Las Vegas, 'the land of the golden chance' as he called it. Then again everything was a 'golden chance' to Slim, who firmly believed that each day, each poker hand, every roll of the dice, held the promise of a jackpot with his name on it. Within twenty-four hours of their arrival in Vegas, every cent Slim had gleaned had been gobbled up by a roulette wheel and the dollar slots.

He left the girls in a cheap motel on the Strip and went in search of a way to support his two charges.

Slim was not afraid of work and would do it if he had to. He could pump gas, pave driveways, or repair air conditioners. He knew how to lay bricks and could cut raw lumber. All else failing, there was always a day's pay to be had unloading produce trucks at a supermarket or cleaning swimming pools. He was always sure to put enough aside to stake himself to the next floating crap game he could find.

That summer the odd little family moved from town to town. When Slim got lucky, they lived in motels, bathed, ordered Chinese take-out, and watched *I Love Lucy*. The little girls would put quarters in the Magic Finger machine beside the bed and vibrate themselves into fits of laughter.

Life was an adventure.

When jobs were scarce and they were down to gas money, they lived in the station wagon. Slim showed the girls how to steal a loaf of Wonder bread while he slipped a pound of cold cuts and a jar of Miracle Whip under his

149

tattered army jacket. 'Now, remember, girls,' he would say as he pulled into the supermarket parking lot, 'just stand in the baked-goods aisle and pick your nose. Nobody can stand to look at a kid pickin' their nose. When they look away, you grab and run.'

Melon made sandwiches on the backseat, slathering the spongy bread with a half-inch of mayonnaise. They rolled along eating their gooey sandwiches and washing them down with plastic quarts of warm RC Cola Slim lifted by the case when they stopped for gas. They sang to the country music that made it through the static on the radio, happy to be headed someplace new and different.

At night Slim pulled over on the shoulder of the road or into a barren field. The backseat flattened down to make a sleeping space for the two girls. He would stretch his lanky frame out on the front seat and talk them to sleep, his voice drawling over the sound of night wind that swirled up over the flat plains of Nevada or Utah. They never paid much attention as to where they actually were. It didn't really matter. They were together and they made the rules.

Each night Slim had another scene, another plan, a dream of riches beyond imagining. Gracie would always curl into a ball and fall asleep. Melon and Slim would then turn to her favorite part of their night talks – spending the imaginary money that would soon rain down on them.

Melon knew it was a game, and after Slim finished his beer and fell asleep, she would lie awake and listen to the wind. Only then did she feel the loneliness and hurt. She thought about her mother and her life before they took to the road. No one had ever explained why her mother left or what it was that Melon had done to make her leave. But she was certain she must have done something.

One steaming July morning, out of funds again and on the lam from an irate and unpaid Carson City motel owner, Slim pulled the wheezing old station wagon into

150

the parking lot of the Blue Belle All Night Diner and Car Wash.

Slim leaned across the front seat and shook Mary Elizabeth's shoulder. 'Wake up, Melon, honey, time for breakfast.'

Sitting upright, she peered over the dusty dashboard. 'I thought you said we were out of funds,' she said in a small voice. That was Slim's somewhat elegant phrase for what to him was always a temporary situation.

'We are, sugar,' he said, grinning, 'but we're gonna have breakfast anyway. Now, get your sister in the back there and go wash up. I'll get a table. And remember, as soon as you've eaten as much as you want, you start to hold your stomach. You know the drill.' He winked, untwisting the piece of coathanger wire securing the driver's side door.

'Yep' – Melon smiled – 'I know the drill. Come on, Gracie,' she said to the rearview mirror. 'Chow time. Move it.'

The girls knew just how long to stay in the ladies' room. By the time they joined Slim in a strategically located front booth, he was grinning at them over a feast of fried eggs, home-fried potatoes, sausage, bacon, and fried tomatoes. As the girls began to eat, he cut and buttered several biscuits, slipped a strip of bacon into each, and popped them into the knapsack that rested on the Leatherette seat by his side.

Melon finished ahead of Gracie, placed her hand over her tummy, and started to rock back and forth. She moaned softly until she attracted the attention of the waitress who had served them.

Seeing the little girl's distress, the waitress rushed over to the table. 'Is there something wrong, honey?' she asked, genuinely concerned.

Melon placed a hand on her forehead and moaned more loudly. 'I don't know, ma'am. I was fine until I ate these here sausages.'

151

On cue, Gracie covered her mouth and began to make retching noises. Slim put his arms around Melon's shoulders and looked plaintively up at the waitress. 'She's never sick,' he said, then looked at Melon. 'You're never sick, are you honey?'

Melon shook her head violently and Gracie bolted for the ladies' room, her hand still firmly planted over her mouth.

'My Lord,' the waitress said with alarm. 'There must be something wrong with this sausage. Here, let me take those.' She whisked the nearly finished platter off the table and ran back toward the kitchen.

In the ensuing commotion no bill was presented. A near-frantic owner and the waitress bundled the little band out to the parking lot amid chattered apologies and suggested home remedies.

As Slim pulled onto the highway, he reached beneath the seat. 'If yawl didn't get enough to eat, there's some mighty fine bacon biscuits there in the sack.'

Melon reached in and pulled out two. She handed one to her sister. 'I like mine with honey,' Gracie whined. From the pockets of her shirt Melon produced half a dozen packets of honey snatched from the diner counter in the confusion.

If their wanderings had any direction at all, it was roughly west toward Los Angeles. By fall the girls would have to go to school, and Slim had a better chance of steady work in a big city.

When they did finally reach L.A., Slim got a job working for a team of window washers. He found a run-down rental in Tujunga. The guy on one side of the house raised pit bulls, and there was a family of bikers across the street. But it was only ten minutes into downtown L.A., and there was a public school two blocks away. Slim lied to the school authorities saying he was their father. No one asked to see any proof, and a week later the girls started grade school.

Even in a school with a population of underprivileged kids, Mary Elizabeth and Gracie O'Flanahan were considered poor.

But Melon was cute. Cuter than dark, dull Gracie, she had her mother's big blue eyes and tip-tilted nose. As she matured, her body developed taut, muscular curves. Her tiny waist and rounded hips made up for the too-short legs and small stature. She had absorbed Slim's cavalier attitude toward life. While it was acceptable in a lanky handyman, such toughness in a tiny blonde girl was startling.

As she had in the back of the old car, she still lay awake nights trying to figure out the funny feeling that seemed to be located deep in her chest. It was an emptiness, a need, a longing for something she didn't have. Slim was kind and looked out for her, but they were interdependent. She was his foil, his shill, and his protective coloration, a prop that made his life easier, his scams workable. He didn't love her. Not in the way she perceived love, and slowly she began to realize that no one, no one in the whole world did. Perhaps, she decided, it was because she wasn't worth loving. She would shiver and burrow beneath the thin blanket. 'It doesn't matter. I don't need to be loved,' she whispered. 'I can get anything I want. Slim showed me how.'

Indeed, Slim had taught her well. He taught her to cry on cue, to bat her eyes and use what he called her 'baby girl' voice, which she found could be used to repel or attract, whichever served her purpose.

'Ain't she cute?' Slim would ask anyone who showed the slightest interest in her. 'Just as cute as a bunny lickin' honey off its paws,' he would say in his prairie drawl. 'As cute as a roomful of Chinese babies,' he would say, grinning. She wanted to believe him with all her heart.

But being cute didn't make up for the ill-fitting thrift-shop dresses and cheap plastic shoes. It didn't make up for her missing mother and the almost palpable hatred that emanated from the girls at school. For she trusted no one with the exception of Slim and her sister. She was so accustomed to getting what she wanted by trickery or lying that to accomplish a goal by simply being honest held no interest. It was boring. There were no thrills on the straight-and-narrow path. And worse – no attention.

By the time she entered high school she had made few girlfriends. However, her blossoming body and provocative ways made her a favorite with the boys. Her quick and acid tongue kept them well in check and even earned her a modicum of respect.

She was insatiably curious about those who had more than she. The girls in school didn't like her constant questions, her pestering them about their personal lives. But the boys liked nothing more than to be asked about themselves.

Early one morning of her fourteenth year she turned in her narrow bed and found Slim lying next to her.

At first she was only mildly surprised, but when she became accustomed to being held and fondled, she actually started looking forward to his visits. What the hell, she rationalized, he wasn't her real father, whoever that might have been. He'd always been kind to her and there were times when she actually felt sexy. Better to do it with Slim than any of those conceited boys.

Throughout high school the longing to be admired by her peers metamorphosed into a fierce competitiveness that made her an excellent student. She had to be the first, the best, get the highest grades, outswim the swim team, and date the best-looking boy. Nothing seemed enough. She achieved her greatest satisfaction on the school newspaper. She convinced the journalism advisor that what the paper needed was a gossip column. Hadn't she spent light-years picking everyone's brains? Information was power, and the attention to be gained from its dissemination fascinated her.

Her first column, entitled 'Grapevine,' caused a

154

sensation within minutes of its being distributed around the sprawling high school.

Her copy was as bitchy and irreverent as the school authorities would permit, filled with blind items on who was dating whom, where the 'in' crowd went for after-school hamburgers, and who didn't have a date for the prom. At last she had the attention she craved.

Her newfound power completely absorbed her. She became an instant addict to it. By the end of her junior year, Jack Murphy, the editor of a neighborhood weekly, approached her student advisor about Melon's doing a similar column for his paper. There were six thousand kids in the school and their parents were bound to be interested in what was going on in their lives.

The morning her first column appeared in the neighborhood weekly she sat at the little table in the kitchen and tore through the paper. She found it quickly. It ran down the full length of the right-hand side of page eleven.

She couldn't believe her eyes. The column was headed 'Grapevine' like the school column, but she had been promised a byline under the title. The space was blank.

Furious, she cut class and demanded Slim drive her to the newspaper. She stormed into the editor's office and demanded to know why her name was not on the column.

Murphy leaned back in his swivel chair and grinned at the tiny, red-faced baby doll standing in front of him yelling at the top of her lungs and slapping his desk with a rolled-up newspaper.

'Honey,' he said calmly after she had finished a verbal onslaught that would have had made a teamster blush, 'you tell me how I'm going to fit Mary Elizabeth O'Flanahan into something one-column wide. I'd have to set it in type so small you couldn't read it.'

'What the hell am I supposed to do?' she nearly screamed. 'Give myself a shorter name!'

The editor righted his chair. 'That's not a bad idea. If you want to see your name in print.'

'Well, I do,' she pouted.

'Okay . . . pick a name.'

She stared at the overhead light fixture for a long moment. She thought about Slim and the way he had talked to her that morning as he awakened her, slipping his hand between her legs and stroking her pubic hair. 'How's your little tuft this morning?' he whispered as he pried her legs apart with his bony knee.

'Tuft!' she said. 'Someone . . . ah . . . someone I like calls me by that name.'

'A what?'

'Tuft,' she repeated.

'What kind of a name is that?' Murphy asked, a frown creasing his forehead.

'Short.'

'Mary Elizabeth Tuft?'

'Melon Tuft,' she corrected him. 'That's my name from now on, okay?'

'Yeah . . , sure, I guess so. If that's what you want, it's okay by me.'

Melon smiled and handed him her column for the following week in which she informed her readers that she had seen a dance instructor at school huddled in a Chevy Nova at the Taco Bell Drive-in with a married science teacher.

'Here,' she said, 'and there's plenty more where that came from.'

'Tuft!'

The city editor of the Los Angeles Tribune shouted above the din of the city room. In April of 1984 Dick Breslauer was middle-aged, married, and had eyebrows that looked as though they were affixed to his face with Velcro strips. He had been slipping away to motels with

156

Melon since she had been on the job, but their familiarity ended in the motel parking lot. On the job he was all business.

Melon, seated at her desk at the back of the room, hung up the phone. She was supposed to be typing the work schedule for the weekend shift. Actually she was calling numbers in the real estate want-ads.

She had had it living in the run-down little house in Tujunga with Slim, who now had a steady job in a print shop on Sunset, and Gracie, who had quit high school to watch television. They were cramping her style. She was out of high school, had her own car (beat up as it was), and she longed to be on her own. She had places to go and things to see, and while she didn't mind working for a better life, she wanted some of the trappings that went with it. That meant her own apartment and some privacy.

'Yo!' she shouted back as she swung around in her chair and trotted up the aisle, her open-toe, backless heels making little slapping sounds against her stockingless feet.

Breslauer watched her as she approached, marvelling at her hip-swinging walk, the set of her shoulders rising above a Daisy Mae blouse pulled low enough to cause heads to shake as she passed. Melon's outfits were the subject of daily water-cooler discussions among the men and withering looks from the women. She wore her hair piled loosely on top of her head. Bright blonde tendrils carelessly escaped around her forehead and cheeks, giving her a look of someone who had just rolled out of bed.

The editor dropped his eyes, hoping to indicate disinterest, and thrust a press release at her. 'Walk this back to Beth Daniels. She might want to do a feature on this shindig.'

Melon took the press release and reading it, slowly walked back toward reporter Beth Daniels's desk.

157

Crystal Kincaid, the glamorous star of television's most popular series, *Distant Mansions*, has commissioned a dealer to auction the contents of her Brentwood estate accumulated during her marriage to former husband, producer Roger Danameyer. The auction will start at 12 o'clock noon. Miscellaneous items will be sold independent of the auction and are offered 'as is.'

Melon felt her throat tighten. She would kill to get inside a movie star's house. And Crystal Kincaid! What incredible things she must have!

The only reason she had taken the crummy job as city room clerk and gofer was in the hope of working her way up to being a reporter. She had been at the *Tribune* for too long – almost two years – but without more than a high school education what she hoped would be a direct route to becoming a reporter was turning into a demeaning dead end.

She glanced toward Beth Daniels's desk. She was nowhere in sight. Melon returned to her desk and checked the daily log. Daniels was covering a fashion luncheon at the Beverly Wilshire. She wouldn't be back until long after the auction was over. She shoved the press release into her bag and sat down, pretending to type.

This was the chance she had been waiting for.

Crystal Kincaid was a B-movie actress who was experiencing a smashing midlife career resurgence. Anything she did, said, ate, or wore was hot copy thanks to the success of her television series. The show, a kind of nighttime soap, got top ratings, and any tidbit of gossip about her, true or not, got headline play all over the world. Melon knew that if she picked up even one tiny item about the star that was exclusive, the paper would use it and hope against hope, put her name on it.

When she saw Dick Breslauer leave for lunch, she made her move.

A sweaty press agent for the auction house was standing at the gate of Crystal Kincaid's estate. He gestured for Melon's cab to stop and stepped to the back window.

When she announced that she was a reporter for the *L.A. Tribune*, his mood brightened. He offered her a personalized tour of the house in which everything, down to omelette pans in the kitchen, was for sale. Only the larger, more authentically antique pieces would be auctioned from the gazebo on the tented back lawn.

Melon joined a small group of reporters for the tour. As they passed through the master bath, she made careful notes. The bathtub was filled to the rim with used makeup. Mountains of linen bearing the star's former monogram were stacked in the hallways. Even drapery hardware was for sale.

It was a good story but with one basic flaw. The house was full of reporters from every L.A. paper plus someone from *Time, People*, the *National Enquirer*, and the wire services. Anything of interest would be picked up by the others. She had to find something none of the others had seen.

As the time for the auction itself approached, Melon slipped away from the group and hurried down the back stairs to find herself in a vast six-car garage. Shoved into one corner next to boxes of a decorator's colour-coordinated books-by-the-yard was a small French writing desk. Glancing around to see that she was unobserved, Melon pulled open the top drawer.

Empty.

She jiggled the next drawer. It was locked. Working quickly, she found a metal nail file at the bottom of her bag and pried open the drawer. It was filled to the top with unbound typewritten pages – a manuscript of some kind. Probably something sent to the star for consideration as a film. She snatched a handful of pages and leaned against a tall carton of books. What she read made the back of her neck tingle.

'Hello?' a familiar voice called from the open garage door. It was the press agent who had noticed her absence from the group. 'Can I help you, Miss Tuft?' he said tightly.

She jammed the manuscript pages back into the desk and heard the lock click into place. 'Oh. Hi, there,' she said brightly. 'I just noticed this adorable old desk. I wonder if I could buy it. Sort of a souvenir. I'm such a Crystal Kincaid fan,' she said pertly.

He scanned the gloom of the garage until he focused on the desk. 'Gee, I don't know why not, Miss Tuft. Let me see if it's for sale.'

Melon sat on the desk and waited for him to return. If the damn desk was more than ten dollars, she'd have to bum a ride back to the paper. Ten was all she had.

'Well, you're in luck, Miss Tuft,' the press agent told her upon returning. There were sweat stains beginning under the arms of his seersucker jacket. 'The auction people say it was set aside because a leg is broken. If that's not important, it's yours for only ten dollars.'

Melon jumped prettily down from the desk and clapped her hands. 'Oh, goody!' she said, moving close to him and tilting her head. She gazed up into his eyes. Then, quickly, as though remembering something, she looked down and pushed out her lower lip. 'Oh, dear,' she sighed.

'Why, Miss Tuft, what's the matter?'

'Oh, nothing. It's just that I really want the desk. I'm moving into a new apartment and it's just what I need for my work but . . .' She took a step closer. Close enough for him to feel her breasts against his shirt and smell her perfume.

'If it's the money, I can certainly let you have ten dollars.'

'Oh, no. That's sweet. I have plenty with me, but I just realized I don't have any way to get it home.'

'That's no problem. Just give me your address and I'll drop it off for you.'

She had to think fast. 'Oh, ah . . . I know a handyman who does repairs. Perhaps you could drop it off there?'

'Of course. When you're ready to leave, I can drop you at the paper and then take the desk.'

'You are adorable!' she squealed. 'Here, let me write it down for you. It's a pretty run-down place. Just leave it on the porch.'

She pawed around in her bag and found one of the business cards Slim printed up for her at the shop as a joke birthday present. The card read: *Melon Tuft, Reporter, Los Angeles Tribune*. She scribbled her own address on the back.

The following morning the stunned city editor of the *Los Angeles Tribune* called an emergency meeting in the publisher's conference room.

Melon sat at a mahogany conference-room table facing her boss, the publisher, and the *Tribune*'s legal counsel. The publisher left word that no calls were to be put through until 'this thing is settled.'

The three men had been sifting through the material Melon had delivered for over half an hour. Occasionally Dick Breslauer looked across at Melon, who displayed no nervousness whatsoever except the annoying clicking of her fingernails on the surface of the conference table.

Little Melon Tuft, the bouncy blonde city room clerk who couldn't spell, had come swinging up to his desk at nine that morning with a million-dollar bombshell in her handbag. Now she sat, cool as a polar bear's tool, negotiating with one of the largest-circulation dailies in the state like a union shop steward with a noon deadline to close the paper down.

Breslauer handed the pages he had finished reading to the legal counsel and picked up another handful. Again he glanced across at Melon. Catching his eye, she reached up and pulled at whatever was holding her hair in place. It cascaded in a mass down around her shoulders. To his chagrin he caught the same expression on her face that he had remembered from the last time they were at the airport Day's Inn Motel. She had been sitting astride him after having moved down from his face, her breasts bobbing in unison like matching fishing floats as she worked herself into a frenzy. Before he could pick up another handful of pages, she slowly wet her lips and half-smiled.

He passed his hand over his Velcro eyebrows to clear the obscene movie in his mind.

The *Tribune*'s lawyer stacked the pages he had just read into a neat pile. He pushed them across the table to Melon and cleared his throat.

'Well, as I see it, what we have here is the love diary of the biggest star in America,' he pronounced.

'Love diary!' Melon shrieked. 'Get real! This is her fuck book! Her scorecard. This is a record of everyone she's ever gone to bed with. We can trace her whole career through blow jobs! It's just like I said when we first came in here. This is the stuff she never said in all the interviews she's ever given. Some love diary!' Melon was half out of her chair, pawing through the pages of the manuscript in front of her. 'Did you see this part about William Holden,' she said, waving a page in the air. 'And the part about her plastic boobs! I mean . . . that alone is worth the front page!'

'Ah . . . Miss Tuft. Please,' the publisher, who until he had walked into the meeting hadn't even known she worked for the paper, spoke in a low, soothing voice. 'Let's all try to stay calm.'

'Look, Mr Thompson,' she said, lowering her voice to a near growl, 'I don't have to stay calm. I don't have to stay, period. I can take this material to any big publication within the English-speaking world. Any publication with balls, that is, which apparently you and your paper lack.'

The lawyer turned toward the publisher as though Melon had not spoken. 'Ah, Bill, I'm having some trouble here with the possibility that this material is stolen. We could be in real trouble if we go with this.'

'It . . . was . . . not . . . stolen,' Melon said, emphasizing each word evenly. 'I bought the desk fair and square. Everything out there was for sale "as is". And that's how I bought the desk – "as is." When I got home, I found the manuscript in the drawer. You don't have to be on the Supreme Court to figure out that this manuscript was abandoned property. I found it. It's mine.'

Breslauer chanced another look at Melon. 'She may have a point,' he said weakly, his eyes fixing on Melon's nipples, which were clearly visible through her thin nylon blouse.

'You can bet your jockstrap I have a point,' Melon said, ignoring the fact that he wasn't speaking to her. 'A damn good one. Now, are you going to run with this or am I going to make a few phone calls? There's a little Mercedes in a lot on Melrose that I'm dying to own.'

The publisher held up his hand. 'Just a minute, Melon. You don't need to threaten us. What you have here is very exciting, and you're a clever girl to have spotted it and brought it to us. Now, when I heard what you had, I got on the phone with our New York bureau chief. This is a copy of Crystal Kincaid's upcoming book for Haddon and Leigh Publishers. Our lawyers there, Roger' – he nodded toward the general counsel – 'tell us that there is nothing to keep us from writing a story about the content of this material. What we can't do is publish the actual words. That would be stealing her material, but hot manuscripts get back-handed to the press all the time. Material gets leaked. That's the way the game is played. New York did some quick figures, and with syndication in the States and abroad a story would be worth several hundred thousand dollars.'

Dick Breslauer cringed. He knew Melon well enough to know that's all she wanted to hear. Now she would really go for their throats.

Melon slapped her palm on the table. 'There. You see! And this is mine. My story, my byline, and' – she shrugged prettily – 'my picture. Why not?'

The publisher continued to address Melon in dulcet, paternal tones. 'Do you think you could extract this material and write, say, five thousand words, as a feature of course, on what Crystal says about herself.'

Melon took a deep breath. 'What's in it for me?' she said.

The publisher looked displeased and cleared his throat again. 'You are an employee of this newspaper, Miss Tuft. You were on assignment for this newspaper when you, ah . . . happened upon this material, were you not?'

'No, I wasn't.'

All three men stared at her.

Breslauer tried to signal her with his eyes. He had hoped the publisher would believe that he had somehow assigned Melon to cover the auction. Now she was going to let the cat out of the bag and he wouldn't look good.

The publisher leaned toward her. 'You were not on assignment?' he asked incredulously.

'No. I'm not a reporter. I'm just a clerk in the city room. I went out there on my own, so technically I don't owe you guys a fart.'

The company lawyer regained his voice. 'Now, look here, Miss Tuft. . . .'

His tone did something to Melon. She felt a sudden urge of fear, fear that these three suits were going to find a way to steal the manuscript. They were powerful men and they were going to screw her out of the best, the only windfall she had ever come close to. Suddenly the fear gave way to anger. She jumped to her feet and furiously scooped the loose pages of the precious manuscript into a ragged pile. She lifted the pile into her arms, clutching it to the front of the blouse. The three men looked from one to another, speechless.

'You know what, guys? I don't think I want to talk to

164

any of you anymore. I gave you a shot and you wimped out. I think I'm gonna take this little bombshell of mine and go elsewhere.'

She shoved the papers into her bag and headed for the door. Instinctively the lawyer and the publisher pushed back their chairs and stood. Breslauer, his mouth hanging open, tried to speak. 'Melon, ah . . . just hold on a minute.'

Melon had reached the door. She had one hand on the knob. She thrust the other one high into the air, her middle finger extended. 'Up yours,' she said briskly, and walked out of the room.

The men were too stunned to speak for a long moment. Breslauer broke the silence, asking. 'Should I go get her?'

The publisher shook his head. 'No. Not just yet,' he said, reaching for his tobacco pouch. He made a production out of filling his pipe before he continued. 'Where, may I ask, did we find that little pirate?'

The editor's cheeks puffed out with a long, tired exhalation of air. 'We ran an ad for a clerk. She just marched in here. Said she'd written for a weekly. I checked it out. She had. High school drivel, but she could type. So I hired her.'

The publisher took a long pull on his pipe. 'Well, go get her, damn it. We'd drive the *Times* crazy if we broke that story. It's golden and we all know it. Go find out what she wants and give it to her.'

'I know what she wants,' Breslauer said. 'She wants money. Enough to set herself up in an apartment. She lives with her stepfather and I take it he puts the moves on her. But more than that, she wants to be a reporter.'

'You seem to know her pretty well,' the lawyer said suspiciously.

Dick Breslauer ignored him; he was in enough trouble already. Besides, he had a soft spot for Melon that went beyond their frisky afternoons in the Day's Inn. He knew she was screwing him because she thought he'd make her a reporter. He wouldn't but that was beside the point. He admired how hard she worked on him and knew her zeal came from being eaten alive with ambition. She wanted to get somewhere someday and she didn't care what she had to do to get there. He liked that. He wished he had been more like that himself when he was her age. He pushed back his chair and stood up. 'Look, let me go talk to her,' he said, hiking up his pants and smoothing his tie. 'I'll offer her a percentage of what we'll make from world syndication and maybe suggest we pay for some night courses. The girl can't spell for shit.'

When he reached the city room, Melon was not at her desk. By the end of the day she had not appeared. He tried phoning her at home until nearly midnight. Finally, on the last call he was going to make, someone picked up the phone. 'Hello!' he almost shouted. 'Melon?'

'No,' a woman's voice said. 'This is her sister, Gracie.'

'Is Melon there? This is her boss down at the paper.'

'Gee. No. I just got home from the movies. Wait. There's a note here on the table. Hold on a sec.'

He waited for what seemed like an eternity. Perhaps Melon's sister couldn't read. Melon had complained once that she was none too bright. If Melon had taken her find to the *L.A. Times* or *Herald* his ass was grass. The soft spot he had for Melon Tuft was rapidly turning white hot as he waited.

Finally, the sister was back on the line. 'Hello?' she said, her voice slightly more excited. 'This is a surprise!' Then there was silence.

'Yes? Hello? What is it?'

'It's a note to my stepfather. It says, "Slim. I've gone to New York. Don't look for your poker winnings because I've got 'em. Good-bye to you, too, Gracie." Aw. Isn't that nice. That's me.'

'Shit,' the editor hissed.

'Sorry?'

'No, I'm sorry. Look, if you hear from her, would you tell her to call me?'

166

'Gee, New York,' Gracie said. 'Is that anywhere near Vegas? I've been to Vegas.'

When Melon left California, she never looked back. In the ten months that had passed since she had arrived in New York, she had never once thought of herself as an uneducated orphan with a retarded sister and an ersatz stepfather. If she ever thought about her chances of success in the real world, she would never have left Tujunga. She'd been free of self-doubt from birth.

She felt she had been born with a steel shell that protected her. That and her perpetual what-have-I-got-to-lose attitude set her free. Maybe someone would hurt her someday. She probably wouldn't recognize the feeling if it happened.

Right now, all she could think about was the ache in her lower back from sitting so long on the hard-backed bench in the draughty Carlyle lobby.

She got up, stretched, and started to stroll around. As she rounded the corner, she saw the desk clerk motioning to her with rapid arm movements. She hurried across the lobby to the desk. 'What is it?' she asked excitedly. 'Is he on his way down?'

His face was red and his eyes slightly popped. 'You better scram, lady. That woman that was here, Miss Motherwell? She knows why you've been hanging around. She just phoned the manager and asked him to call the cops.'

7

Up until that point, until her photograph had appeared in the *Post* every victory, every good thing that had happened to Sloane, every step farther along the road to success, had been engineered, promoted, and advanced by Noreen.

Ironically, the very day Sloane was to learn she had an interview with Warner Bromley himself, a letter arrived from her mother. It was more of a note than a whole letter, and it was accompanied by a picture of Noreen wearing a strapless evening gown and long, dangling earrings. She was seated at a large round table with several recognizable faces: Tom Selleck, Merv Griffin, and Dinah Shore sitting next to a handsome and familiar face Sloane couldn't immediately identify. Next to Noreen was a tanned and smiling Mark Reynolds. The pouches Sloane remembered under his eyes were no longer there, and he looked as though he was wearing a hairpiece. It was clearly some sort of award dinner where a hired photographer moved from table to table taking pictures one could buy later.

The note, hastily scribbled, read, *Fun evening with gang. Hope everything going well in the Big Apple. Love, Your Mother*.

The competitive message was not lost on Sloane. She pressed a corner of the picture into the mirror frame, her mind a jumble of conflicting emotions. There she was on the verge of a very real career breakthrough, one that she had achieved without Noreen anywhere in sight. Still, the one person she longed to call with the good news would have been her mother.

Sloane had been waiting at home for some kind of word about the job all day. When Alan had repeated every single word he had heard while doing Layla's hair, she had been ecstatic. Her break had finally come.

Turning away from her mother's photograph, her hands wrapped around a mug of warm tea, she listened to rising heat expanding metal somewhere in the old building. A wind had come up from the Hudson. It sent bits of flotsam and trash clicking against the high windows. Far in the distance an ambulance siren keened into the night. The momentary euphoria she'd felt upon hearing Alan's news had passed. In its place lurked a feeling that something was missing. Shouldn't there be someone special to share the good news with? Alan was happy for her, but not the way she *needed* someone to be happy for her.

The ringing phone interrupted her thoughts. She debated picking it up. It was probably someone who wanted to take her out at the last minute. She didn't want to go out. She didn't want to stay in either. After the fourth ring she couldn't resist. Maybe Alan had forgotten to tell her something.

'Sloane?' a familiar voice said. 'This is Cole Latimer. Sorry to call so late. I hope I didn't wake you.'

'Oh, Mr Latimer! Why no. Not at all. I . . . it's not late.' She was jabbering like a ninny but she was so surprised.

'I spoke to Ms Bronz this evening and we would like to set up an appointment for you with Mr Bromley some-time tomorrow if possible. Are you available?'

'Yes . . . of course. Sure. Where should I be?'

'I'd like to have you meet Ms Bronz first. Perhaps you could stop by the *Realto* office and then you and I will go to the Carlyle. Mr Bromley has a suite there. I've spoken

169

to your representatives at Snap. They'll have their lawyer there to answer any legal questions that might come up.'

'Gee, I'm speechless. I didn't think things were going to happen this fast.'

'I know we're rushing you, but Mr Bromley is here for only a few days and we need to move on this project. Shall we say ten o'clock at the brownstone? Same place as this morning.'

'Fine . . . fine, I'll be there, Mr Latimer.'

'Cole.'

'Cole,' she said. 'And thank you. Thank you for just everything, I'm really excited about all this.'

'So are we, Sloane,' he chuckled. 'So are we.'

She was awake by six. She rolled out of bed in her sweat suit and slipped a Bob Marley tape into place. For a full hour she worked out on a floor mat. When her sweat suit was soaked through, she stepped into the shower. She felt as though she had taken amphetamines.

She needed a full hour for her makeup and hair. The night before she had picked out and steamed a simple, beautifully draped cashmere dress with a huge cowl collar. The hemline fell well over the tops of her grey suede boots. Her only jewellery was thick gold cube earrings and a chunky gold wrist bangle. To complete the simple, clean look she chose a long pewter suede trench coat.

At the brownstone, as she walked down the hall headed toward Layla Bronz's office, she checked herself one last time in the oval gold-framed mirror.

She had never looked better.

Her meeting with Layla Bronz was brief, if not downright chilly.

The woman was businesslike and pleasant but she seemed distracted. She called her 'Susan' twice and took four phone calls during their fifteen-minute meeting.

When she left the brownstone with Cole for the short ride to the Carlyle, she had the distinct feeling that the magazine publisher not only didn't like her but didn't care whether she was chosen as the spokeswoman for Bromley or not. It would not be right to mention her feelings to Cole. He himself had been nothing but sweet to her. He would hardly speak against his colleague and boss.

Layla's big Rolls purred to the curb in front of the Carlyle. It was one of those New York winter mornings, cold but blessed with dazzling sunlight. A high wind swirled around them as they made their way toward the revolving door of the hotel.

Sloane entered the lobby ahead of Cole, and blinded by the sudden change of light, she hardly noticed the woman who rushed toward him.

'Cole!' she shouted, accosting him as he emerged into the lobby. She began to tug at the silk scarf hanging loosely under his Burberry.

Cole reeled back and stared down at her. 'Hello, Melon,' he said briskly. Sloane could tell he was not amused.

'You're going up to see Warner Bromley, aren't you?' she said breathlessly.

Cole reached up and pried her fingers from his scarf. He glanced over at Sloane, who was watching the curious scene a few steps to the side. 'Ah . . . Melon, this is Sloane Taylor,' he said, trying to distract her. 'Sloane, Melon Tuft. Melon is, ah . . .' He paused, as though unsure how to describe Melon. 'Melon is a writer,' he said.

Sloane extended her hand. Melon ignored it.

'Thank God you're here,' Melon said to Cole.

'Having a breakfast interview, are we, Melon dear?' he asked. His mouth smiled but his eyes were cold.

'You've just got to take me with you. I've got to meet him. Please, Cole. I'll do anything. Please, please.'

'Anything?' he responded, raising his eyebrows in a leer.

171

'Anything,' she said without batting an eye.

'Well, I'll tell you what, precious. You go sit down over there on that little thing by the elevator, and when we're finished our business, I'll let you know.'

Like a dutiful puppy Melon scurried back to her seat.

As Cole and Sloane stepped into the elevator, Melon leaned around the door and simpered. 'Nice to meet you, Joan.'

After the elevator closed, Sloane said, 'People seem to be having a hard time with my name today.'

Cole smiled across the elevator cab at her. 'Don't worry about it, dear. After today no one will be able to forget your name.'

Sloane held up both hands and crossed her fingers. 'I hope you're right,' she said. 'It would help if you could tell me what Mr Bromley is like.'

'Like a movie star,' Cole answered nonchalantly.

The door opened silently on the penthouse floor. Cole paused and let Sloane pass.

'Really?' she said in disbelief. 'Somehow I pictured a fat tycoon with a foot-long cigar.'

Cole gestured toward the red lacquered door at the end of the long, carpeted hall. 'He's hardly that. You'll see. Warner Bromley is without a doubt one of the best-looking men in public life,' he said. 'A real charmer. Tough businessman but what my mother used to call a real dreamboat.'

Rose Motherwell answered Cole's knock. Her crisp demeanour encouraged nothing more than quick formalities.

Cole introduced Sloane. Rose nodded and indicated that they were to follow her into a room that served as a dining and conference room.

There were people already seated around the large oval table. When Cole and Sloane entered, all fell silent and stood up. She was introduced around the table. There was an agent and a lawyer from Snap. There was also an attorney from Solters & Roskin, which was a powerful public relations firm Sloane had heard of, an advertising consultant with a serious comb-over, and the art director from *Realto*, who would be laying out the ad pages for the magazine. Sloane nodded and smiled at all these strangers who were simultaneously sizing her up. Later she realized that stepping into that room was more intimidating than any beauty contest she had ever been in.

After a few minutes of excruciating small talk, Ms Motherwell left the room as if responding to some secret signal. A moment later Warner Bromley entered the room.

Cole was right. He certainly was attractive. He was wearing a blue-black European-cut suit, high under the arms and slightly nipped at the waist. His custom-made shirt was pale blue. His tie was a formal silver and dark-blue silk stripe. He had a strong, prominent jaw, a long, straight nose, and wide-set grey eyes under black eyebrows. On either cheek there were deep creases like elongated dimples that deepened when he smiled. His dark hair was slightly longer than that of the other men in the room, highlighted by touches of silver at the temple.

His presence electrified the atmosphere in the room. It was as though someone had called, 'Lights! Camera! Action!' Everyone present, with the exception of Ms Motherwell, who stood by the door like a guard, seemed more animated, in better spirits, eager to put their best behavior on display.

Bromley moved from one person to the next, shaking hands, smiling, and saying nothing more than 'Hello' or 'Nice to see you again.' He reached Sloane last. She extended her hand and smiled, waiting for him to speak. As tall as she was, he was a good head taller. She was prepared and looked up at him with the same expression she used for the camera, fixing her eyes on an imaginary point behind his own, inside his head. She was caught by

173

his clear, steady gaze. A smile flickered at the corner of his mouth as he extended his hand.

'Hello, Sloane,' he said, holding her eyes. His voice was deep, well modulated, and as intimate as a whisper. She felt a rush of heat rising under her shoulder blades and encircling her midsection. At first she attributed the feeling to the fact that he was the most powerful man she had ever met and at that very moment held her future in his hands.

She had expected an ordeal. Hours of sitting around being grilled and judged, squirming while the agents and lawyers tried to one-up each other and cut a deal that would end up profiting themselves more than herself.

Instead, Warner Bromley took charge the minute he sat down. He seemed to have taken Cole Latimer's selection of Sloane as beyond discussion. She was already the Bromley Woman.

He announced that the contract was for one million dollars and all expenses. Her duties were fully spelled out in documents Rose Motherwell handed around the table in bright red folders with the Bromley crest. In less than half an hour it was all over.

Sloane stood by the door smiling and shaking hands again with everyone as they filed out of the room in little clusters.

She turned to pick up her bag and realized that she and Warner were alone in the room.

'How was that?' Warner asked, standing at the far end of the conference table.

'Very pleasant,' she said. 'And mercifully fast.'

'I don't believe in wasting time,' he said, moving toward her. 'And with that in mind, will you have dinner with me tonight? We should get to know each other. I hope you're free.'

'You bet,' she said.

Perhaps she sounded too eager. She wanted to please him and she knew he wouldn't have asked her to dinner if it wasn't something he wanted to do.

'I like that,' he said, laughing. 'Most women I ask to dinner say they have to check their calendar.'

'I don't have a calendar. Not for dinners.' She smiled.

'I'll send my car, then. Say, seven-thirty?'

'Why thank you. Let me give you my address.'

'I'll get it,' he said. 'I think Mr Latimer is waiting for you.'

'I'll see you tonight, then,' she said over her shoulder. 'I'm looking forward to dinner.'

As she joined Cole waiting at the elevator, she saw that her hands were trembling. She quickly plunged them into the pockets of her coat.

As they moved through the lobby, she once again heard the blonde writer yell, 'Cole! Cole! Cole!' from her seat by the elevator. He didn't slow his pace. Sloane looked over her shoulder to see Melon running toward them.

Cole turned as he spun the revolving door into motion. 'I told you I'd let you know when we finished our business, Melon.'

'Yes? And?' she asked expectantly.

'We're finished,' he said, and moved out onto the street.

'She's *what*?' Layla flat-handed the top of her desk, speaking through a cumulus cloud of smoke.

'She's having dinner with him,' Cole said. He was sitting on the couch in Layla's office after lunch filling her in on the morning meeting.

'Shit,' she hissed. 'With who else?'

'That's it. At Le Cirque.'

'Just the two of them?'

'Correctomundo, contessa.'

'How did you let that happen, Cole?' she said menacingly.

'*Moi*? I didn't find out about it until I got back here.

175

Rose called for her address. She wasn't too thrilled about it either.'

'But she had to know about it when the two of you left the meeting.' Layla scowled. 'You mean she didn't mention that he asked her to dinner?'

'Not a peep.'

'What do you make of that?'

'Perhaps she figures her personal life is personal.' Cole shrugged.

'I don't like it, not one bit,' Layla said. 'I saw that girl this morning. Believe me, I know the type.' She leaned forward. 'Cole, she's a killer.'

'She's really a terribly sweet kid, Layla. Lay off.'

'Yeah. *Sweet*.'

'Yes, sweet,' he insisted. 'And naive as well. I'll bet she never dated anyone but the captain of the football team.'

'Ha!' Layla barked. 'I'll bet she wears teddies under her panty hose and flosses after every meal. That kind fucks like a bunny if there's something to be gained. Don't kid yourself.'

'Darling, calm down.'

Layla nervously flicked the lid of her Fabergé-egg lighter up and down, making an annoying clicking sound. 'So old Rose called for her address, huh? What's he doing, sending his car?' she asked, pulling a sour face.

'E . . . yop.' Cole nodded.

'And he'll drive her through the park after dinner. I know the drill.'

'That would be a pleasant thing to do,' Cole said lightly. He wasn't going to be party to Layla's temper tantrum. He was happy for Sloane and hoped she had a wonderful evening.

'Crap. She'll be diving for his fly before they make it around Bethesda Fountain.'

'Layla. Now stop this!' Cole said as he pulled himself out of the low sofa. 'The man is about to invest millions in the girl. He has a right to see where his money is going.'

176

'Well, he won't have the energy for more than conversation. Not after last night,' she said, smiling lasciviously.

'By the way,' Cole said as he walked toward the door. 'I saw Melon at the Carlyle. She's got the lobby staked out.'

'To interview Warner?' she asked, surprised.

'Looks like it.'

Layla rubbed her chin and slowly nodded. 'That's ballsy. I'm going to have to keep an eye on that girl. And Cole,' she said, reaching for the ringing phone, 'check around this afternoon. See if you can find anyone we know who's going to be at Le Cirque tonight. I want a full report.'

Cole was relieved to get back to his office. For a brilliant woman Layla could be completely insane on the subject of Warner Bromley. Worse, she was lethal if anyone got near him. Sometime soon he would have a chat with Sloane. An introductory dinner with Bromley was certainly in order, but she should know that things could go no further. If it did, he knew what Layla would do, and none of them would survive it.

Sloane had dinner with Warner Bromley for the next four nights in a row. The rest of the week she had lunch *and* dinner with him, went to a Broadway opening, and accompanied him to a private dinner at the Park Avenue duplex apartment of one of his executives. Someone took their picture arriving at the theatre and it appeared in the *Daily News*.

Sloane floated through the week slightly dazed at the attention and glamour of it all. She bought a new answering machine, one that she could beep into from a pay phone to check on whether Warner had called. He invariably had.

By the weekend her apartment had begun to look, as Alan described it, like a well-kept grave. In pots, vases, milk cartons, and glasses there were lavender roses. They had arrived by the dozen every day since that night at Le Cirque.

By the time the flowers began to fill the bathtub, she asked Warner not to send any more. Deliveries to the loft continued, but the packages were smaller: tiny boxes from Cartier, Harry Winston's, Van Cleef & Arpels, and finally Bulgari.

She opened each box as it arrived, gasping at the lovely things, holding them to the light and putting them tenderly back into their boxes to be returned.

Alan had merely shrugged until he saw the ruby bracelet from Bulgari. 'Baby, you can't!' he said in horror.

'Can't what?' she said, curling the skein of brilliant stones back into the tissue paper.

'That's exactly the colour of your red suede coat.'

'Rubies don't go with suede,' she said smugly, popping them back in the box.

Alan groaned. 'Rubies go with everything. So do diamonds and sapphires. And gold. The gold that man has dropped on you could wipe out the Brazilian national debt. You could at least keep something!'

'No, I can't.'

'Sometimes you make me so angry, Sloane Taylor. Why not, for God's sake? You're sleeping with him, aren't you?'

Sloane rose and walked behind the kitchen counter. She pushed the containers of flowers to one side so that she could see Alan lounging on the couch. 'No, I am not sleeping with him, I'm just going out with him. Like lunch and dinner. I'm getting a little sick of fancy unborn food. Last night we had little teeny tiny carrots the size of cashew nuts —'

'Stop avoiding the subject. You know you're going to have to sleep with him eventually.'

She pulled a high stool up to the counter and sat down dejectedly. 'Alan, what am I going to do? He's so . . .'

'Old?'

'Well, kinda.'

'I asked around. He's fifty. That's not so bad. He's great looking, dresses beautifully, he's rich, powerful, handsome. And I suppose he's sexy. Doesn't ring my bell, but he's not sending me rubies either,' Alan said. 'I have to ask you. Is he sexy?'

Sloane shrugged. 'Well, yeah, kinda. He doesn't make my knees weak like Fernando did, but I'm a big girl now and I know nothing will ever be like that again. I might as well stop looking.'

'Jesus, girl. What more do you want?'

'Guess?'

'Beats me,' Alan said, swinging his feet clear and reaching for his drink on the coffee table. 'You have a contract, right? The big press conference is next week. The tour starts on April first. You'll be too damn busy to worry about him. Why don't you take a bauble or two, drink a lot of champagne, and hop in the feathers. You might just like it.'

'I want more than a job and jewellery, Alan.'

'What more is there, girl?' he said, waving his arms in frustration.

'Promise you won't go crazy on me?'

'Promise.'

'I think he wants to marry me.'

Alan stared at her trying to see if she was serious. He shook his head. 'You'd do that! You get the icks about sleeping with him because he's so old. Now you're telling me he wants to marry you like you're actually giving it some thought. You realize if you marry the man, he's not going to get any younger or sexier.'

'Then it would be different.'

'Oh, sure,' he said snidely. 'Isn't the power you're going to have as the Bromley Woman enough? The money? The fame? The men waiting just around the corner? That's not enough for you?'

She slid off the stool and leaned her elbows on the countertop. 'Alan, I'm alone, except for you. There's no one who knows me as I really am, and Warner seems to. I'm something completely new for him and he adores me. Besides, the life I could have with him would be beyond description. Cars, houses, planes, dinner with the most powerful and famous people in the world. Wouldn't I be crazy to say no?'

'And Noreen would be pleased.'

'That too,' she said.

'I think you've lost your furry little mind.' Alan took a long pull on his drink. 'You know, one of these days you're going to meet someone who curls your toes. What are you going to do then if you're married to Warner Bromley? He strikes me as the kind of guy who would give his wife everything but the freedom to sleep with someone else.'

'I'll chance it. I can *make* myself fall in love. I wish you would try and understand.'

And Alan understood. He hated it but he understood. All he could do was watch what was happening. He watched the way he would watch a car crash or a luxury liner sinking or a spider weaving a tight silken web around a fly. Sloane did not make a move that wasn't calculated. By the second-week anniversary after their first evening at Le Cirque, Sloane accepted a tiny gold bumblebee pin with sapphire eyes and pavé diamond wings.

She was wearing the little bee on the lapel of a new black Chanel suit when she boarded the Bromley company jet that whisked the couple to Bermuda for the rest of the weekend.

Sloane called Alan from a villa there the following day. She said Warner was playing tennis. She was lying on the terrace under a huge umbrella being waited on by Mr Bromley's butler. 'And guess what, Alan?' she asked breathlessly after describing the scene.

'Can't.'

'We did it!'

'You *did* it!' he said. 'You mean you made love. You had sex. You let him put his thing in you? Jesus, Sloane, you can take the girl out of Bakersfield but you . . .'

'Well, what am I supposed to say – "we fucked"?'

Alan sighed. He wasn't going to argue with her vocabulary, but there were times when her naïveté was unreal. 'Okay. How was it?'

There was a long pause on the line. He could hear the ocean in the background. 'It was wonderful. Absolutely wonderful. We made love for hours. He's amazing.'

Alan didn't really want to hear it.

'I think I'm in love, Alan. Honestly I do.'

He knew that was coming. The old guy probably gave her a real bouncing around and now she was all starry-eyed and wet. He wondered if sex was better after a ride in a private jet and knew it was. 'That's great, Sloane. I'm happy for you.'

'There was a white rose on my pillow this morning,' she continued. 'Just one rose. Can you believe it? I think that's more precious than jewellery. Don't you?'

'Take the jewellery.'

'Oh, Alan,' she giggled. 'You don't mean that.'

'I mean it,' he sighed. 'When are you coming back?'

'Tomorrow. My press conference is Thursday morning. I haven't a clue what I'm supposed to say.'

'Don't worry about it. There'll be a dozen people to tell you.'

'Will you be available, Alan? The saltwater and sun are ruining my hair. I'm going to need you desperately.'

'Yes, Sloane,' he said sadly. 'I'm available. You know that. Bye, honey.'

He sat smoking quietly, thinking about Sloane and what she was doing to her life. There wasn't any doubt that she would marry Warner Bromley. The poor rich bastard didn't stand a chance.

8

After saying good-bye to Alan, Sloane set the remote phone down next to her iced tea and stretched her long legs full length on the chaise. She had not felt such contentment since she left California. Her freezing loft, the mean streets, the uncertainty of her career, were all but forgotten. Even the Bad Girl Game that brought such a rush of excitement only to be replaced by feelings of guilt and shame was like a bad dream. For the last twenty-four hours she had been in paradise.

At the sound of the terrace door's sliding open, she looked up. Warner was standing over her, his lean, broad-shouldered body momentarily blocking out the sun.

'Happy, darling?' he said, bending to kiss her forehead.

'Blissfully.' She smiled up at him. He was wearing his tennis whites with a towel looped around his neck.

'I hope I had something to do with that.'

'Everything,' she said. 'I have never in my life been in such a beautiful place. How can you bear to leave it, ever?'

'No choice.' He shrugged. 'I leave so I can pay for it. But if you like it here, wait until you see my place in California.'

'Bigger, better, nicer?'

'Bigger and better. Nicer only if you were there, my love.' He removed the towel and wiped his forehead. 'I'm going to shower and dress. I thought we'd have champagne here when you're dressed and then go to the club for dinner. There are some people I want you to meet.'

Sloane lay back and pulled her straw hat over her eyes. Warner had been so sweet last night, so loving and gentle. She had lied, a bit, to Alan. They hadn't exactly made love all night. Twice, actually. What they had really done was talk all night. Rather, Warner talked. He knew everything about everything – art, music, politics, the economy, and high-level gossip about people she had only read about. She loved the way he told her things. He didn't lecture or talk down to her. He made everything sound as though these were things that surprised him, too. As though he had just found out something interesting and wanted to share the information with her.

When he came into her room in his silk, crested robe, she didn't know what to expect from their lovemaking. She knew it would not have the passion of spontaneity or the erotic excitement of the reckless sex that she craved. She had hoped that being with Warner might be something like it had been with Fernando, but it wasn't like that, either. Whatever they did, she had never lost control or the awareness of what she was doing. Still, it was lovely being told she was beautiful, to be touched and held. She knew she was bringing him pleasure. And after all, why would she even be here if she had not wanted to do that?

Afterward, as she lay in his arms, she was content, not transported exactly, but happy and serene.

When she looked at Warner, she could not help but see the life that surrounded him, one in which every need was anticipated, every care was solved by someone else.

On the plane ride from New York they had been accompanied by Warner's administrative aide. He was a pleasant man not much older than Sloane. In his blazer and horn-rims he looked like any one of the yuppie clones who hit on her in clubs around town.

183

The yuppie and Warner's uptight secretary, Ms Motherwell, had sat in the front of the plane at a white lacquer desk fitted out with state-of-the-art phones, computers, and fax machines. Warner had stayed with Sloane in the plush second compartment, but he spent most of the trip on the phone while she read magazines. They were served Bloody Marys and omelettes lighter than air by two handsome uniformed stewards. The pilots, the stewards, even the yuppie, wore the Bromley crest on their jacket pocket.

Upon landing they had been met by the airport security people, who'd stood respectfully at the foot of the plane stairs. The Jaguar that pulled right up to the steps of their plane was driven by a man wearing a uniform with the same crest on the pockets. To her relief the car dropped Motherwell and the yuppie at the Hamilton Inn. While the aide was nice enough, Ms Motherwell made her uneasy with her tight-lipped efficiency and subtle disapproval.

Warner's house was on a secluded spit of land that meandered out into the emerald-green ocean. It was a sprawling glass and redwood arrangement that looked as if it were about to take flight. At the very point of land farthest into the sea there was a huge satellite dish. She imagined it relayed information to the office in still another wing of the house.

As soon as they arrived, Warner had apologized and left for his office while a silent maid showed Sloane to her room in a wing by the pool. Having her own room was a surprise. She had assumed that after the weeks of holding him off, he would now insist they sleep in the same bed. She learned later that Warner used his own room only to shower and dress. Separate arrangements were out of deference to the staff.

The first, silent maid left her in the hands of her own personal maid, a sweet, motherly woman who unpacked her suitcase and pressed her silk things, hanging them on

184

scented, padded hangers. Without being asked, the maid had also drawn a perfumed bubble bath before slipping out of the room.

The huge bathroom was filled with the most wonderful array of cosmetics, all Bromley, of course. The towels were larger than bedspreads and as thick and creamy as frosting. In the house the Bromley crest was replaced by Warner's own monogram. Everything seemed to have WB on it; even the white sand in the terrace ashtrays was pressed with a metal gadget that marked the surface with his initials. Now, as she rose from the chaise where she'd called Alan to go and dress for dinner, Sloane thought again what it would be like to live like this all the time, to be a part of it for real and not just a pampered visitor. After last night she knew it was not an unattainable goal. There was only one person to focus on, to please, to make happy. All she really had to do was let it happen.

Warner was waiting for her, seated by the seawall on a comfortable wicker love seat. He sipped champagne and watched the sun dip into the cobalt sea.

She stepped onto the terrace knowing she had never looked better. The day spent in the sun had brought a golden glow to her limbs and face. She had selected a flowing caramel satin pyjama outfit that showed the lines of her figure. As she passed a blooming hedge, she picked a huge white blossom and tucked it into the twist of her upswept hair. She had taken extra care with her makeup, enlarging her eyes and glossing her lips. She never felt more confident than when The Mask was so firmly in place.

As she crossed the flagstones to join Warner, the butler stepped from behind the bar and headed toward the seawall with a silver tray of champagne and slivers of hot lobster showered with coconut dust.

Warner turned and beamed when he saw her, the soft evening breeze pressing the thin fabric against her breasts and hips.

185

'You take my breath away,' he said, standing to greet her with a brushing kiss on the cheek. At the last minute she had splashed on a Bromley fragrance she had found on the glass shelves in the bathroom.

He breathed deeply. 'Ah, you're wearing Heaven. On you it smells as I intended. I think I'll change the name to Sloane. Would you like that?'

She pulled away, her hands resting lightly on his shoulders. 'Are you serious?'

'Absolutely. It would just take a phone call.'

'No more phone calls, Warner darling. I want you all to myself tonight,' she said with a pout, and reached for a champagne flute on the tray.

'And that you shall have.' He signalled the butler who was back behind the bar. 'James, did you bring out the package?'

'Yes, sir, Mr Bromley,' the butler said with a subdued smile as he reached under the bar, then walked toward them holding a robin's-egg-blue box tied with white satin ribbon. He handed it to Warner. Warner held the knot of the ribbon in two fingers and placed it in her hand.

'Warner! You really shouldn't,' she protested. 'Just being here is —'

'Shhhh. . . . Don't comment until you see what it is. You might be surprised.'

There would be no refusing whatever was in the box. Not now. Not after last night.

She kept her eyes on him while she untied the ribbon and opened the lid. Nestled in the square box was another domed leather affair with a catch. She pressed the catch and lifted the top. Inside, rising out of the velvet, was a blaze of diamonds. One large emerald the size of a pigeon egg cut through the middle. It was surrounded by smaller but no less impressive diamonds.

'Oh, Warner. It's the most beautiful thing I've ever seen! What can I say?'

'Here,' he said, 'let me.' He lifted the ring out of the

186

box. He held it between his thumb and forefinger, letting the light catch in the stones. It seemed to be alive as each stone bounced little flash points of light against the satin of her blouse.

'I've never seen anything like this in my life!' she said, staring at the ring.

'And you won't.' He smiled, taking hold of her chin. He turned her face toward his and looked into her eyes. 'Sloane Taylor, will you marry me?'

Without warning, she burst into tears.

'My darling!' Warner said, alarmed and upset. 'What have I done?'

Sloane threw her arms around his neck. 'I'm sorry,' she sobbed. 'I'm just so overwhelmed. I don't know what to say.'

'Just say you love me, again,' he said. 'Say it the way you said it last night.'

She was embarrassed in front of the butler but he seemed oblivious, busying himself with things behind the bar.

'Oh, I do love you. I do. I do. So much,' she whispered. 'Just hold me.'

He held her as he had the night before when she had said those words to him for the first time. Before, she had said those words to another man out of passion. That passion had brought her excruciating pain and devastating loss. Before, those words had left her trapped, impotent, and alone. Now, as she said them, she felt sheltered and safe. What could be wrong in telling him what he wanted to hear?

As they sat and watched the sun disappear far out to sea, she dismissed the little doubts she had to the back of her mind. Whatever her misgivings, Warner was going to save her.

It seemed such a small price to pay.

On the flight home from Bermuda on Monday morning, Sloane began to realize her life would never be the same.

As on the flight down, Warner was on the phone behind his desk in the back cabin. Ms Motherwell and the yuppie, whose name Sloane had learned was Brian, sat in the front going over papers. Sloane sat by herself pretending to read magazines. Each time the steward passed her armchair he silently refilled the wineglass at her side. She smiled up at him and took the fresh drink, holding it in the patch of sun coming through the small window over her shoulder. The light caught and held in Warner's ring.

When she had returned to her room after dinner the night before, she had called Alan and told him she was going to marry Warner. Alan had dutifully acted as if he were deliriously happy for her.

After hanging up with him, Sloane had sat for a long time on the edge of the bed knowing she had to call Noreen. Again, the old conflict loomed. She wanted her to hear good news, and yet she didn't want to risk a negative, dismissive reaction. Reluctantly she picked up the phone and dialled the number of Noreen and Mark's new condo off Wilshire. Although Noreen had sent her the number weeks before, this would be the first time Sloane had used it or heard her mother's voice since she came to New York.

The phone rang three times before the service picked up. Disappointed and relieved at the same time, Sloane left a message for her mother to call her in New York when she returned. Little Mary Sloane couldn't imagine getting married without her mother there. Grown-up Sloane wasn't so sure it would be a hot idea. Her problems multiplied the more she thought about the actual service. How could she marry a man as famous as Warner Bromley with only her hairdresser in attendance? Who would stand up for her? None of the girls at the agency were close enough to ask. The thought of

Rochelle with her teased hair and big mouth was unthinkable.

Suddenly both stewards sped up the aisle single file. She glanced toward the back of the plane and saw that Warner was standing behind his desk. Evidently anytime he stood up it was the sign that he wanted something. The tall, blond steward swung the hinged desk to one side so Warner could pass. Warner said something to the other, who moved in quick time back up the aisle and stepped behind the bar.

Warner strode toward Sloane smiling broadly. 'Now. That's settled,' he said, sitting down in the armchair opposite her. The steward who had run to the bar swirled to pick up a napkin and glass of wine, which he then placed on the side table in one smooth motion. Then he stepped back to his station at the bar.

Sloane reached forward and laid her hand on top of Warner's. 'What coup have you effected now, darling?' She smiled.

He leaned forward and kissed her lightly. 'Oh, just getting things organized for you.'

'For *me*?'

'Um. The Carlyle has a little suite for you. It's just below the penthouse with a connecting stair that's been sealed. They'll open it for us.' He wiggled his eyebrows meaningfully.

This was a complete surprise to Sloane. 'A suite? Am I moving?'

'Of course, my dear. You can't stay in that dreary loft. Not now. I'm having my New York public relations firm announce our plans to the press Wednesday, to take advantage of your press conference Thursday morning.'

'Wait, wait, wait!' Sloane laughed. 'Slow down. Announcement? Press conference? My head is spinning.'

'Now, now. Don't panic, darling. Everything will be taken care of. The PR people will handle everything. All you have to do is get settled at the hotel when we get back.

They'll tell you what they want you to do on Thursday. We've set the press conference for the Plaza. You'll read a little statement they're writing for you, answer a few questions, and let them take as many pictures as possible of your beautiful face. We want to have all this out of the way before the wedding.'

'Whew! Everything's moving so fast,' she repeated.

'Relax, darling. You'll do fine.' He patted her knee and noticed her glass. 'Raymond, more wine for Miss Taylor.'

'Ah, Warner . . .'

'Yes, dear?'

'About the wedding . . . when – I mean, how . . . well, you know. How's all that going to work?'

He threw back his head and laughed. 'That's what I love about you, Sloane. First things first.'

'I would like to know how I can help. There should be a lot to do.'

'I'm going to leave all that up to you, my sweet. I thought we'd have it in the suite with just a few close friends. Ask anyone you choose, of course. But I want this to be your happiest day and you can do anything you like. Flowers, food, music, decor, anything at all you want. I'll ask my old friend Judge Crawford to marry us. The rest is up to you. All you have to do is pick up the phone and call the catering manager. Rose has made arrangements with all the good stores – Saks, Bloomingdale's, Bergdorf's. You won't even need a charge account. Just have things messengered to the hotel. The stores know what to do. Spare no expense and surprise me when I get back.'

'Back? Back from where? Oh, Warner, you're not running off somewhere, are you?'

'I'm always running off, my love. Get used to it. This is a short trip, though, just to London. I'll be back in a week. That's why I set the wedding date for Saturday the ninth.'

March ninth! Sloane counted ahead. 'That's not even two weeks,' she said with some alarm.

'Right. Think you can handle it?'

She paused, but couldn't bear to disappoint him by admitting how frightened she was. 'Yeah. Do you think Ms Motherwell could help?'

'Sorry, love. She'll be travelling with me. Always does.'

Sloane took a deep breath and slowly exhaled. 'Okay.' She smiled weakly. 'I think I'll get through it.'

'Of course you will, my darling girl. You can do anything. Now, let's have a little lunch.' He raised his arm and nodded to the steward.

Sloane pretended to be studying the stewards as they flurried about setting up a table with crested linen and silver on which they served a cracked-crab salad in crystal bowls. The wine was changed to champagne.

Both stewards stood at atttention after the table was set. One of them asked Warner, 'Would you and Miss Taylor like to listen to some music while you dine, sir?'

Warner looked at Sloane for approval. She nodded, glad for the distraction. She wanted to think.

'The Mozart "French Horns" would be nice, thank you.' Warner smiled across at Sloane.

Almost instantly the compact disc in the communications console sent beautiful music swirling around them.

As ever, when she felt overwhelmed, Sloane told herself to just take things one at a time. Make lists. Don't panic. She felt as though the minute Warner had given her the ring she had stepped into a world where everything was free. She didn't have to think about the cost of anything. 'The stores know what to do' – she loved that. Only last month she had hung a coat she loved back on the rack after trying it on because she saw the price tag. Not to mention telling the deli man she would pay him tomorrow because the extra slice of Muenster on her sandwich cost more than she had with her. Perhaps Warner assumed too much. Maybe she wasn't up to all this, but it was terribly important that she not disappoint him. He thought she could do anything. Well, damn it, she would try.

She lifted her champagne flute to eye level. All this drinking before lunch was making her fuzzy-headed. 'When is the last time I told you I love you, Warner Bromley?'

His fork paused in midair. 'Let's see. I think about six this morning.' He beamed, remembering.

'You shouldn't have to wait that long,' she said, gesturing with her glass. 'To the man I love.'

Warner's glass met hers. 'And to the woman I adore.'

Warner's driver dropped him at the Carlyle and proceeded down to Warren Street with Sloane to collect her things.

As she pushed open the sheet-metal door to the loft, she could hear the phone ringing. She flung her bag and coat on the couch and dove for it.

'Hi!' she said excitedly, sure it was Alan wanting the very latest details.

'Hello, Sloane. This is your mother,' Noreen said crisply.

'Mom! Oh, my gosh,' Sloane said, breathless with exertion and surprise.

'I hope I didn't disturb you,' Noreen said formally. 'But you did leave word that I should call.'

'Yes . . . yes . . . I know I did, Mom . . . ah, how are you?'

'We're fine,' Noreen said, undoubtedly referring to Mark as well. 'And you?'

Damn! Sloane thought. *Why does she have to be like that? After everything that's happened. She doesn't have to keep up the offended-mother act. I'm the one who should be offended!* She was going to make this short and sweet and to hell with it! 'Mother, I'm getting married,' she said quickly.

The pause on the line was so extended she thought her mother might quietly have hung up. Then Noreen said,

192

'It's nice of you to let me know, Sloane. Would you like to share with me just who it is you're marrying?'

'A man named Warner Bromley, he's —'

'I know who Warner Bromley is, Sloane. I read the papers,' Noreen said sharply. 'Sloane, you're only eighteen years old! Warner Bromley is older than Mark!'

Sloane decided that no matter what, she wasn't going to let Noreen get under her skin. She was a big girl now and she could handle it. 'I'd like to have you here, Mother,' she said, ignoring Noreen's remarks. 'It's going to be at the Carlyle on the ninth.'

'The ninth of what?'

'The ninth of March.'

'O, my . . . we couldn't do that,' Noreen said as though Sloane had invited her to a backyard barbecue and not her only daughter's wedding. 'Mark's addressing the National Association of Film Distributors in Rio that weekend. We've had plans for weeks, everything is arranged. I don't see why you couldn't have told me sooner, Sloane.'

Sloane picked up a pencil and bit it so she wouldn't grind her teeth. 'He didn't ask me sooner, Mother,' she said.

'My, we're in a big hurry, aren't we?'

Sloane didn't want to talk about it anymore. She didn't want to explain Warner's lifestyle, she didn't want to be squeezed into making excuses or apologizing. She wanted to get off the phone so she could throw it through the window. 'Well, if your plans change, Mom, let me know. I'll be staying at the Carlyle.'

'Before the wedding? You're staying at the Carlyle?'

She could hear the grand-lady tone in Noreen's voice. 'Yes, Mother. I'm living there now in my own suite.'

'Just don't forget, Mary Sloane, you are all you have. Take care of yourself.'

'Good night, Mother. Thank you for calling back,' Sloane said. 'Say hello to Mark for me.'

Sloane put down the phone without waiting for Noreen's reply. She was grateful for the darkness in the street when she returned to Warner's car. It wouldn't help anything for his driver to see her crying.

9

No one would have understood Sloane's ambivalence.

After months of struggling against the cold indifference of New York, she had just spent two of the most incredible weeks of her life with a man who, to most of the world, was larger than life. That simple unposed newspaper photograph had led to a million-dollar contract, chauffeured limousines, private jet flights, and a proposal of marriage from a man who could fulfil her every fantasy.

Marrying Warner Bromley and all that implied would have answered the prayers of a million women. Yet, as she sat alone late on Monday afternoon in the flower-filled suite at the Carlyle, toying with the growing pile of expensive baubles he had presented her with, Sloane felt a dark uneasiness about her future.

How simple it was just to defer to Warner's judgment, his plans, his grand view of her career and their future life together. He clearly knew what he was doing and made decisions he felt were in her best interests, decisions that showed his love and concern for her. Why then did she feel left out, isolated in some undefinable way? She could not shake the feeling, when she was with him, that she became diminished, incapable of controlling things that directly affected her, whether it was as important as the direction her career should take or as simple as ordering from a restaurant menu. Several times Warner had actually told a waiter what she would be having for dinner. She always let it pass, but it still rankled when she thought about it.

She dropped the ruby-and-diamond bracelet she had been absentmindedly clasping and unclasping back into the velvet-lined box especially made for her new 'toys.' She shouldn't be such an ingrate, she admonished herself. She had everything anyone could possibly long for and here she was being picky and petulant like some spoiled brat.

Suddenly the air in the suite felt stuffy and overheated. She had to get out before the walls actually closed in on her. A walk. She would take a walk and clear her head.

She would walk the few blocks to Central Park. Walking down Madison Avenue at any time of day was a crowded chore. She needed elbow room and trees. It was lovely in the park in the late afternoon; with fewer people around, it always reminded her of a private estate.

She pulled on a lined raincoat against the winter chill in the air and tied a Hermès scarf over her head.

The park was as empty as the streets were full of rush-hour pedestrians. She picked up her pace and moved briskly along the winding walkway that ran along the rim of the Sheep Meadow. By the time she reached the pond at the edge of Central Park South, she was tired. She spotted an empty bench dappled with the rays of the setting sun and sat down, feeling both invigorated and contented.

Along the walkway on the other side of the pond she noticed a young man wearing a stylishly cut dark suit. He was strolling toward her. As he drew closer, she fleetingly remembered her promises to herself never to play the game again. As she locked eyes with the approaching stranger, the vows slipped away, dismissed, forgotten in the surge of lust that enveloped her. She had made those promises before her life had completely been subsumed by Warner and his world. Looking into this man's eyes, she felt the hunger for a moment of control. She craved just a taste of what it used to feel like to make her own decisions and act upon them.

She turned her body toward him and smiled. She could almost see his breath catch as he moved closer, unable to break eye contact. Now she knew she had him, as surely as if she were some regent summoning a subject to do her bidding.

'Darling! Over here!' she heard a voice calling from behind her. The expression on the man's face turned from growing expectancy to deflated disappointment.

Sloane looked over her shoulder to see a young woman in a raincoat not unlike her own, moving briskly toward them from the direction of a stand of trees. Within seconds she had slipped her arm through his. They turned and walked back toward Central Park South. As they moved away, he turned and looked back at her as though apologizing.

She felt her lips tightening into a hard, thin line. 'Damn,' she whispered to herself as she pushed up off the bench and headed in the direction of the zoo. All her good feelings had vanished.

Feeling thwarted and helpless once again, she pounded her heels into the hard pavement, cursing silently to herself. When she reached the zoo, she cursed again. It was closed. She should have remembered. The zoo was closed for renovations. The entrance was blocked by sawhorses. Rubble and construction equipment lay stacked haphazardly about.

From the other side of the blocked entrance she saw a group of Hispanic workmen shambling toward her. The grime of a day's work stained their clothes. She stood and watched them chatting among themselves in Spanish. One spotted her in the fading light and called out, '*Señorita bonita!*' and another shouted something that seemed to offend one of the others.

'Hey, man, chill out,' he said, using his cap to slap the arm of the man who must have said something dirty.

Sloane ignored them. As she turned to go, she heard the offended worker telling the dirty-mouthed one he should apologize. The suggestion was greeted with catcalls and laughter.

Suddenly, the man was by her side, holding his cap in both hands. 'Excuse me, miss,' he said. 'Don't mind those jerks. They don't know a lady when they see one.'

Touched, Sloane turned to look at him. He was in his early twenties. He had wonderful straight teeth and lovely blue-black eyes and hair. There was a boyishness about the way he looked at her. She looked deeply into his eyes. In what was left of the sunlight she saw something behind the sweetness of his expression. Had it been there all along? Or had it developed when he looked at her?

'You really shouldn't be in the park this late,' he said, still holding her gaze.

'Thank you.' She smiled. 'It's quite all right. I was just leaving.'

'Let me walk you out. You never know who's hanging around looking for trouble.'

Sloane smiled. She knew he wasn't referring to her, but he could have been. From the way he was looking at her she knew she had him hooked.

She began walking up the path leading toward Fifth Avenue. He followed a few paces behind. At the end of the path, instead of turning right toward the entrance of the park, she quickly turned left and walked up a slight incline toward a grove of trees. When she reached the secluded clearing between the trees, she turned and leaned against a large oak. Her coat was open, her posture sending out a clear invitation. He hesitated for an instant, as though he couldn't believe his incredible good luck. Sloane reached toward him, palms up, in a gesture of eager submission, and he was in her arms, kissing her neck, his pelvis pressing against hers.

This was what she had been looking for. As he reached

under her coat and pulled her closer, she knew she would never have admitted it to herself when she went for a 'head-clearing walk.' As his impatient hands ran down her body, his breath coming in rapid, panting gasps of desire, she imagined what an addict must feel when a deadly drug courses through the bloodstream. This was her drug. These moments of utter freedom, locked in the erotic embrace of a man who demanded nothing more of her than that she let him fill her with his passion. The thrill of the chase, the ease of the conquest, was a fire racing through her and restored her sense of power and control over her own existence.

He slowly unbuttoned her blouse and eased her bra up to expose her breasts to the cool night air. He kissed each one hungrily then, his tongue tracing a wet line down her body. Lowering himself to his knees, he pulled down her panties and gently separated her thighs.

Sloane threw her head back in ecstasy as he buried his head between her legs, his tongue working its magic.

As he brought her to near frenzy, she lowered her head and opened her eyes. Had she heard something? A branch breaking? Someone coming? It was just a small click, but it snapped her out of her transport.

She stared out through the foliage, squinting into the blue-purple twilight. There, standing only a few yards away, half-concealed by low branches, was a woman and a camera with a long, almost obscene, barrel-shaped lens against her eye.

Sloane froze. Her rising passion was instantly replaced by terror. She had been seen. Someone had photographed her acting out her secret. Roughly, she pushed her oblivious lover's head away and pulled down her skirt.

As she ran, she could hear herself screaming silently. Her chest ached and perspiration began to soak through her blouse. She couldn't look back. She didn't care what he might have thought. What if she looked back and saw the woman still taking pictures? *You thought you could get away with it, didn't you?* the sane Sloane screamed somewhere in the back of her mind. *You deserve this. You're sick! You're going to lose everything now.*

By the time she reached Fifth Avenue and darted into the street there were tears streaming down her face. *Please,* she pleaded to any force that would listen, *please, please don't let me get caught. I won't do it again. I promise. Never again. It feels so wonderful when it's happening, but I'm so tired of being afraid and ashamed.*

By the time she reached the Carlyle she was soaked through despite the cool air. Her clothes were mussed and she knew her hair and makeup were a mess.

'Good evening, Miss Taylor,' the doorman said, smiling, and touching the brim of his cap.

'Yes . . . yes, it is,' she blurted out. 'Thank you for asking.'

A tiny cloud of confusion passed across his wide Irish face.

'Sorry,' she said, moving past him. 'I'm in such a rush.'

'Yes, of course, miss,' he said.

What could he think of her, looking the way she did, babbling incoherently? What if he mentioned something about her state to Warner?

Now there was one more possible witness to her shame.

Layla noticed Warner's Bermuda tan the minute he entered the restaurant at the Carlyle. Thanks to Rose Motherwell's report that morning, she knew he had gone to Bermuda and taken Sloane Taylor with him.

Waiting for him, she had sipped her drink and stared at the juge jardiniere of country flowers on the table in the middle of the elegant room. Inside each blossom she pictured the face of Sloane Taylor as she mentally ripped the head of each flower. She had imagined a tiny scream of pain as she slaughtered first a wild rose, then an anemone.

Rose Motherwell's report on the trip to Bermuda had been less than satisfying. She had been stuck away at the Hamilton Inn with perky little Brian and could tell her nothing of what had gone on at the house. 'Damn it all to hell,' she cursed under her breath, snapping a swizzle stick in half as Warner approached the table.

His progress was slowed by the people at other tables greeting him, jumping to their feet to shake his hand. She was used to Warner's celebrity, to the constant public interruptions wherever he went. What she wasn't used to was so direct a threat as Sloane Taylor. Her jealousy was only magnified by her feelings of total impotence. If Warner was falling in love with the girl, what could she do to stop it? There had to be something. If Sloane had been a contemporary, she could sic one of her bulldog reporters on her. Everyone had something they wanted to hide, but the girl was too damn young to even have a past! There had to be a way. If only she could think straight. It was as though all her normal self-preservation responses had suddenly come unplugged.

She hoped the two 'greenies' she had gulped before leaving the office wouldn't make her overreact to whatever Warner was going to tell her about his weekend. She had to be calm.

Not wanting to spoil their meal, she deliberately waited until dessert was served to bring up the subject. 'Do anything interesting over the weekend, darling?' she finally asked.

'As a matter of fact, I did.'

'How *was* Sloane Taylor?' she said, taking a deep drag on one of her last cigarettes.

'I'm going to marry her, Layla.'

Layla froze. She felt a chill run down her arms and then extend to numb her entire body. Her last bite of lemon soufflé caught like a rock in the centre of her throat. She knew she looked obviously shocked and surprised, something she hadn't allowed to happen for decades.

201

'When?' she asked, trying without success to control the trembling in her voice.

'Soon,' he said quietly. 'First she has to get that press conference out of the way. Then I have to make a short run back to London and wind up the Pacific Oil merger. So we're planning the wedding for the ninth of next month. I thought we'd have the ceremony here in the suite.'

Layla sat speechless. By now they were the only customers left. Even the waiters had all left for the night. Marco, the bored captain, stood lonely sentinel at the back of the room, where he was working on the reservations list for the following day.

Composing herself as best she could, Layla cleared her throat and said, 'I can't believe we sat here all evening before you sprung this on me.' She probed for another cigarette. There were none. She crumpled the empty pack and held it in the fist of her left hand.

'I dreaded telling you, Layla,' he said softly. 'But I wanted you to know before the publicity broke. We're announcing on Wednesday to take advantage of the publicity before Sloane's press conference.'

Layla stared straight ahead, squeezing the crunched cigarette pack until he reached over, put his hand over hers, and removed it.

When she started to weep, he handed her his silk handkerchief. 'Why?' she whispered. 'Why her? Why now? What can being married possibly do to improve your life?'

Warner turned toward her. 'Why do you ask things that you know will hurt, darling?'

'Because I have to hear you say it.'

'All right. I love her. I'm going to marry her because I want her and that's the only way I can have her.'

'Don't tell me she's playing that game! The oldest one in the book. And you fell for it!'

'Don't be naive, Layla. I had to beg her to marry me.

What I meant was, I have to marry her to keep her in my life.'

'She does that much for you?'

'Amazingly, yes. All the clichés in the book are true. She makes me feel good. She's shown me that there is no joy in having what I have if there's no one to share it with.'

'Did it ever occur to you that you could share it with me?'

'Layla, you and I are special. My marrying won't change that. We're a part of each other's history. If we were meant to marry, we would have done it years ago. This is something new and I want it.'

'You are breaking my heart, Warner.' Her fury was mounting. She took hold of his face with one hand, digging her long nails into his cheeks. 'Does she give good head? Huh? You always liked that. Remember those rides in your limousine? Remember that night in Rome when you found out I ran off to Amalfi with that boy? Remember what we did for two days when you found me? Do you remember!'

'Layla, don't.' He jerked his head free of her grip.

'Does she squeeze her legs together real tight just before you come? You always like that.'

'Layla!' He spoke so loudly that the captain looked up from his work. 'Cheque, Marco, please,' he called.

'You go, Warner,' she said, not moving. 'I'm staying.'

'You can't stay here, Layla, they're going to close.'

She turned to him, her eyes black and mean. 'I'll do whatever I fucking well please. I always have and I always will.' She raised her hand and waved. The captain, who was in the aisle, was struggling into his coat. 'Bring the cheque for Mr Bromley and I want a bottle of Veuve Clicquot, please!' she commanded. 'One glass. And find someone in the kitchen who can go out and get me a pack of Marlboros.'

When a completely confused captain reached the side

of the table with the cheque, she pulled a ten-dollar bill from her bag and handed it to him.

'But Madame . . .' he protested.

'Right away, please!'

'I'm not staying, Layla. I have a conference call coming in from New Delhi. You're upset. Come up to the suite and we'll have a nightcap,' he pleaded, pulling himself up from the banquette.

'I don't want to talk to you anymore, Warner. I want to get drunk. It's nice here, or at least it was. It will get nice again after you leave.'

The captain stood in the aisle in front of the table looking from Warner to Layla and back, waiting to see who would prevail.

Layla didn't move. Finally Warner shrugged and turned to go. He backhanded a hundred-dollar bill into Marco's hand. 'Thank you for everything, as usual, Marco,' he said. 'Get Ms Bronz anything she wants and put it on my bill. Put your overtime on there as well.'

A harried busboy slid a saucer onto the table containing a pack of Benson and Hedges but no change. It was the wrong brand, but she paid no attention. She ripped open the pack and yanked out a cigarette.

She sat silently smoking, drinking her champagne. Everything she had was due to Warner. She wondered how in the world she was going to go on without him. Or even if she wanted to.

Layla had worked her way through the magazine world starting right out of high school as a lowly typist at *Vogue*, teaching herself how to write by reading. She sold her first magazine piece to the long-defunct *Coronet* by wangling an interview with Fabian, telling his press agent that she already had an assignment. She moved on to editorial jobs at *Glamour*, *Cosmopolitan*, and *Harper's Bazaar*, free-lancing in her spare time. All the way she hungered for more control, the ability to shape her own individual product. But in the closed, clannish world of magazine women, she was considered, though brilliant, abrasive and autocratic. She knew she would be satisfied only when she had her own magazine. It was just a matter of time.

It had been her father who had convinced her the world would someday be hers – even though he wouldn't be the one to give it to her. It was all he could do to raise a motherless daughter and put food on the kitchen table of their tiny aluminium-sided house in Floral Park.

Zack Bronz was a slick and fascinating man who spent most of his time at the racetrack. He filled his innately intelligent little girl's head full of the possibilities 'out there' for someone with brains and guts – only he said 'balls' and winked.

Zack was one day rich and the next day poor, and though he adored his headstrong daughter he loved the thrill of chance more. She learned early that while she could count on him for moral support, financially she was on her own.

When he was broke, he would take a job as a security guard. It was low-impact work that permitted him time to read his beloved gambling books in his endless efforts to beat the system.

Her father firmly believed that the appearance of money was almost as good as having it. 'You can always borrow money if people think you have it,' he would tell her, picking an imaginary piece of lint from one of the dapper suits he wore to the track.

With that in mind, upon Layla's reaching adulthood, father and daughter conspired to give her the appearance of being rich. It was a plan that got her hired at *Vogue*, where her competition was all trust-fund Muffys and Binkys in pastel sweater sets and Mummy's pearls. Layla competed with voluminous black cashmere, stacks of silver bracelets from thrift shops, and dramatic makeup. Her signature became attention-getting hats when no one was wearing them. She wore giant disks double the size of a 33⅓ record, fake-fur cones to rival a palace guard's, pillboxes dripping with silk fruit, and floppy fake-pony-skin tams topped with plaid pom-poms. Her favorite was a crimson gaucho hat that tied under the chin.

She made veiled allusions to an upbringing 'on the Continent' and had a Village artist paint her portrait sitting sidesaddle on a rearing horse. In return she sorted out his tangled income taxes, found him a gallery to show his work, and an agent/manager to sell it.

By the early seventies, she felt she knew the magazine business backward and forward. Now all she had to do was find the someone who owned a magazine and would let her run it.

Opportunity presented itself when she was assigned by a news syndicate to interview the young communications tycoon Warner Bromley. Bromley had just purchased the failing old literary publication *Realto* and announced he would turn it into the must-read publication of the decade. His plans called for an all-new format with a heavy concentration on those who set trends in the news. Ironically, his meeting with Layla would be the only interview he granted in his career. Many had tried since, most recently that craven Melon Tuft.

The interview lasted well past the appointed hour, and charmed by the aggressive and savvy reporter, Bromley invited her to drinks.

During the days and nights of seeing him that followed, she never mentioned her desire to run a magazine and was infuriatingly secretive about her background. Warner was intrigued. By the time their relationship had become sexual, she made her move. She arranged for them to dine at an out-of-the-way restaurant in the Village. She told him she wanted to tell him something important, something she could only tell him in a restaurant where the tables were far apart and they couldn't be overheard.

What she shared with him over the calamari and

Chianti was an enormously successful lie. She told him that she was the illegitimate child of the then-governor Nelson Rockefeller. It was a perfect ploy. There was absolutely no way he could check the story out. To prove her claim once and for all she told him she had to drop by the Rockefeller town house on West Fifty-fourth Street to pick up some papers having to do with her trust fund.

'Wouldn't it just knock the staff's eyes out if I arrived in your big car,' she said, rubbing the inside of his thigh under the tablecloth. 'They're sure to tell my father. He'll see the company I keep and that I can be trusted with an increase in my allowance.'

Warner bit. Impressed but sceptical, he agreed to drive her there in his limousine and wait in the car. He told himself if she actually gained entrance to the Rockefeller private residence, her story had to be true.

An hour later the big company-owned limousine pulled to the curb in front of the town house on West Fifty-fourth Street. Layla skipped up the steps, rang the bell, and was admitted instantly by the security guard. Once inside, she and her father took their time chatting about the events of the day. A half-hour later he handed her a manila envelope stuffed with nothing more negotiable than the morning's edition of the *Times*.

She climbed back into the car and was greeted by a completely overwhelmed Warner. She apologized for taking so long, complained of having to triple-sign several documents, then reached for the zipper of his trousers.

That night in front of the fire in her apartment on Morton Street, he asked how she would like to take over as editor-in-chief of his new acquisition, *Realto* magazine.

She rolled over on the lumpy pull-out couch and buried her face into the pillow to hide her reaction. This was what she wanted more than life's breath. She was afraid he could hear her heart pound as she said, 'Well . . . maybe. With certain conditions.'

It took most of the night and two more bottles of red wine to drive her bargain home. As dawn streaked the sky, she had his promise of a contract that would virtually give her a job for life. She would be, for all intents and purposes, 'fire-proof.' At the time it seemed better than any marriage license.

Her first few months on the job were a bloodbath of firings as she and Warner revamped the entire publication. They raided other magazines for fresh people and signed big-name writers as contributors. To launch the first issue under their stewardship, Layla produced an interview with a former mistress of the Shah of Iran. It was a feat that earned her a signed photograph of the Shah and his family sent by a noncomprehending Farsi-speaking press agent.

The communications industry quickly realized they had a sparkling new team to watch. Layla Bronz and Warner Bromley had formed an alliance that was to become one of the most successful in the business.

Eventully, she told Warner who she really was. His response was to laugh until tears ran down his cheeks. The following week she moved into the apartment at the top of the *Realto* town house. Waiting for her was an enormous vase of lavender roses. Into the leaves of one was tucked a huge amethyst ring surrounded by diamonds.

She mistakenly took the gift to mean a proposal of marriage was in the near future. It never came. The subject of marriage was never discussed. For years Layla had gone about her hectic life – and waited – loving him beyond definition. When the waiting turned her love into obsession, she made a private arrangement with Rose Motherwell to spy.

She needed to know where he was, what he was doing, whom he was with. In case, just in case there was a threat to what they had, no matter how small, she wanted to be able to head it off. She had been successful. She always had advance warning when someone was getting too close.

Until now. Until this beautiful girl out of nowhere slithered up on the love of her life and was about to carry him away. The thought of losing him filled her with despair. She felt that without him her life had no meaning. Something would have to be done.

By two o'clock in the morning she was very, very drunk.

Marco was asleep in his chair, still wearing his coat.

'Marco!' she called.

The weary captain bolted awake at the sound of her voice. 'Would you call my driver, Marco?' she slurred.

'He's right outside, Madame. He's been here for some time. I heard Mr Bromley phone to have him bring your car when he left.'

Marco reached to help but she pushed him away. He managed to get her sable coat over her shoulders and followed her out the Madison Avenue entrance of the hotel. Her imposing Rolls sat at the curb. Yitzak was asleep behind the wheel. Marco eased Layla into the backseat and quietly closed the door.

She threw her head back as if to clear it and opened the glass between the seats. 'Yitzak. You drove that girl home a couple of weeks ago, right?'

'Which girl, ma'am?'

'The tall, dark one. The model. She was at the house with Mr Latimer.'

'Oh, that one. Yeah, I remember.'

'Where does she live?'

'Down on Warren Street, ma'am. It's like an old factory building. I don't know the number but it's right off the corner.'

'Take me there,' she commanded.

Yitzak turned around to look at her full face. 'Down there? It's after two.'

'Do it, Yitzak,' she growled.

209

He shook his head and started the engine. 'What do you want to go all the way down there for, ma'am? It's not such a nice part of town.'

'Well, I have not such a nice bit of business to transact and this is as good a time as any.'

As Yitzak pulled up Madison and circled around to head downtown on Fifth, Layla pulled the half a pack of cigarettes she had left out of her bag. 'Benson and Hedges,' she snorted. 'What kind of a candy-ass cigarette is that?'

'Pardon, ma'am?'

'Nothing, Yitzak,' she sighed, staring out the window at the empty streets.

'Are you all right?'

'No, I'm not all right. My fucking life just exploded in there.'

'Ma'am?'

'Mr Bromley is getting married.'

There was a long silence. Yitzak had been with Layla for over a decade and was not unaware of the importance of what he was hearing. 'That's a surprise. You think he'll really do it?'

'Oh, he'll do it. The trick is, will she do it after I get through with her.'

Yitzak looked at Layla in the rearview mirror. 'Ms Bronz, can I say something?'

'Of course, Yitzak.'

'You're in no shape to go down there. She's gonna tell Mr Bromley you made a fuss. It won't stop him from marrying her,' he said gently. 'If I may say so, ma'am, it's not gonna make you look good.'

'I don't care, Yitzak,' she said. 'You know what Warner means to me.'

'I do, ma'am. But there's a part of a man's anatomy that's got no conscience.'

'Do you think that's what it is, Yitzak? Sex? Is that why he's doing this?'

210

'That . . . and fear. This girl helps him not to be afraid.'

'Afraid?' she snapped. 'Warner's never been afraid of anything.'

'Beg to differ, ma'am.'

'All right, what's he afraid of?'

'Dying. Man like that, all that money. He has everything except a beautiful young wife. Guess he figures he oughta have that too before he goes. Some men think youth is transmissible, like some kinda disease.'

Maybe that's what it was. Maybe Warner just had some kind of a disease and would get over it, Layla thought. She peered out into the dark street. 'Where are we, Yitzak?'

'Twenty third Street, ma'am.'

Suddenly she felt bone tired. 'Take me home, Yitzak. You're right. This was a bad idea.'

Yitzak nodded and swung a left turn in the next light. As they headed uptown on Park, Layla told herself there was a better way to handle this situation. She had caught him with stealth, she had kept him with cunning. That had to be the way to get him back.

10

Melon gave up staking out the Carlyle on Saturday, when she saw Bromley and his bodyguards leaving with luggage and the beautiful girl who had first come to the hotel with Cole. She had seen the model several times since, and she completely ignored Melon's attempts to talk to her. The no-necks accompanying her would wave Melon away every time she approached, notebook in hand. She made a mental note to call Randy and get a line on the girl. If she couldn't get to Bromley himself, perhaps she could track down the girl on neutral turf and get through to Bromley that way.

On Monday she arrived at the sex-phone office late as usual. She liked the morning shift. Guys didn't seem to have the hornies much after nine o'clock. Then she started to get the shut-ins, gimps, and hospital patients who weren't easily satisfied and hung on the phone for up to an hour with the meter running clickety-click all the while.

She was leaning back in the swivel chair in her cubicle pleading into the ear of a regular who liked to talk about tying her up with her pantie hose. Her job was to beg him to untie her. She had just gotten to the part where he says she has been a 'bad, bad doggie' when she became aware of a pair of grey flannel legs standing just in back of her right shoulder. Her feet crashed to the floor. She swivelled around to see a man, medium height with dark, slicked-back hair, wearing a too-sharp suit with a vest. The split-second thought that streaked through her mind was that one of her clients had decided to come down and see what she looked like. Any outside communication was strictly forbidden and dangerous. Without another word she slammed down the phone.

'Get the fuck out of here, mister!' she said in her toughest, most-menacing voice. 'Now, or I'll push this button.' She gestured to the space under the desk where there was no button. 'The cops will swarm this place before you can even get your pecker out.'

The man stared at her for a moment and then threw back his head and laughed.

Shit! she thought. A sicko for sure. She thought of the long, steel letter opener in the top drawer. It would take only a second to retrieve it. She wouldn't hesitate to stab this turkey if he moved an inch closer.

Pulling himself together, the man said, 'What button? I didn't know we installed buttons in here.'

'Trust me,' she said evenly.

'What's your name?' he asked.

'Not your business, mister. I said go.'

'I'll go when I finish checking the payroll books,' he said. 'Then how about you and me having some lunch? You're some hot ticket.' His black eyes moved up and down her body, taking in her baby-chicken-yellow sweater and black leather miniskirt. Her high-heeled black pumps and black mesh stockings emphasized her well-rounded legs.

'Payroll?' she said. So that was it. This jerk was going to rob the place. 'There's no payroll here.'

'Sure there is, back in my office. I'm Matty Chiga. I own this dump.'

Melon dropped her head into her hands. 'Shit. I'm sorry, Mr Chiga. I didn't know.'

'Perfectly understandable. You were great! I like knowing I've got an employee that treats a stranger like that, Miss . . .'

'Tuft. Melon Tuft. How do you do.'

'I do great but let me ask you something. What would you have done if I'd put some heavy moves on you?'

'Stabbed you,' she said pleasantly, fluffing her hair with both hands. She watched his eyes drop to her breasts as expected.

'You're kidding? With what?' he said, laughing again.

'Foot-long letter opener in the desk here.'

'Damn. You *are* a pistol.' He smiled. 'Wouldn't have worked on me, though.' He tapped his chest with his forefinger. It made a thumping sound.

'What is that? A bulletproof vest?'

'Yup.'

'Then I would have stabbed you in the crotch.'

'That does it,' he said with a chuckle in his throat. 'I order you to have lunch with me. Anyplace you wanna go. You name it. The ritzier the better.'

'Le Cirque,' she said without a moment's hesitation.

'You got it.' He formed his hand into a gun and aimed it at her. 'Pick you up at twelve-thirty.'

She watched as he lumbered down the hall toward the closed doors at the back of the suite. Matty Chiga, she thought. Wow. The other girls had told her he owned the place, but she didn't believe it at first. Matty Chiga, the tabloids' favorite gangster, wouldn't deal in such small potatoes as a sex-phone shop. Then she read that he had a corner on every sex-phone operation on the East Coast. Matty Chiga was a busy man who had never done a day in jail. He was involved in your basic loan-sharking, extortion, numbers, and funeral parlors with the duplex coffins so they could secretly bury a fresh hit under your dead aunt Rose. The media liked him. He was polite in a blunt sort of way and was always good for a colorful quote. Not yet forty, he was one of the most powerful mob bosses in town. And she almost stabbed the guy. Whew! Wouldn't that make a headline or two. She would have liked that. But even better would be if he let her interview him.

Now she wished she hadn't been such a smart-ass and asked to go to Le Cirque. They would never get in there. It was practically a closed club. Ordinary people got in if they reserved for the following year. Never notorious gangsters. She kind of liked him and now she would have to see him embarrassed.

She need not have been concerned. Sirio, who guarded the gates of the chic restaurant as if it were the jewellery vault at Chase Manhattan, was standing at the curb to help them out of the cab. They were escorted directly to a premier table with much smarmy small talk about hopes and wishes for his health, inquiries into the fun he might have had on his last vacation, and grovelling requests that he ask anyone in the restaurant's employ for anything his heart desired. The pleasure to wait and serve and run and jump and kiss butt that the great Mr Chiga could provide seemed boundless. And what in all the world of difficult service could they provide Mr Chiga and 'the beautiful lady' to start their lunch?

'Martinis. Doubles. Vodka. Up. Dry. Twist,' Chiga ordered without consulting her. 'Later we'll have the duck, real crispy, and I want some of those little red potatoes. You know, where they peel 'em just around the middle. Tell 'em to make 'em nice and brown. You can forget the baby vegetables and crap and bring us a Caesar salad, heavy on the anchovies.' He paused while the captain, standing on tiptoe in back of Sirio and craning his neck to hear, scribbled madly on a pad.

'You got any of those little cheese thingamajigs?' Matty asked.

'You mean our Brie twists, Mr Chiga?' Sirio fawned.

'Yeah, yeah, whatever. Make sure they're hot.'

'Always, Mr Chiga.' Sirio bowed. 'Will that be all for now, sir?'

'Yeah. No, some wine.' He looked across at Melon. 'What kinda wine you like, babe?'

215

'Actually,' she said, rubbing her chin, 'I'd really like a beer.'

'Two beers, Sirio.'

Melon noticed an almost imperceptible twitch around Sirio's nostrils. 'Right, Mr Chiga. Will Heineken be all right?'

'Okay by you, kid?' Matty asked Melon.

She nodded at Sirio as he backed away from the table with the unneeded menus, lowering his eyes in deep respect.

Melon scanned the room. There was a recognizable celebrity at nearly every table.

She loved it all. Just being here was exciting, but being here with a man like Chiga was something else. She liked his total take-charge attitude. She liked a man who ate real food while others picked at dry, unsauced fish and spidery greens. She liked a man who drank double martinis at noon in a world of wimps sipping Perrier and white wine.

As their drinks arrived, two elegantly dressed men stopped at the table to talk to Chiga. He seemed anxious to get rid of them and didn't introduce her. She studied his face as he listened to the two men pitching something about real estate she didn't understand. He wasn't half bad looking. Overbarbered, perhaps, but she liked the look. He had a slightly moon-shaped face and his skin had the poreless, creamy look heavily bearded men achieve by daily hot-towel soaks and professional shaving. His eyebrows and hair were thick and black, and his fingernails were buffed, not polished. His moves were quick and definite. When he reached for a cigar, there was no patting and digging around in pockets. Just one swift move produced what he was looking for. His shoulders and chest were so broad it made his arms look too short, and when he walked, head high, he had a rolling gait peculiar to heavy men. To Melon, that walk was a sure tip-off that a man was a terrific dancer.

He dismissed the two men with a flick of his hand and turned to her. 'You're a foxy-looking broad, you know that?' He grinned, pulling on his cigar as the drinks arrived. No one around them was smoking, and yet not a soul approached to tell him to put it out.

'Why, thank you, Mr Chiga,' she preened.

'Matty, please. The only people who call me Mr Chiga are guys from the D.A.'s office.'

'You have a lot of dealings with them, do you?' she asked, batting her eyes over her martini glass.

'Not if I can help it,' he said.

'You ever kill anybody?' she asked, snapping off a piece of Brie twist.

'Hey!' He laughed. 'You don't mess around, do ya?'

'Well . . . have you?'

'Naaa, not personally.'

'You mean your, ah . . . men do it.'

'Look, my men get hit, too. I've lost a runner, three bookmakers, two drivers, and a chef. Damn fine chef, too. I miss him. Made the best *bresaola della Valtellina* I ever put in my mouth,' he said, kissing his fingertips.

'Why would someone kill a chef? That's so mean.'

'He heard something he shouldn'ta heard. What can I tell you? Ain't these cheese things great?'

'Umm. Exquisite,' she said between bites.

'So,' he began, tucking his napkin between the second and third button of his shirt, just above the line of his undershirt. 'What else do you do? A bright dame like you. Talkin' dirty on the phone ain't a career.'

'I'm a journalist.'

'Whoa!' he said. 'You aren't gonna write down anything I say, are you?'

'Of course not,' she said, trying to look hurt. 'This is social. I wouldn't ever do that.'

'So, who do you write for?'

'Anyplace that will buy my stuff. I do mostly profiles and interviews. Right now I'm trying to interview

217

Warner Bromley, but I'd really like to do an interview with you.'

He held up both hands, palms out, his cigar clenched between his teeth. 'No way. I don't talk to the press. They're leeches and liars. They suck up to you and then take what you say and turn it all around.'

'Not all of us,' she protested. 'For instance, if I was ever going to interview you, I would tell you first so you would only say the things you wanted me to hear. Some of us have ethics.'

'Ha!' he barked. 'How far would you go to interview Warner Bromley?'

'Lie, cheat, and steal.'

'You make my point,' he said with a cool smile as he smoothed his napkin. 'I tell you what, pretty lady. I won't let you interview me, but I can put you in touch with Warner Bromley.'

'You're kidding!' she said, leaning forward and resting her breasts on the edge of the table. 'Is he a friend of yours?'

Matty Chiga smiled a slow, sly smile. 'Let's put it this way. Bromley owns companies that use trucks, right? Think about it.' He shifted his weight and tugged at his alligator belt. 'When I ask Bromley to do something, he likes to be of help.'

'I think I'm going to faint.'

'Don't do that, doll. I've got the rest of the day planned out. First, we're going to the Bronx to look over a plant I have up there. Then we're going out to the airport and chopper down to A.C. for the dinner show.'

'Atlantic City?'

'Yeah. There's an act I gotta catch. Tonight Sinatra and Sammy Davis are coming in special. You'll enjoy them. You game?' He finished the martini and signalled the waiter for their beers.

What she said was, 'Well, ah, sure. That would be interesting.' What she was thinking was, *Oh, boy-*

218

howdy, am I game! Game for whatever this guy has in mind.

Melon was naked. She sat astride her exhausted employer, her arms out straight against his chest for support. Her hair tumbled over her face as she tried to wind down. Guys always loved her to get on top, but now Matty was protesting.

'You gotta get off, babe,' he mumbled into a pile of the king-sized pillows provided by the Carousel Casino and Yacht Club in Atlantic City. 'You're gonna kill me, you sexy broad.'

She threw her head back and bit her lip. 'Bet I can get you going again,' she teased, and wiggled her hips.

'No. I mean it,' he moaned. 'I'm pooped.' He reached up, took hold of her shoulders, and eased her to the mattress. Their bodies made a sweaty, sucking sound as they separated. He rolled over and pulled a pillow over his head. 'Gotta take a nap, babe. You wear me out.'

Melon lay propped up on several pillows smoking and looking around the most outrageous room she had ever been in. The decor of the duplex suit was Tel Aviv Aztec High Roller, all Mediterranean blue and Day-Glo orange with arches and brocades and ball fringe everywhere. There wasn't a fibre found in nature in the entire suite. There was a full-sized pool in the middle of the living room and a white baby grand piano beside the fountain in the foyer and smoked glass by the yard. Even for a girl raised in cheap motels and a tumbledown shack in Tujunga, this was beyond vulgar.

The evening had started with a heart-stopping helicopter ride that was straight out of a mobster movie. Then there were the ringside seats where Matty held court, an introduction to Sinatra and Sammy Davis, and so many men wearing tuxes and star sapphires on their pinky fingers she lost count.

219

On the way into the lounge Matty spotted a dress in a garish boutique in the lobby and insisted on buying it for Melon to wear on the spot. The dress was short and strapless and bottle green with a marabou cuff at the bust and hem. The stiletto pumps she had been wearing all day and the dark hose worked with the outfit. The lady who ran the shop promised to send her other clothes to their suite.

Dinner was an even more frantic re-creation of their lunch. She was introduced to everyone as 'My friend Melon Tuft, the writer.' The act he had flown in to see was an aging singer Melon thought was dead. She still had a good set of pipes and delivered one ballad directly to Matty at ringside.

Between the noise, the fawning, and what seemed like several gallons of good champagne, they had stumbled to this suit in a stupor.

Amazingly, she was the one to make the first move. Matty Chiga might be a mobster and a criminal, but he was also a gentleman. Melon was sure that if she hadn't lurched toward him and started unbuttoning his shirt, he wouldn't have touched her. There were several other bedrooms in the duplex. She could have slept anywhere but she found herself really wanting to sleep with him.

She had to admit, as she blew a long stream of smoke toward the triple-tiered chandelier over the bed, she was good. Damn good. The best he'd had in a long time, she hoped. She wondered if he was married. It wasn't the kind of question one asked a man like Matty.

She had showered and dressed in yesterday's clothes and was exploring the obscene suite when she heard him calling. She trotted back into the bedroom and sat on the side of the bed.

Matty ran his hand up her thigh. 'You got dressed,' he said, sounding disappointed. The thick black hair on his chest looked like a fur T-shirt.

'You said you were through.'

'Not through, just resting,' he said, rubbing her arm. 'You are some piece of work, lady.'

'Well,' she said sweetly, 'you turn me on.'

'I do? So, take those clothes off.'

She pulled away. 'No, Matty. I really have to get back. I have to work and tonight I have to go stake out the Carlyle. Warner Bromley got back from his trip today according to a very well-greased bellboy, and I gotta be there.'

Matty propped himself up on his elbows. 'Are you nuts? You can't go back to that crummy job. How much were you making on those phones?'

'The most I ever took home was two hundred a week.'

'I'm going to pay you five hundred a week not to do it. I'll put it right in your bank every Friday.'

'I can't do that.'

'Whatdaya mean, you can't do that? Nobody turns down money. I'll make it a thousand. You should be writing.'

'Matty, we just met,' she protested. 'Why would you want to do that for me?'

' 'Cause you're a stand-up broad. I like you. You've got smarts and ambitions and you're legit. I don't know any women who are legit. I know hookers and showgirls and ball-busters.'

'Come on, Matty, I'm just a one-night flip.'

He pulled himself up and brushed her cheek with his fist. 'Don't say that. You got brains. I can talk to you. Guy like me can always get pussy. That's coin in my world. Besides, I like your style. You don't take any bullshit.'

'And I don't take money from men. I want to earn it doing what I want to do.'

He sat up and swung his legs over the side of the bed. He sat with his back to her. 'Well, goddamn,' he said, shaking his head.

'Sorry, Matty. I don't want to hurt your feelings, but I've been on my own since I was a kid. I like it that way.'

221

She slid her arm around his ample waist. 'Doesn't mean I don't want to bounce you around as often as I can, though guy.' She planted several tiny kisses on his hairy back. 'You make me feel reeeeeal good.'

Matty sat for a long time, his elbows on his knees. 'All right. I'll make a deal with you. I'll get you to Warner Bromley so you can write your article. In the meantime I'll make you a loan against your fee. You can pay me back. But you gotta promise me you'll quit with the phones. I hate to think of you talking like that with those creeps. It ain't dignified.'

'That's all well and good,' she said. 'But what happens after I write the Bromley story? That money won't last forever. I'll still have to keep doing interviews.'

Matty stood up and pulled on his silk shorts. He took a fresh cigar from the night table and lit it with his fat gold lighter. 'Okay. Okay,' he said through a stream of smoke. 'I know when I'm whipped. I'll make you a promise.'

'What?' she said, rolling over on her stomach and staring up at him.

'If you're not famous enough and loaded with assignments from your Bromley piece, you can interview me.'

'Matty!' she squealed, pulling herself across the bed until her head was even with his knees. 'You would do that for me!'

'Yeah, yeah, yeah. You at least I trust.'

'Come here,' she said reaching for his fly.

Instinctively he crossed both hands over his crotch.

'I mean it, come here!' She pushed his hands away, being careful to avoid the burning cigar. She shoved her hand into the opening in his shorts.

'Baby, I can't. You wore me out.'

Melon worked away for a moment. 'Liar. Look what I have here. Alive and well and ready to go.'

11

On Wednesday morning, Kayzie Markham sat at her desk trying to dislodge an imbedded piece of clay from under her thumbnail using a bent paper clip. When her evenings had begun to drag, she had signed up for a West Side pottery class and it was playing havoc with her nails.

The feeling of gloom around the office had been palpable all week. Warner Bromley was going to marry Sloane Taylor. Randy was on to the news first thing Tuesday morning when he heard Layla telling someone she had dinner with Warner the night before and what had happened.

Since then Layla had been out of sight, busy with something every second. She had also been nearly impossible to deal with.

Now Kayzie looked up to see Randy struggling through the door with the Wednesday papers. He looked like an ant with a loaf of bread. He plopped the papers on the front of her desk with a thud and a sigh. 'There you go, dearie. Read 'em and duck.'

She tossed the paper clip into the wastebasket and righted the sliding pile. 'Why? What's happened?'

'Today all three New York papers and the *Washington Post* are running the Bromley wedding news on the front page.'

'Argh. Duck is right. What am I going to do? She's going to ask for the papers. I can't exactly hide them all.'

'You could stall. Mr Latimer is taking her to lunch.

Maybe she'll drink herself under the table and she'll go straight up to bed. Tomorrow is another day,' he chirped, and sailed out of the office on his little sneakered feet.

Kayzie grabbed the *Daily News*. Under a headline that read 'Bachelor Billionaire to Wed Model,' there was a picture of Warner Bromley and Sloane Taylor standing against a wall of Chinese wallpaper and smiling into each other's eyes. The story began:

Billionaire bachelor Warner Bromley will marry a former child model early next month, his corporate media director announced today. His bride to be is Sloane Taylor. Ms Taylor was voted Miss Teen California and Miss Junior Santa Monica and holds many other contest titles. She started her modelling career at the age of four as the tiny television spokesperson for Happy Snappy apple juice. Ms Taylor is continuing her modelling career with a million-dollar contract with Bromley Cosmetics to act as the Bromley Woman in an extensive print and television advertising campaign. Originally from Bakersfield, California, her father, Jack Taylor, a high school football coach, is deceased. Her mother, Noreen, is married to entertainment executive Mark Reynolds, currently president of Cinetech Productions in Los Angeles.

Bromley Industries media representative Hildy Bornstein told the *News* that the wedding will take place in the Bromley penthouse suite at the Carlyle on March 9th.

Bromley maintains other homes in Los Angeles, London, the south of France, and Hamilton, Bermuda. In 1984 *Forbes* magazine named him one of the ten wealthiest men in America.

The couple will honeymoon briefly in France before making their home at Bromley's Bel Air estate, which is estimated to have cost $24 million.

Ms Bornstein added that Ms Taylor will announce plans for her national tour for Bromley Cosmetics at a Plaza Hotel press conference on Thursday, February 28th.

The story went on to detail Warner's rags-to-riches business career and only on the next-to-last line mentioned that among his multinational holdings was an unspecified financial interest in *Realto* magazine.

Well, I'll be darned, Kayzie thought, closing the newspaper. Warner Bromley and Layla were more than just friends. They were some kind of partners. But women didn't go bananas when partners got married. Why didn't she just give a cocktail party for the happy couple and send Kayzie out to buy a great present? That's what her father did when his law partner got married. He certainly didn't slam around the office throwing small objects, biting people's heads off, gobbling those little green pills she had squirrelled away in Battersea boxes all over the office – and then disappearing. That was the worst of it. Kayzie couldn't get any answers or even mail signed.

The office line rang and Kayzie snatched up the phone. 'Ms Bronz's office,' she answered.

'Kayz? Melon.' She sounded out of breath.

'Hey, Melon. What's up? Where've you been? I've called and called.'

'I can't talk. Just tell your boss that if she wants an exclusive interview with Warner Bromley, I've got it. He'll sit down with me anytime I want for as long as I want!'

'Melon! You did it! I don't believe it! How?'

'Can't say, but it's definitely on, and considering the story in this morning's paper, maybe she wants to tear something out of next month's issue to use it. Tell her it's going to be a blockbuster.'

Kayzie was floored. She knew Melon had been hanging

225

out at the Carlyle, but Bromley had gone away for the weekend. How in the blazes had she managed to get to him? 'You don't want to tell me more? It might be helpful.'

'Later, Kayz. I gotta run.'

'All right, I'll tell her. She's going to be very, very surprised to say the least. By the way, you never told me where you were.'

'I choppered down to A.C. with a mobster to catch a lounge act. Met Sinatra and Sammy. Spent a wild night with the gangster in a high-roller suite and choppered back.'

Kayzie laughed. 'You're so funny. It's a good thing you're a writer. It gives you an outlet for that active imagination.'

'Whatever you say,' Melon said, chuckling. 'But I've got a piss-green strapless trimmed with marabou and a ten-pound wheel of provolone to prove it.'

Since the morning papers, the phones at Solters & Roskin, which was Bromley Cosmetics' public relations firm, had been going crazy.

Account Executive Hildy Bornstein, a slender redhead with the kind of looks that last well beyond menopause, had a phone on each ear all morning on Wednesday. Reporters, both print and TV, who otherwise wouldn't have been interested at all suddenly wanted to come to the Thursday press conference. They knew that a young model walking off with one of the world's richest men was good copy, and they wanted a look at her. So, apparently, did the producers at the *Today* show, *Live at Five*, *Good Morning America*, and a dozen other talk shows. On orders that any bookings would have to be cleared with Bromley himself, Hildy called the Carlyle only to find him tied up in meetings.

As the press list grew, she could see that the small

reception room they had booked at the Plaza simply wouldn't do. She called and rebooked. Only the ballroom would be large enough to handle the crowd. Hildy was an old hand at managing the media and she knew a feeding frenzy when she saw it building. They would need extra security to discourage the crashers and creeps who invariably showed up when something like this was announced in the paper. She made an appointment for her assistant to meet with Sloane Taylor to discuss what she would wear and say, then proofread the short statement for Sloane that would mention her campaign and tour for Bromley Cosmetics. That would be their only chance to get publicity for the product. Once the conference was thrown open to a question-and-answer session, the press would shift its focus from lipstick to love and start quizzing her about her upcoming marriage to Warner Bromley. He had given instructions for Hildy to keep that part brief. All he wanted Sloane to say was that they met when she interviewed for the job. They fell in love and were going to be married. They are very happy. Sadly, her parents wouldn't be able to attend. Thank you for coming, we love you all, please mention Bromley Cosmetics anytime you write about us. Over and out. Get the security people to take her out the back way and then, Hildy smiled, have a quart of vodka for lunch with her husband, Al, who thought she had a superficial job.

She made a note to come up with some other reason for the absence of the bride's parents besides what Sloane had told her on the phone. A stepfather's illness and a mother who wouldn't be able to leave him just didn't cut it. Hildy would think of something.

She reread her list. That should do it. She would be there to see that it was kept short and sweet with lots of pictures. Pictures! Damn. She knew she'd forgotten something. The agency would need their own pictures to circulate to the out-of-town press.

She buzzed her assistant. 'Daisy, who's that free-lance photographer who did the original shot of Sloane Taylor? The one the *Post* ran. You know, the one with the weird name?'

'You mean Caramia Dell'Aqua?'

'That's the one,' Hildy said. 'Give her a ring, would you? I want her to cover the press conference Thursday. See that she gets credentials so that she can wander. I want tons of black-and-white shots. And see if you can get her to wear something other than that fake-fur jumpsuit. Security will think she's a street freak.'

Caramia was delighted.

She barely remembered the model they wanted her to shoot on Thursday and was completely unaware that it was her photo that had been the start of Sloane Taylor's career.

But she could use the work. Touch Me Softly greeting cards was cutting back and hadn't bought anything from her for weeks. Recently she had taken to walking up to people on the street and saying, 'Got any spare change?' Amazingly, a lot of people gave her money. Maybe they gave because she wasn't threatening. Then again, maybe it was the way she looked. One lady handed her a few bills and said, 'Here, honey, go touch up those roots.'

The job for Solters & Roskin would more than pay the rent. PR firms always bought everything she shot and overpaid. Piece of cake.

The press conference was at eleven A.M. Thursday morning. At ten Caramia stopped by Hildy Bornstein's office and picked up her pass and a carton of free film.

'Interesting outfit, Caramia,' Hildy said, handing her the credentials.

'Your assistant said I shouldn't wear the leopard jumpsuit.'

'Yeah, well, that one is certainly an eye-catching colour.'

'It's called magenta,' Caramia said.

'Turn around.'

On the back of Caramia's jumpsuit was a logo that ran from shoulder line to waist that read INDIANAPOLIS 500.

'Smart,' Hildy said dismissively. 'Now, wear that pass on this chain around your neck so you don't get hassled. It will get you anyplace in the room you need to go. Try to use available light. A flash would be too distracting to the audience.'

'Got ya.' Caramia smiled, shrugging her heavy camera bag onto her shoulder. 'You won't be disappointed.'

The crowd pouring into the ballroom of the Plaza was highly unusual for a routine promotional press conference. All the networks were there with film crews and recognizable stand-up reporters. The AP had a photographer and a reporter, and *Women's Wear Daily* sent two reporters.

All the photographers had been shunted over to one side of the stage on which there was a long table with glasses of water in front of six chairs. A wooden lectern with a microphone attached was set off to one side.

Caramia received a disgruntled reception as she joined the group. There wasn't a photographer there that she hadn't bashed, stomped on, or shoved at one time or another. The guy from the *Post* greeted her with a snarl, no doubt remembering she had slam-dunked him into a street trash can to get a better shot of Joan Collins coming out of the Côte Basque.

As Hildy Bornstein walked to the lectern to introduce Sloane Taylor, Caramia could see that the *Daily News* reporter would be blocking her first shot. 'Down in front, dickhead!' she shouted, aiming her long lens at the far side of the stage where Sloane would enter.

The *Daily News* photographer whirled around, then saw who was addressing him and skulked off to one side.

As Sloane walked out onto the stage followed by six Bromley executives, Caramia could see she wasn't going to get any good close-ups from where she was standing.

She crouched down and duck-walked behind the curtain while the others fired at Sloane smiling and waving from behind the lectern.

'Boring, boring, boring,' Caramia muttered as she crawled through the backstage darkness. She located an opening in the curtain. Now she was only a few feet away from Sloane. She screwed on a macro lens that could pick up an open pore and focused. Squinting through the viewfinder, she realized she was looking at a remarkably beautiful woman. From her vantage point the light fell on the planes of Sloane's face highlighting the high cheekbones, huge eyes, and perfectly sculpted jawline and lips. She wore nothing under her simply cut black suit jacket. The dark fabric emphasized her pale, flawless skin.

Damn. This girl's got it! Caramia thought as she started to shoot. From years of photographing faces Caramia knew the secret was bones. No matter how much plastic work anyone had done, there was nothing much doctors could do about your bones. You either had 'em or you didn't.

For years she had photographed a famous couple as they arrived at Broadway openings. Each year they had their faces lifted again until finally, in their seventies, they looked exactly alike. Their eyes and mouths could barely close. Shortly before their deaths she photographed them getting out of their limousine at the opening of *Les Misérables*. Little wizened Chinese heads, one with a fright wig, the other with no hair at all. She had made a montage of their faces over the years and called it her Dorian Gray Ensemble. Magazine art directors around town admired her work but were too repulsed to buy it.

Suddenly she snapped to attention. Sloane was taking questions from the press. Something about getting married. The expression on her face had changed from all-business grim to one of rapture. The transformation was startling. At the first question Sloane raised her head just a bit higher. The light just above her fell starkly along the line of her profile, throat, and neckline. The rest of her body was in darkness. Caramia held her breath and fired off an entire roll of film.

'Bingo!' she whispered.

That night Caramia stood in her bare feet at the large developing trays in her makeshift darkroom. Her living room was pitch-black save for a dim red bulb burning over her head. On a clothesline that stretched across the room she had hung the pictures she had already developed. Now working on the roll that had Sloane Taylor's profile, Caramia had a strange feeling. Call it déjà vu or simply a professional hunch, but as she watched the outline of Sloane's face begin to appear, she knew she had seen it somewhere before. But where? It wasn't the face she shot for the *New York Post*. She had photographed this face in a more furtive and subtle way.

She hung the last picture in the roll to dry and stepped back to study them all. They were truly beautiful pictures. She knew Hildy would be pleased.

She opened some tuna fish, sat down on the rump-sprung couch, and forked it right from the can. She continued to study the drying photos. 'Damn,' she said. 'Where have I seen that face?'

Suddenly she remembered! She walked to the hallway between the living room and the tiny kitchen. It was lined with photo files.

After a few minutes search, she found what she was looking for – the outtakes she felt Touch Me Softly would find too raunchy for her lovers series.

She pulled out the file and lugged it back to the couch.

She looked at the third picture in the file. Two figures entwined in a passionate embrace. The woman was leaning against a tree in Central Park letting a guy work away, his head between her legs. Caramia had taken the picture only a couple of days before. She remembered it clearly because the girl had seen her, pushed the guy away, and run like hell. It was a good shot despite the low

231

light. What made it particularly memorable was the expression on the woman's face. It was a look of pure rapture Caramia seldom captured.

The woman in the picture was Sloane Taylor, all right. No doubt about it. She would recognize those bones anywhere.

She flipped through the rest of the pictures. There were a few more of Sloane, taken before she'd bolted. Carefully, she slipped the Sloane pictures into a clean file folder. Now she wouldn't worry about wheedling an extra assignment out of Hildy. With Sloane Taylor's newfound fame Caramia was sure there would be a market for the very unusual lovers series. She would show them to David Inwood at the *Post* in the morning. She had an appointment to show him a particularly good shot of John F. Kennedy, Jr., running in the park. Perhaps David Inwood would be interested in these as well.

Caramia began to hum.

David Inwood hadn't said a word for more than five minutes. He was studying each of the black-and-white pictures Caramia flipped onto his desk with an illuminated magnifying glass. Finally, he tossed it aside and leaned back in his chair, rubbing his eyes.

'Great stuff, Cara me girl,' he said. 'Almost porno. And weird. Stunning shots, though.'

'Thank you.' Caramia smiled.

'You're right. The girl is certainly that model. Checking it against your press conference pictures, there's no doubt about it.'

'So? Can you use them?' Caramia asked hopefully.

'Ummmm. I don't think it would be wise. You know she's about to marry a very powerful man.'

'So. It's a news story, damn it! Or better, buy them now and run them after they get married. I can see the headline now.'

'Listen, Cara, no one is more addicted to a sleaze-factor story than I am. I spent fifteen years on Fleet Street, remember. Now, if I was buying for the *Sun* or *Sunday People*, you'd be a rich woman. But I'm not. The management here, unfortunately for us fun-loving folk, are susceptible to outside pressure. Sorry, luv.' He handed the pictures back to Caramia with a sad smile.

'Shit,' Caramia hissed. 'You got any idea who might be interested?' How about the *National Enquirer*?'

'These are too up-market for them. Now, if you had Madonna, they'd love it. But this girl is an unknown except for the fact that she's marrying one of the richest men in America, and a very private one at that,' he said, handing her back the file.

'Then maybe I need a publication that writes about rich people.'

'So take them to *Realto* magazine. They might just snap at something like this.' He flipped through his Rolodex, found the card he wanted, and studied it. 'Here.' He scribbled a name and number on the back of the payment voucher for her pictures of JFK, Jr. 'Call this lady, Layla Bronz. She's the publisher and a friend. Tell her I sent you. I'll bet she'll run 'em. She's got one more ball than I do.'

The morning after Sloane's successful press conference, Kayzie looked up to see an extremely odd creature standing in her office door – a woman in a fuzzy leopard jumpsuit and orange hair tied into ponytails on either side of her head with thick fuchsia yarn.

'Yes?' she said primly. 'May I help you?'

'I'm Caramia Dell'Aqua. I called. You remembered my name from my *New York Post* picture.'

'Oh, yes, of course. Come in, Caramia.' Kayzie stood and gestured toward the chair in front of her desk.

'Is Ms Bronz here?' Caramia asked, sitting down. She was clutching a plastic folder to her chest.

'Ah, no. I'm sorry, she had an emergency at the printers. She won't be back today.' Kayzie consulted her daybook. Because Caramia had used the name of Layla's friend, the *Post*'s photo editor, she had agreed to see her after lunch. 'I know you had an appointment, but I didn't know how to reach you. I'm truly sorry we've inconvenienced you.'

Caramia looked disappointed. 'This is real important.'

'Is there anything I can do for you in the meantime?'

Caramia looked about the office. She hugged the plastic folder closer to the front of her jumpsuit as though she feared someone would rip it out of her hands. 'Well, I suppose I could leave these,' she said. 'I have an assignment out at Newark Airport. Springsteen's coming in. It's going to be a zoo. I hate to carry these around.'

'Well, if you leave them, I can promise you I'll keep them in my desk. Ms Bronz could look at them first thing Monday morning and let you know,' Kayzie said, trying to reassure her.

'Gee. I don't know,' she said, still rolling her eyes around the room furtively. 'These pictures, well, David Inwood felt sure the magazine would be very, very interested.'

Kayzie's curiosity was piqued but she didn't want to be pushy. 'Ah, do you want to tell me what they are?'

Caramia's eyes grew wide. 'I couldn't do that. Really. it would be better if only Ms Bronz sees them.'

'I tell you what, Caramia. Let me give you a signed receipt for them. I'll put them in Ms Bronz's safe until Monday morning. She may even drop by over the weekend, she often does. I'll leave her a note about them. How would that be?'

Caramia hesitated, thinking it over. 'Okay. I really would feel better if you locked them up.'

'No problem,' Kaysie said, writing out a receipt. 'Do you have a number where we can reach you?'

Caramia gave her phone number, picked up a camera

234

case that must have weighed a hundred pounds, said she could find her way out, and left.

Kayzie worked straight through the day, lunching at her desk and trying Melon's number every so often. It was still on the machine and by noon she had given up. She was beginning to feel the whole world was doing something else and she wasn't invited. Both the day of the press conference and again today Cole had called to say that Layla wouldn't be in. He said she had meetings, luncheons, the printers, on and on. Kayzie was grateful for the quiet and the break from having to tiptoe around Layla's black mood of late.

She had just tossed the empty peach yogurt container in the trash when Randy came la-dee-dahing through the door with the out-of-town papers. He dropped them from his favorite spot, three feet above her desk. Instead of swanning out of the room, as usual, he flopped down on the couch.

'Dish?' he said, resting his chin on his shoulder and striking his best Truman Capote pose.

'What, Ran . . . deeeee?' Kayzie extended her neck and made a Donald Duck mouth.

'You don't like me, do you?'

'I like you, Randy. Mostly because I don't want you for an enemy.'

'Oh, good,' he said, unfazed.

She could see he was settling in. 'All right. What's the dish?'

He pointed toward the ceiling. 'She's been up there for two days.'

'How do you know?'

'I can tell. The light on her bedroom extension's been going off and on constantly. I'm surprised you hadn't noticed. Cole's been up there. So has Nina with trays and things. I've heard the elevator running. Haven't you?'

Kayzie leaned forward. 'Randy, I would have to have been in the hall of the house to see her private line light up. It doesn't light on my desk, or yours for that matter. You can't hear the little elevator running unless you're on the second-floor landing. We've been a busy boy, haven't we, Randy-poo?'

'Well, someone has to pay attention around here,' he said.

'So what's it all about? Is she sick or what?'

'If you'd been waiting for the man you love to marry you for years and he suddenly marries a girl who's the same age you were when you met him, wouldn't you be sick?'

'I'm her assistant, not her shrink,' Kayzie said briskly. She busied herself with papers on her desk.

She was interested in the information, but she didn't want to give Randy the satisfaction of knowing it. She wondered how many times he'd been through *her* desk drawers and hoped he had found the box of Tampax and the half tuna sandwich.

Randy could see she didn't want to play. He rose to go. 'You're no fun,' he pouted. 'But remember where you heard it. She's done this before. It's like an army general going on a retreat before he blows his enemy into smithereens. She's plotting something. I just know it.'

Kayzie looked up. 'Oh, Randy, to you life is a plot.'

'Bet you a bikini wax I'm right,' he sang as he disappeared out the door.

Kayzie neatly organized the papers the way Layla liked them and carried them into her office. The room always smelled of Layla's cigarettes and Heaven, her favorite perfume. Caramia's plastic folder lay at the edge of the desk. She picked it up and started to walk to Layla's safe.

What the hell, she thought. *Layla will show them to me. If they're so hot, I might as well have a look now.*

She peeled open the Velcro strip that held the flap in place and pulled out a pile of eight-by-ten black-and-white glossies. She looked through the first few prints. Suddenly she stopped and walked to the triple window in back of Layla's desk. She removed the horn-rimmed glasses from her nearsighted eyes and studied the woman in the pictures. And then the man. 'Oh . . . my . . . God,' she said under her breath.

12

As soon as Kayzie got home, she rang Melon's bell. She had to tell someone. She had ridden the subway in a state of semishock over the pictures of Sloane. All she wanted was someone to help her figure out what was going on.

Melon answered the door wearing an orange terry-cloth robe several sizes too large. 'Hi, kiddo,' she said, grinning. 'Come on in. I've got some great cheese.'

'Pleh,' Kayzie said, sticking out her tongue. 'I don't want food, I want a drink.' She tossed her coat over the back of the couch and flopped down with a deep sigh.

'What's up, cookie? You look beat,' Melon said.

'Melon,' Kayzie began, 'the most outrageous thing happened today.'

'Goody. Tell me while I fix us a drink.'

Kayzie launched into the story of the pictures and talked nonstop until Melon raised her hand.

'Hold it, hold it,' she said. 'Are you sure it was her? And are you sure about what they were doing?'

'I'm positive,' Kayzie said. 'Melon, please promise me, I mean, on your eyesight, promise you won't tell anyone.'

'I'm not going to tell anyone, Kayzie,' Melon said. 'Holy shit! This is wild. What did she look like? I mean, did it look like she was enjoying it? It didn't look like a rape or anything?'

'Melon, I don't know what a rape looks like.'

'Of course you do. Rape victims look annoyed, to say

238

the least. Women who are enjoying themselves look like, well, like they're enjoying themselves.'

'She didn't look unhappy, that's about all I could tell. Except for one thing I did notice.'

'What? What?' Melon said, nearly beside herself with excitement.

'It didn't look like she was wearing any makeup. I noticed because I've never seen her without a lot of face on.'

'Wow,' Melon breathed, leaning against the mantel of the nonworking fireplace. It was lined with dozens of stuffed toys, dolls, and kitschy knickknacks that she had liberated around town. 'I wish I knew what that meant.'

Melon helped herself to a slab of cheese from the largest privately owned wheel of provolone Kayzie had ever seen, washing it down from the case of Heineken the new man in Melon's life had sent to go with the cheese. Clearly the man knew the way to Melon's heart and bed was through food.

'You know,' Melon said, drinking her beer straight from the bottle, 'I just love sexual deviation. It fascinates me, always has. There are people who like to screw in public. It's a kind of exhibitionism. But to do it with strangers in the park? That's downright dangerous.'

'Well, we don't know that he was a stranger. But clearly she likes dangerous sex,' Kayzie said.

'Hmm,' Melon said, scratching her chin. 'Makes the announcement of her impending nuptials open to speculation. Doesn't it?'

'Maybe Warner Bromley is kinky. Now, there's your story.'

'Nah,' Melon said. 'My gut feeling is that she's on some dark, private sex trip. Warner has nothing to do with it.'

'I wish I knew her. Cole says she's delightful, one of the sweetest people he's ever met. None of this makes sense.'

'Maybe the idea of getting murdered turns her on,' Melon speculated.

Kayzie shuddered. The whole conversation was depressing her. Her growing conviction that people who seem to have so much really have so little was being confirmed.

Melon popped open another Heineken. 'These pictures could cause a sensation.'

'Sensation? It could destroy her career, Melon. What if they did get published? Could she sue?'

'For what? She meets the test of "public figure." She's got a press agent. She's openly courted celebrity. Her picture is all over the papers today. Anyway, these pictures were taken in a public place.'

Melon's Garfield the Cat phone on the end table rang. She lifted the arm and spoke into the paw.

Kayzie hoped it was Melon's new man. Melon had hinted that he had some underworld connection. Kayzie hoped Melon wasn't putting her on. She had never met a mobster, let alone known someone who dated one. 'Invite him over,' she whispered, half-kidding.

Melon listened for a minute and pressed her finger to her lips. 'Yes, Ms Bronz,' she said, a little louder than necessary. 'You did . . . you are! I will . . . yes, of course, I'm thrilled. Right . . . sure . . . tomorrow at eleven? Certainly. Thank you . . . yes. No, I can't believe it either. Beginner's luck, I guess. Wait. Let me get a pencil . . . okay.' She cradled the cat arm and scribbled something on a notepad that had a line drawing of a couple in the missionary position with the notation *Things to Do Today*. 'I got it. Right . . . see you then.' She hung up and jumped into the air with a whoop.

'She wants the article?' Kayzie asked, as excited as Melon was.

'Hot damn!' Melon shouted, and went back to pacing. 'She got your message when she got in and was astounded.'

'She was at the printer's all day.'

'Must be the ink fumes. She sounded high as the

Goodyear blimp. What's she do? Speed? She was going a hundred revolutions a minute.'

Kayzie shrugged. She was feeling disloyal already for having told office secrets to Melon. She wouldn't compound it with tales of Layla's Battersea boxes full of little green pills.

'She wants to see me at eleven tomorrow morning. She said I should start setting it up right away.'

'On Saturday! Damn, I won't be there. Did she say what she'd pay?'

'No. We'll talk about that tomorrow, I'm sure,' Melon said, cutting another piece of cheese. She was talking rapidly the way she did when she got excited. 'But . . . but . . . listen to this, pally.' She held up one finger for emphasis. 'She says she has some unpublished, exclusive pictures to go with the article.'

'God, she's seen them!' Kayzie said, falling back among the pillows of the couch. 'If she's going to use them, that means she wants you to trash both Warner *and* Sloane.'

'Sure looks like it. Isn't that delicious!'

'I feel so awful.'

'Why, for Christ's sake? You haven't done anything.'

'Those poor people. Just starting a new life and all.'

'Give me a break, Kayz. Warner Bromley is a robber baron. He's fucked over more companies and fired more employees than half the *Fortune* five hundred. As for his glamorous baby-girl bride, she's some kind of pervert. We know that much, right?'

The combination of the cheese, beer, and subject was making Kayzie's stomach roll. 'I guess,' she said, wishing she were home in bed.

Melon walked to the end table and picked up the scratch pad she had written on. 'Layla wants me to call this person if I need photos during the interview. Ever hear of Caramia Dell'Aqua? Damn. It sounds like one of those sick-making Italian liqueurs.'

Saturday morning there was a tapping on the steel door of Kayzie's studio even before she'd opened her eyes. She threw back the covers and padded to the door. 'Who is it?' she called apprehensively. It was only seven o'clock.

'Me, Mel. Help.'

She opened the door on the chain and peered out. Melon was standing under the light of a bare bulb with her arms folded for warmth across her chest. She was wearing a slip and a pair of Bullwinkle down slippers. Large moose horns drooped from the top of each foot.

'Kayz, you gotta help,' she pleaded. 'I've tried on five different things. Nothing works.'

Kayzie leaned against the edge of the open door in her Lanz granny nightgown, one bare foot on top of the other. 'All you need is something simple.' She yawned. 'Something ladylike that doesn't make you look like you're going to the Beaux Arts Ball. But you're not due at the magazine till eleven. Why are you dithering around so early?'

'I can't sleep. Too excited. I was up most of the night spending the money. What's the most Layla ever paid for an article?'

'Ummmm. Not much since I've been there,' Kayzie said. 'But Randy the office reptile said she paid fifty thousand dollars for an exclusive interview with Claus von Bulow. Barbara Walters beat her out of the story, though.'

'Barbara Walters? Does she pay?'

'Randy says those television people all lie and say they don't because they're journalists,' Kaysie said, making a face when she said 'journalists.'

'Boy-howdy, fifty thousand smacks! Bromley has gotta be worth that, don't you think? What I could do with that kind of money!' Melon's eyes glazed with wistful longing.

'Are you in or out, Mel? It's freezing!'

Melon turned. 'I gotta go back. Would you just come over and look at my closet? I have nothing!'

Kayzie grabbed her keys off the hook on the centre column and pulled the door closed behind her. 'Okay, but I've got to get dressed myself.'

Melon's closet was truly amazing. There wasn't an item in it that could remotely have been called safe. Kayzie dug around until she found a black wool suit with a short jacket and one of Melon's few knee-length skirts. The only problem with the suit was the row of rabbit-fur pom-poms running down the front of the jacket.

'Here,' Kayzie said, ripping off one of the fur balls. 'We'll just get rid of these.'

'What are you doing?' Melon screamed. 'That's my favorite suit.'

'It's a good suit. Nice hand to the fabric, good cut, but these dead bunnies have to go.' She tugged off the rest of the puffs and dropped them in the Snoopy wastebasket.

'I put those on myself,' Melon moaned.

'Figures.' Kayzie held the suit up in front of Melon. 'I have some nice flat black buttons I took off a coat. We'll whip them on and you'll look like Dina Merrill.'

Melon relented. 'Kid, you are a pal, I mean it. When I get paid for this gig, I'm going to buy you something terrific.'

By ten-thirty Melon looked terrific. The transformation from bimbo-bambi to New York professional was quite effective. The black-and-white-checked silk blouse she found to go with the refurbished suit was proper – not too crisp, not to feminine. She had smoothed and tamed her hair into a calm, sleek pageboy. Completing Melon's new look was a long strand of very good pearls Kayzie hadn't seen before.

Melon saw her eyeing them. She lifted them into the light. 'You like?' She smiled.

'New, right?'

243

'They arrived by messenger right after you left last night. The guy had hair on his fingers.' She giggled. 'Do you think they're real?'

Kayzie aimed the lamp full force on the pearls. They were lustrous and heavy with a pale pink sheen. 'I'm not an expert but they sure look real to me. They're extraordinary, actually.' She dropped them back in place on Melon's blouse.

'Good,' Melon said, admiring them herself again. 'He's got good taste.'

'Your gangster?'

'I think we should start referring to him as Matty now.'

'I don't know how you girls do it,' Kayzie said, shaking her head.

'Do what?'

'Get guys to give you jewelry like that. The only thing a guy ever gave me was an Elvis Presley rabbit-foot key chain. The chain turned my *keys* green and the foot molted.'

'We don't ask, you know. They volunteer. There's always strings, though.'

'You know, it's time to go,' Kayzie said. 'You ready?'

Melon smoothed her hair and pulled back her shoulders. 'Ready as I'll ever be.'

As soon as she entered Layla's office, Melon noticed that there were black-and-white glossy pictures spread across the entire surface of the publisher's desk.

'Melon,' Layla began, 'thanks for coming in on such short notice.'

Melon nodded. Layla continued. 'Let me introduce you to Dedrick Holly, our lawyer. And you know Cole Latimer.'

Melon nodded again.

'I'll get right down to business. First let me say that I was flabbergasted to hear that you had lined up an interview with Warner Bromley. He assured me that he plans to see you as soon as possible.'

'Thank you.'

'I don't suppose you want to share with us how you accomplished this feat?'

'No, Ms Bronz, I don't,' Melon said calmly. She noticed Layla shoot a look at Cole.

'Fine. I like that. Never reveal a source – that's the heart of effective journalism.'

'*Ha*, Melon thought. *If Bromley didn't tell her he had mobster friends, why should I?*

'I interviewed Warner Bromley once,' Layla said, leaning back in her chair. She was wearing a teal-blue ultrasuede suit and a choker of pearls that looked like eight rows of the strand Melon was wearing. 'That was back during the Crimean War, you understand. To my knowledge he hasn't granted one since. Why do you suppose he decided to talk to you?'

'Well, perhaps because he's gone public with his personal plans lately, so to speak. Maybe he thinks it's good PR.'

Layla hesitated for a moment as though thinking about Melon's answer. Melon glanced at the two men, wondering when they were going to say something. They were sitting stark still with their eyes focused on the same midpoint of the rug. Clearly, this was Layla's show.

Without warning, Layla scooped up the entire display of photos and handed them to Melon. 'Would you take a look at these, Melon, and tell me what you see.'

Melon took her time looking at each picture, telling herself to cool it. Layla was up to something. Melon looked at the last one, patted them into a neat pile, and handed them back. They were just as Kayzie had described them. 'I see a beautiful woman making love to a dark man in what looks like a city park.'

'And do you know who that woman is?'

'I'm afraid not.' *Let her tell me*, Melon thought. *She's dying to, anyway.*

'That woman is the soon-to-be Mrs Warner Bromley. Her name is Sloane Taylor. She's an up-and-coming model.'

'Oh,' Melon said. 'Are those modelling shots? They're quite artfully done.'

'No, these are random pictures taken by the free-lance photographer I mentioned to you, Caramia Dell'Aqua. The magazine has purchased these pictures from her for a considerable sum. What we would like you to do for us, for a fee we'll discuss later, is to write an article to be illustrated by these pictures and others.'

Melon looked first at Cole and then at the lawyer. No reaction. 'You mean, do the Warner Bromley profile using these pictures of his . . . well, new wife? She will be by that time, right?'

'Right.'

'Excuse me for being thick, Ms Bronz, but I don't get it. These are pretty erotic snaps here. I don't see how they work with a piece on Bromley.'

'We don't want you to do a piece on Warner Bromley, Melon. Oh, you'll need to interview him, of course, as planned. We want you to do a profile on Sloane Taylor and whatever her . . . umm . . . her problem is,' Layla said. 'After your, shall we say, remarkable work in the Crystal Kincaid matter, all of us thought you'd be right for this project.'

At last the lawyer showed some signs of life by crossing his legs and clearing his throat with a little tut-tut-tut sound.

'Dedrick?' Layla said to the lawyer. 'You wanted to say something?'

'Ah, well . . . Miss Tuft,' he said, leaning forward stiffly and facing Melon. 'By the time you've done your article Ms Taylor will qualify as a public figure. Still one must be careful about the libel laws and —'

Melon cut him off. 'Libel is when you lie about someone in print, sir. I don't write lies.' She was grateful for the interruption. It would give her a minute to absorb what Layla was doing. This had to be one of the damndest things she'd heard.

'That's fine, Miss Tuft,' the lawyer continued, not appreciating being smart-mouthed by some free-lance writer. She wished he knew she was wearing a mobster's pearls. 'But we want you to be aware of the . . .'

Melon tuned him out as he gasbagged on about second sources and matters of taste in a magazine like *Realto*. He was just running his meter. It was all a bit much, going on about 'taste' when his boss was about to destroy Sloane Taylor with sexy pictures. She let him drone on, fascinated with her first real look at the monster everyone said lurked behind Layla Bronz's glamorous façade. She knew everything he was saying and wanted to get on with the real business. He was into an ass-numbing speech about freedom of the press and respect for individuals when she pulled forward on the couch and said in a loud voice directed at Layla, 'How long do you want this to run?'

The lawyer stopped midsentence and lined up the toes of his shoes. He looked hurt. Melon glanced at Cole for an instant. He was maintaining the same zombielike expression, his eye still fixed at the centre of the rug. He didn't look happy.

'The longest piece we run is ten thousand words. But if you have the material for more, perhaps arrangements can be made,' Layla said, as though glad to get back to the subject at hand.

Melon was getting the distinct feeling that there had been a heated conversation between all of them before she had entered the room. Whatever the controversy, Layla had won.

'What's my deadline?'

'As soon as you can crank it out,' Layla said. 'We'll give you all the support you need. We'll set up interviews with

247

her family for you, school friends, former employers, the whole schmear. I want a complete, total, in-depth profile that will include the story behind this kind of behavior. We'll put you in touch with shrinks for comments.'

'What if she turns out to be a dull, pretty girl who made her way in the big city?' Melon asked.

'Then we have a dull, pretty girl who managed to marry one of the ten richest men in the world after less than a year in New York. Not unimportant to your story is the fact that during this time, these pictures were taken,' Layla said, tapping the pile of pictures with a long orange nail.

Melon got the picture. 'I want seventy-five thousand. Half on signing. Half on completion. All expenses. First-class travel. Hotels. Fax. Long-distance calls. Final typing fees,' she said, imitating the way Matty ordered a martini.

The glances between Layla, Cole, and the lawyer ricocheted around the room.

Cole was the first to speak. 'The most we've ever paid here is fifty thousand, Melon.'

Layla leaned across the desk and said, 'What if I told you that we would be able to get you a job travelling with Miss Sloane on her publicity tour?'

'Doing what?'

'Oh, press aide, public relations operative, whatever.' Layla waved her hand, sending her bracelets into a frenzy of clinks and clanks.

'All under cover, I assume,' Melon said. This was a new wrinkle. It certainly would get her up close and personal.

'Yes, of course. No one, absolutely no one is to know you are working on this piece.'

'In that case I'll have to have eighty-five thousand dollars and the services of a hairdresser.'

They all started to talk at once with Cole prevailing. 'Now, Melon. Really. That's more than most book advances.'

'Do you know anyone else who can do the job?'

No one answered.

'Do you know anyone who has a guaranteed interview with Warner Bromley, without which this story could not be done properly?'

Silence. Melon thought she saw the lawyer's cheek twitch.

'Do you know anyone who is willing and able to take a month-long tour pretending they are something they are not and writing press releases about cosmetics they don't even like or use? And lastly, do you know any spies who can write a ten-thousand-word article that will sell your magazine in record numbers?'

Cole raised his hand like a traffic cop. 'All right, all right, Melon. You've made your point. We can offer you sixty-five and expenses. No hairdresser.'

'Eighty,' Melon shot back.

'Seventy, not a penny more.'

'Seventy-five and I'll do my own hair.'

Layla nodded at Cole.

'All right, seventy-five, Melon.'

'And expenses?'

'Yes. Yes.'

'Great. Then we're back to eighty-five — just what I asked for in the first place.' She smiled. 'When do I start?'

Everyone looked confused.

'I said seventy-five, Melon.'

'I know,' she said pertly. 'But when you add the ten grand you still owe me for the Kincaid piece, that brings it to eighty-five.'

Layla frowned at Cole. 'Cole? What is she talking about?'

Cole had his hand over his eyes. He removed it slowly and said, 'I completely forgot. Our deal with Melon was another payment when and if she did another article.'

'Not a good deal, Cole. I'm surprised at you.'

'Layla, may I remind you of the crunch we were under

to get the Kincaid piece in the next issue. If you put your mind back to the chaos around here at the time –'

Layla cut him off. 'All right, all right. Eighty-five, Melon.'

'Terrific!' She smiled. 'When do I start?'

'I think you'd better start with the Bromley interview,' Layla said. 'He'll be going on an extended . . . ah . . . honeymoon' – she said the word as though it were obscene – 'and will be out of touch. You won't have to reserve the right to a follow-up interview. I have the feeling Mr Bromley will be begging to talk to us when he realizes what kind of article you're doing.'

'Fine. I'll call his secretary right away.'

'And Cole,' Layla said, 'would you call Hildy Bornstein at Solters and see about getting Melon on that tour.'

'Check,' Cole said, easing up out of the couch.

The lawyer rose, limply shook Melon's hand, mumbled something polite to Layla, and departed with Cole.

Melon rose to go as well. 'Thank you. This is going to be quite a project,' she said.

'You're quite welcome, Melon, but I think the person we should both thank is Matty Chiga.'

Melon fingered her pearls for the one beat it took for Layla to know she had the advantage. She smiled and slowly nodded her head. 'Right. I'll tell him tonight. When I thank him for these pearls.'

'They're hot,' Layla said as she waved her fingers and smiled.

Dying for the last word, Melon said, 'So's Matty.'

As soon as she was out on the street, Melon called Kayzie from a pay phone. 'We eat tonight!' she announced as soon as Kayzie picked up the receiver.

'You got it!' Kayzie answered.

'I got a lot. And you've got a dinner at "21."'

'Oh, Miss Melanie, I never ate no dinner at "21,"'

Kayzie said, doing her Butterfly McQueen imitation. She dropped her voice and said, 'Can you get a reservation?'

'I can't. Matty can.'

'Will he be there?'

'Yup. I want you to meet him. For a killer he's very cute.'

'Great,' Kayzie said with little enthusiasm. 'Tell him not to bring a fella for me.'

Cole waited until he heard Melon's heels clicking down the hall toward the front door to return to Layla's office. He marched past Kayzie's desk without a word.

'Don't start,' Layla commanded from behind her desk as he closed the door and leaned against it.

'Excuse me, darling,' he said tightly, 'but where the fuck are we going to get that kind of money? You know damn well anything over fifty thousand dollars is vouchered straight to Warner. I don't want to be on the same planet if he gets wind of what you're doing.'

'I can get around that,' Layla said, aimlessly re-arranging the papers on her desk.

'Pray how, O Mighty One?'

Layla leaned back in her chair. 'I'll pay for it.'

Cole dropped back onto the couch. 'Layla, you've gone mad. You're losing it,' he said, shaking his head. 'What are you going to do, sell some of the IBM Warner put you into before it split?'

'Let's not talk money, Cole, dear. It's tacky.'

'Tacky!' Cole screamed. 'I'll tell you what's tacky! Destroying this girl is tacky, Layla, and you know it!'

'Cole!' Layla barked, her voice even louder than his. 'I don't want to talk about this anymore.'

'Neither do I,' Cole sighed. 'I just want to be left out of this whole obsessive scheme of yours.'

'Fine. Do what you always do when you can't stomach something.'

'And what's that?'

'Pretend it isn't happening.'

Cole knew he had been dismissed. He rose to go with the sinking feeling that nothing he could say or do would change her mind. The roots of their relationship went too deep for threats. He couldn't quit. The magazine was his life. Layla might have a contract that said she couldn't be fired without walking with a huge financial package from Warner, but he didn't. He had pushed his case as far as he could, and a job, after all, was a job.

13

Sloane looked around the little jewel box of a suite at the Carlyle. Both rooms were furnished with English antiques and brilliant Chinese rugs.

She was exhausted. In the last few days she had moved all her belongings to the Carlyle, seen her marriage announced on the front page of every paper in town, held a press conference for two hundred pushy reporters, and managed, somehow, to keep herself looking good enough to please Warner. He had surprised her with a reception in his suite the night after the press conference. She hadn't known a soul. She wished she could have invited Alan. It amused her to think of cute little Alan with his blond ponytail and bizarre Japanese designer clothes moving through that crowd of bankers and lawyers and real estate tycoons and their proper wives.

Warner had never left her side during the party, his hand gently resting on the small of her back as he ushered her around the room to meet everyone. By the time it was over, her cheeks ached from smiling. She had done the best she could. Warner said she charmed everyone.

They had spent a lovely day together on Friday, although Warner had spent too much of it on the phone. And then, early Saturday morning, Warner left for London. Before going, he told her again how terribly proud he was of her. Her press conference pictures were all over the papers. He was ecstatic and kept his entourage waiting in the lobby while he kissed her again and again.

After he was gone, with promises to call hourly from wherever he was, she sat on the edge of the big canopied bed in her suite trying to collect her thoughts. She hadn't been truly alone since they'd left for Bermuda. She decided to take a long, luxurious bath and begin the day by making her list.

She was just getting out of the tub when the phone rang. She picked up the bathroom extension on the first ring. That would be Warner calling from the helicopter to JFK.

'Darling?' she said.

'Excuse me for bothering you, Miss Taylor.'

'Oh! Excuse me, I thought this was someone else,' she said.

'Quite all right. This is the hotel operator. Mr Bromley asked us not to put any calls through, but your messages are piling up here and I thought you should know.'

'Messages. From whom?'

'Do you want me to read them to you?'

She stepped out of the tub, slipped into a long terry-cloth robe, and sat on top of the closed john. 'Please.'

'Let's see . . . got a pencil?' the operator asked.

'That many?'

'I'm afraid so.'

'Hold on, hold on.' Sloane ran to the living room and sat down at the little French desk. Finding a pad and pen, she picked up the extension. 'Okay.'

'All right. In order of time received. ABC, CBS, the *Today* show . . . ah, *People* magazine, the *Donahue* show, the *Washington Post*, the *New York* –'

Sloane stopped scribbling. 'Wait, wait, wait. What do all these people want?'

'I suppose they want to interview you, Miss Taylor. They all called yesterday and spoke with Mr Bromley. But they're not stopping now just because he's gone. You're quite a celebrity.'

She thought for a moment. 'Look,' she said, 'would it

be too much trouble to have someone bring all those up to the suite. I'll sort them out here.'

'Right away, Miss Taylor. And should we send the flowers up as well?'

'I'm not expecting flowers.'

'Well, they're here,' she chirped. 'The concierge didn't have any room up front so they put them here in the phone room. Five boxes. Probably roses from the size of the boxes.'

Sloane smiled. 'Yes, yes, send them up, please.'

At first Sloane had been angry with Warner for stranding her like this. How could she stay angry at a man who hadn't been out of sight for an hour before he sent five boxes of flowers?

A few minutes later a bellman struggled through the door with the flower boxes and her messages. The boxes obscured his face.

'Just put them on the coffee table, please,' she said, holding the door.

He set the flowers down and handed her a stack of pink phone slips. 'Will there be anything else, Miss Taylor?' he asked.

Sloane looked at him for the first time. Their eyes held. He was young with very white teeth and high cheek-bones. She started to speak but couldn't for the nearly deafening inner voice screaming, *Don't do it, Sloane. It's too easy. It would be all over the hotel in an hour.*

'Miss Taylor?' the bellman repeated. 'Are you all right?'

She pulled her eyes away. It took every bit of strength she could find. 'Ahh . . . no! she said too loudly. 'That's fine. Ah . . . a tip. Yes, a tip! Here.' She grabbed her bag from the writing table and thrust a twenty toward him. 'Thanks a lot!'

He held up a white-gloved hand. 'Oh, no, Miss Taylor. Mr Bromley takes care of all of us each Christmas. Besides, that's much too much.'

It was much too much. Embarrassed, she stuffed it back into her bag.

She closed the door behind him and leaned against it, shaking. 'God help me,' she whispered. 'I must be suicidal. How could I even think of it now?'

She had sworn all that was over. The erotic thrill of the chase and conquest wasn't worth the devastating guilt, the searing shame. Warner was a gift too great to risk. The whirlwind of the last weeks must be getting to her for her even to think about doing it.

She knew, as well, that trying to control the panic of planning the wedding, handling the press, and changing her life so drastically was more pressure than she had ever sustained.

She needed help, fast.

She paced the floor in her silk robe. Alan wouldn't do. He was working, anyway. The hotel catering manager? Sure, Warner had a kingdom of people to smooth his way, she thought resentfully. She had no one.

She glanced down at the magazine beside the desk. Kathleen Turner smiled out from the cover of this month's *Realto*.

'Cole Latimer!' she shouted. 'God, why didn't I think of him?' Her Filofax was in her makeup kit. She raced back to the bathroom phone; it was still dangling where she had left it. She hung it up, looked up the home phone he'd given her right after she signed the *Realto* deal, and punched in his number.

Cole awoke with a terrible hangover, grateful that he wouldn't have to go to the office. His screaming match with Layla on Friday had left him depressed and anxious. He had holed up in his apartment for the weekend, feeling sorry for himself, drinking, and watching old movies.

Layla's scheme to 'get' Sloane bothered him

256

immensely. The reverberations of what she planned would have earthquake proportions in the industry. It would mean a higher profile for the magazine. Layla's peers in the media would be beside themselves. She was famous for taking risks, but taking on the bride of the man who owned her magazine was either dazzling in its stupidity or brilliant independent journalism. It might not get her Warner back, but it would do the next best thing: feed her enormous ego.

Now that he was home for the weekend, Cole wanted to forget the whole thing. When the phone started to ring, he had a bad premonition. He tried to ignore the shrill bell, hoping it would stop. On the fourth ring he gave up, picked it up, and grumped, 'Hullo.'

'Cole? Is that you?'

He struggled higher on the pillows. It was Sloane Taylor herself.

'What can I do for you, dear?' Cole asked.

'Cole, I just got a pile of phone messages from half the reporters and television bookers in the Western world,' she said, sounding as though she was on the verge of crying. 'I'm sitting here nearly paralysed. Warner's gone to London and left me to make all the arrangements for the wedding. I don't even know where to start!'

'Now, calm down, honey,' Cole said soothingly.

'I can't calm down,' she cried. 'I think I'm going to freak out if I don't get some help.'

'Well, we'll just have to get you some help, dear. That shouldn't be too hard,' he said. 'Let's see, it's Saturday. Perhaps I can find someone who can work with you tomorrow. How would that be?'

'Oh, Cole, could you?'

'No problem,' he said, not having a clue as to whom he could get, but something had to be done for the poor girl. 'I tell you what. You take the day to relax. Shop, call a friend for lunch. Have your hair done. Whatever you beautiful girls do to relax. I'll have someone there tomorrow morning who knows how to do this kind of stuff. In the meantime, forget the media vultures. They'll still be around when you need them.'

'Thank you, Cole,' Sloane said. 'Thank you from the bottom of my heart.'

'Not at all. Now, get out of that stuffy hotel room. It's a beautiful day. Why don't you start with a stroll in Central Park?'

Cole lay back into the pillows with a low moan and a creeping sense of foreboding.

To Kayzie's utter discomfort, Matty *did* bring a date for her.

The man with Matty in the lobby of '21' when Melon and Kayzie arrived was tall, sandy blond, and had thick eyelashes and a nice mouth. Matty introduced the women to Ryan McKenna as 'my friend the lawyer. A very smart man.'

Melon, who was standing just behind Matty's shoulder and out of his eye range, signalled madly to Kayzie that all this was a big surprise. She was wearing Matty's puke-green dress; in the soft light of the foyer at '21' it didn't look all that bad. The hot but real pearls lay against the marabou trim.

Kayzie shook Ryan's hand, smiled, and went silent. Somehow he looked as uncomfortable as she felt.

The captain could have been a clone of Sirio at Le Cirque for all his fawning and falling about. He escorted them up the stairs to the second-floor dining room, which was considered less rowdy and more elegant than the checker-tableclothed bar downstairs.

For all of its chic reputation in song and story, '21' was nothing more than a big, noisy steak house. Granted, Kayzie recognized a lot of important faces around the room. They were the kind of faces that didn't recoil at twenty-dollar hamburgers and fifty-dollar lobsters because their companies were footing the bill.

In the din, conversation was next to impossible. The evening dragged on, punctuated only by Melon's incredible baby-girl pronouncements about Matty. 'Isn't he adorable? Oh, Matty, you're so smart. Kayzie, listen to this. Matty did the wildest thing! Tell Kayzie about the time . . .'

Kayzie and Ryan sat hunched over their food, trying to ignore all the grabbing and ear-blowing and goo-goo talk going on between their dining partners. Finally, Ryan turned to her and said, 'You want to dance?'

'Huh?' she said, bewildered. There was no dance floor at '21', even a hick from Massachusetts knew that. She stared down into her plate. It looked like the scene of a ritual slaughter from the leavings of a medium-rare sirloin she already wished she hadn't ordered.

'I said, let's dance.'

Kayzie looked around the room. 'Where?' she said.

'Someplace else,' he said, unfolding his lanky body and tossing his napkin onto the table. 'Matty?' he said across the table. Matty had his entire face buried in Melon's hair, which had resumed its usual exploding-dandelion configuration since her meeting with Layla that morning.

'Matty!' Ryan shouted.

'Yeah, yeah,' Matty mumbled after removing his tongue from Melon's ear.

'Kayzie and I are going to dance,' Ryan said.

'Sure, sure,' said Matty, his eyes glazed with love. 'Have a ball, you kids.' He turned his face and placed it back in Melon's hair just under the big green velvet bow.

Kayzie stood, still not sure what was going on. Ryan took her elbow and guided her wordlessly down the stairs and into the street. She didn't care where she was going, just as long as she got some air and space. Being with Melon and her gangster was a price more dear than she cared to pay for a free dinner. She knew both Ryan and

259

she were there simply as an audience to whatever Melon and Matty were having – a love affair, a thing, or as Melon called it, 'a little dingdong.'

They pushed into the cold street looking like patients, too long disconnected from a life-giving oxygen tube, taking great gulps of air. When they had their fill, they turned to each other as survivors of a near-suffocation and laughed.

'Where would you like to go?' Ryan asked.

Hit man, consigliere, whatever he was, he had a lovely smile. 'I thought you wanted to dance,' she said as she pulled the collar of her thin wool coat up under her chin.

'That was an escape tactic. Forgive me.'

'*Au contraire, monsieur*. Bless you. Let's go have a drink somewhere and you can tell me about crime in America.'

'How about Sardi's bar?' he asked. 'It's a brisk, brain-clearing walk. Five minutes, tops.'

'Sounds fine.'

They headed up West Fifty-second Street at a matching pace. He adjusted his longer stride to hers as they walked, without speaking. He quickened the pace as the cold began to bore. When they reached the corner of West Forty-fourth and Broadway, they were almost running.

They could see Sardi's lighted marquee a half a block away. 'Drag you for beers,' Kayzie said. 'Winner buys.'

'You're on,' he said, and bolted down the block.

Sensibly, Kayzie had worn flats. She gathered steam and within seconds roared even with him. By the time they reached the restaurant they were in a dead heat. They collapsed against the door gagging with laughter.

The bar was almost empty. Ryan explained that most of the drinkers run to the theatre at eight o'clock and one can always get a seat.

They hiked themselves onto barstools still wearing their coats. After Ryan ordered them both gin stingers on ice, he turned to Kayzie. 'So, what are you doing with those *people*?'

260

'Those people? I thought you were Matty's, ah . . . chum. How's that for delicacy?' In the different light she could see his coloring more clearly. It might have been the run in the cold air, but he seemed to glow with blondness. His clear blue eyes crinkled at the edge, and a lock of sandy hair fell over his forehead. He had a great, strong jaw and large, wide hands.

Their drinks arrived. They clinked glasses and took a long sip.

'Truth time,' he pronounced, putting his drink down.

'Shoot,' she said. 'No pun intended.'

'I met Matty Chiga for the first time today at a deposition. I'm the attorney for a legit company he has a piece of that's being sued. It was late when we finished, and in the men's room he asked if I'd like to come to dinner and meet a pretty lady.'

'He didn't even know me,' Kayzie said.

'So? He was right. Anyway, *Miami Vice* is in reruns. I was hungry. He's a funny man, and unethical or not, I said yes. I'm glad I did.' He smiled. It was one of those little-boy smiles that sent a ripple of warmth down the back of her neck. She leaned closer. He smelled like cinnamon and clean, sun-dried cotton.

Kayzie did not miss the buzz phrases. Lives alone, hungry, no one to cook. Lawyer. Sense of humor. Thought Melon and Matty were funny but vulgar. And my, my, my those hands. She took another long pull at her stinger and wondered how those hands would feel working their way up, and down, her body.

Out on the street four stingers apiece later, they found a cab and tumbled in. She babbled her address and the cab headed up Broadway.

Ryan leaned his head against her shoulder. They knew everything about each other now, family, school, siblings, hopes and dreams, one divorce (his), one abortion (hers), favorite music, and movies.

'Can I come up and play?' he said as they approached

261

her corner. 'It's Saturday night and my mom lets me stay up late.'

Kayzie looked down at his hands holding hers, resting in her lap. She probably answered too quickly. 'You *did* ask me to dance.'

14

Kayzie and Ryan lay entwined in each other's arms under a snarl of sheets and blankets.

They were watching Sunday-morning cartoons and singing along with a cookie commercial.

Kayzie paused and let Ryan take the upcoming bass part.

'If you're a grown-up or plan to be one . . .' he boomed.

'Damn,' she said, interrupting his big finish to catch the ringing phone. 'This has to be a wrong number. No one calls on Sunday morning. It's not civilized.'

'Want me to get it?' Ryan grinned. The phone was on his side of the bed.

'No, thanks,' Kayzie said, laughing. 'It might be my mother and I'm not up to the inquisition.' She picked up the receiver and pulled it back under the covers. 'Hello.'

'Kayzie? This is Cole Latimer. I'm sorry to bother you.'

'Oh, hi, Cole. No bother. Is anything wrong?'

'Yes and no. I have a little problem and I wondered if you might be able to help me out.'

'Sure . . . sure,' she said, pushing Ryan's head away from her left breast. 'Quit!' she whispered.

'I *am* disturbing you,' Cole said.

'Ah . . . no, really. The cat jumps on me a lot,' she lied, feeling a bit silly giving in to her residual Yankee morality. 'What's up?'

'Sloane Taylor called me yesterday. She's staying at the

Carlyle until the wedding,' he said. 'She has to plan the whole thing herself and I'm afraid she's a tad overwhelmed,' Cole explained. 'I was wondering if you would mind stopping over there this morning and giving her a hand.'

Intrigued, Kayzie sat up and pulled the blanket up to her neck. 'Well, sure. But like, what does she need done? Invitations, stuff like that?'

'I don't think she knows herself. Warner is off on a business trip and she's expected to have everything ready by the time he gets back.'

'I'm not sure I know much more about planning a wedding than she does, never having done it,' Kayzie said.

'Well, from the way she sounded, just having someone to supply moral support would help. Do you mind terribly?'

'Of course not,' Kayzie said, folding the edge of the pillow over Ryan's face to drown out the soft meowing sounds he was making against her shoulder. 'What time do you think she wants me?'

'You are an angel, Kayzie,' Cole said, sounding much relieved. 'Say noon?'

'Fine.'

'I'll call and tell her to expect you,' Cole said. ''Oh, and Kayzie, don't forget to feed that cat. He sounds very large and critically hungry. Perhaps home fries and eggs up with a side of bacon?'

'Thank you, Cole,' she said sarcastically, and hung up.

She slid back down under the covers. 'I'm mortified,' she said into the blond hair on Ryan's chest.

'What was all that about?' Ryan said, pulling her close.

'I gotta go do something for the office.'

'Rats. When?'

'Have to be at the Carlyle by noon.'

Ryan lifted his arm and checked his watch. 'Great. Two hours. Let's see how many more times we can do it between, say, now and eleven-thirty.'

'Okay,' Kayzie said, grinning up at him. 'You start.'

When Kayzie was reluctantly ready to leave a couple of hours later, Ryan saw her to the crosstown bus. Once aboard, Kayzie found herself surrounded by Sunday shoppers headed for Bloomie's and mothers with children on their way to the Metropolitan Museum.

Kayzie clutched an overhead strap to avoid banging into the woman seated in front of her and wondered what Sloane Taylor was really going to be like.

Kayzie had heard of little else than the current adventures of Sloane Taylor for weeks. What she was up to had become the office soap opera with daily instalments directed and fuelled by Randy. Now that Kayzie had seen the secret sexy pictures of Sloane she was more than curious to meet her.

She wondered what it must be like to go through life looking like Sloane Taylor.

I'll never have to worry, Kayzie shrugged inwardly. Thank God for hereditary clear skin and whoever invented soft contacts. She had long ago given up cursing her plainness and concentrated on other things, like being a 'good sport.' That was her brother's way of paying her a compliment about her looks. There were times, growing up, that being plain had hurt. Particularly when boys started asking her friends to the movies and asking her to play centre field. It might be nice to try waltzing through life without having to actually *be* a good sport. People had to get to know you to find that out. Someone who looks like Sloane didn't even have to speak and people fell all over themselves just looking at her. Not that Kayzie would trade places – but then again, maybe a long weekend looking like that would be nice. Okay, maybe a month. A month on the Riviera. How about looking like that for a year in Paris at the same time Robert Redford was making a movie in the apartment next door? How about this? she pondered. How about looking like that the next time Ryan picked her up for a date? She'd open

265

the door and – *Voilà! Me in Sloane Taylor's body!* she hadn't needed to look like Sloane Taylor last night, she thought, and smiled to herself. Now, *there* was some consolation.

The bus reached Madison and Kayzie got off to walk south to the Carlyle. She'd better stop daydreaming and start thinking about what her attitude toward Sloane would be. Was she her peer? Certainly not. They might be the same age, but Sloane Taylor was a celebrity. Was she an employee sent to do some work and not get personal? Probably not that either. Helping someone plan their own wedding was a pretty intimate assignment. Then there were those pictures of Sloane in the park. She couldn't get them out of her mind. Was Sloane some kind of nymphomaniac who had sex with men in public? There had to be a better explanation than that. She shouldn't judge. It wasn't fair. She would just be pleasant and helpful and above all a good sport.

Sloane called room service and asked to have her breakfast tray removed. She was nervous about meeting Kayzie Markham and wanted to make a good impression. A half-gnawed melon and a basket of cold croissants lying around was not the way to start.

How she wished she were already close friends with this woman. If only she had someone to talk to about what happened last night, she wouldn't be so anxious.

Last night the Bad Girl Game had backfired.

All day she had resisted the idea of a walk through Central Park. She fitfully filled the long hours trying to nap and read. By dusk she could stand it no longer.

She threw her raincoat over her skirt and sweater and left the hotel by a side door. She quickly covered the distance from the hotel to the pond where children sailed miniature boats. By the time she reached the boathouse she had seen only a few joggers and a man walking a Great Dane.

As she crossed the drive to the walkway that led to Bethesda Fountain, she saw a man loading a van with wooden barricades put in place for a marathon earlier in the day. As she approached, he turned and their eyes met.

Sloane smiled and moved closer, trying to make out his features in the light from the streetlamp. The day alone with her thoughts made her eager for the sound of a human voice. If he wasn't good-looking, she wanted at least to stop and speak to him.

He moved around to the side of the van and leaned against it, still staring at her. The light was brighter and she could see his face. He was not as young as she would have liked, a little too stocky, but he had a nice chin and high cheekbones. But it was his eyes! There was something in his eyes she couldn't resist.

'Hello, pretty lady,' he said in a low voice. The air was damp and chill. He must have noticed how tightly she was clutching the fabric of her thin raincoat around her neck. 'You shoulda worn something heavier. Kinda nippy out here tonight.'

She slowed her pace, still studying his face. *You weren't going to do this again*, she told herself. *You promised you would stop*. She cleared her throat to drown out the warning voice. An electrical current was passing between them now. It was time to draw him in.

He slid open the door panel on the side of the van. 'I got my heater going. Hop in.'

Without a word, Sloane stepped into the van. Wooden barricades were stacked against the back door. In the space between them and the two front seats lay an old mattress covered with tools. She climbed over the mattress and sat down in the passenger seat.

He climbed in behind her, closed the door, and flopped into the driver's seat. Wordlessly, he reached into a compartment under the dash and extracted a steel flask and unscrewed the top. 'How about a shot of whiskey?'

he asked. Wiping the neck of the flask with the sleeve of his plaid jacket, he handed it to her.

Ah, she thought, *just what I need*.

'I'm Jim,' he said as she took a large gulp and handed the flask back.

She swallowed hard, feeling the sharp burn streak down her throat. Instantly she felt light-headed. She caught her breath and said, 'I'm – she paused – 'Sally.'

He took a long pull at the flask, coughed, and recapped it. He turned toward her and roughly pushed his hand up her skirt, tearing at the waistband of her panty hose.

'Hey,' she said, 'not so fast!' She liked kissing first, lots of hot kissing before anything like hands up her skirt.

'Whaddaya mean, not so fast,' he growled. He reached around her with his other hand and pushed some mechanism on the side of her seat. The back reclined abruptly and she fell backward with a jolt. Before she realized what was happening, he was pulling her off the seat and onto the dirty mattress. She didn't like what was happening. He had taken complete control. This wasn't the way to play the Game! As she opened her mouth to protest, he covered it with his. He smelled bad, a sour mix of sweat, whiskey, and old cigars.

She was scared. He was going too fast. He was too rough. Something sharp was puncturing her shoulder blades. Her skirt was up to her waist and he was tearing away the fabric of her panty hose as if it were made of spiderweb strands.

She heard a zipper ripping open.

She gave up struggling against the weight of his huge chest. He stopped kissing her. She gasped as he entered her with a painful thrust. He grabbed her legs, pulling them upward, trying to change the angle, stabbing deeper, harder. He seemed possessed. He was no longer aware of her. He grunted obscenely as he jammed himself into her again and again. *Please make him stop*, she prayed, panic beating against the inside of her skull. She felt as though she was blacking out. This wasn't sex or pleasant danger, this was an assault. She was being raped. What if he were diseased? Somehow the thought had never occurred to her with the others. But they had behaved. They had done what she wanted; therefore they were good. This one was evil and with evil came more evil and pain and disease. The last thing she heard before she passed out was the sound of her own voice screaming.

She had no way of knowing how long she was unconscious. The first thing she was aware of was a vibration under her. She lay still on the dirty mattress among the scattered tools. Her jaw and throat ached and her mouth tasted rancid. *Good Lord*, she thought, *what did he do to me while I was unconscious?*

The van was moving too fast to be on a city street. She kept her eyes tightly closed and tried to keep her breathing even, terrified that he might look back and see she had come to.

She felt the van moving up an incline and then turning left. Her body shifted involuntarily as the van came to a sudden stop. *This is it*, she thought. *This is when he kills me*.

She heard the driver's door slam and the side door sliding open. She willed her body to go totally limp as she felt his hard hands lifting her under the arms and dragging her from the mattress. Her legs flopped to the ground like those of a broken doll. He dragged her a few feet across rubble-covered ground and dropped her with a painful thud.

Her mind went blank with fear. She couldn't even pray. It was over. The Bad Girl Game had finally gotten her murdered.

In disbelief, she heard the engine of the van fire up and tyres screeching.

She lay on the ground for what seemed like an eternity listening to the sound of cars and trucks swooshing past before she dared to open her eyes.

Slowly, with great pain, she pulled herself off the ground. Her raincoat was wet and torn, and long threads of her panty hose dangled down her legs. She felt the pocket of her coat. Her little change purse and room key were still there. Cautiously she looked around, still half-believing he was hiding, watching her. She was in some kind of vacant lot. Beyond was a highway and beyond that the river. She recognized the Pepsi-Cola sign in Queens and realized she was looking at the FDR Drive. Only two nights before she had stood with Warner and some of his friends at the high gallery windows of a penthouse apartment on Sutton Place looking at the same view. Now she stood, raped, sodomized, bruised, her clothes torn to shreds in a filth-strewn empty lot not ten blocks away.

She shook herself slightly. Nothing seemed to be broken. She wasn't bleeding. She could make it to a side street and hail a cab.

She took a deep breath and ran her hands through her matted hair. She felt overwhelming relief and to her amazement, a shivering excitement.

When she was once again safe inside the suite, she was so shaken and exhausted she had barely been able to shower and make it into bed. It wasn't until this morning that she had seen the ugly purple bite mark low on her neck. Slowly, gently, she managed to cover it with a heavy matte base she usually put under her eyes. A high turtleneck sweater would do the rest.

When the desk rang to say a Ms Markham was on her way up, Sloane nervously checked herself in the mirror by the door. She ran her fingers under her turtleneck sweater, wincing at the pain. Carefully she pulled the collar back into place, horrified at what the Game had come to.

Last night she had no longer been in control. That alone had been the heart of the game. The fact that this was the first time she had ever been marked made her realize once again how much she had to lose.

She couldn't think about it any longer. Not today. Today she would make a new friend. Today there was no room for remembering nightmares.

As soon as she opened the door of the suite and saw Kayzie Markham smiling at her, she felt relieved.

'Hi, Miss Taylor,' she said. 'I'm Kayzie.'

Sloane took in Kayzie's outfit: the plaid kilt, the monogrammed Shetland sweater under a beat-up Burberry. She had expected someone entirely different to be Layla Bronz's secretary. Rather than a stiff middle-aged lady, Layzie could have been her own sister. 'I could hug you!' she said, holding the door wide. 'Come in, come in, please. And call me Sloane, for heaven's sake.'

Kayzie stepped into the small foyer and slipped out of her coat. 'Wow, isn't this a beautiful room!' she said, her eyes sweeping her surroundings.

Sloane hung up Kayzie's coat. 'Come on, let me show you the bedroom and terrace. You can see the reservoir in the park from here.'

It took only a moment or two to walk Kayzie through the suite. Sloane had not realized until then how starved she had been for someone her own age to talk to. She liked Kayzie instantly. She was relaxed and funny and as familiar as a soft, well-worn housecoat one longed for on a dark, cold night far from home.

She liked Kayzie even better for the frank way she refused Sloane's offer of tea.

'To tell the truth, Sloane,' Kayzie said, holding her forehead, 'I was introduced to several stingers last night and I have a King Kong-sized hangover. I think I need something just a tad stronger.'

'How about champagne?' Sloane asked eagerly, clapping her hands. She turned toward the phone to call room service.

'Champagne at the Carlyle? I'm afraid that's a bit over my head, swollen as it is,' Kayzie said, laughing.

'That's no problem. Warner has his own champagne

271

by the case in the wine cellar. I think he brushes his teeth in it. He owns a vineyard in the Loire Valley. If we don't drink it, somebody else will.' She hoped Kayzie wouldn't think she was showing off. Warner *did* keep his own wines in the hotel and she wanted to please her new friend. Here she was giving up her Sunday even with a hangover.

'All right, if you're sure,' Kayzie replied, curling up in the big wing chair next to the fireplace.

Sloane called room service and ordered a bottle of Warner's wine to be opened right away and an extra for later. 'I'll put it in the bathroom fridge, just in case. You hungry? Of course you're hungry,' she said, not waiting for Kayzie to answer. She turned back to the phone. 'And a tray of those crustless salmon sandwiches, and some cold chicken with tarragon mayonnaise, and . . .' She looked at Kayzie for any suggestions she might have.

'Chips?' Kayzie said, raising her eyebrows.

'And some potato chips.' She covered the phone. 'They have hot homemade ones, okay?'

'Fabulous.'

Sloane finished giving room service the order and hung up feeling very pleased. This was the first time she had been able to use Warner's position to do something for someone else. It almost felt as though the money were hers. 'I think they shot the last bag of store-chips that tried to get into this hotel. You'll like the hot ones.'

'That,' Kayzie said with a smile, 'I don't doubt.'

Sloane pushed back against the pillows of the couch and pulled her dressing gown around her knees. 'I can't tell you how much I appreciate your doing this, Kayzie. I guess I must have sounded frantic to Cole. Actually, I was.'

'I don't blame you. When is the wedding, anyway.'

'Next Saturday.' Sloane grimaced.

'Krikees! We're going to have to work fast. Who's invited?'

'Mostly Warner's friends.'

'How many from your side?' Kayzie asked.

'Ah . . . there's only my mother, but she won't be able to make it. But my friend Alan will be there.'

'What a shame. Why can't your mother come?'

'Her new husband has to make a speech in Rio,' Sloane said, hoping Kayzie wouldn't pursue the subject. It still hurt that Noreen wouldn't come. 'This whole thing happened so fast she couldn't change their plans.'

'Okay, Now, how many do we plan on?'

'Fifty,' Sloane answered, grateful to move on.

'Fifty!' Kayzie looked shocked. 'In this little suite? Someone will have to stand in the shower.'

'Oh, no, no, I'm sorry,' Sloane said, waving her hands as though to erase the words from the air. 'We'll use Warner's suite. It's upstairs in the penthouse and it's humongous. We'll go look at it after lunch.'

'Okay,' Kayzie said, reaching for a notepad and pen on the end table. 'Have you made a list?'

'Not really. I played around with one until I got paralyzed thinking about it. I'm afraid I'm not the most organized person in the world.'

'Well, we'll start one now.' Kayzie began making lines and numbers on the pad.

'Warner says we can use the hotel caterer for things.'

'Great. He can do practically all of it. Flowers, drinks, food, cake, nut cups . . .'

'Nut cups?' Sloane said, puzzled.

'Just kidding.' Kayzie smiled. 'Music?'

Sloane nodded tentatively. 'Now there, I'm lost.'

'I went to a gallery opening Ms Bronz didn't want to go to last week. They had this wonderful group. Just three people, two violins and a bass playing Brahms and Mozart. Why don't I try to find them?'

'Perfect! Mozart is Warner's favorite.'

'Now. How are you going to invite people? It's only a week away. We can't mail anything.'

'Gee, I don't know. Phone?'

Kayzie shook her head rapidly and frowned. 'Not proper for the future wife of Warner Bromley,' she said with mock schoolmarm prissiness. 'How does this sound? When Ms Bronz gets out of her spur-of-the-moment urges for a grand dinner, she has invitations hand-delivered in little red lacquer folders with ribbons. We could use white. I order really heavy creamy paper and the folders from a shop on Madison and write them by hand. The hotel could deliver them for us.'

'Some of these people are overseas or in California.'

'Those we'll overnight express mail. I'll put down my office number and they can respond by phone to your "secretary."'

'The Sultan of Brunei?'

'Why not? They have phones in Brunei.'

'Of course they do.' Sloane laughed. 'You know, Kayzie, maybe this thing can be done after all.'

'Now,' Kayzie said, holding up one finger. 'The pièce de résistance!'

'Oh dear, have I forgotten something important?'

'Your dress.'

'My God. I am losing my mind,' Sloane said, aghast. 'I hadn't given a thought to what I'd wear.'

'Well, it's too late to have one made,' Kayzie said, tapping the end of the ballpoint on her chin. 'Tell you what. Bronz has a personal shopper at every store in the city. When she wants something special, she calls up and they have a private showing for her. She just points to what she likes. I'll call Bloomingdale's lady and set up an appointment. This afternoon we'll pick up the notepaper and your entire ensemble.'

'Let me get that,' Sloane said, responding to a discreet tap on the door. 'Kayzie, you're wonderful,' she said, opening the door. 'This may just work after all.'

After Sloane scribbled her name on the bill and the

waiter had gone, they surveyed the table he had presented.

Kayzie lifted the silver lid of a platter heaped with tiny sandwiches and replaced it. 'I feel like I'm in one of the ads in the magazine,' she said, shaking her head in disbelief at all the food. 'If this doesn't cure my head, nothing will.'

The two new friends laughed and giggled and gossiped through both bottles of champagne and all the food. By two o'clock Sloane was falling about the sofa, laughing hysterically. Kayzie was finishing a story about Randy the Office Reptile and the time he slithered into Layla's private bathroom to check the medicine cabinet and locked himself in.

Sloane sat up and wiped her eyes. 'Oh, God, Kayzie, we're smashed!' she said through her giggles.

'Speak for yourself,' Kayzie said, pulling up out of her chair and proceeding across the Chinese rug in a knee-buckling gait that set off another burst of Sloane's hysteria. 'I always walk this way,' Kayzie slurred, steadying herself against the edge of the breakfront by the door.

'I better order some coffee,' Sloane said, reaching for the phone.

'Nah . . . we're not that far gone. Come on, girl. Put something on and we'll go find you the most drop-dead wedding dress in New York City.'

By the time they left Bloomingdale's, the night security guard had to unlock the side door to let them out.

Their condition had made them somewhat reckless with Warner's money. Sloane had completely lost count of what she had spent. Halfway through their spree they talked themselves into the fact that Sloane needed a honeymoon wardrobe, honeymoon lingerie, honeymoon shoes, and honeymoon luggage, and because Warner had planned that they go to his villa in the south of France, several honeymoon hats to keep the sun off, as Kayzie put it, 'your honeymoon face.'

The dress the personal shopper found was perfection. A Givenchy column of pale-peach watered silk with enormous jewel-encrusted sleeves. A head-hugging cloche of pearl- and diamanté-covered silk would be made and sent directly to the hotel with all their other purchases.

As they stumbled, dazed and giddy, onto the East Fifty-ninth Street sidewalk, Sloane realized the extra-ordinary afternoon was coming to an end. She didn't want it to. She suddenly pictured her hotel suite, empty and lonely without Kayzie's company.

'Kayzie, I don't know how to thank you,' she said, hoping to prolong the day. 'Please, let me take you to dinner.'

Kayzie pursed her lips and hesitated. 'You don't have to thank me, Sloane. I've never had such fun. This was unbelievable. Do you have any idea how much we spent?'

Sloane shook her head. 'No. Not really. I guess I should have kept count, huh?'

'I can tell you if you want to know,' Kayzie said, reaching into her bag and withdrawing a sheaf of receipts. 'Not including your bridal-hat thing, which will run about five hundred, it will come to twelve thousand four hundred and —'

Sloane put her gloved hands over her ears. 'I don't want to know,' she said. 'Let's worry about it over dinner. My treat. Pick someplace fabulous.'

Kayzie sighed. 'Sloane, I have to tell you. Last night I met this really terrific guy, and I promised . . .'

Sloane felt terrible. She had taken Kayzie's entire day and now had presumed to take her evening as well. 'I'm sorry, Kayzie. How selfish of me. Of course, I under-stand.'

'Any other time, really. It's just that I met him only last night, and well, he's pretty delicious. I don't want to give him a chance to get away.'

'Now, that's exciting.' Sloane smiled.

'Look,' Kayzie said, holding her arm out to attract an approaching cab. 'Let me drop you at the Carlyle. Then, if you don't have plans tomorrow, how about coming over for brunch. I'm sure Layla will give me a little extra time. And the morning off to help you with your wedding plans. I'd like you to meet my neighbor Melon Tuft. She's a writer and like nothing I've ever met.'

'I know Melon Tuft,' Sloane said, surprised. 'At least I met her. She was trying to get an interview with Warner, wasn't she?'

'Right! I think she actually got it. That makes it even neater. I know she'd love to meet you. One of her hobbies is liberating food. Tomorrow we'll make a big smorgasbord out of her recent take.'

Sloane thought for a moment. Monday stretched ahead as bleak and lonely as Sunday had threatened to be before Kayzie. 'I'd love that!' she said brightly. 'I'd just love that.'

'Great!' Kayzie said, pulling open the cab door. 'Wear jeans. We'll sit on the floor and sort out the rest of the wedding plans.'

Sloane let Kayzie take the cab. She wanted to walk a bit before going back to the hotel. Kayzie waved good-bye through the back window as the cab pulled into the early-evening traffic.

She stood on the curb long after the cab disappeared. The chill night air made her shiver. She pulled the collar of her polo coat around her neck. The thought of brunch tomorrow with her new friends, women her own age, warmed her. She wondered what Kayzie's new man was like. *Funny,* she thought, *here I am about to marry Warner Bromley, every girl's fantasy husband, and I'm feeling a little envious of Kayzie's romance.*

Monday morning Melon opened her refrigerator door and surveyed the take. There was the remains of her huge

'21' steak plus the untouched sirloin Matty had ordered when she asked the waiter for a doggie bag. On the shelf below were two whole cold lobsters from Umberto's Clam House, where they had eaten last night. Matty thought her habit of snagging food was so cute he was now ordering two meals. One to eat in the restaurant and one to go. She still had plenty of provolone and beer left to complete her contribution to Kayzie's brunch.

When Kayzie told her she was not only helping Sloane Taylor put together the Bromley wedding but had invited the bride to her apartment, Melon was ecstatic. It was a perfect way to establish a friendly rapport with the woman before they left on the tour.

She would have to be careful, however. Her inclination would be to pounce and interrogate Sloane. That would never do. If she controlled herself, she'd have it made. Now, if only she could swing an invitation to the wedding!

She listened at the door of Kayzie's apartment before she knocked. It was important to her that she did not arrive ahead of Sloane. *Don't look too eager*, she counselled herself, be cool, nonthreatening. There was too much to lose.

It wasn't just the money. Now there was Matty's adoring respect. Being a writer made her different. He flaunted her career among his mobster pals and bragged about her as if she were living proof of how desirable his own intellect must be.

Melon didn't want Matty's intellect. She wanted Matty.

For the first time in her life a man was making her feel good about herself. In his world, so peopled with bimbos and gum-cracking beehived mobettes, she was treated like Sophia Loren.

It was a joke. She was realistic enough to know that. Her career was just getting started and no one, really, knew who she was. Not on the level to which she aspired. But to Matty, she was already the star she craved to be.

'It's unlocked,' Kayzie called from inside her apartment.

Melon backed through the door with her arms laden with food. Out of the corner of her eye she could see Sloane sitting on a pile of pillows by the fireplace. She was wearing faded jeans, a navy turtleneck sweater, and sneakers. She was in full makeup, which seemed odd to Melon. Maybe models never go out without it, she thought as she dumped her armload onto Kayzie's coffee table with a thud.

'Good Lord, Melon. Have you taken to holding up supermarkets?' Kayzie asked as she sorted through the doggie bags.

'Surf and turf, anyone?' Melon offered, pulling one of the cold lobsters out of a bag.

'Melon,' Kayzie said, gesturing to Sloane, 'this is Sloane Taylor.'

'Hi. We met,' said Melon pleasantly.

'Of course.' Sloane smiled. 'In the Carlyle lobby as I recall. Congratulations. I hear you got your interview with Warner.'

Melon dropped to the couch and reached for a beer. 'I did, indeed. I hope to see him before you guys go on your honeymoon. Maybe you could put in a word for me?'

'I'll do my best,' Sloane said sweetly. 'What kind of an article are you planning?'

'Oh, just a profile, really,' Melon said lightly. 'You know, one of those question-and-answer, how-did-you-become-a-success things. Nothing sexy.'

'Maybe I could give you the sexy bits,' Sloane said, laughing.

'Boy, wouldn't I love that. Unfortunately it's not going to be that kind of a story,' Melon said. She thought for a minute. Perhaps this was the time to tell Sloane she would be going on her tour with her. It would be awkward if she let it wait and she found out. Better to get off on the right foot from the start. 'I'll take one of your Coronas if they're cold, Kayz,' she said.

279

When Kayzie handed her the beer, she took a big slug and said to Sloane. 'I've got news, girls,' she said.

Sloane and Kayzie looked toward her.

'Layla's assigned me to Sloane's tour.'

'You are kidding?' Sloane said excitedly.

Kayzie went back to dicing the steak.

'As what?' Sloane said. 'I mean, what will you do besides keep me company – which I would love.'

'Oh, handle the press, write releases, see that you get to studios on schedule, that kind of stuff.'

'I am so excited!' Sloane said as though she really meant it. 'I was beginning to get nervous about it, but with you along it will be a party!'

Kayzie finished checking out the food supply and carried it to the kitchen against the wall. 'I'm going to make red-flannel hash out of this steak unless one of you hates beets.'

'Let me help!' Sloane said eagerly, lifting herself off the pile of cushions. 'I better get into practice anyway.'

'You really think you're going to have to cook for your new husband?' Kayzie laughed over her shoulder. 'Cole tells me his house in California is so big they haven't even found the kitchen.'

Sloane and Kayzie stood side by side working at the tiny kitchen counter. They had their backs to Melon. As they chattered away, she noticed Sloane's handbag sitting on the bathroom floor.

' 'Scuse me a sec,' she called. 'This beer works fast.'

Neither seemed to hear her over their conversation about the wedding. She slipped into the bathroom, locked the door, and turned on the water full blast.

Sloane's bag was predictable. A wallet, tissues, change purse, a small comb and brush, and a little zippered makeup case. Melon opened it and poked through the contents. At the bottom was a well-used tube of Cover-Mark.

Cover-Mark, she thought. Why would someone with

that kind of skin use an industrial-strength blemish concealer? She dropped the tube back into the case, zippered it, and made a mental note to manœuvre Sloane into a better light and get a close look at her face.

Kayzie served the crispy hash, beer, and cold lobster salad on the Parsons table by the window. The day that had started somewhat gloomily had turned bright and sunny. High clouds scattered across the sky over the Hudson.

The conversation was almost exclusively about Sloane's wedding. *Better*, Melon thought, *let them talk. My mouth always gets me in trouble*. The light was perfect for scrutinizing Sloane's face.

The skin on her face was like glass, perfect.

It was her neck, just under the jawline and above the fold of her turtleneck that held Melon's interest.

Cole had told Kayzie to take the whole day to help with the wedding, so she and Sloane spent the rest of that afternoon writing and addressing wedding invitations on the Parsons table where they had had brunch.

'Melon's nice,' Sloane said, smoothing another creamy page flat.

'Um,' Kayzie answered without looking up as she carefully scrolled 'Mr and Mrs David Rockefeller' onto a heavy card to be slipped under the white watered-silk ribbon on a white lacquer box. 'She was a bit subdued today, I thought. Usually she's off the wall.'

'She's kind of cute.'

'Um,' Kayzie responded again, and looked at the next name on the list Ms Motherwell had supplied Sloane. 'My goodness,' she said softly. 'President and Mrs Reagan! Is this for real?'

Sloane nodded shyly.

'Whoa!'

'Warner says the President won't come. Too much security and traffic mess.'

'Rats.' Kayzie smiled.

'But Mrs Reagan has already told him she'll be there. Let's send it anyway. You have to know Rose Motherwell. If she put it on the list, she wants one sent.'

Kayzie tapped her finished pile on the tabletop. 'There,' she said. 'That's that.' She reached over and took some of Sloane's.

'Kayzie?'

'Uh-huh.'

'Can I ask you something?'

Kayzie looked up quizzically. 'Sure.'

'I don't want to embarrass you.'

Kayzie put her pen down. 'Embarrass me?' She frowned.

'Well, it's just . . . it's just . . .'

'Sloane, just ask. Don't worry about it. Bride stuff, right?'

'Yes, how did you know?'

Kayzie tapped the side of her head. 'I think I know the answer already.'

'You do?' Sloane blinked.

'Yup. Now, don't be shocked,' she said smugly. 'The girl gets on the bottom and the boy gets on top. Then later, when you get bored, you can switch.'

'No, no, no,' Sloane said through her laughter.

'Sorry. I guess you knew that.'

'Kayzie, will you be my maid of honor?' Sloane blurted out.

Kayzie dropped her pen. 'Me?'

'Please?'

'Sloane, I'm speechless.'

'I like you so much,' Sloane said, her lower lip trembling. 'My only close friend here is Alan, my hairdresser. I've really never gotten terribly friendly with the girls at the agency, and . . . weddings are so special. I thought it would be nice to have someone –'

Kayzie thought she was going to cry and interrupted

her. 'Hon, you don't have to justify asking. I'm so flattered I'm beside myself. Of course I'll stand up for you. It would be the most exciting thing that's ever happened to me!'

Sloane leaned across the table and pressed her cheek to Kayzie's. 'Thank you, Kayzie. I'm thrilled.'

Kayzie clapped her hands with glee. 'This is so much fun,' she said. 'Who's standing up for Warner? Is he cute?'

'Actually, he is. He's been Warner's attorney for years. He's a little older, but he's very handsome. We had dinner with him the night before and he's single, too.'

'Rats, if I'd known that, I wouldn't have fallen in love last night.' Kayzie laughed.

'Oh, Kayzie, I meant to tell you yesterday. Please bring him to the wedding.'

'You serious? Could I?'

'Of course. The bride's side is going to need some fluffing up.'

15

On Tuesday evening, Layla was propped up in bed with her cat, the papers, and her pain.

She snapped open *Time* magazine and tried to focus on whether Brooke Shields's advice that girls should hold on to their virginity was the beginning of a trend. If she weren't so distraught, she would have asked someone to do a survey of college girls for the magazine.

She had to get out of the office. One more minute in the cloying current atmosphere and she would have needed an insulin injection.

Cole, in all his goody-two-shoes wisdom, had volunteered Kayzie's services to plan Warner's wedding. Layla had agreed at the time, thinking the arrangement would at least give her a pipeline into what was going on.

Pipeline! she seethed. It had become a raging storm stewer. Warner's little fear-of-aging squeeze had gone and asked Kayzie to be her maid of honor and Cole to give her away! If Warner knocked her up, she'd probably ask Randy to be midwife.

She had listened to Kayzie on the phone with the wedding guests all day. Every call was from someone she knew. They were her friends! After slamming her door twice to shut out the chatter, she gave up and stormed out, only to have Kayzie hand her a message from the Bornstein woman at Warner's public relations firm. She wanted to meet with Layla about coordinating the issue with Sloane on the cover with her promotion tour.

The bitch had not only deprived her of Warner, she had now succeeded in taking over her office, her staff, and her telephones.

When she'd reached the top floor, Nina had handed her a white lacquered box that looked like the invitations she used for dinner parties. It had been hand-delivered to the town house that morning. She opened it, saw what it was, and flung it across the room.

Now, alone in the privacy of her room, her agony over Warner's betrayal sprang back full-blown, like a monster in her head.

She knew she was drinking too much, taking too many pills, biting people's heads off. She couldn't help it. Since the night Warner had told her he was marrying Sloane, her life had been out of control. Never, in her wildest dreams, had she imagined a life without Warner. If he had died, she could have handled it. This was worse. Her jealousy of Sloane – and she had to admit that was the word for it – was like acid slowly dripping onto her brain, burning an ever-widening, bloody, festering hole. She couldn't breathe, she couldn't sleep. She had to do something to punish both Sloane and Warner, but what would be painful enough? How could she irrevocably hurt them?

When she first saw the pictures of Sloane with that man in the park, the adrenaline rush was like a jolt of electricity. The monster in her head had taken a break while she plotted how best to use them. She was consumed with shaping the plan for her revenge.

But today, surrounded by all the chatter and giggling about the wedding, the pain had returned. She had no choice but to take it up to bed and wrestle with it on her own turf.

She was unable to articulate her despair, even to Cole. Everything she had acquired and accomplished in life was hers because of Warner. She achieved for an audience of one. Now she had lost him in the cruellest way a woman her age could lose a man. The years meant nothing to him. Poof! Out with the old, in with the new.

She replayed their conversation again and again. Warner, by his own admission, was marrying the girl to keep her from other men. That admission kept popping into her head. It lodged there like a fish bone in her throat. How could she use that against her, against him?

Then came the pictures. From nowhere, like a sign! She knew the moment she saw them that these were her weapon, her jewelled sword. She wrote out a $100,000 cheque on the spot. When Layla handed it to that strange woman who looked like Raul Julia in drag, the photographer had gone into a swoon and crashed to the office floor. She didn't even mind paying Melon's outrageous fee.

Layla was mesmerized by the pictures. This was the way to obliterate Sloane Taylor. She would prove to him, in the most public way possible, that the woman had a sexual kink so bizarre, so repellent, that as besotted as he was he couldn't ignore it.

He would argue, perhaps, that all this happened before he came into her life. But what if she kept it up? What if Layla could prove, by letting others braid the hangman's noose, that even as Mrs Warner Bromley she pursued her sick game? That, he would not abide. Warner was a proud man. A man with a consuming ego who might tolerate private betrayal. But a public humiliation? A scandal of such sleazy magnitude that he would be laughed at, humiliated? Never.

'Ahhhh,' she sighed, sinking back into the pillows. Just thinking about it made her feel better.

To make it all work, Sloane would have to be watched. What perfect timing to be able to make use of Melon Tuft's savage tenacity. Melon wouldn't win any popularity contests in life, but there was something about her that fascinated Layla. She was like a small, voracious animal able to consume things ten times her size. Melon

286

reminded her of herself back when she'd started. The drive, the need for attention and power, the disregard for the rules. Melon had one thing Layla had not had in those days, however. It was that essential quality of a good reporter; she was not afraid to make a fool of herself.

It also amused her that, according to Rose, Melon was involved with Matty Chiga.

The Chiga family controlled a couple of the unions involved with printing and distributing the magazine. When *Realto* started to move ahead of the competition, she had her run-ins with Matty. He was a man of such charm and slamming energy, and yet the couch pillows in his office were stencilled with pictures of his mother.

Matty muscled his way into powerful women's lives like a refugee trying to catch the last helicopter out of Saigon. After he picked their brains and enlarged his vocabulary, he rolled off on the balls of his feet with that odd rocking gait of his. No doubt he would do the same to Melon. Tra-la.

'Tra la, tra-la, tra-la,' she sang out loud, trying to ward off the returning monster. Hot tears were building at the back of her throat, triggered by the thoughts of happier times. She pictured the monster, sitting in the steaming pool of acid this time. Usually he stood, leaning on the side of her brain mocking her, clouding her vision, spitting poison into her veins.

What was in her that kept her from going to Warner before it was too late and throwing herself at his feet? Why couldn't she beg? A passionate, skin-stripping beg that would set the clock back to the day he had called her from the Concorde and sent the lavender roses and had not yet met Sloane Taylor?

Her stomach began to churn. She threw back the covers and stumbled toward the bathroom to be sick.

As she splashed cold water on her face, she glanced up and saw the Gianni Versace dressing gown she had given

287

him one Christmas. It was well-worn and had never left the room.

In a white rage she snatched it from the hook, wishing he were wearing it, and tore it to shreds.

'Kayzie, Goddamn it! You've just got to, that's all.' Melon was screaming into the pay phone on the corner of Forty-second and Lex. She was early to meet Matty for lunch and thought she'd try one more time.

'Mel, I can't,' Kayzie pleaded. 'I simply can't do it. You've only met Sloane once, for heaven's sake.'

'Twice!' Melon corrected.

'Okay, twice.'

'I met her before you did!'

'Melon, I would do it if I could. I can't ask her. It just wouldn't be right.'

'Fuck right!' Melon bellowed. 'You're her maid of honor, for shit sake. If you asked her to invite me, you know she would do it.'

'If she wanted you to be there, she would have asked you yourself,' Kayzie said. 'Lord knows there are few enough people from the bride's side.'

'That's my point, damn it, she *needs* me.'

'Melon, give me a break,' Kayzie pleaded. 'I don't understand why this is so damned important to you. It's just a little wedding in a hotel suite.'

'A little wedding!' she screamed. 'The fucking world is going to be there! They're closing off the side streets for Nancy Reagan's goddamned Secret Service contingent! Malcolm Forbes is sending a helicopter to get to the airport! You've got Brooke Astor, the Kissingers, the Sultan of Brunei . . . Jesus!'

'He's not coming,' Kayzie interrupted.

'Not funny.'

'What did you do, Mel? Go through the invitation list when I had my back turned?'

'Of course,' Melon said nonchalantly. 'What's wrong with that?'

Kayzie let out a low moan. 'Melon, ask me anything else. Ask me if you can borrow my espresso maker . . . again . . . after you return it. Ask me if you can sleep with Ryan.'

'Okay.'

'Okay what?'

'Okay, send Ryan over to get the espresso maker and I'll sleep with him.'

'Be serious, Melon,' Kayzie growled.

'I *am* serious. Serious as cancer. I'm going to get into that wedding. With you or without you. Some friend.'

'I'm sorry, Melon, truly I am.'

'Well . . . fuck you!' Melon screamed. She slammed down the phone with such force a man passing the phone booth jumped and covered his face with an upraised arm.

She'd get in, she told herself, somehow, some way she was going to observe that wedding if she had to offer to screw every one of Nancy's Secret Service men to do it.

'Hey, ease up, Baby,' Matty chortled. 'I don't like to hear you talk dirty. Gettin' into that shindig is a lot simpler than that.'

They were sitting at a dark corner table at Sparks Steak House, for years a favored wise-guy watering hole.

'What do you mean simple?' Melon snapped. 'I told you what it was going to be like. Police. TV crews, Secret Service at every door . . .'

'Baby. Baby. Baby.' Matty said, slowly shaking his head. 'When you got a problem, why don't you come to Matty, here?' He thumped his chest with his fist.

She reached across and smoothed the back of his hand. 'Darling, I know you can do just about anything, but this just can't be done.'

'Wanna bet?'

Melon's mouth flew open. She knew him well enough to know he wouldn't hint at something he couldn't do.

Matty put one knuckle under her chin and closed her mouth. 'There are a couple of restaurants in that hotel, right?'

'Yeah . . .' she said expectantly.

'Restaurants make a lot of garbage, right?'

'Yeah . . . yeah.' She nodded eagerly.

'And commercial garbage in this city is taken away by private contractors,' he teased, drawing it out.

'Matteeee, you're making me crazeeee,' she singsonged, threatening to stab the back of his hand with a fork.

'We got the contract for the Carlyle's hauling. That makes us real friendly with the staff.'

'Oooooh, Matty!' Melon squealed. 'I'm getting the picture! You are incredible, you big huggy thing, you.'

She reached under the tablecloth, unzipped his pants, and slipped her hand inside his shorts.

Matty stiffened, swivelling his head about the room, his eyes wide and rolling about in his head. 'Hey! Hey!' he said in a hoarse whisper. 'What the hell are you doin'? You crazy broad!'

She leaned toward him. Her face was less than a half-inch from his. 'You know what I'm doing, Mattykins-Boo-Boo-Bunny-Bear.'

'Quit it!' he whispered, truly panicked and turning redder by the second. 'Not here!'

'You know you don't mean that,' she cooed, working away on him until she had his full erection outside his pants. 'Matty, darling,' she breathed, pressing her cheek against his. 'Is anyone looking this way?'

Matty scanned the room. 'N . . . n . . . nnno,' he stammered.

'Then would you excuse me for a moment, dear?' she said, lifting the floor-length tablecloth and disappearing under the table.

*

Matty Chiga liked doing things for women. Women had done so much for him.

His father, Gino Chiga, had been a careless loan shark who was found floating inside an oil drum just off the Christopher Street pier when Matty was a senior in high school. After his funeral there had been a council meeting at the Chigas' semidetached two-story house in Howard Beach. Young Matty, to his great pride, was included for the first time.

Matty's uncles were also in the money-lending business. His cousins were in dope, which they referred to as pharmaceuticals. The rest of his extended family was in the construction trades and real estate. One of the several Chiga-controlled buildings in Manhattan was the sixty-four story Galaxy Towers apartment complex on the East Side.

At the meeting that night it was decided that young Matty would begin his career there as an assistant to the superintendent. He soon learned that his duties would entail those of a shakedown artist, payoff handler, and enforcer. In a building the size of the Galaxy Towers there were endless petty details to be attended to. Elevator inspectors had to be bribed, food inspectors for the two restaurants on the ground level had to be shown how to look the other way, demanding, rich tenants had to be placated when water leaks from shoddy plumbing destroyed carpeting and wall treatments.

The stocky young assistant super with his swarthy good looks and even, gleaming teeth soon became the pet of the building tenants. Most particularly the women.

Until he got to the Galaxy Towers, Matty had known only two kinds of women. Mothers with their hair in a bun and a wooden spoon in a pot, and bimbos with beehive hair, stiletto heels, and hips that moved in counterpoint to their cracking gum. The women at the

291

Galaxy Towers were another piece of work altogether. The thought of them kept him awake nights.

Awash in fur and trailing expensive perfume, they slipped passed his widening eyes on the glistening marble of the opulent lobby. Their long crimson-fingers were usually curled round the chests of tiny dogs and shopping-bag handles. Their golden-auburn-titian-pale-spun-sugar whipped-velvet hair tumbled down their backs and made it difficult for Matty to breathe.

They wore silk dresses that clung to their long, glazed legs and spoke in a voice that melted over his skin like dark, warm honey.

Matty wanted them all. Some had rich husbands, others were daughters of wealthy men, but the women he fantasized the most about were the ones who had earned their own wealth. Like Tania Jenkins-Twelve-A, a jewelry designer, or Ms Zabriski-Nineteen-D, who owned a chain of handbag stores. Then there was Mrs Bagdikian-Penthouse-C, who, so the story went among the staff, had been a nightclub singer who, when her husband died, bought a dive on Third Avenue that she turned into one of the most successful celebrity watering holes in Manhattan. Matty soon learned that when someone famous stepped out of a car in the circular driveway, they were generally headed to Penthouse C.

As he watched these ladies come and go, he hungered for all of them, though he would have considered single-limb amputation a reasonable price to have just one. He might as well have been invisible. His longing was rewarded with only an occasional smile and several twenty-dollar bills pressed nonchalantly into his sweating hand at Christmas.

Many a long night he would lie wide-awake on the lumpy cot in his basement room dreaming about them. Someday, he promised himself, he would have one on either arm. He would have one for breakfast, another for lunch, and two more for dinner and afterward. He would burrow under their silks and furs and smother in their perfume, and when he finished, they would cling to him and beg him not to leave. 'Don't leave me, Matty,' they would plead. 'Do it again, Matty.'

'Have a gold watch, Matty.'

'Have a round trip ticket to my villa in Málaga.'

'Matty, you're the best! Do me, Matty. Do me, pleeeese!'

In his dreams Matty would 'do them' like they'd never been done before, if that's what they wanted. He certainly knew how. He had been doing bimbos under the boardwalk at Coney Island since he was twelve. It wasn't the sex he cared about. He wanted to be part of the kind of world women like that lived in.

If he kept his nose clean and did this piss-boy job right, his uncle Rico would set him up in some of the family businesses. Someday he would have all the money he could spend. That wasn't the point. He wanted something the mob could never provide: the kind of woman he saw every day at the Galaxy Towers.

So he decided to begin by studying their men.

He took careful note of the clothes the men wore. Each morning he searched the building incinerator for discarded men's fashion magazines, studying the pages and tearing out pictures of suits and jackets and coats.

He offered to work overtime as a night doorman so he could hear them speak, study their haircuts and jewelry, and see how they treated their women.

He lost weight and began to work out until he was as tight and trim as any of the models in *Gentlemen's Quarterly*.

The clothes he would need would cost money. He began to build a little nest egg he didn't have to account for to anyone. The doorman's job gave him the opportunity. There were vendors to squeeze for use of the sidewalk in front of the building. There was stuff to fence for a guy on the twenty-fourth floor, girls and blow to provide for anyone who asked.

Soon word worked its way through the huge complex that Matty was the man to see for an unusual errand. His tips increased. He was quick to run out for liquor when a party ran dry or, in the case of Thirty-seven K, keep track of daytime visitors for a suspicious husband. If someone's driver went sick on Matty's day off, he made himself available.

'Saratoga, sir?' he would ask with a boyish grin. 'No problem.'

'Newark Airport? Twenty minutes tops, ma'am.'

His real break came in the form of Mrs Bagdikian-Penthouse-C and her Yorkshire terrier. The squirmy, foul-breathed, nearly hairless animal turned out to be Matty Chiga's ticket to the big time.

Mrs Helene Bagdikian, a tall, fine-boned blonde on the sunny side of fifty, swung through the front door of the Galaxy Towers on Sunday night on Matty's watch. She had a deep skier's tan and a cast on her left leg. Matty held the door while she repositioned her crutches. Her driver followed with the balding Pookie in his arms.

Mrs Bagdikian didn't even have to ask. Matty saw his chance and hopped aboard. For fifty dollars a day, her offer, Matty would be thrilled to walk Pookie. Mrs Bagdikian's big grey eyes filled with tears of gratitude when he said of course he'd take Pookie to the park. No problem.

The park was a long five blocks away and who knows if Pookie was turned loose in the basement storage room three times a day to do his thing. Dogs, thank Christ, couldn't talk. Besides, Matty needed time away from his other duties to prolong his visits when he returned Pookie.

His visits grew a moment or two longer each week. It was all a part of Matty's plan.

After the third week, Matty hosed down the storage

room, slicked back his blue-black hair, and put on a fresh black T-shirt tight enough to show the results of his daily push-ups on the basement floor. He scooped up Pookie and rode the elevator to Penthouse C, a half-smile playing on his cherubic face.

The maid answered his ring and beckoned him inside. He found Mrs Bagdikian with her leg up in the sun room and deposited the squirming dog gently in her lap.

'Matty, I don't know how I would have managed without you these past weeks.' She smiled up at him, her diamond bracelet glinting in the morning sun as she stroked the dog.

'Please,' Matty said, holding up his hand, palm out. 'I really love the little mutt. No problem.'

'I know,' she cooed. 'Isn't he adorable?'

Matty shifted on one foot and then the other. Time for the kill he thought. 'Ya know,' he said, ever so lightly, 'you've done me a great favor.'

'You mean the money? Think nothing of it.'

'I've decided I'm going to really treat myself to something I've always wanted.'

Mrs Bagdikian's thin face brightened with interest. 'How's that, Matty?'

'You're the only one I could tell this, Mrs Bagdikian,' he said, curling the corners of his mouth into a practiced boyish grin. 'Is it okay if I sit down?'

'Oh, my! Where are my manners,' she said. 'Please.'

Matty sat down on a low hassock rather than the club chair opposite her. He wanted to be able to look up at her as he spoke. 'You see,' he began just a touch sheepishly, 'I have a chance for a real good job at a friend's nightclub. Sort of a manager, ya know? I'm going for the interview next week and I need a suit real bad.'

'Why, that's wonderful! Now you have the money to get a really nice one.'

'Well,' he said, looking down at the floor, 'I thought so until I saw this picture.' He pulled a carefully folded page torn from a recent fashion magazine from his hip pocket. 'I really love this suit. I went to Korvette's, I tried Macy's — nobody carries it and I don't think I'd be happy with anything else.'

'May I see?' she said sweetly, holding out her hand. She took the page and studied it for a long moment. 'Why, Matty, you're not going to find this suit in any of those places. This is a Dici-Milano. You would only find it in the boutique on Madison. I'm afraid his suits are terribly expensive.'

She wasn't telling Matty something he didn't already know.

'I'm afraid what I pay you to care for Pookie isn't nearly enough for a Dici-Milano suit.'

Matty took back the picture, lovingly folded it, and put it back in his pocket. 'Boy, I feel like a real fool,' he said softly, standing to go.

She clapped her hands, startling Pookie off her lap with a yipe. 'I'll tell you what. I have a wonderful idea. I'm going to take you to my late husband's tailor. He can copy anything in the world. You've been so wonderful, I won't take no for an answer.'

Matty pushed his hands into the pockets of his black chinos. 'Jeez, Mrs Bagdikian, I couldn't let you do that. It wouldn't be right.'

'This isn't a moral issue, Matty. You need a suit to get a better job and I know someone who can get it for you. It's a business deal.'

Matty thought for a long moment. He bit his lower lip as though pondering her offer. What he was really thinking about was how long it was going to take him to get Mrs Bagdikian into bed. The way she was sitting, even with the cast on most of her leg, was giving out signals he well understood.

'Well,' he said, nodding his head, 'if you put it that way, Mrs Bagdikian . . .'

'Please.' She smiled up at him, her grey eyes twinkling. 'Call me Helene.'

It was at Helene Bagdikian's Fourth of July party at her house at the Hamptons that Matty met three senators and the chairman of the board of the New York Stock Exchange.

Back in Howard Beach, his uncle Rico and his cousins were becoming increasingly impressed with the new friends Gino Chiga's kid was making.

In the decade that followed there were dozens of Helene Bagdikians in Matty Chiga's otherwise rough and brutish life. He had even married one, an interior designer he elbowed away from her mob-lawyer husband. After their second child she began to look more like the women in Howard Beach than these on Park Avenue, and he began to stray in earnest.

It was not until he met the kick-ass little blonde who was working away so expertly on him under the table at Sparks Steak House that he stopped dead in his tracks.

She didn't have the long, graceful legs of the federal judge he had recently dumped nor the smarts of the tiny, dark Broadway producer he almost divorced his wife for. What Melon Tuft had that made her different from all the others was a fire in the belly that matched his own.

She was younger and noisier and far more infuriating in her personal habits than even the most neurotic women who caught his fancy. She didn't have the connections or the social clout that usually attracted him, although her involvement with the media had real potential. What Melon had was an attitude that for her there were no rules. If she wanted something, she went after it. He wondered if the day would come when he might find himself in the cross hairs of her emotional gunsight.

He didn't want to think about it. Right now he didn't want any negative thoughts to interfere with how good what she was doing felt.

16

Sloane knew she couldn't have survived the week before the wedding without Kayzie.

She was wonderful. She took all the responses from guests, kept the press at bay, worked with the Carlyle staff, and somehow managed to find the most stunning dress, which Sloane insisted on paying for.

Sloane found herself missing Warner and looking forward to his return Thursday night before the wedding. Kayzie had typed a neat list of the wedding arrangements. Sloane placed it on the library desk in the penthouse and sat down to wait for him. She was anxious to see how pleased he would be with all that they had accomplished in only a few days.

Sloane stood when she heard the front door.

He was in midconversation as he stepped into the foyer. He looked tired but tanned and handsome.

When he saw her, he quickly introduced her to his entourage, two Japanese businessmen and the head of the international banking department of the Bank of England. Standing behind them were Brian the Yuppie and of course, Miss Motherwell.

After pleasantries were exchanged, Warner handed his briefcase to Brian and asked to be excused. He turned to Sloane and without another word, guided her into the library and closed the door.

They flew into each other's arms. He smothered her mouth and eyes and neck with kisses until she was breathless. 'God, I missed you,' he said through clenched teeth.

Sloane laughed. 'We spoke every night, darling.'

'Not the same,' he said, crushing her with his long, strong arms. 'Oh,' he said, shuddering, 'you feel so good. Let's go to bed.'

Sloane tilted her head and smiled up into his face. 'Right now? You've got a roomful of people out there.'

'Let 'em wait,' he growled. 'They like waiting for me. Gives them time to scheme.'

With a single motion he picked her up and swung her into his arms.

'Where are you taking me?' She giggled, her arms tight around his neck.

'To the bedroom, of course.'

'Let's do it here on the rug,' she said mischievously.

He carried her toward the bedroom door at the other end of the library. 'You shock me!' he said in mock horror.

'I'm serious, Warner. It would be kind of sexy.'

'I shall not make love to you on the rug when we have a perfectly luxurious king-sized bed a few feet away,' he said grandly, pushing open the bedroom door with his foot.

As he approached the bed, she said, 'Don't you want a shower after your long trip? We could do it in the shower.'

He gently placed her on the bed. 'I showered on the plane.'

'The Concorde has a shower?'

Warner smiled down at her. 'I sent for my own plane. Had to cart back all those people out there.' He slipped out of his jacket and started to unbutton his shirt.

Sloane sat up and began to undress.

Somehow the spell was broken. The passion she had felt only a moment before had ebbed away. It didn't matter, she told herself, the minute Warner touched her she would feel it again.

Naked, he slipped into bed beside her and pulled her into his arms. For a while she snuggled against him, absorbing his smell, the warmth of his body, the safety she felt just being with him. 'I'm so glad you're back, darling,' she whispered against his shoulder as she ran her hand down his chest. She reached farther but he didn't respond. The sound of his breathing caught her attention. She pushed herself up on one elbow so she could see his face.

'Darling?' she said tentatively.

Warner was sound asleep.

When he awoke an hour later, befuddled and embarrassed, Sloane had showered, redone her makeup, and changed into the dressy silk suit she had brought to the penthouse, assuming they would be going out to dinner.

She was sitting in the wing chair by the window looking out at the lights going on around the edge of the park.

'Welcome back, darling,' she said brightly.

He pulled himself up in the bed, moaned, and lay back down again. 'What a jerk I am,' he said. 'Can you forgive me?'

Sloane laughed. 'Don't apologize. You must have been exhausted. We have a lifetime to catch up.' She stood and walked to the edge of the bed.

He reached out and stroked her hand. 'I can't believe I did that,' he said lightly. 'Here I am in bed with the most beautiful woman in the world and I conk out.'

Sloane smoothed his hair into place. 'I do love you so, Warner Bromley.'

'Grrr,' he said, burrowing his face into her stomach.

'Those men are still out there,' she said.

'To hell with 'em.'

'We really should go in. Miss Motherwell will have them drunk by now.'

'I hope so,' he said, releasing her. 'They'll be easier to get rid of.'

'Are we going out to dinner?'

He nodded. 'Ummm. I asked Rose to book Lutèce. I'm going to send them on ahead. I want to be alone with you,' he said, swinging his feet over the side of the bed. 'But first I want to go over your wedding plans. Is everything on schedule?'

'Absolutely,' she said. 'I think you're going to be pleased.'

It didn't take long for Warner to shower and dress, and they were soon settled in the library, where a waiter appeared with an iced bottle of Warner's private champagne.

Warner sat behind the large Regency desk, set perpendicular to the flickering fire, checking Kayzie's list. Sloane sat in the leather chair across from him, sipping her champagne and waiting.

The only sound in the room was the occasional snap from the fire and the *tap tap tap* of Warner's gold Mark Cross pen on the leather desktop.

He turned the single sheet of paper over and studied the blank back, then looked around the desktop as though there were pages missing. Removing his gold half-glasses, he asked, 'Who did you say helped you with this?'

'Kayzie Markham, Layla Bronz's assistant.'

'Ah . . . right. Right.'

'Is there something wrong?' she asked, concerned at the puzzled expression on his face.

'Do you mind if I make a few changes, darling?'

'Of course not,' she said. Her throat felt constricted – the way it had when she realized a teacher was about to discover she hadn't done her homework.

'I see you girls plan to use the hotel for just about everything.'

'Well, yes, darling. You said to.'

'Yes, but I thought the manager would know who I use for things like flowers and music . . .' His voice trailed off. 'I also think this menu is a bit too light for late afternoon.'

Sloane's mind was racing. All the work, all the phone calls and details were worked out. The wedding was set for five o'clock Saturday and here it was Thursday night. She was about to speak when Warner held up one finger.

'Would you excuse me for a minute, darling,' he said, putting his reading glasses back on. He lifted the phone and depressed the intercom button. 'Rose, would you step into the library for a moment?' he said.

Before Sloane had swallowed the next sip of champagne, Rose entered the room carrying a notebook. 'Yes, sir?' she said, ignoring Sloane's presence.

He showed her Kayzie's list, holding it while she read it over his shoulder. 'Do we still use Marina?' he asked, pointing to some notation on the page.

'Not since we did the Armco board dinner. The greens were half dead and the centerpiece didn't arrive until the second course. We switched to Hadley-Waltham.'

'And you like them?' he asked, looking up at Rose.

'Very much,' she said with a nod.

'Good, ring them,' he said, looking up over the top of his glasses at Sloane. 'What colour is your dress again, darling?'

'It's a very pale peach.' She brightened, happy to be included in what seemed an almost coded conversation.

'Right,' he said. 'Rose, get a swatch of the dress from the store. Tell Hadley-Waltham I want everything in as close to peach as they can get – roses, peonies, gladiolus, orchids if they have to. Stress that everything should be no more than one day past full bloom.'

Rose nodded.

He moved to the next item. 'I don't know this group. It says here two violins and a bass – sounds like some college amateurs. Um. Call Peter Duchin. I know it's short notice, but he'll understand. We want a small orchestra, ten musicians should do it.'

Rose was now furiously making notes.

'Get Mrs Rutledge from housekeeping up here first

thing in the morning. I want all the furniture out of the drawing room by noon. Oh, and when you speak to Hadley-Waltham, tell them I want green swags braided with peach velvet streamers around all the windows. Peach candles in standing floor holders, nothing small or low. A few hundred will do. Potted ferns in peach ceramic pots, a peach runner, or pale pink, whatever. And see what you can do about this menu.' He pointed to the next item on the list. 'We'll have Sirio do the buffet. Cancel the hotel food. We'll keep their waiters and bartenders. See that Waterford is used on the bar, not those dreadful hotel glasses. Also ask security to hold one elevator just for guests. I want everyone met by valets at the curb and escorted, Okay?'

'Right away,' Rose said, smoothing the curve of her immaculate silver pageboy.

Sloane thought of all the work under way in the kitchens downstairs. She had checked with the banquet manager earlier in the day, and they had already started preparing the food. Now, here Warner was cancelling it. He must be aware they would charge him for it. It didn't seem to matter.

'Did you reach Jean-Baptiste?' Warner said, still addressing Rose.

'Yes. He will be at the Nice airport to meet you. They're all ready for you at the villa.'

'Did you arrange for a personal maid for Sloane?'

Rose's lips tightened as she nodded. 'Yes.'

'Excellent,' he said, smiling for the first time since he and Sloane had entered the room. 'One more thing, Rose. Would you call Lutèce and tell them we're delayed. I want to spend a few more moments with Sloane.'

Sloane waited until Rose left the room. She felt like a naughty child who was about to be punished.

'I'm sorry, Warner,' she said softly. 'We really tried.'

'You did beautifully, darling,' he said. His voice was a bit too loud. It was a parent's voice speaking to a proud, unknowing child who had just washed his tuxedo in the bath tub.

'I thought you would be pl –'

'Now,' he said. He wasn't even listening to her. He swivelled his chair around to the wall safe beside the desk, spun the combination, and took out a long, flat object.

Oh, Lord, she thought, *what's coming now? Is he going to spank me with a ruler?*

He stood and moved around the desk with it in his hand. 'I'm sorry Rose didn't have a chance to have this wrapped, but I want you to have it now so you can wear it on Saturday.' He handed her a long, flat leather box. 'Happy wedding day, my darling girl,' he said, gently brushing his lips against hers.

It was a bib of diamonds. Dozens and dozens of diamonds mounted at intervals on gold chains as fine as angel hair so that when she held it against her skin the chain seemed to disappear.

'Darling!' she said, truly astonished at the beauty of the necklace.

'I thought you'd like to wear it with your wedding dress,' he said.

'Of course,' Sloane said, bending as though to look at the necklace but wanting to hide her expression of deflation. *Isn't he going to let me do anything?* she thought, holding back tears that she knew would only confuse him. What was wrong with the plans she and Kayzie had made? It wouldn't have been so bad if he hadn't asked in the first place, but he had, and now he was changing everything. Did she have such terrible taste?

She rubbed her thumb against one of the diamonds. She looked up at Warner, who was still beaming, moving his gaze from the necklace to her face. The expression of pure adoration on his handsome features made her feel guilty. He hadn't meant to demean her. He couldn't have.

Not the way he was looking at her. He was just a man who had always done things his own way.

Her heart melted. All the bad thoughts disappeared as she reached for him. 'Of course,' she repeated with more enthusiasm. 'Of all the wonderful things you've given me, this is the most beautiful. I love it and I love you.'

He kissed her lightly on the cheek and returned to his desk.

Sloane watched him as he passed the bar. 'Darling,' she said lightly, 'while you're up, would you pour me a brandy?'

He turned and frowned at the champagne flute she'd left on the coffee table. It was still half full. 'You don't want your champagne?'

'Ah, well, sure . . .'

'Then finish your champagne and I'll get you a brandy.'

She stared at him, debating whether to say anything. All she could manage was a soft, 'Yes, Warner.'

Cole awoke Saturday morning with a throbbing head, as usual, caused by martinis followed by wine, followed by champagne, and lastly after-dinner brandy. He had managed to imbibe all this liquor at one of the most unusual prewedding dinners he'd ever attended. Warner's best man had originally intended to fete the small wedding party with a gala dinner at Bellini's. Sometime around five o'clock, however, Kayzie got a call from Rose Motherwell saying that the groom and his lawyer, who was also the best man, were tied up in some crucial negotiations with some visiting Japanese. There was a business crisis and they wouldn't be able to make dinner.

Without Warner present Kayzie felt the younger group would be more comfortable at a more relaxed restaurant, and she moved the festivities to Joe Allen's, a pub in the theatre district.

When Cole arrived, he had found Kayzie, Ryan, Sloane, and Alan, Layla's hairdresser. Kayzie introduced Cole to Ryan and was about to do the same for Alan when Cole interrupted and said they were acquainted. Cole had never paid much attention to Alan when their paths crossed in Layla's dressing room, but now, in this light, dressed as he was in a smashing designer outfit, Cole could see that the young man deserved closer inspection.

They seemed to have been standing at the bar drinking for quite a while and were having a riotously good time.

Cole deliberately took the empty stool next to Alan. Cole felt a stirring he had not experienced in years. The boy was a beauty.

As Ryan held the girls' rapt attention with a long shaggy-dog story, Cole and Alan fell into an easy conversation. It was really the first time they'd talked. Cole's only contact with Alan before had been hurried greetings as he rushed in and out of Layla's dressing room lugging his hairstyling supplies.

'We're all drinking champagne,' Alan said. 'How about you?'

'Sounds good.'

'And the price is right,' Alan said laughingly. 'Kayzie and Ryan are buying.' He signalled the bartender, who was already wiping off another champagne flute.

'How long have you been doing Sloane's hair?' Cole asked.

'Oh, I'm not her hairdresser, really. We both escaped L.A. together. We were high school chums.'

Cole studied Alan as he rattled on about their days growing up in Los Angeles. He was looking at Alan carefully for the first time, smiling to himself. Sitting there next to him with his tight little athlete's body and outré blond pigtail was the beautiful boy Cole had spent the seventies searching for in Rio at carnival, New Orleans before Lent, the Greek islands, in the bathhouses, the

Pines and Provincetown, in Village bars and the park Ramble.

He would stagger home from the magazine, eat dinner, and set his clock for four-thirty in the morning so he could arrive at the downtown discos fresh. Those still dancing were stoned and young enough to have lasted the night. He would stand at the back of the dark dance floor until he spotted Mr Right. He had to be blond, have a sweet face and a tight athlete's body. He left many discos with many boys. All of them Mr Not Quite Right.

By the early eighties, Cole ran out of steam. There was so much sex and not a breath of love. The jackbooted clones that marched down Christopher Street each night began to look like human dildos to him. The baths seemed fetid, oozing invisible microbes. It was all so meaningless. Cole's change of heart came, ironically, as the Black Plague with its tortured, inappropriate name started to strike down the boys.

Then Gary, his art director and former lover, started getting spike-high fevers and spending more and more time at home. 'Gay cancer,' he told Cole after Cole insisted he see a doctor. That's what they called it then. Occasionally he heard the phrase 'Karposi's sarcoma.' A writer for the magazine in San Franciso told him there were over a hundred cases there. Gary held on for a year, and in the spring of '83 he died. Deaf and blind, he had weighed eighty pounds. Cole was devastated. He sought out and read everything published about AIDS, a lot of it infuriatingly conflicting. As he put each publication aside, he told himself he should be checked, but his sense of denial in those days was still aggressively functioning. Layla hectored him to be tested. His argument against it was, 'If I've got it, I don't want to know.' Her argument was, 'If you've got it *I* want to know.'

Then Sherman, what whom Cole shared a summer rental in the Pines, died. Soon Ed and Dennis and Paul and Philip got sick. Cole spent his days at work and his nights at hospitals trying to be droll and witty. He went to funerals and memorials, and finally, he went to the doctor for a complete workup.

Somehow he got through the days of waiting for the test results. They were the worst in his life. Valium and vodka became his new best friends. During those dark, endless days he promised himself that if he escaped, he would become a monk. He would go back to the church. He would take in the homeless, tithe to the Gay Men's Health Crisis, and start to jog. He was ready to make any pact with the devil or God, whichever had the guarantee of a longer life.

'You're fine,' the doctor had said over the phone one rainy Friday afternoon. 'Your blood pressure's a little elevated. Mind your salt intake.'

Cole's first reaction after he hung up was anger. Didn't the damn fool know what he had been through? Didn't he have any sympathy for his days on Death Row? He had poured himself an enormous brandy with shaking hands.

Later he sat in the very back of a nearly deserted bar and sobbed quietly. He cried for himself, for his friends, for the Mr Right he would never know, and for the extra time he had been given. He tried to remember the old litany. 'Hail Mary, full of grace . . .' he had begun.

'And how about you?' Alan asked.

Cole started. 'Huh?'

'Where did you grow up?'

Cole took a mouthful of champagne to get his head together. 'Sorry, ah, here, on the East Side. East Sixty-fourth Street, as a matter of fact. My father was a banker.'

'So you were here in the seventies, you lucky guy,' Alan said.

'Yeah, lucky. One big party. But as the Marvelettes used to sing, there were too many fish in the sea.'

'You been tested?' Alan asked abruptly.

Cole turned and stared at him. He wished the boy didn't have those huge blue eyes. He wished he were an ugly troll of a thing that he could dismiss. Of course he would ask a question like that. He was Sloane's age, for God's sake. 'Yes. I'm fine,' he said softly.

Alan grinned at him. 'Me, too,' he said. 'I'm fine too and I'm going to stay that way.'

'Hey, you guys,' Kayzie's voice called from the door leading to the dining room. 'We're starved. You joining us or what?'

Cole reached for his champagne glass and slipped off the barstool. 'We joining them, or what?'

'Let's join them and worry about "or what" later.'

Cole's heart stirred. Maybe life wasn't all work after all. Maybe Mr Right wasn't dead after all. He had just been busy growing up in California.

As soon as they were seated and more champagne was poured, the toasting began.

Ryan started with a very funny and slightly blue limerick dedicated to the happy couple. Then Kayzie toasted Sloane sweetly, speaking of new friendships and dreams coming true. Alan, designating himself 'best boy', reminisced about Sloane's decidedly unusual childhood.

Cole had never seen Sloane more relaxed and animated. He wondered if she would have been quite as loose if Warner had been there. It was not until Alan started telling tales about Sloane's mother, Noreen, that Cole noticed Sloane's mood changing. She stopped smiling and stared into her champagne glass.

In the middle of Alan' story Sloane suddenly interrupted him. 'We haven't heard from the father of the bride yet,' she said, gesturing toward Cole.

On the way to the restaurant he had kicked himself for getting suckered into a major role in this melodrama. He both admired and felt sorry for Sloane. Kayzie had told him a bit of her background: father dead in some freak accident when she was just a kid, pushy stage mother who organized her life and remarried just when Sloane needed her the most. Maybe that's what provided her with some deep inner core that sustained her. She was a winner. Cole liked winners. What else could explain his years of loyalty to Layla? Every time he was ready to throw in the towel on *Realto*, Layla did something gutsy and brave. He saw a little of that in Sloane Taylor. She had taken on the toughest town in the world alone at eighteen and here she was marrying Warner Bromley. Was it a match made in heaven? Probably not. Was it breathtaking in its scope and worth a ringside seat? You bet.

Alan reached for his drink, refilled by the waiter when he saw Cole stand, and glanced across the table. Alan watched him intently. For Cole just looking at Alan dispatched any lingering misgivings about being there.

Everyone at the table was waiting for him to speak. He cleared his throat and raised his glass toward Sloane. 'To the future Mrs Warner Bromley,' he said. 'May your new life be as beautiful as you are.'

Everyone cheered and raised their glasses. 'To Sloane,' they all cried in unison.

Cole sat down, glanced at Alan, and shrugged as if to say, 'That's the best I can do.'

Alan grinned and patted his palms together in silent tribute, probably to Cole's brevity. If he was feeling the way Cole was, the quicker this whole charade could be wrapped up the better. What was left of the evening, he hoped, belonged to discovery for both of them.

Ryan, who was getting visibly drunk, started to sing and everyone joined in. In the racket of good feeling around the table Cole noticed that there were tears in Sloane's eyes. He attributed it to bridal jitters.

He had planned to say something about how lucky she was.

Something had stopped him.

Lying in bed now, recreating the evening, he realized

310

what had stopped him was the image of Melon Tuft's pugnacious little face.

He rolled over and checked the illuminated time. The menacing little clock read 2:33. He was bushed.

In the back of his mind he had hoped that he and Alan would get together after the party. Now he was glad they hadn't. It was better this way, more intriguing.

He drifted off smiling as he remembered the look on Alan's face as they said good-night outside the restaurant. Alan had handed him a slip of paper. Cole didn't have to look at it to know it was his phone number.

17

Warner had arranged for a long, pure-white limousine to transport the wedding party from Kayzie's house to the hotel. Sloane had not wanted to spend her last night alone in the Carlyle. After the wedding dinner, she and Kayzie had gone back to the little apartment, where they would dress for the late-afternoon ceremony.

Cole, looking smashing in black tie, picked them up at four o'clock sharp in the block-long car.

When they reached the corner of Madison and East Seventy-sixth Street, the side street was blocked by police barricades. Only vehicles with riders whose names were on a guard's checklist were permitted onto the block. New York City police and private security guards kept the press and TV cameras well back from the entrance of the hotel. Secret Service agents mingled about on the sidewalk with walkie-talkies in hand.

The white limousine was waved through immediately and slowed to a stop under the canopy of the Carlyle.

Cole stepped out first and offered his hand to Kayzie. She looked very pretty in a rust-colored silk sheath. Alan had swept her dark blonde hair on top of her head and ingeniously entwined a cloud of baby's breath. Cole had never seen Kayzie in full makeup and made a point of telling her she should do it more often. She looked quite glamorous.

The reporters, sensing that Sloane would be next,

312

surged toward the car door, hollering, 'Here she comes! That's her.'

As she alighted from the car, motor drives whirred, microphones stabbed the air around her, and guards bellowed, 'Stand back, stand back.'

Sloane stood beside the car for almost five minutes, collecting herself as the photographers recorded her image. She seemed unfazed by the commotion, as cool and regal as a lily. Her dark hair was pulled back under a head-hugging cap of peach silk and jewels that matched the jewels embroidered on the huge puffed sleeves of her dress. The low afternoon sun flickered rainbows of light off the rows and rows of diamonds that cascaded from throat to cleavage.

Gawkers and sidewalk onlookers gasped, then spontaneously broke into applause.

Sloane smiled and waved tentatively. She moved, swanlike, up the white canvas runner that ran from curb to door. Cole felt he would never see anyone quite as awesome again. She was more than a bride. She was like some fairy-tale princess come to life.

A wedge of hotel security men surrounded them as Sloane, Kayzie, and Cole, followed by the hotel photographer, were quickly escorted through the lobby. Along the sides of the lobby stood the hotel staff. They also applauded at the sight of Sloane.

The party was led to the private-for-the day elevator and were whisked to Sloane's suite one floor below the penthouse.

To Cole's delight Alan was waiting in the living room when they entered.

Sloane squealed and ran to him. 'Alan! How did you get here?'

'Oh . . . my,' he said softly, holding her at arm's length for a moment. 'Let me look at you! You are incandescent. I think I'm going to cry.'

'I'm so glad you're here,' she said. 'You said at the apartment they wouldn't let anyone up.'

'She put the fix in.' Alan grinned, pointing to Kayzie.

'I thought you'd want Alan here until the last minute,' Kayzie said, handing Sloane a glass of champagne.

'Where's Ryan?' Sloane asked.

'Upstairs looking for the scotch.'

They had hardly finished their first glass of champagne when a guard appeared at the open door. 'Mr Latimer?'

'Yes?' Cole said, turning toward the door.

'They're starting, sir. Would you take your party upstairs now? We're holding the elevator.'

'So soon?' Kayzie said, setting the glass on the coffee table. 'Quick, Sloane. Let me check you out. Cole, get the flowers, would you? They just arrived. They're on the counter in the bathroom.'

Cole stepped to the bathroom and carefully lifted a trailing sweep of white roses and baby's breath wrapped in cellophane from the counter.

'Don't forget the short one,' Kayzie called. 'That's mine. Your carnation is in there, too.'

They rode to the penthouse in silence.

As they stepped off the elevator, they could hear the Peter Duchin orchestra playing Mozart from the drawing room. Through the double door Cole could see that the room was full. It had once been a rooftop ballroom, and emptied of furniture, save several dozen gold chairs, the acoustics were that of a vast concert hall.

Hundreds of freestanding candelabra were set at intervals around the entire room. It was just turning dusk. The blue light from the sky over the park beyond the high, arched windows was the colour of lapis lazuli. The masses of candles were the only other source of light. Hundreds and hundreds of flickering points of fire were repeated in the high gloss of the floor and the window glass. The effect was so ethereal Cole thought he was about to step into a golden dream world.

Kayzie, holding a nosegay of roses and baby's breath, positioned herself to step off ahead of the bride.

'There's Mrs Reagan,' Cole whispered over her shoulder. 'Way down in front with the black mink hat.'

A man from the Carlyle staff wearing a tuxedo addressed the group. 'All set,' he said.

Cole checked himself in the long, gilt mirror of the foyer. 'All set,' he said.

The man in the tuxedo signalled the orchestra.

Cole turned to Sloane. 'You ready, love?'

'Can you see Warner? He's down there, isn't he?' she said anxiously.

Cole chuckled. 'Yes, my darling, he's there.'

The orchestra struck up Mendelssohn's 'Wedding March.' Quickly Sloane turned to Cole and kissed his cheek. 'Thank you, Cole,' she said. 'Thank you for being here for me. You'll never know how grateful I am.'

He found himself unable to respond. His throat closed. For the first time in many years he tasted the beginning of sentimental tears and had to look away from her radiant face.

As heads turned to face the door, he stepped forward. Sloane floated beside him, head high, shoulders back. Her eyes were fixed on the tall, greying man standing ramrod straight at the end of the aisle.

Cole had to admit he wouldn't have missed this for the world. This had to be the wedding of the year, and he was thoroughly enjoying being a part of the supporting cast.

As they moved through the golden light, awash in music, he glanced down at the shimmering creature on his arm. Suddenly he felt very protective. The thought of Layla's plan to do a destructive article on Sloane floated like a tiny black cloud across his mind. He had long experience in Layla's reaction to being talked out of something she had set her mind on, and it wasn't pleasant. Perhaps there was some way to talk her out of it, but figuring out how to do it would take more concentration than he was capable of at the moment. They had nearly reached the end of the aisle.

As they approached the flower-bedecked altar, Warner took a step toward them. He reached for Sloane's hand as Cole released her and stepped aside, silently grateful that the service, at Warner's request, would not include the old who-giveth-this-woman routine. That would only have compounded Cole's guilt.

As the black-robed judge began to speak, Cole fixed a smile on his face, hoping anyone watching would believe he thought little Mary Sloane Taylor from Bakersfield, California, was the luckiest girl in the world.

In the library, just off the ballroom, Melon's scalp was beginning to sweat. She forced her index finger under the vinyl wig and scratched.

In a moment or two some of the most important people in the world would be gliding into the room. White-gloved waiters stood at attention against the far wall. The long table behind which she was standing was laden with more elegant food than any freeload she had ever crashed.

When she heard the music triumphantly signalling the end of the wedding service, she straightened her white lace collar and quickly removed a speck of béarnaise from her black nylon uniform.

She watched as Sloane and Warner, Warner's best man, Kayzie, and Cole formed a small receiving line in the foyer and began to greet their guests. She had to squint to see through the cheap white plastic frames perched on her nose. When she thought anyone was looking her way, she kept her head down and rearranged the already perfect alignment of the silver meat servers on the tray of sliced filet mignon that she was assigned to tend.

From time to time she smiled at the two cute Secret

316

Service men stationed on either side of the library door. They had thin white wires running from one ear to their lapels. As soon as Nancy Reagan, escorted by Gregory Peck, came through the line, the agents followed her into the room, maintaining a discreet distance as she chatted with other guests.

Once through the line, people moved past Melon and headed toward the bar. She stepped back a pace as Warner and Sloane swept by arm in arm, gazing into each other's eyes as though they were the only people alive.

Behind them walked Kayzie and Ryan. Then came Cole escorting Layla Bronz in a black Chanel suit dripping with chains and ropes of pearls. Melon knew Layla would come.

People seemed to want to talk and drink first, and there was little action at the end of the buffet. She looked up from refolding a pile of cocktail napkins and saw Cole making his way straight toward her.

She took a smaller plate and served him a slice of filet. Silently he gestured to the sauce boat of béarnaise. He shook his head and began to move on to the cold cracked crab.

She couldn't resist. '*Pssst*,' she hissed.

Cole's head snapped toward her. 'I beg your pardon?' he said, looking perturbed. 'Did you hiss at me?'

'It's me, Cole,' she said in a stage whisper.

Cole squinted at her in the candlelight. 'Melon, is that you? Jesus wept!' he explained. 'What in the world do you think you're doing?'

'Sh!' she said, pulling her head down as Malcolm Forbes stepped to the table. She served him a slice of filet and plopped on some béarnaise. He nodded at Cole and stepped around him.

'This is outrageous, Melon!' Cole said sharply. 'Good God! What's that on your face?'

'Warts.' She peeled a rubbery spot off her chin. 'Kids love 'em. I got these at Woolworth's when I got the wig.'

Cole handed his plate of red meat back to Melon. 'Here. I think I'm going to be sick.'

'You look great in the monkey suit, Cole,' she said, scraping his untouched meat back onto the serving platter.

Cole watched in disgust. 'Does Layla know what you're doing?' he asked.

'Sure. That's why she's here. When I told her what I was going to do, she said she wouldn't miss this for the world.'

'But why, Melon? The place is crawling with cops. You're going to end up in the slammer and if you dare . . .' He shook his fist at her. 'If you tell them you're here on assignment for Layla, I'll deny it and you can rot!'

Melon didn't like being threatened. 'Cool your jets, Latimer,' she said in a low, menacing voice. 'I can't do a piece on Sloane unless I'm at her wedding.'

'I should call the cops,' he said, looking around the room.

'What for? I didn't spit in your food. I'm here as a legitimate waitress. Go ask the banquet manager, asshole.' Suddenly her face brightened. She had another customer. As she smiled, she could feel one of the rubber warts moving higher on her cheek. 'Hello!' she crooned. 'May I serve you some delicious filet? It's from Le Cirque.'

Mrs William F Buckley and Kitty Carlisle shook their heads politely and moved on, champagne flutes in hand.

'Don't know why I bother,' Melon said, tossing the serving fork back on the platter. 'Those women never eat. Look at them!'

Cole took a long, deep breath and exhaled slowly. 'All right, Melon,' he said. 'But for pity's sake, behave.'

She ignored him, looked over his shoulder, and cooed, 'Hello! May I serve you some delicious filet? It's from Le Cirque.'

'Don't tell people it's from Le Cirque,' Cole said after the guest walked on.

'Why not?'

'Because it's tacky!'

'Yeah, I know,' she said, tugging at her wig. 'It shakes 'em up.'

Cole flattened the heel of his hand against his forehead and walked away.

As the guests began to move back into the other room to watch Sloane and Warner take the first dance, Melon glanced around to see that no one was watching.

She slipped the platter of prime filet mignon over the side of the table and tipped its contents into a large plastic shopping bag.

As a crescent moon hung over Central Park, a tiny helicopter fluttered like a dragonfly over the wide terrace atop the Carlyle. Alerted by the sound and the sweeping landing light that flashed through the ballroom windows, guests stopped dancing and rushed excitedly to watch.

The tiny craft hovered in midair, suspended directly above the broadest part of the terrace, seesawing back and forth as though the pilot were making up his mind where to put down. As the excited guests cheered, it began its descent onto the flagstones of the terrace directly in front of them. The roar of the rotary blade all but drowned out the music. Its arrival was Warner's surprise for Sloane for which he had received special FAA permission.

Sloane and Warner walked arm in arm through the ballroom followed by Kayzie and Ryan, who had slipped away earlier to help the couple change and prepare to leave.

Security guards opened the French doors leading out onto the terrace. The crisp night air billowed the damask draperies as people reached to hold them back.

As the bridal couple reached the side of the helicopter, they turned and waved.

The pilot stepped out and shook hands with them both. He handed Warner the helmet he was wearing. Sloane and Warner both wore long trench coats that whipped around their legs in the high wind. Warner helped his bride into the passenger seat, then stepped in himself and took the controls.

The waltz music ended, and as Warner revved the engines, the magical little bubble started to rise. A rocking 'Your Love Lifts Me Higher' boomed into the night air. Even Nancy Reagan stood on tiptoe and jumped ecstatically up and down with the other guests as the craft rose into the night sky, turned, banked, and swept out over the East River.

At JFK they would board his private jet. By dawn they would have landed on the azure coast of southern France.

Ryan put his arm around Kayzie's waist and guided her back into the ballroom. Pinned to the shoulder of her dress was the tiny bumblebee pin with ruby eyes and pavé diamond wings Sloane had given her moments before.

Cole watched the dramatic departure from the window near the bandstand with a lump in his throat.

Alan stood just behind him, so close his chin brushed Cole's shoulder. 'Lucky girl,' Alan said wistfully.

'Um,' Cole said, looking straight ahead. 'Lucky. I sure hope she's going to be able to handle all that luck.'

Dawn was breaking over the sea far below as the Citroën climbed higher and higher into the hills above Cap Ferrat to Warner's estate, Vue à Vol d'Oiseau. The whole world was layered shades of blue. Far, far out where the skyline met the Mediterranean Sea the water was indigo. Nearer the shore, it was powder blue like the sky. The air rushing into the backseat smelled of the lavender blooming along the edge of the road.

The crisp, thin air was helping to clear Sloane's head of the wedding champagne and drinks on Warner's plane.

Fortunately, she had been able to nap in the double bed in the rear compartment during the crossing.

There hadn't been much else to do. After drinks and dinner, Warner excused himself and spent most of the trip on the phone to Tokyo and London. The business deal that kept him from their wedding supper was now delaying their honeymoon.

She half-expected to see Rose and Brian on the plane. To her great relief there was only the flight crew and the two stewards she remembered from the flight back from Bermuda.

As the car reached a flat meadow in the hills, she sank back into the plush leather of the backseat and rested her head on Warner's shoulder.

'I hope you like the old place,' he said, burying his face in her hair. 'I bought it in the midseventies from an ancient old count. His family had lived up here since the sixteenth century. I had a pool and an office wing put in, but other than that very little else had been done to it.'

'It's so beautiful up here,' Sloane said. 'And so high. I feel as though I'm still in the plane.'

'Ah, nice work, Jean-Baptiste,' Warner said, addressing the driver as the car slowed and turned into a driveway marked by an arched stone gate.

Warner turned to Sloane. 'Jean-Baptiste seems to have had the gate whitewashed in your honour.'

Sloane leaned foward. 'Thank you, Jean-Baptiste. They look beautiful.'

'*Madame Bromley dit, merci, Jean-Baptiste, la porte est belle,*' Warner said.

The driver nodded, staring straight ahead.

'That's the first time I've been called that.' Sloane smiled, squeezing his hand. 'The stewards on your plane all called me madam.'

'What would you prefer to be called, darling?'

'How about just plain Sloane?'

'Ummmm. I think not, sweetheart. Particularly not

321

here. All the servants are terribly Old World. They'll want to call you *madame*, too.'

'All the servants?' Sloane said, surprised. 'I thought it was just Jean-Baptiste and a maid for me, although heaven knows what I need her for.'

'Oh, no-no-no. The house has some thirty rooms. And the grounds alone take a half-dozen men. Then there's the mill, the vineyards, and the cattle.'

Sloane was beginning to learn that she should assume nothing about her new life. Warner seemed to enjoy surprising her and told her very little beforehand. It was not like her to ask a lot of questions. She felt perhaps that was why Warner loved her, because she accepted things unquestioningly.

'So how many others will be on our honeymoon?' she asked, carefully keeping her tone light.

Warner chuckled. 'In the house itself there is a cook, and of course Jean-Baptiste, who is butler, driver, majordomo. Then there are three girls from the village who clean and do the marketing with the cook. Don't fret, my love, you won't even know they're there.'

As soon as the car pulled up in front of the house, two black-and-tan Dobermans bounded out of the front door and leapt on Warner. Jean-Baptiste subdued the over-joyed beasts and shooed them back into the house.

The outside of the mansion reminded her a little of Fletcher's transported château from so long ago. Inside it was quite another story. She didn't know what she expected. Something a bit more modern, maybe. This wasn't exactly a crumbling ruin, but it looked as though it had not been painted for a century. The weathered stone on the outside was partially covered with vines and a grey-green moss. From what she could see from the great reception hall where Jean-Baptiste piled their luggage, the rooms were large and spare with a few very old French country pieces scattered about. The floors were made of wide wood planks worn smooth by years of foot traffic. All the rooms had high-double windows that were opened to the steady lavender-scented breeze that moved the sheer white curtains in cloudlike billows.

She could see why Warner loved it so. There was a feeling of serenity about the broad meadows, the endless sky, and silver-leafed cypress trees that stood in long, straight rows like sentries around the property. From the front of the house, far in the distance she could see the great curve of a bay. Still farther out, on the horizon line, she saw two huge tankers that looked like bathtub toys making their way east to Genoa and on to Istanbul.

Warner introduced her to the unsmiling staff standing at respectful attention in the foyer. They wore rough country clothes and spoke not a word of English. Sloane could see that if they were going to spend much time here, she would have to learn to speak French.

Each servant bowed to her in turn, and then they all vanished to carry on with their duties. The cook returned to the kitchen wing, the village girls went back to whatever they dusted or swept. A pretty teenage girl in a black dress and thick cotton stockings stayed behind to see to Sloane's bags.

Warner kissed Sloane tenderly as the young girl waited on the stairs with her back discreetly turned. 'The maid will show you up to our room, darling. You get some rest,' he said. 'I'll be up in a bit. I need to check the telex in the office.'

'I'd love to see your office, Warner. Where is it?'

'It's an exact replica of the one in Bermuda,' he said, releasing her. 'Nothing exciting. You go on and get unpacked. I promise I'll be right up.'

Sloane was just about to fall asleep when she felt his weight on the other side of the linen-covered bed. She stirred and turned over into his arms. No words were needed to express what they both were feeling. At last they were together. There were no phones in the room, no meetings to rush to, no pressing business to attend to.

They had their own world at last, endless time in the blue air moving up from the sea to explore each other. As his hands caressed her body, she melted into him. How she loved this man who had brought her to this beautiful place, this beautiful life and safety at last.

They made love and slept most of the day. As darkness fell, they rose as if sleepwalking. They bathed and dressed without speaking, neither wanting to break the magic that engulfed them.

Jean-Baptiste was waiting beside the car in the drive-way, but Warner told him he could go. It was a beautiful evening and they wanted to walk to the village. They dined under the weeping willow trees that surrounded the terrace of a nearby centuries-old country inn. After dinner Warner asked her if she wanted to walk through the village.

They both knew the answer was no. They both wanted to go right back to bed.

The bedroom had been tidied and the linens changed in their absence. An iced bottle of champagne and two glasses sat on the night table. The last thing she noticed before she was in his arms again was the trail of their hastily removed clothes leading from the door to the bed.

The next two days were the happiest of Sloane's life. They saw no one but fleeting glimpses of the servants. They drove the winding country roads in an old red jeep, stopping to drink wine in the little inns, to walk on the pure white sand of the beach, and sleep away the hazy afternoons. When Warner reluctantly had to go to his office, she would stretch out in a hammock under the cypress trees and read or daydream.

Wednesday Sloane awoke and tried to open her eyes. She couldn't. She was paralysed with fear. She thought she was suffocating. When she opened her mouth to scream, no sound came out. Someone in white was standing over her holding a gas mask on the nose and mouth. Worse than not being able to breathe was the panic. She was held down by wide leather straps across her thighs and chest. Even her wrists were bound with something. Through the blinding light that surrounded her she heard a voice saying, 'It's all right, Mrs Taylor, we'll have your little girl's tonsils out in no time.'

Sloane's eyes flew open. The glaring white tile of the hospital room in her dream disappeared. She looked around her, completely disoriented. She didn't recognize the room. 'Where am I?' she said to no one.

'*Oui, madame?*' a soft voice somewhere outside the room answered.

'Hello! Who's there?'

'*Je m'appelle Clementine,*' said the soft voice.

'Oh,' Sloane sank back against the pillows in relief. The village girl stood in the door. Evidently she was saying her name was Clementine. Surely she wouldn't enter the room with the two of them in bed! 'Warner,' she said, turning. The other side of the bed was empty.

'What time is it please, Clementine?' she asked.

The girl didn't answer or move.

Damn, Sloane thought. Of course, the girl spoke only French. Her watch was still on the bathroom shelf where she had left it. She could tell from the sunlight outside the open door leading to the balcony that it must be late morning.

She wished she knew how to tell the girl she didn't need anything. Why hadn't she paid attention in high school French. 'A . . .' She racked her brain and came up with. 'Ah . . . *merci, Clementine,*' she said haltingly. 'Ah . . . *au revoir.*'

The girl looked baffled, turned, and disappeared. *Oh, God,* Sloane thought. *I've just told her good-bye! She must think I'm either rude or crazy.*

Sloane swung out of the high bed and sat on the edge for a moment to collect herself. She padded to the tall armoire on the far wall. When she opened it, she felt even more guilty about what she had said to Clementine. As usual, the beautiful things she and Kayzie had bought that silly, tipsy afternoon at Bloomingdale's were all pressed and hung. Next to them on a row of shelves were her accessories, hats, scarfs, and lingerie carefully folded in tissue paper. Her shoes and handbags lay beneath the shelves in perfect order. Everything was color co-ordinated like a department store display.

She slipped into the silk robe that matched her nightgown and walked to the bathroom to get her watch.

Two o'clock! No wonder Warner wasn't around, the day was half over. How could she have slept so long? She smiled, telling herself that being well loved and worry free is the world's best sleeping pill.

She dressed quickly in a pair of white linen slacks, sandals, and a black cashmere T-shirt. She pulled a comb through her tangled hair, swept a blusher brush over her cheeks, carefully outlined her lips, and added a dark pink gloss. It wouldn't do to think that just because they were married she was letting herself go. She expertly applied eye makeup, lengthening her already long lashes with mascara. She smiled at her reflection and had to admit she looked wonderful, more relaxed and happier than she had in a long time.

The only sound from outside was from a slight breeze rustling the leaves of the cypress trees. In the distance, somewhere in the valley below the house, she could hear a dog barking.

As she crossed the beamed dining room to reach the office wing, she heard voices. Mercifully, they were speaking English.

She stopped for a moment. It was a familiar voice.

Now a man was speaking.

She stepped through the door to see Warner seated at the long table that served as his desk. Seated on the other side of the table with their backs to her were Rose

326

Motherwell, Brian the Yuppie, and the red-haired public relations woman who had arranged her press conference. Sloane could hardly believe her eyes.

Seeing her enter, Warner stood. 'There you are, my sleeping beauty!' he exclaimed exuberantly. He stepped around the desk and opened his arms. 'Come, darling, and say hello to everybody.'

Sloane stepped into his embrace and hugged him for a moment. 'Why didn't you wake me?' she said softly. He quickly released her. She glanced around the table trying to smile as though she were delighted to see everyone. 'Hello, Rose . . . Brian,' she said, then paused.

'You remember Hildy Bornstein, don't you?' Warner boomed.

Sloane nodded at the red-headed woman. 'Hello, Hildy,' she said, 'this is a surprise.'

Hildy rose half out of her chair to shake hands and said, 'Hi, Sloane. Congratulations.'

Sloane stood awkwardly beside the table wondering if she should sit down.

'Darling,' Warner said. 'Please, join us.'

Sloane took the only empty chair.

'Actually, Sloane, this meeting is about you,' Warner said. 'I was going to wake you up in a moment.'

'Me?' Sloane looked from face to face in bewilderment.

'There was a telex from Rose last night. Your tour has been moved up. I asked Rose and Brian to bring Hildy over for a meeting. No way was I going to ask you to leave here.'

'When did you arrive?' Sloane asked Rose, once again overwhelmed by Warner's power to make people jump.

'This morning on the Air France flight to Nice,' Rose said, sounding inordinately pleased with herself.

Sloane wondered how Rose stood the indignity of flying a commercial airplane. She turned to Warner. 'But why was my tour moved up? What happened?'

'You see, Sloane, dear,' Hildy said in a too-brisk voice

327

designed to impress Warner, 'we've been stalling the media since your press conference, thinking we had more time. It now looks like we can't keep them on hold. We've already lost the *Today* show. We have *Good Morning America* but –'

Rose interrupted, reading from her ever present spiral notebook. 'We're in the process of booking thirty cities. You'll leave a week from today on March nineteenth. In each city you'll have a press conference and do the local TV and print interviews, as well as in-store promotions. Layla Bronz is arranging for you to have a press aide on the tour.'

'I know. Melon Tuft told me,' Sloane said. 'I was delighted.'

'Layla has also volunteered to pay Melon a fee as well as taking care of Alan Wade's expenses. I think having your own hairdresser along is essential.'

'Goodness, she's awfully involved in all this,' Sloane said, hoping she didn't sound ungrateful.

Rose looked at Warner. He cleared his throat. 'She's a very old friend, darling,' Warner said. 'She suggested it as a wedding present at the reception. I agreed for you. Of course, under the circumstances I would have agreed to anything.'

There were knowing chuckles all around the table from everyone except Sloane. She loved the idea of both Melon's and Alan's travelling with her, but she would have liked to have been consulted. It seemed as though Warner and Layla were acting like nervous parents organizing a child's first trip to camp. She tried not to let her irritation show. She wasn't crazy about having all these people descend on her honeymoon in the first place. Now she got the feeling they all knew things she did not. There was nothing she could do about it. They wouldn't be here if Warner hadn't asked them.

'Now,' Warner said, taking a folder Rose handed him. 'Rose has been working with a consultant on your wardrobe.'

Her wardrobe? Now they were telling her what to wear! She thought she had gotten rid of that sort of treatment when she left Noreen. She looked beseechingly at Warner. 'Darling, do you really have to talk about all this now?'

Warner looked slightly surprised at her assertion of a complaint, then nodded. 'Sorry, darling,' he said, then looked down the table at the others. 'Look, everybody. You must all be exhausted and I have to return these Tokyo calls. Why don't we call it a day and go over the details at dinner this evening.' He pushed back his chair and stood, signalling a temporary halt to arranging Sloane's life.

Sloane watched as everyone gathered up their things, joked as to whether they should say 'good night' or 'good day', and followed Jean-Baptiste to their bedrooms in another part of the house.

'I wish you had told me I'd have a working honeymoon,' she said to Warner when they were alone.

'I'm sorry,' Warner said, bending to brush her lips with his own. 'This is really terribly important. Brian read me the figures. They're pretty bleak. We stand to lose the company by the end of the year if we don't do something really spectacular. It all hinges on you now.'

Sloane studied her hands in her lap, fighting to hide her disappointment.

'Don't look so sad, my sweet. I'll make it up to you, I promise.' He lifted her chin and looked down at her, his eyes soft with concern.

'I thought we would have more time together, that's all,' she said in a small voice. 'I love you so much.'

'And I love you,' he said. 'Now, kiss me and let me get some work done.'

She stood and dutifully kissed him.

'Why don't you finish the book you're reading and we'll have drinks around eight?'

'All right, darling. Happy phoning,' she said, and left the office.

She didn't want to read. She knew she wouldn't be able to concentrate. If she didn't walk off her anger, it would show, and that's the last thing she wanted.

As she headed off down the driveway toward the open meadows, the Dobermans trotted reassuringly by her side.

So this is the way it's going to be, she thought. *I've married a man who has all the money in the world and no time.* Time, something she once had so much of, was becoming a precious thing. There were only twenty-four hours in a day, and even Warner Bromley wasn't powerful or rich enough to borrow it from some other alternate universe. Things were important. Things had to get done. Sometimes some things had to be done instead of other things. There were layers of projects and meetings and flights and phoning, so that each single project dovetailed neatly into the next in a seamless treadmill that produced money. He needed money to pay for the projects, and flights and meetings, and phones. If she was to be a part of his life, she would have to take the space allotted to her. Being the Bromley Woman was that space. Being Mrs Bromley came second. Warner didn't need her as a wife anyway. The idea of cleaning and mending and cooking heart-shaped meat loaf for a man like Warner was ludicrous. He wanted her in his life because he loved her. What woman in the world could ask for more?

She turned off the road and crossed the meadow leading to a hill that overlooked the valley below. She found a smooth, flat boulder jutting out of the hillside and sat down. The Dobermans curled up at her feet.

Had she truly thought her life would be one long float on a luxurious worry-free cloud? The only reason she met a man like Warner in the first place was because she was a professional. What made people professional was their ability to get up and get on with whatever work was theirs to do. One didn't whine about it, one didn't complain. At least Noreen had taught her that.

330

She remembered how disgusted she had been with the ladies-around-the-pool as she called them. The women with rich husbands and perfect tans and fingernails who watched her parading around in fashion shows in stiff, hot clothes and aching feet. The hours in front of cameras holding a pose, smiling until she thought her face would freeze in a deathlike grin forever.

Just because she had a rich, powerful husband didn't give her a free ride. An important part of his business was in trouble and he needed her.

She wasn't too thrilled that others seemed to be calling the shots. She had seen him huddled with Layla Bronz at the wedding reception. They had spent so much time together Ryan had finally gone over and asked Layla to dance. This wasn't the first time Layla had done some behind-the-scenes manoeuvring of Sloane's own life, and she wondered what the woman really was to Warner other than the publisher of his magazine.

A sudden, chilling breeze swept up out of the valley. She shivered in her thin silk blouse. *All right, Mary Sloane*, she told herself, *grow up! You had three dreamy days with a wonderful man who loved you so much he married you. Now it's reality time and you have work to do.*

She stood and beckoned to the dogs.

First on her list of things she must do was to get back to the house, get dressed up in the most dazzling outfit she had, and charm the socks of everyone, even if they were sharing her honeymoon.

18

Alan had never seen anything remotely like the Bromley company jet.

The only other airplane he had been on in his life was the one that brought him to New York. Although Sloane had described it to him in great detail, he never dreamed he would find himself traveling the country in it. It wasn't so much a plane as it was a flying apartment, complete with a bedroom, phones, and television, even a bathroom with a shower! To top it all off there were two cute guys serving drinks and gourmet food.

'I've died and gone to heaven,' he said as he took his seat on the first day of the tour. Sitting opposite him was a woman named Melon Tuft, who had been hired by Bromley Cosmetics to assist Sloane and act as a press aide.

She smiled across the aisle at Alan. 'Can you believe this?' she asked him, equally in awe of their surroundings.

Alan had met Melon earlier that morning when he'd found her sitting in the backseat of the radio car that would take them both to the airport. The schedule so far called for visits to Chicago, Pittsburgh, Minneapolis, and St Louis, then on to New Orleans, San Francisco, and Los Angeles. The plan was to return to New York, every weekend and go back out on the road each Monday.

Alan had been beside himself when Sloane returned from her brief honeymoon and asked him to come along.

She told him the cosmetics company would pay him a handsome fee and all expenses while he saw the country by private jet. Adding to his delight was that he could spend some time with Sloane.

He missed her in his life. Before she met Warner he wouldn't hesitate to call her at midnight or six in the morning just to giggle and gossip. Now that she was the famous Mrs Warner Bromley, those comforting times were over and he missed them dreadfully. Even at the wedding he had seen how his life would change. Warner's friends were older, powerful people and she would have to live in his world now. The opposite was impossible. The thought of Warner sitting around with people like Kayzie Markham and himself, eating chili and watching old movies on the VCR, was beyond laughable.

Across the aisle Melon eyed the Gucci case sitting next to his chair. 'Is that all you're taking?' she asked, accepting a Bloody Mary from the steward.

'I have a handbag in the back, but I keep the tools of my trade with me for emergencies,' he explained, smiling. 'With this I can make Margaret Thatcher look like Princess Di.'

'And that's all you have to do for Sloane? Just her hair?'

Alan nodded and took a Bloody Mary from the proffered tray. 'Ummm,' he said. 'Hair and makeup. You'd be amazed at how much work that is. Sloane's got to be fluffed after every appearance. Makeup melts, and you know what they say — never let 'em see you sweat. I also carry bags, press gowns, and run out for Chinese.' He took a sip of his spicy drink and thought how incredibly nice all this was. 'What about you, Melon? What are your chores, exactly?'

'I'm supposed to keep her on schedule. All the arrangements are made by the public relations people. Everything is broken down into daily segments, hour by hour,' she said, holding up a leather-bound folder. 'I'm supposed to keep her on time. Then there's her clothes. They have to be coordinated for each appointment. She's got twenty suitcases on the plane!'

Alan pulled off the jacket of his Comme des Garçons suit. The steward soundlessly stepped forward and lifted it from his hand, simultaneously turning to Melon to ask, 'May I put your bag out of your way, Miss Tuft?'

The outsized handbag Melon had been clutching since she got into the taxi was still on her lap. She looked up at the steward, pulled the bag even closer to her chest, and shook her head. 'No!' she snapped. 'This stays with me.'

The steward nodded politely and scurried off to hang up Alan's jacket.

Alan thought Melon's reaction was a bit odd. Then again, Melon was somewhat odd herself. She was dressed as though she had made a great effort to look like something she wasn't. She was wearing a navy-blue blazer, grey flannel skirt, and an I've-got-an-MBA-and-you-don't white Oxford shirt and floppy bow tie. To Alan's practiced eye the getup wasn't her. The makeup and nails were pure Joan Collins, which this woman clearly wasn't, and his fingers itched to do something with her hair.

Melon leaned forward and batted her eyelashes. 'So, Alan, tell me,' she said. 'How do you know Sloane Taylor?'

'We went to high school together,' he said.

'You did? Where? In Los Angeles?'

'Yes, the Dearfield Academy. We were sort of best friends.'

'Then you must have known her parents.'

'Sure.'

'What was her mother like?' Melon inquired.

'Noreen?' Alan laughed. 'She's something else.'

'How do you mean?'

'Just that she really ran Sloane's life.'

'I heard she was a child model. Are you saying her mother ran her personal life or her career?'

'Both,' Alan said.

'She must have been very popular in high school. Did she have a lot of boyfriends?'

Alan frowned and took a sip of his drink. 'Not really,' he said. He wanted to change the subject. She was making him uncomfortable. He felt disloyal discussing Sloane. Why was this woman asking so many questions, anyway?

The inquisition was interrupted by what he saw out the window over her shoulder. In the distance, a limousine was moving toward them across the tarmac. As it turned and moved up under the wing, he saw the Bromley crest on the driver's-side door. ·

'Here they come!' he said excitedly.

Melon turned in her seat to see what he was looking at. 'Wow!' she shouted. 'Major stretch there! I like the way it just drives right up to the plane.'

They watched as the driver opened the door and three men stepped out. They were followed by Sloane in an ankle-length sable coat. She was carrying an alligator clutch bag and a Vuitton makeup case.

Alan stepped across the aisle to get a closer look. 'Who do you suppose the suits are?' he asked.

'They must be the guys from the cosmetics company,' Melon said. 'The people at the PR office mentioned they'd be coming along.'

After Sloane and the men came aboard, they greeted everyone and moved to the office in the front of the plane. They were there to brief Sloane on whom she would be seeing on their first stop in Chicago.

As soon as everyone was sitting down and buckled in, the pilot started the engines. Alan raised his glass to Melon and smiled. 'Here's to an adventure,' he said.

'I'll drink to that!' she agreed with a gleeful laugh.

Within minutes they were in the air headed out to see America.

*

At first Alan had been excited about seeing so many different cities. After the first few days, however, he realized they could all be the same one – except perhaps for San Francisco and New Orleans. In most cities, a highway was a highway, high-rise buildings had no geography, and airports and restaurants were interchangeable. Every morning he would check the hotel notepad on the night table to see where he was.

Days and nights became a blur of limousines, mountains of luggage, hotel suites, television station green rooms, and mobs at local department store cosmetic counters where Sloane would promote the Bromley line.

To Alan's dismay, iridescent blue eyeshadow was still alive and grotesquely in use from coast to coast. Poor Sloane had to smile and say the same thing over and over and over again like a cracked record. Most of the people who interviewed her wanted to know more about her private life than the cosmetics she used. What a pro she was! She never stopped smiling. She answered their repetitive and inane questions as though each reporter who interviewed her was a potential Pulitzer Prize winner. She never seemed to lose her patience with people and was just as fresh and beguiling at a boring nine P.M. dinner with local Bromley reps as she was doing a morning TV talk show.

His earlier suspicion of Melon and her inordinate interest in Sloane, particularly her past, vanished by the end of the first week. He found himself liking her. She was funny and irreverent and good company. She also redeemed herself in his eyes by doing a bang-up job for Sloane. She never left her side, anticipated her every need, and fended off potential screwups without fuss or complaint.

Sloane was never late for an appointment, except the time they got stuck in the elevator at the Beverly Hills Hotel. Sloane worked hard to be sure she knew everybody's name before she met with them. She never found a belt missing from a dress or shoes left at the last hotel. By the time they arrived back in New York after the second week, they all considered themselves an effective team running a smooth operation as though they had done it all their lives. They succeeded in getting Sloane and Bromley Cosmetics fabulous publicity in every city, which was after all the point of all the racing across the country.

But all the while Alan looked forward to the times Sloane didn't need him to repair her face or hair. It gave him time to call Cole back in New York.

Since Sloane's wedding Cole had been in his thoughts night and day. And from the messages he found waiting for him at the registration desk of each new hotel, it looked as if Cole felt the same way.

At first, the only drawback of going on the tour was that it meant leaving this new relationship. Once out on the road Alan realized that just being out of town didn't change it; if anything, it made it better. In the course of their nightly telephone conversations and brief weekends together, they both realized they were living through the first heady days of falling in love. Like everyone who has been burned by romance gone wrong, which was the case for both of them, they were cautious at first. That had not lasted long. Due in part to Alan's being out of town during the week, the relationship intensified each weekend until every meeting, meal, and conversation was freighted with a special significance to them and them alone. Code words, snatches of songs, punch lines without the jokes, and shared moments of tenderness were accumulating on the shelves of Alan's mind like Cole's collection of millefleurs paperweights, each one more valuable and precious than the next.

In every hotel gift shop and airport souvenir stand, Alan searched for goofy postcards on which he wrote cryptic messages in their shared secret language. One day in Pittsburgh he sent a dozen cards, each with a different word on it that formed a sentence for Cole to figure out.

Miraculously, they had yet to have a serious argument. Alan had become so used to the constant bickering and screaming that went on during the last year with Brad Rampart that he half-expected the same treatment from Cole. When it didn't happen, he began to think that maybe – just maybe – this time was for real. He had, at last, found Mr Right.

True love or not, it was making his life incandescent. That, more than anything else, kept him out of the clubs and discos on the road.

Every Friday night, as soon as he stepped off the Bromley jet, he raced to Cole's apartment, his suitcase full of things that would please him. They were always little things, a shirt he knew he would like, a funny poster, a box of pralines he knew Cole craved. Once in a dusty antique store in Los Angeles after a particularly brief and dreary visit to his mother's apartment, he spied a millefleurs paperweight unlike any Cole had. His heart leapt at the sight and sank just as quickly when he read the price sticker. It was obscenely expensive, but he couldn't resist and pulled out his Visa card. That Friday when the Bromley jet delivered them all safely to JFK once again, he couldn't wait to give the paperweight to Cole. At Cole's apartment he found the table set, candles lit, and wine breathing. He waited until they both had their drinks before he handed him the package. He sat waiting to see Cole's reaction as he opened it.

Cole gently lifted it out of the box and placed it on the palm of his hand. He stared at it without saying a word. He leaned forward and placed it on the coffee table and resumed sipping his drink. It was only then that Alan saw that Cole's face was wet with tears.

That had been the moment. It had freeze-framed in their hearts and sealed their feelings for each other.

In that moment both their worlds were altered.

Alan was kinder now. More patient with small delays and major foul-ups on the road. More caring about others' feelings and needs. That moment became another of their coded messages that described a feeling only they understood. 'Millefleurs, Alan,' was all he wrote on the next postcard he sent home from the road.

If Sloane was pleased and feeling confident about her performance on the road, Warner was ecstatic.

Their first two weekends together during the tour had been bliss. His desk in the Carlyle suite library was piled with clips and tapes of her interviews in the cities she had visited. The cosmetics company's marketing department sent glowing reports on how well the campaign was going. Bromley products were beginning to move in the better stores around the country, and thanks to Sloane's efforts a whole new and younger generation was beginning to buy.

'Our whole image is changing, darling,' Warner said on their second midtour Sunday together when she walked into the library. He put down the sheaf of profit reports he had been studying and rose to kiss her. 'Thanks to you, beautiful girl.'

She returned his kiss and then helped herself to a cup of coffee on the sideboard before turning to join him by the desk again. 'I'm so glad it's doing some good.' She smiled, curling up in the leather wing chair. 'But I hate being away from you so much.'

'It's just another week. Then we can settle down,' he said. 'For the foreseeable future I'll be spending a lot of time on this Japanese deal. Being in L.A. will make travelling so much more convenient.'

'So we *are* going,' she said. She should have sounded more enthusiastic about the move, but recently she had hoped they could stay in New York. The feedback from the tour was making her realize how much she wanted to concentrate on her acting.

'It's all set.' Warner beamed. 'You're going to love the

house. It's almost as though I had you in mind when I built it. Now I can't imagine it without you.'

'Thank you, darling,' she said. 'I can't wait.'

'You know, anything the company needs you for can be done just as easily there as here.'

'Yes, I know,' she said, watching the freshly laid fire burn.

Warner excused himself to take a call. It was chilly for the end of March, so she pulled a coat from the closet by the window to step out onto the terrace with her cup of coffee. She leaned against the wall that encircled the terrace and looked out toward the park. The bare branches of the treetops in the park were beginning to turn a delicate green. The brisk air held a definite promise of an early spring.

So, she thought, *we really are going to go.*

She wasn't ready to return to L.A., not yet. The pain was too fresh. She had lived without Noreen in her life for too long to open up all those wounds. Here in New York there was a chance of getting whole again, of finding who she really was. Did it really matter that Warner was not exciting? He loved her. He gave her everything a woman could dream of.

The response she was getting on the road was thrilling. Only when she was alone with her thoughts did she dare think what it would be like if she were just another model chosen for the role and not his wife.

Within her there was still the hunger for something she couldn't even define. Since the wedding she had been awakening in the middle of the night from nightmares. Had her black dreams disturbed her sleep, or was it a kind of longing, a need she could not name? These were thoughts she could never articulate to Warner. It would be cruel to tell him she wasn't completely happy without being able to explain why.

She looked down at the pathways under the trees in the park and closed her eyes tight against the disturbing scenes that flashed in her mind.

'No more,' she whispered to herself. 'Never again.' People gave up addictions every day. Somewhere they found the strength to give up the liquor or the drugs or the gambling that threatened to destroy them. Surely she could be that strong. Hadn't she already proved she could be? Those first two weeks of the tour had shown her that. She could quit! She *would* quit. Now, while it was still her secret. If she quit now, it would be as though it had never happened.

Now she truly had something to lose if she continued. Her tour as the Bromley Woman had been the most fulfilling days of her life. People took her seriously. She wasn't just another pretty face but was a sought-after expert on how to improve one's appearance. Women in department stores would stand in a circle listening raptly to her every word, then rush to buy the things she recommended. Television audiences cheered and applauded, truly interested in her tips. To anyone else — except perhaps Kayzie or Alan — it was a small thing, but to her it had been an enormously satisfying experience.

The constant, steady work exhilarated her. From predawn television talk shows to midnight radio call-ins, she was on the go. There had not been a time to concentrate on anything except what was on the minute-by-minute schedule. It felt wonderful to have a real purpose other than just looking good.

Best of all was that the urge to play the Game had completely left her alone. She awoke each morning feeling good about herself and guilt free.

She turned and stepped through the sliding doors to the library. Warner was momentarily off the phone.

'Pretty day,' he said without looking up.

'Ummm,' she said. 'I bet it's even prettier in California.'

He smiled at her, his eyes soft with love. She knew she had pleased him.

*

The Monday morning of what would be their last week on tour, Melon was not in the radio car when it picked Alan up for the trip to the airport. The driver told him she had not answered repeated buzzings of the intercom at her apartment. By seven-thirty everyone was on the plane waiting and wondering what they should do about Melon. Just then a taxi screeched up to the side of the plane and she tumbled out.

She came aboard, out of breath and disheveled, dragging her bags and clutching the big handbag that never left her sight. Her hair was flying and her makeup was smeared. Everyone on the plane cheered as she stomped down the aisle without explanation.

She was barely in her seat when the pilot revved the big jet engines and started to taxi down the runway.

Alan looked over at her and smiled.

On closer examination, she looked even worse. Her eyes were puffed and her nose looked rubbed raw as though she had been crying – a lot.

It was impossible to talk over the roar of the engines as the big jet lifted off and began to climb out over the Atlantic. He would wait until they leveled off before asking what was wrong. Funny, he thought, a month ago he would have been annoyed at having to comfort a relative stranger. He had been so wrapped up in his own worries and insecurities he had never seemed to have room in his mind and heart to deal with someone else – unless, as with Sloane, he was very close to them.

Since Cole, all that had changed.

The big jet thrust upward through the grey layer of clouds over Manhattan. Bright sunlight streamed through the oval windows. He watched while Melon undid her seat belt and stepped to the bar. She poured a cup of coffee from the carafe and carried it with both hands back to her seat.

'You okay, kid?' Alan inquired.

Melon stared into the coffee cup. She shook her head.

'Wanna talk about it?'

'Not really,' she said.

'Okay. I've got big shoulders when you do.'

'Oh, Alan, it's a man. What would you know?'

He couldn't help himself; he threw back his head and laughed. 'Try me,' he said.

Melon took out a handkerchief and loudly blew her nose. 'Shit!'

'That bad?'

'I keep calling him and calling him from the road and leaving messages and he never calls me back.' She stuffed the tissues between the arm of the chair and the cushion.

'I take it, whoever this guy is, he *lives* someplace. Can't you just go and confront him?'

'That's what I did,' she snuffled. 'I found out where he lives. I rented a car and drove out there yesterday afternoon. Way the hell out in godforsaken Queens.'

'This guy lives in Queens? He must be married.'

'You're a regular Sherlock Holmes, Alan,' she said sarcastically. The steward whipped up to her chair, removed the wedged tissue, and spirited it away between forefinger and thumb.

'So then what happened?'

'I sat in the car all night, watching the house. I figured he'd either come in or go out, something, anything. I was crazed. Finally, the sun is coming up and I'm going nuts because I gotta get my act together, drop the car, and get to the plane here. I guess I dozed off. The next thing I know someone is tapping on the window. I look out and all I see is someone wearing a sweater with sequins and crap all over it. I rolled down the window and this woman puts her face in and goes, calm as you please, "Excuse me, miss, but do the police have your finger-prints?"

'I'm like real confused. I don't know what she's talking about. So I say, "What's it to you?" and she says with this real mean face, "Because they are going to need them to

identify your body when it washes up in the Sound."
Well, that scares the crap out of me and I begin to roll up
the window and she's got this baseball bat. She sticks it in
the window so I can't get it up. When I see the bat, I'm
about to freak and she says, "I'm Shirley Chiga, and if
you've been sitting out here all night looking for my
husband, you're out of luck. Now get the fuck out of the
neighborhood before I smash your cheap face." '

Alan sat stunned. 'I hope you left.'

'Like a shot! I damn near wrapped the rented Toyota
around a stop sign. Now, you know she's going to tell
him I was there,' Melon said, fresh tears sparkling on her
mascara-clotted lashes. 'And I'll never see him again.'

Alan whisked a handful of tissues from the box on the
end table and handed them to her. 'Don't be so sure,
sweetie pie,' he said. 'Men are strange creatures. He
might just be flattered that you cared enough to risk
getting smacked with a baseball bat just to see him. Don't
give up so soon.'

Melon brightened a bit. 'Oh, I don't know,' she
moaned. 'I wish there was something I could do. I *have* to
get him back. I'm crazy about him.'

'I have an idea that might work.'

'What?' she said eagerly.

'Well, what does the man like? Is there something he
absolutely can't resist?'

Melon thought for a moment. She mentally ran
through the things Matty had to have in his life – like sex,
power, money, excitement . . . 'Food!' she said. 'The man
loves to eat.'

'Great, now we have something to work with.' Alan
smiled, warming to his Dr Ruth role. 'How does he feel
about his mother?'

'His office is full of pillows with her picture on them.'

'Aha! That's a valuable clue,' Alan said excitedly.
'Okay, I'm going to give you a plan. You have nothing to
lose, right?'

'Right.' She nodded. 'I've already lost him.'

'Don't be so sure. Now, don't call him. Don't send him notes. Don't hang out waiting for him. Don't even put your machine on while you're away.

'But what if he calls!' Melon cried.

'No, no, no,' Alan said, waving his hand to erase her words. 'You have to be totally unreachable. Do that until the end of the tour –'

Melon groaned and held her head. 'I don't think I can do it.'

'Listen to me. You can,' Alan said, reaching over and squeezing her wrist. 'When you get home for good, send him brownies.'

'Brownies!' Melon shouted. She stared at him in disbelief. 'Brownies? Get outta here.'

Alan ignored her lack of enthusiasm; he knew what he was talking about. 'Big, moist, double-chocolate brownies clogged with nuts and covered with an inch of dark chocolate frosting. Have them delivered with a little note like "Thinking of you." Nothing mushy. Then stand back for the results.'

'I think you're crazy,' she sniffed.

'Now, we have to go deeper. Brownies are just to get his attention. Let me ask you what you think he most liked about you in the first place.'

'Well, on our first date he told me he thought I was a stand-up broad.'

'Then be one. Don't go wimping around calling, hanging out, pestering the man. You're making yourself resistible. That's not sexy. Be your own person. He's got to think he has to work to get you.'

Melon stared out the window, twisting her fingers and looking sad. Reluctantly she turned to face him again. 'Okay. Okay. I'll try anything.'

'Trust me. I know what I'm talking about.'

'How come you know so much about men, Alan?'

'It's a hobby?' he said, smiling.

345

It was during the last week of the tour that Sloane's luck began to run out.

In Dallas, their plane had been delayed due to weather and they were two hours late getting to the hotel. The crew put the wrong stickers on the bags they needed and the luggage was misdelivered. Alan's bags went to another hotel. Melon's went to Alan's room, and they were still sorting out where Sloane's things were.

Tired and irritable, Sloane had to step out of the shower covered with soap to answer the phone. She said a little prayer that this was the desk saying her bags were on their way to the room. She had nothing to wear but the clothes she'd been in all day, let alone a nightgown.

'Hello,' she answered.

'Sloane, can I come up for a minute? It's important.' Alan was speaking quickly, his voice tight with urgency.

'Of course. I'm just getting out of the shower. Is there something wrong?'

'I think so, very.'

'Let me guess. The bags have gone to Peru.'

'No. No. This is much worse.'

'Good heavens, Alan, you're scaring me. What's up?'

'We don't have much time. I have to show you something.'

'Okay, come right now. I'll leave the door unlocked.'

She stepped back into the shower and rinsed off the soap feeling very uneasy. What could Alan possibly have to show her?

She was slipping into the hotel robe hanging on the back of the bathroom door when she heard the living room door open and close. 'I'll be right out, Alan,' she called as she twisted a towel around her wet hair.

When she walked into the living room, he was sitting on the couch. Next to him was a familiar bag. His face was milky white.

'Hi, what's that?' she asked, pointing at the bag.

'This is Melon's bag. The one she hangs on to all the time,' he said ominously.

'I thought I recognized it. What are you doing with it? She must be frantic.'

'Has she called about it yet?' Alan asked.

'No. The last time I saw her she was on the phone in the lobby calling New York. She must have set it down and it got scooped up with all the others.'

'If the phone rings, don't answer it. I don't want her to know it's here for a bit.'

Sloane sat down next to Alan and the bag. 'What in the world is going on, Alan?' she asked, frowning.

'After I called the desk to tell them they'd sent up the wrong bags, I decided to put them outside the door so I could shower. When I picked up this bag, it was heavier than I thought and I accidentally dropped it. When it hit the floor, I heard this.' He reached under the leather flap of the bag, pushed something, and watched.

There was a whirring sound for a moment, and then they heard Sloane's voice speaking conversationally. Sloane recoiled from the bag as though it were alive. 'Wha. . . !' she gasped.

'Shhh! Listen,' Alan said.

Another voice was speaking. This time it was Melon's.

'Alan! What is this?' Sloane said, alarmed. She picked up the bag and flipped open the large flap that covered the zipper. It was heavier than a leather flap should be. She squeezed it and felt a hard lump inside the double fold.

'It's a goddamn tape recorder, Sloane,' Alan said angrily, peeling back the opening in the fold to reveal a hand-sized machine. 'Melon Tuft has been taping you without you knowing it.'

'But why?' Sloane gasped, completely bewildered. 'There's no reason to tape me. This sounds like a conversation between the two of us. I could see it if it were a talk show or something, but Alan . . . I don't get it.'

Alan pushed up off the couch and started pacing the carpet. 'What did Melon do before she was hired for this tour?' he asked.

Sloane thought for a moment. 'Well, she was a writer, a journalist. As I recall, she had managed to get an interview with Warner, something he never does. He told me she called just before we left and postponed it.'

'Where was the interview supposed to appear?'

'Why, in *Realto* magazine.'

'And who hired her for you? The PR people?'

'No . . . Layla Bronz suggested her. As a matter of fact she insisted. She and Warner are friends so he . . . oh, my God, Alan . . . I see what you're saying.'

Alan continued to pace, his hands plunged deep in his pockets. 'She's spying on you, Sloane,' he said.

'But why? Certainly not for an article on Warner?'

'I don't think she's doing a piece on Warner. I think she's doing a piece on you.'

Sloane's mind was racing. This was crazy. 'But Alan, if she wanted to do a piece on me, why didn't she just ask? I'd give her an interview, that's my job. How many nice chatty interviews have I given already? Fifty? Sixty?'

'I don't think she wants a nice chatty interview about Bromley Cosmetics. I think she's doing a nasty profile on you for some other reason. Let's listen to some more.' He moved the tape forward and pressed the play button. They heard Sloane's voice again, but now she was talking to a man.

'That's the host of that Cleveland talk show,' Sloane said. 'I remember, that was after the show while we were waiting for the car. He asked me to have dinner with him.'

'Do you remember where Melon was?'

'Not with us. That I'm sure of.'

'That means she probably set the machine, put her bag down close enough to catch what you would say, and walked off somewhere.'

'Alan, this is frightening,' Sloane said. She rested her head in her hands and tried to think. Nothing like this had ever happened to her. Maybe Melon wasn't doing a piece, maybe she was spying on her for someone. 'Alan,' she asked, grasping at straws to make sense of it all, 'you don't suppose she's working for Warner, do you?'

'No, that doesn't make sense. Has he ever been jealous or paranoid? I mean, he trusts you completely, doesn't he?'

'Of course,' Sloane said. 'You're right. It doesn't make sense.'

'On the other hand, it doesn't make sense that Melon has to sneak around taping you. You don't have anything to hide.'

Sloane glanced up at Alan for an instant and then looked away.

'Well, do you?' he asked with a slight chuckle.

'N . . . no,' she said. 'Nothing at all.' She had to get out of the room. She jumped up from the couch. 'Excuse me for a sec, Alan. I've got to run to the john.'

She didn't register his reply. As soon as she made it to the bathroom, she closed the door and sat down on the edge of the tub. Her hands were trembling uncontrollably and her knees felt as if they had floated away. She grasped her elbows, hugging herself, and rocked back and forth to try and lull the panic that was engulfing her.

How could they know? How could anyone know? She thought of Melon. She had liked her so much and here she was part of some sinister thing. Melon's betrayal was bad enough. Not knowing who was behind it was worse. Who could she talk to? Surely not Warner. He treated her as though she were born the day before they met.

Layla! Layla Bronz. Somehow that woman was behind this. Sloane was sure of it. Layla always acted as though she owned Warner, anyway. He always took her calls, no matter what else he was doing. Sloane had seen him come out of important meetings to talk to her. Layla would be

349

jealous; after all, they had been friends for years, but still . . . She'd talk to Cole, that was the answer. No. Not Cole. As sweet as he had been, his loyalties were with Layla. He wouldn't tell Sloane anything.

One thing she knew for sure. She wouldn't sleep through a night until she got to the bottom of this.

Somehow, Sloane stumbled through the next two days. She made Alan promise not to say a word about the situation. If Melon suspected they were on to her, she might stop and they would never find out.

Alan and Sloane watched her for the next two days in fascinated horror. Now that they knew what she was doing, it was painfully obvious. The black bag was never more than a few feet from Sloane when she was talking to anyone.

One evening they even let Melon leave the bag in the limousine when Sloane went to dinner with a Bromley rep.

It was the most difficult two days of Sloane's life. By the time they landed at JFK on the Friday night that marked the end of the tour, she knew what she had to do.

That night Warner threw a little surprise party at L'Orangerie. It was a combination victory and welcome-home celebration. Many of those invited had been at the wedding. Melon, of course, was asked. At first glance, Sloane didn't recognize her out of her serious on-the-road outfit. She was wearing a strapless hot-pink gown and a chubby little fur jacket that stopped just under her well-exposed breasts.

Sloane watched her carefully to see whom she talked to. Sloane hoped she could catch her talking to Layla Bronz, who arrived looking somewhat overdressed in one of the Christian Lacroix that was all the rage. But Layla stayed only a few minutes, saying a somewhat tight-lipped hello to Sloane and Warner. She chatted

350

briefly with a *New York Times* reporter and left with a group Sloane didn't recognize. At no time did she speak to Melon.

Sloane watched what she drank. She wanted to have her wits about her. After the party, she and Warner went directly home to her suite.

'Let's have a nightcap, darling,' Sloane said disarmingly to Warner as they arrived at the door of the penthouse.

'That's a switch,' he said, grinning. 'Usually I'm the one who wants a good-night pop.'

'Well, I missed you. I want to catch up.'

She knew he was feeling mellow. The party had been a great success and he had glowed with the compliments people paid both of them.

They settled into their usual places in the library, and Warner handed her a crystal snifter of brandy. She let him chatter on about various people at the party, waiting for her opening. When it came, she spoke lightly and without any real apparent interest. 'Tell me about Layla Bronz, dear. You've known her a long time, right?'

'It seems like all my life,' he said.

'Were you lovers?' she asked, knowing the question was risky.

Warner stared at her with a level gaze, swirling his brandy slowly as though sizing up his answer. 'Why do you ask?'

Sloane laughed. 'Don't be cagey, sweetheart. It would be nonsense for me to be jealous of a man who has led the kind of life you have. I'm just curious.'

'Yes.'

'There, that didn't hurt,' she said. 'You'll notice I have not run from the room weeping hysterically.'

She could tell from the chuckle that followed that she had disarmed him. She was on the right track. 'What's your relationship with Layla now?'

'Nothing, other than the fact that she publishes my

magazine,' he said. 'Does a fine job of it, too. I dread the day I have to tell her I'm going to sell it.'

'Are you?' Sloane asked, a bit surprised.

'Umm. I've been thinking about it. If this Japanese deal goes through, I'm going to have to divest a bit. There are too many loose ends. The canning factories should go, some of the small newspapers we own out west. My financial people say it makes sense to throw *Realto* into the pot.'

'Won't that upset her?'

He rubbed his chin. 'Terribly, temporarily. But business is business. She's a wealthy woman. She'll manage.'

'Kayzie told me *Realto* is her life.'

Warner threw up his hands in a what-can-you-do gesture.

'How much of her life were you, Warner?'

'My goodness, aren't we a persistent girl!' he exclaimed teasingly.

'Well, I'm interested,' she said, effecting a playful pout. 'It's delicious to know other women love my man.'

The blatant flattery worked. Warner put down his brandy and crossed his legs. 'Layla is a gutsy, fearless, brilliant woman. I've not met her like before or since. If she had a failing, it was that she was a compulsive-obsessive. After a while people who are like that can remove all the oxygen from a relationship. We were very close for some years. Then, I guess I got so I couldn't breathe and began taking her in smaller and smaller doses.'

'She must have felt pretty bad when you suddenly married me,' Sloane said, trying to get to the heart of how Layla must feel about her.

'She was, as the Brits say, not amused.'

'Do you think she would ever do anything to, oh, I don't know, to . . . get revenge.'

Warner chuckled again. 'It's possible. She carries grudges and I suppose she has a certain power. Anyone with access to the printed page can make life difficult if they have a mind to.'

'What would you do if she tried something like that?'

Warner shrugged. 'Oh, who knows. Slap her down, I guess.'

'Well, you've just said you're going to sell her magazine out from under her. That should do it.'

He rose, yawned behind his fist, and stretched. He walked over to her chair and lifted her chin. 'Darling girl. Why are we talking about this? Layla's not someone I worry about. And if, by some wild stretch of the imagination, she tried anything, I'd just sell the magazine sooner rather than later. Now, come,' he said, extending his hand. 'I had a video made of the interior of the Los Angeles home. I thought you'd like to see our piece of Shangri-la.'

Sloane smiled at him. He had told her as much as he was going to. It was enough.

On Monday she would make an appointment to see Layla Bronz. At least she had some ammunition.

19

When Sloane rang *Realto* on Monday morning to ask if she could drop by the office, she let Layla assume her visit was to discuss the Bromley Woman cover that was in the works. Of course Sloane could stop by. No problem. Layla would cancel a scheduled meeting and be available at four that afternoon.

If there was one thing Sloane hated more than not pleasing people, it was a confrontation of any kind. She supposed the two were all part of the same feelings about herself. If you confronted people, they wouldn't like you. She wanted Layla to like her. Layla, in her own way, had been greatly responsible for Sloane's current success. And yet, the woman frightened her, made her nervous and uneasy. She was so . . . in control, Sloane decided. Layla led a life in which she was the only star onstage. If something was happening that she objected to, she knew how to manipulate people and events to turn things around to her own advantage. What did it take to get to that point in life? Sloane wondered. Time? Experience? Attention to detail? Or just plain self-centred ambition for your own wants and needs?

Whatever had made Layla the way she was, it was no longer important. Sloane had to deal with the woman she was today. Only Sloane herself had to know how incapable she felt of the task.

She left a note for Warner with Rose saying she was out shopping. He was closeted with the Japanese businessmen as usual. Rose had booked Mortimer's for dinner and Sloane planned to meet him there.

No matter how rich Warner was, the few blocks between the Carlyle and Layla's brownstone didn't justify a taxi. She would walk and try to get her thoughts in order for what she knew would be the most difficult conversation of her life.

Sloane had spent the entire weekend in a fit of anxiety, which, of course, she'd had to hide from Warner. Sunday night she had slept little. As she thrashed about, trying not to wake Warner, it occurred to her that her paranoia was groundless. No one could know about the Game. Her partners were always, always anonymous. That was essential to its success. And if Layla and Melon didn't know that about her, what else was there? Surely the revelation that she sometimes used Preparation H on her eyelids to reduce a champagne puffiness wouldn't stop the presses. How about the dark truth that she used to save on panty hose by cutting them in half when one leg had a run? She had never shoplifted, she wasn't hiding an illegitimate child, she had never been thrown out of school for cheating. Her secret life was secret still. Without direct knowledge there was no reason for her to be afraid. The whole neurotic business was just a way for Layla to get back at her for marrying Warner.

Still, she felt uneasy.

Suppose one of the men she had been with recognized her picture in the paper and somehow got ahold of Layla? New York could become a tiny town if you got famous.

Look what just one picture of her in the *New York Post* had led to. For every good thing publicity brought you there had to be some bad. She couldn't shake the feeling that whatever Layla was up to was definitely something bad. But what?

She had to stop torturing herself. Second-guessing wouldn't solve anything. *Get a grip on yourself, Sloane,* she scolded, *and start thinking straight.*

Analyse the enemy. What were Layla's motives? Jealousy? Layla was a woman scorned. Attention: Layla's ego demanded a constant supply of explosive events that she could manipulate. Revenge: Warner's marriage was a rejection of her after all these years.

By the time Sloane reached the steps of the brown-stone, she knew what her position would be. She would tell Layla to go ahead and have her followed around. There was nothing she had to hide. The only reason she had asked for the meeting was to make Layla aware that she knew what was going on and didn't like it. Not one bit.

When Kayzie looked up from her desk, she broke into a broad grin. 'Hey! You're back!' she said. 'How was it?'

Sloane leaned over the front of Kayzie's desk and kissed the air near her left ear. 'Great,' she said. 'I wish you could have come along. I missed you.'

'Me, too. I loved your notes. You should think about writing a piece on the tour,' Kayzie said, shutting off her typewriter. 'The bit about the stuck elevator was hilarious!'

Sloane pulled off her black kid gloves and stuffed them in the pocket of her sable coat. 'Not if you were there,' she said, rolling her eyes.

'Were you really going to hoist Alan through the trapdoor in the ceiling?'

'We would have if he hadn't started carrying on about how he was in love and didn't want to die.'

'What? Alan's in love?' Kayzie said, her eyes widening.

'You haven't heard about Alan and Cole?'

'Noooo,' Kayzie whispered. 'You mean . . .'

'Umm-hummm.'

'Well, I'll be. That's kinda neat,' Kayzie said. 'Boy, there must be something in the water. Cole and Alan, Warner and you, me and Ryan. The only one having a bad time is Melon.'

Sloane was puzzled. 'Melon? What about Melon? I've

been with her for a month. She never mentioned anything.'

'I think she's having problems with the Italian stallion,' Kayzie said, eyeing Sloane's outfit. 'Wow! Great coat!'

Sloane twirled around in a full circle, grateful not to have to discuss Melon any longer than necessary. 'You like?' she said. 'Actually, it's not mine. The company loaned it to me for the tour. I'm taking my time about giving it back. Maybe Warner will take the hint and buy it for me.'

Kayzie glanced at the grandfather clock by the door. 'Ms Bronz said you could go in as soon as you got here. She's waiting for you.'

'Thanks, hon,' Sloane said absentmindedly. Something Kayzie had just said was distracting her. As laid back as Kayzie was, even she called Layla 'Ms Bronz.'

Kayzie walked Sloane the few steps to Layla's door. 'Call me now that you're back,' she said. 'We'll have a girlie lunch. I want to hear about the south of France, the tour, all the Sadie-Sadie Married Lady stuff, and what it feels like to be famous.'

'I'll call,' Sloane said, and stepped through the office door to face her tormentor.

Layla was seated with her back to the light. As Sloane entered the office, she stood and extended her hand. She was wearing a bright hunter's-pink jacket with black velvet lapels and brass buttons over a black turtleneck cashmere sweater. Sloane had to admit the woman knew how to put herself together.

'Sloane. You look well.'

'Hello, Layla. Thanks for seeing me on such short notice.' She shook Layla's hand.

'Please, sit down.'

Sloane took the chair directly in front of Layla's desk rather than the couch. She wanted to be able to look her directly in the eye.

She assumed they would begin with some small talk

about the tour, but before she could get the words out Layla spoke.

'I'll save us some time, Sloane,' she said, lighting a cigarette with a big jewelled egg. 'I know why you are here.' She snapped the lighter shut with a sharp *pop*.

Sloane jumped imperceptibly. 'You do?'

'You found out we're planning a profile on you.'

Sloane was aghast. Warner had said she was brilliant, but he didn't say she was clairvoyant. She cleared her throat. 'That's right. How did you know?'

'The people I hire aren't stupid. Melon noticed that her tape recorder had been rewound after her bag went missing on the tour. She put two and two together. Besides . . .' Layla paused to take a deep drag on her cigarette and rested the holder against the side of a gigantic crystal ashtray engraved *United States Senate*, 'why else would you come rushing over here to see me? I knew you didn't want to talk about your cover. We both know that's being handled by Cole and the art department.'

Sloane took a deep breath and exhaled. 'Why are you doing this piece, Layla?' she asked. 'There's nothing in my life that would interest your readers for more words than you'd need for a picture caption.' She was struggling to keep her voice as inflection free as possible. 'I could sue you, you know.'

'Anyone can sue, Sloane.' Layla smiled. 'After the fact. By then it will be too late.'

'Too late?' Sloane said. 'Too late for what?'

'Too late to keep the world from having seen these,' Layla said, opening a drawer in her desk and removing a folder. She flipped it onto the desktop. 'Once these are published there will be no grounds for a suit. The damage will be done. There's not a lawyer in the world who can get the toothpaste back in the tube.'

Sloane stared at the folder. It lay on the desk between them, like a ticking time bomb. *What in all that's sacred does this woman have in that folder? She doesn't even have the decency to hand it to me,* Sloane thought. Slowly, she leaned forward and picked it up. Inside was a stack of black-and-white glossies. 'You want me to look at this, I take it,' she said.

'I think you better.'

Sloane began to look through the photographs. Her mouth went dry. She felt a tightening in her chest and a sharp jab of pain just under her left breast. She had to swallow hard to speak. 'Where did you get these?' she asked, horrified.

'Freelance photographer. We bought them,' Layla said evenly. She picked up her cigarette holder and sat with it jutting out of her clenched teeth.

Sloane prayed she wouldn't cry. She couldn't give in. She thought of acting class. Somewhere inside her there was something she could draw on. She tried to recall a time in her life as terrifying as this and could not. Even the most risky of Bad Girl encounters did not fill her with such dread. She finished looking at the pictures, more out of her need to stall for time than from any desire to see all of them. They made her sick. 'Look,' she began slowly, 'I know you love Warner. I know you want to hurt me, or hurt him through me. But this' – she tapped the top of the folder – 'is absolute, cold-blooded blackmail.'

Layla removed her cigarette from the holder and angrily ground it out in the ashtray. 'You and Warner discuss me a lot, do you?'

'Only once.'

'Why do you say this is blackmail, Sloane? I'd be blackmailing you if I showed you the pictures and asked you for something to stop me from publishing them. I'm not doing that.'

'Let's turn it into blackmail then. What do you want?'

'A good story. Our readers will eat this up.'

Sloane had heard people calling others monsters in her life. Now, for the first time, she was sitting in the same

359

room with one. 'How were these pictures taken?' she asked.

Layla leaned forward and tented her long, tapered fingers. 'Serendipity,' she said. 'Plain old good luck.'

Sloane couldn't help herself. 'I think you're sick,' she said.

'I'm sick!' Layla boomed. 'What kind of sickness do you see in those pictures?'

Sloane slapped the folder aginst her knee. Her impulse had been to rip it to shreds, but she knew reprints could be made before she could get back to the Carlyle. 'I don't care to discuss what I see in these pictures with you, Layla. Why should I? This is something I have to work out for myself.'

'Oh,' Layla sneered. 'So you admit you have a problem. How interesting.'

Something went *ping* between Sloane's eyes. A reddish mist seemed to pass across her sight line. She knew what she had to do. At last, all those acting classes were going to pay off.

She jumped to her feet and flung the folder onto Layla's desk. 'Now listen to me, lady,' she growled. Her voice sounded like someone else's. 'You can go ahead and publish your garbage. You can destroy me and my marriage. You can make Warner so sick with fury he'll never be the same man, but you can't do it for two months. That much I know about this gutter business. After that it will be too late.'

'What are you talking about?' Layla said in a voice that implied she wasn't really interested.

'Warner is planning to sell your precious magazine.' Sloane remained standing and gripped the back of the chair to keep her hands from trembling. Somehow she must have known this was her trump card. She was startling herself by actually using it.

They faced each other in silence and Layla blinked. 'He what?'

'You heard me,' Sloane said in a still, cold voice.

'Warner is going to sell *Realto?*'

Sloane sensed the subtle shift in the balance of their discussion and knew, at least for the moment, she had seized the high ground. The look of stunned disbelief on Layla's face gave her renewed confidence. 'Now we both have a problem, Layla,' she said quietly. 'I can't say mine is any bigger than yours. At least now the playing field is level.'

Layla's expression remained the same. 'I don't believe you,' she said.

'Maybe you'll believe *him*,' Sloane said, nodding to the phone. 'He's at the Carlyle. Let's call him right now and ask him.' She was playing it close to the edge. It was risky to suggest calling Warner. He probably wouldn't be back from his meeting, but she couldn't be sure.

Layla slammed her hand down on the top of the desk. 'That bastard,' she bellowed. 'That sneaky goddamned bastard!'

The intercom lit up and Kayzie's voice popped into the room. 'Ms Bronz, you okay?'

'It's fine, Kayzie, fine,' Layla replied briskly. She looked back at Sloane, her finger still depressing the intercom button. Then she sighed. 'Get me Melon Tuft. If she's not at home, find her.'

'Right away,' Kayzie's disembodied voice responded.

Sloane sat down. 'Why are you calling *her?*'

Layla leaned back in her chair. She pinched the bridge of her nose between two fingers and closed her eyes for a moment. When she spoke, she employed an enlightening-a-dull-witted-child voice. 'I . . . am . . . calling . . . Melon . . . Tuft . . . to . . . call . . . her . . . off . . . the . . . story.'

Sloane was silent for a moment, trying to sort out what was happening. Finally she asked, 'What are you going to do with these pictures?'

Layla flicked a glance at the folder. 'Take them,' she said. 'We won't be needing them.'

Sloane picked up the folder. She would hide it until she could burn it all in the fireplace at home. 'Where are the negatives, Layla?'

'I'll give you the photographer's name. You can contact her. I'll call her and tell her to give them to you.' Layla's voice was deadly calm. She seemed spent, as though all the fight and self-confidence had drained away in the last few seconds.

'Call her now and have them messengered to the desk at the Carlyle — *in my name*. If they aren't there by six, I'll be back.' The last thing in the world Sloane wanted to do was come back to this office, but she had to threaten or she might not get the negatives. They were crucial.

'All right,' Layla said quietly. 'If that's the way you want to do it.'

Sloane picked up her bag and the folder. 'I think I'd better go,' she said.

Layla held up her hand, her eyes still closed. 'No, wait, Sloane,' she said. 'Please sit down for a minute.'

Reluctantly, Sloane sat down on the edge of the chair, indicating that her stay would be short-lived. 'What is it, Layla?' she asked. She felt spent. All the adrenaline that had been building up seemed to have drained away.

'You probably think I'm a shit, don't you?' Layla said. Her tone was different now, softer, less confrontational.

'That's not the word I would use, but frankly, yes.'

'I don't blame you, Sloane. All I ask is that you try and understand how crazed I was when Warner told me he was getting married. I went on a real binge of self-pity. I was so depressed I felt that the only way I would ever get whole again was to take some sort of revenge on you both. I knew Warner would be furious if I published those photos, but he couldn't fire me. The contract he gave me makes me unfireable, but there's not a word about what happens to me if this magazine is sold. All I've ever needed in the world was this magazine and your husband. I've finally accepted the fact that I've lost him, but now you're telling me I might lose the magazine, too. It puts a whole new light on this cheap-shot scheme of mine.'

'I can understand that,' Sloane said evenly.

'I'm glad, because I want you to help me hang on to this magazine, Sloane.'

'Two minutes ago you were hell-bent on destroying me. This is quite a remarkable mood swing. I may be naïve, Layla, but I'm not stupid. Why should I lift a finger for you . . . ever?'

'Because you have your whole life ahead of you and I don't, not if I lose this magazine.'

Sloane met Layla's gaze. 'How can I trust you?'

'Have you ever been in love, Sloane? I mean completely, totally, obsessed with one man? I mean to the point where your every thought, every action, every moment, had the same goal — to hold on to that man because you knew you'd die if you lost him.'

Fernando's handsome face flashed through Sloane's mind. She looked down at her hands clutching the evil folder. 'Yes,' she said softly. 'Yes, I have.'

'And you lost him, right?'

'Yes, I lost him.'

'Why? Because he stopped loving you?'

'Not really,' Sloane said. 'I lost him because others took him away from me.'

'That's my point,' Layla said. 'Now, picture that happening after nearly twenty years.'

Sloane studied the obvious pain etched on Layla's proud features. 'Layla, you can't blame me for taking Warner away from you. It happened. I didn't even know about you and Warner, really, until Friday night. I was the one who brought you up. I knew I was coming here, so I asked him about you.'

'What did he say?'

'He said you'd been lovers for a long time, that you were the most unique woman he had ever known. He said you were brilliant.'

Layla's face began to crumble. 'He said that?' She covered her face with both hands and held them there.

It wasn't until Sloane saw her shoulders shaking that she realized this tough, unsentimental, rock-hard woman was sobbing.

Sloane couldn't stand it. Layla's pain must be overwhelming for her to let Sloane see her like this. She leaned forward and pulled a few tissues from a box on the desk and brushed them against Layla's knuckles. 'Here,' she said meekly. 'Don't . . . please. We're both hurting. Let's try and work something out.'

Layla took the tissues and patted her face, careful to avoid smearing her elaborate makeup. 'Damn!' she said.

'Look,' Sloane said. 'I can't give back Warner, but I will ask him not to sell the magazine. I can tell him that after I finish being the Bromley Woman I want to work here. I've never asked him for anything. He won't deny me.'

Layla noisily blew her nose. 'You would do that? After what I've tried to do to you?'

'Don't,' Sloane interrupted. 'You called off Melon. You gave me the pictures. I promise I'll speak to Warner. It might not be right away. It may have to wait until we get to California. He's swamped right now with some big acquisition in Japan. But you have my word.'

'When do you leave?' Layla asked.

'Soon.'

'Here,' Layla said, turning to the table at the back of her desk. She whirled a large Rolodex and removed two cards. 'I'm going to give you a couple of names. When you get settled in L.A., I want you to call both these people.' She quickly jotted names and numbers and handed the slip of paper to Sloane.

Sloane read the first. 'Stella Altman? Why are you

giving me her name? She's the most famous drama coach in the country.'

'By the time you reach her, I'll already have called. She'll take you as a private student as soon as you like.'

Stella Altman, Sloane knew, didn't take just anybody. You had to be either very, very good or highly recommended. 'You're serious about this?' Sloane asked, amazed.

'Completely,' Layla said. 'The same goes for the other person.'

Sloane read the name aloud. 'Dr Vincent Rollo?' she asked, puzzled. The name seemed vaguely familiar.

'Vince Rollo is absolute top in his field.'

'And that is?'

'Sexual obsession and aberrant behavior. I could have used him myself in the past. I was too arrogant.'

Sloane didn't know whether to laugh or be angry. 'And you think I should see him?' she asked.

Layla lowered her gaze and looked directly at Sloane. 'Don't you?'

Once again Sloane gathered her bag. She lifted the folder, looked at it, and then turned back to Layla. 'Yes,' she said softly. 'Yes, I do.'

As Sloane walked back to the Carlyle, her feelings were a mixture of relieved satisfaction and mild guilt. What she hadn't told Layla was that Warner hadn't sounded terribly serious about selling *Realto*. She knew it would be a small matter to have him drop the idea. She hadn't lied, really. And more important, she'd gotten the folder that was now hidden under the voluminous sable coat. She was aware that something had happened between Layla and her just now. A truce of some kind, between two women fighting for things they each wanted desperately. In a way, they both had won. There was no real threat to Layla's magazine. Sooner or later she would find that out. In the meantime Sloane was safe. Safe from humiliation and discovery, safe from the old fanged demons she seemed to have under control.

365

This was her brilliant new life. She'd be damned if she would see it destroyed by the bad old one. Maybe, just maybe in taking charge of her own destiny she may have made a new friend in Layla Bronz.

When Melon hung up from Layla's call, she screamed. 'Shit!' so loudly it left a stinging feeling in her throat. She flung herself down on the couch and screamed 'Shit!' again. 'What the fuck does that bitch think she's doing to me?' she asked the empty apartment.

She jumped up and ran to her desk. It was covered with typed pages and dozens of cassettes of tape she had been furiously transcribing since she had returned from the tour.

'She thinks I'm going to hand over all this work?' she yelled. 'She thinks she can kiss me off with a crummy kill fee after I've worked this hard? Well, fuck that!'

She scooped up everything on the desk that had to do with the Sloane story, stuffed it into a large manila envelope, and locked it in the bottom drawer of her desk.

She scrambled around to find Caramia Dell'Aqua's number in Tudor City, only to be told that Layla had called her, too. She had already taken the negatives to the desk at the Carlyle.

Furious, Melon slammed down the phone. Something was going on. Some deal had been made and she wouldn't be surprised if some money had changed hands. Now she would never get to interview Warner. Her byline wouldn't appear on the most sensational story since Miss America posed nude. No fame, no fortune. 'No shit!' she shouted, snapping the tab on a can of beer.

Later that night when she left again to stalk out the apartment she'd discovered Matty had on the East Side, she left a note on Kayzie's door.

Tell your boss in the morning I burned all my notes.
She'll know what I'm talking about.

She pushed through the lobby door into the cool night
air. It might be early April but the nights were still damp
and chill. She should know; she'd spent the last two
freezing on a fucking East Side fire escape.

She hurried to the Seventy-ninth Street crosstown bus,
muttering to herself on the way. 'No way am I handing
back that stuff, goddamn it! I'll use it someday, somehow.'

She patted her handbag. The high-powered field
binoculars were still there.

Last night, freezing on the fire escape of a boarded-up
theatre on Third Avenue, she had watched Matty and
two naked women fooling around until he turned out the
light.

So much for Twinkle Toes Alan's advice!

The very day she was back from the tour she had tried
making brownies. She miscalculated the baking time and
they came out like reinforced cement. She gave up in
disgust and spent thirty-four bucks at Zabar's for
enough brownies to keep the Harlem Boys Choir happy
for a week. She packed them in a huge tin so they
wouldn't get stale and left them at the front desk of the
porn-phone office where she knew Matty would check in.

Nothing. No response. Zipola in the phone department. She knew he got them because she checked with the
girl at the desk the next day. How could he be so cruel?
All she wanted was a frigging phone call. No, she
thought, that was a lie. She wanted more than that. She
wanted Matty. All of him. Every day. She didn't care if he
was married. Big deal, married. That didn't seem to
cramp his style.

When she reached the East Side it was dark. No one
was around as she stepped into the alley, pulled the
weighted ladder of the fire escape down, and clambered
aboard.

She settled into the corner of the third-floor landing and peered through the binoculars. Her heart skipped when Matty's shiny head crossed the living room across the street. There was a dark-haired woman sitting on the couch. Melon adjusted the lenses to get a closer look. They were drinking coffee. Heartsick, she saw Matty lift her tin of brownies and offer one to his companion.

She dropped her binoculars from her eyes. The only thing Alan left out with his Ann Landers routine was that she should inject each goddamned brownie with rat poison.

20

When they'd first arrived at Sans Souci in the hopeful spring of 1985, the Bromley helicopter bearing the newlyweds and the ever present Rose circled the Bel Air estate slowly so that Sloane could get a better look at what was to be her new home. As they began their descent, Sloane was filled with excitement. She was so looking forward to this new world. Even though, geographically, she was returning home, Bel Air was a completely different world than the Santa Monica life of her childhood.

As they hovered above the blue-green velvet lawn beside the tennis courts, Sans Souci looked like some sort of exclusive resort. The house itself sprawled across a third of twelve acres in the middle of Bel Air. There was a courtyard that could park fifty cars, electronic monitors, hidden cameras, and a gatehouse that held security guards around the clock.

An Olympic-size pool and elaborate pool house lay to the south next to the clay tennis courts. Beyond were the stables and show-ring. Inside, Warner promised, were more glories to behold, installed since she had seen the video of the interior.

After Warner bought the estate, he wanted more lawn for his satellite dish and purchased the mansion next door and had it demolished. Directing a team of decorators from his offices and the Bromley jet had become a kind of hobby he enjoyed telling her about in fond reminiscence.

She sensed that he was sorry the work was now finished, even though she knew he was eager for her astonished admiration.

As they alighted from the helicopter, they were greeted by Warner's butler. The rest of the staff consisted of four maids, a cook, a handyman, and a groom. Three Japanese gardeners took care of the greenhouse and grounds, and a yardman tended the pool and tennis courts.

Sloane gasped as she toured the results of Warner's insistence on perfection. In all there were thirteen bedrooms (six of them equipped with steam rooms and Jacuzzis), a game room, a dance studio and gym for Sloane, as well as an office off the library for Warner and Rose. There were two kitchens, 'one for summer, and one for winter,' Warner explained, beaming. Sloane refrained from asking what the difference was in the southern-California climate. Her mind reeled with the thought that organizing the army of servants would fall on her.

The living room, dining room, and library were enormous and furnished with massive sofas and chairs in muted tones of peach and white and beige. There were marble fireplaces everywhere, including the two kitchens.

She smiled to herself, remembering Warner's remark when she had complained that she didn't even cook.

He had just laughed and said he prayed she would never have to.

It was all overwhelmingly beautiful. But after the first few days she realized it would never feel like a home.

Sloane never knew where to sit, where to just be. Eventually, she asked Warner if she could make a little office for herself in one of the bedrooms on the second floor. She needed someplace to keep track of things that had to be done each day to keep the house running.

He agreed, and finally she had a room of her own with walls that didn't make her feel as if she were in Yankee Stadium. The furnishings were simple, made up of leftovers in storage from the decorating job. There was a couch, an easy chair, a desk with a good lamp, and some bookshelves. From behind the desk she could sit and look out toward the tennis courts and the swimming pool beyond.

Only in this room did she feel cosy and secure. The room was her sanctuary.

The day after she arrived she called Stella Altman at her studio on Sunset, only half-believing that the great lady would take her call. To Sloane's amazement the famous drama coach came right to the phone. She had already set up a schedule for Sloane's sessions. They were to begin the first of May. Layla had actually done what she'd promised. Sloane was thrilled. Her dream of acting would be so much more attainable if she was an Altman studio graduate.

Tingling with excitement and gratitude toward Layla, she immediately called New York to thank her.

'Sloane!' Kayzie squealed with delight. 'Wow, it's good to hear from you. How's everything going? Do you love it out there?'

'I think so,' Sloane said, laughing with delight at her friend's enthusiasm. 'This house is kind of overwhelming. There are rooms I haven't even been in yet. You really must try to come out, Kayz. You could have your own wing. I miss you.'

'Me, too. But don't tempt me. It's chaos here,' Kayzie said. 'But how are you? I mean, how are you, Sloane, not the Mrs Warner Bromley you? Are you doing a lot of stuff for Bromley Cosmetics?'

'Not at the moment. Warner is talking about another tour, maybe Europe next. But listen to this, Kayzie. I'm so excited. Stella Altman is going to take me as a student. I just talked to her. She's arranged a whole schedule for me. I'm starting the first of the month.'

'Sloane! That's fabulous. How did that happen?'

'Would you believe your boss got me it?'

'You're kidding.'

'Nope,' Sloane said. 'That's why I'm calling. To thank her. Is she in?'

'Oh, this is so great, Sloane! Hold on a sec. I'll get her. She's just about to go to lunch. And call me, will ya, huh? At home where we can really chat.'

'Okay, I promise. Soon.'

Within seconds Layla burst onto the line. 'Darling! How can I thank you!' She was practically shouting. 'I'm delirious. I was going to call you this afternoon to thank you. You are a fabulous, adorable girl!'

Sloane was stupefied. Layla was gushing. What in the world was she so excited about? 'I'm sorry?' Sloane asked.

'Hold on,' Layla said. 'Let me close the door. Kayzie just turned on the copier and I can't hear a thing.'

Sloane frantically searched her mind for what she could have done to have Layla calling her 'darling' and 'adorable.'

'I'm back,' Layla said. 'I got Warner's memo this morning. I almost jumped out of my skin. The idea of buying *City Living* magazine and combining it with *Realto* is absolutely brilliant!' Fortunately, Layla wasn't giving Sloane a chance to respond. Her words tumbled on. 'You must have done some selling job, Sloane. I've wanted to take a go at *City Living* for the last three years. Not only did you get Warner to keep *Realto*, but he's putting money into it as well! God, I'm going out of my mind with happiness. Anything, anything I can ever do for you, darling girl . . . well, you just have to whisper.'

So that was it! At first Sloane felt a wave of relief, then a quick twinge of guilt. She hadn't, of course, done anything to produce Layla's joyous mood. She'd never even heard of *City Living* magazine. 'I didn't do anything, Layla, truly,' she said.

'Maybe not to you. You know Warner would rehang the moon if you asked him. Last night I had the first good

372

night's sleep since you two left for California. This will be our little secret, okay?'

'Sure,' Sloane said tentatively. 'Listen, Layla . . . I'm actually calling to thank you for the introduction to Stella Altman. I start the first of the month. Maybe now I'll get my career off ground zero, thanks to you.'

'I'm happy you're happy, dear. Haven't things worked out marvelously for us both? Now,' Layla said, taking a more serious note, 'let me ask you one question.'

'What's that?'

'Did you call Dr Rollo?'

Sloane took a deep breath. She hadn't called.

'Hmmmm?' Layla prodded.

'No. I'm sorry, Layla. I'm just not ready. Not yet.'

'That's because things are going well right now, Sloane. But really dear, you *must* do that.'

'I know. I know. I will. I promise. I just want to get settled out here. It's all pretty overwhelming at the moment. I haven't figured out where the light switch for my dressing room is,' she said, laughing nervously.

Layla chuckled as she eased up on her. 'All right, sweetie, I understand.'

'I will call him, though. Soon.'

Layla thanked her profusely several more times and filled her in on New York gossip, including the news that Melon had gone freelance with a vengeance and was in Washington interviewing a cute young senator. 'I feel sorry for the guy,' Layla said, laughing. 'She's bound to trash him if she can.'

Sloane listened with half an ear. The mention of Dr Rollo had clouded her upbeat mood. There were things that she knew she had to deal with. But not now, she thought, please not now.

If she ignored them, perhaps the demons would die in their sleep.

*

Mornings she forced herself to do the paperwork involved in employing so many people. She drew up meticulous lists of things to be repaired and supplies to be ordered. She made phone calls to track down everything from a missing pool filter to a shipment of feed for the stables. Everything she did was accomplished under the pressure of pleasing Warner, for unlike the penthouse at the Carlyle, where one called room service, or the villa in Cap Ferrat, which he considered rustic and relaxed, Sans Souci was the place Warner thought of as home. His tastes were to be reflected in even the most mundane detail. Whenever he travelled, he expected her to fax a summary of everything she was doing in the management of the house, which was now her responsibility as his wife. She wanted to live up to his expectations for her, but it was hard, headache-producing work she had never thought would be required of her, ever. There were two things that sustained her over the first months at Sans Souci. First, her long heart-to-heart calls to Kayzie to talk about her life, assured that Kayzie wouldn't tell Layla that she was unhappy. Eventually, whatever Layla knew might get back to Warner, who thought Sloane was blissfully happy. And second, there were her afternoons at Stella Altman's studio.

At one o'clock each afternoon she would walk her notes to Rose in the office wing. If Rose was traveling with Warner, she put them on the fax machine herself. Then she would go to the bedroom and change into leotards and ballet slippers and meet her exercise and dance teacher in the gym.

After a two-hour workout she would shower and drive to the studio. Layla could not have imagined how great a gift she had given her by introducing her to such a woman. Stella was a short, squat Hungarian of uncertain years who spoke heavily accented English. She wore her salt-and-pepper hair in a severe blunt cut that emphasized her beautiful, deeply lined face. Each time she left one of their sessions Sloane felt challenged and enriched. She cherished their meetings and began to read and study as she had never done before.

It was only in the evening hours when she was alone in the vast, silent house with Warner on yet another one of his trips that she thought about her life. She sat in her little office, looking at the grounds eerily illuminated by lights hidden in the hedges, and she listened to the silence surrounding her.

It was in this little room that the real drinking started. Before that it had just been wine. One night she had turned on a television movie and recognized a man she had picked up one night in New York. During their brief conversation he had mentioned he was an actor. Now here he was on her gigantic television screen in a terrible remake of some South Seas adventure in which he played a native king, all glistening and mahogany, with a row of animal teeth and feathers around his neck.

She quickly slipped a blank tape into the VCR not so much to preserve the dreadful movie as to be able to replay his image. As soon as he came on the screen, she was filled with such an overwhelming melancholy that, in order not to weep, she padded down to the elaborately equipped and unused bar on the ground floor and took a glass and a bottle of brandy back upstairs.

By midnight most of the bottle was gone.

Drinking wine had started earlier, during Warner's first extended trip to Japan. At first she had politely sat at the massive Italian lacquered dining-room table that could seat sixty, feeling tiny and foolish as Conchita, the cook, and Warner's butler fussed over her. The first night the butler placed a stemmed glass and a bottle of Bordeaux next to her plate. After the first glass she felt warm and less alone. After the second she felt peaceful and grateful to be living as she was.

The next night she had a drink before dinner and tried eating at the butcher block table in the kitchen just to

375

have some company, but Conchita didn't speak enough English to hold a conversation.

The following evening that she asked Conchita to put her dinner on a TV tray in the library but found the room unnerving. Warner had turned it into a shrine of mounted pictures of herself matted in watered silk and framed in fruit wood. To eat being stared at by dozens of pairs of her own eyes gave her the creeps. That night she finished all the wine.

Now she took all her meals in the little office. After she realized brandy gave her a terrible hangover, she started sipping vodka after dinner as she read in bed. Often she would wake with a start in the middle of the night to find the lights on and her book tangled in the bedclothes.

One night, she was nodding off around nine o'clock when the bedside phone rang. Usually one of the night staff would answer it, but Sloane was so hoping it might be Kayzie she snatched it on the first ring.

'Sloane?' said the deep, instantly recognizable voice of Stella Altman.

'Miss Altman?' Sloane answered, completely surprised. Her coach had never called her for any reason, let alone at night. 'Are you all right?'

'Of course, my dear,' Stella said pleasantly. 'I hope I'm not disturbing you. I'm at dinner at the Volker Rhules'. Something has come up that I didn't want to let go until I see you tomorrow.'

'Oh my goodness. What?' Sloane asked, wide-awake and excited.

'May I put Volker on? He can explain.'

'Ah . . . of course. Please.' Sloane's heart began to thud against her chest. Volker Rhule was both a playright and a very successful television producer. Sloane had only recently read lines from one of his plays in class. She was racking her brain for the title when suddenly he was on the line.

'Miss Taylor. How do you do?'

'Fine, thank you, Mr Rhule,' Sloane managed to say.

'Forgive the hour. My old friend here hasn't stopped talking about you all evening. She thinks you would be perfect for our next project.'

Sloane cleared her throat and swung her legs over the side of the bed. 'How exciting. Why don't you tell me a little about it?' She hoped that was the appropriate thing to say.

'We're going to do *Anna Karenina* as a miniseries for the fall. Based on Stella's infallible recommendation, I'd like you to read for the lead part,' he said.

'M-m-me?' Sloane stammered. 'I'd be absolutely thrilled. If that doesn't sound too eager.'

Rhule chuckled. 'I appreciate eagerness, Miss Taylor. How does the day after tomorrow sound? Say, four o'clock at my office? Stella will give you the details and I'll see that a script is messengered over to you in the morning.'

Sloane thanked him, hung up, and leapt out of bed. She threw both arms above her head and spun around the huge bedroom until she was dizzy from singing, 'It's happened! It's happened!'

She didn't care if she woke up the whole house. She wanted to run out onto the vast lawn shouting at the top of her lungs.

She had to call Alan! Or Kayzie! She had to tell someone or she would burst with the news. She didn't care if it was midnight in New York. She tried Alan, but he was out. Kayzie just had to be home or she would explode.

Kayzie was indeed home. The two friends laughed and gossiped and giggled until well after two A.M. When Sloane finally hung up, she was exhausted but too exhilarated to sleep. It wasn't until she turned off the light and plumped the pillow that the empty space on the other side of the bed reminded her. Four o'clock the day after tomorrow. Warner was due back from Europe around

377

six. They were to entertain some business types at Chasen's.

She punched the pillow one more time. That was okay, she thought. She could leave word and meet him at the restaurant.

She hoped he would be half as excited as she was.

Warner, the man who built two kitchens in his new house, always chose to dine out. He preferred Chasen's, where he was always given the same table, for business dinners. For social entertaining he liked the Bistro Gardens for the 'old Hollywood money' crowd, and on Sunday nights they 'roughed it' at Spago or Morton's. Whenever they went to Spago, he would mutter about 'the element' there, by which he meant the younger, faster-track crowd he knew Sloane found amusing.

Tonight was a Chasen's night. She knew that meant she would be bored out of her mind.

The evening seemed interminable. As anxious as she was to share her wonderful news that Volker Rhule wanted her for the lead in a miniseries, Warner's guests made it impossible for her to tell him. There were two guests. The man next to her on the banquette was a German industrialist with teeth like praying hands. The man seated next to Warner and across from her was a London barrister who had the annoying habit of leaning across the table and speaking three inches from her face.

From time to time during the eternal meal Warner would slide his hand under the table and pat her knee as if to say, 'Courage, darling. This too shall pass.'

By midnight they had finished their brandy and coffee. Sloane had affixed a frozen smile on her face and completely tuned out of the thrill of leveraged buy-outs and talk of megamergers, whatever they were.

At last she and Warner were alone in the back of the big Bentley he liked to use for business dinners. With a sigh she moved closer to him and put her head on his shoulder. 'I had wonderful news today, darling,' she said, gazing up at him.

Warner listened carefully while she told him about Stella and Volker Rhule and the miniseries, saving the best until last. She was just about to tell him that she got the part that afternoon when he interrupted in a tone she knew by now meant he hadn't really been listening.

'How is Volker? I haven't seen him since the Heart Fund dinner last year.'

'He's terrific,' Sloane said, fighting being wet-blanketed out of her good mood. 'I liked him very much.' Warner didn't seem to be listening but Sloane plunged ahead. 'He wants me to start right away,' she said. 'Darling, do you think one of the Bromley lawyers could do the paperwork? Here I am with an offer for the lead in a miniseries and I don't even have an agent.'

'You know, Volker did a Broadway play last season. Something about the French Revolution?' Warner said, sounding as though he were talking to himself. 'Terrible flop as I recall. Took a real bath. He came back to L.A. and went in with the people from Tel-Planet . . . I almost bought that company . . .'

'Warner?' Sloane ventured.

'Sorry, darling. You were saying?'

'They're going to start shooting the exteriors in Czechoslovakia this fall. Mr Rhule says the architecture looks more like Moscow than Moscow does. He said they'd need me for about a month.'

Now Warner was listening. 'Whoa! Hold on, sweetie. What's all this? Czechoslovakia, Moscow. . . ?'

Sloane shifted away from his shoulder so that she could look him in the eye. 'Darling, I've been trying to tell you. I've been offered the lead in Mr Rhule's remake of *Anna Karenina* for a television series.'

Warner rubbed his chin. '*Anna Karenina*? That's pretty heavy stuff. Do you feel you're ready for something like that, darling? I know you're with Stella but . . .'

Sloane bit her lips for an instant and said, 'I read for him and he offered me the job. Stella says I'm ready. What more do I need?'

'Well, dear,' Warner said, running his hand along her arm, 'this sounds like something we'll have to discuss further. I tell you what. I'll call Volker in the morning. Ask him to the club for lunch. See what this is all about.'

Sloane leaned back against the seat and took a very deep breath. It helped prevent her from doing what she wanted to do, which was scream. Why was all this so familiar? Why did she feel she had lived this all before?

She was staring out the window at the deserted streets when it dawned on her. *He's Noreening me!* she gasped inwardly. *He's doing the same damn thing my mother used to do. Taking over. Lying in wait for a triumph that I got on my own and lifting it right out of my hands.*

She squeezed her eyes shut so tightly her temples began to throb.

Warner made love to her that night. She called it making love for lack of a better phrase. What it felt like to her was having a brief sexual exercise. All she could think about as he tried to arouse her was what she was going to do if he didn't let her take Volker Rhule's offer.

As it turned out, Warner had to leave the next day for an emergency in Washington. He wouldn't be back for a week, and Sloane spent the time reading the script of *Anna Karenina* three times, underlining, memorizing, and speaking the lines out loud to Conchita in the kitchen. The cook, whose only function was to fix Sloane's salads and cook for the help, smiled sweetly but understood nothing.

The more Sloane studied, the more ironic it seemed that her first real acting job would be portraying the story of an ill-fated marriage.

She got the actual Tolstoy volume from the Los Angeles public library, plus a biography of Count Tolstoy himself, and began to read them. By the time Warner was due back she felt as though she could go on a lecture tour on the subject.

The light was just beginning to fade in her little office when she heard tyres crunching the gravel in the driveway.

She glanced out to see the driver helping Rose out of the backseat as Warner strode toward the house. He had arrived back in L.A. that morning and phoned to say he was going straight to his club to have lunch with Volker Rhule. She had been able to think of nothing else for the rest of the day.

She quickly showered and dressed. Their routine, when Warner was in town, was for her to join him for a cocktail in the downstairs library before they went out to dinner.

She entered the library and took the drink the butler silently offered from a tray. Warner already had his and was just getting off the phone.

'Ah . . . my lovely.' He smiled, walking toward her and bending to brush her cheek. 'Every time I look at you I swear I'm going to stop traveling.'

'Do, darling,' she said, returning his kiss. 'Stay right here with me always, always.' She carried her drink to the couch and curled up in one corner. 'So?' she asked tentatively.

'So?' Warner said, tilting his head as though to hear her more clearly.

'How did your lunch go?'

'Lunch? Oh, Volker! Sorry, darling. My mind was still at the hearings in Washington,' he said, joining her on the couch. He reached for the television remote control on the end table. 'Actually, it was most enjoyable. His project sounds quite doable. Perhaps he's a bit premature to be casting it, but he seems to have things under control.'

Sloane nervously twisted the tassel of a cream satin throw pillow. She tried to keep her voice calm. 'So you're satisfied, darling?'

'Ummm,' he said just as Tom Brokaw's face appeared on the giant screen reporting the day's events. He lowered the sound but didn't turn it off. 'I'm sure it'll be a successful project. It's too bad his timing is off.'

'Sorry?'

He hit the mute button and turned to her. 'We're going to need you for our big European push for Bromley Cosmetics in October and November. Too bad, darling. But Volker understood. He assured me he would keep you in mind for his next project.'

Sloane was too stunned to comment. Warner had only mentioned a fall tour for Europe. It was never anything definite. Now, suddenly, it was a big-deal 'push.' She couldn't think. She tossed the pillow aside and rose from the sofa. 'I'm going to let you watch your news, dear. I still have some paperwork to do upstairs.'

'Fine, fine,' Warner said, staring at the screen. He turned up the sound.

Sloane waited until she was well down the hall before she started to run. She charged up the staircase and into her office. It took all her self-control not to slam the door behind her.

She fixed herself a stiff drink from the minibar and sat down behind her desk. She knew if she started to cry she wouldn't stop for days. She had to do something. She couldn't let him take this away from her without a fight. She wished she knew more about fighting, standing up for herself, getting what she wanted. She wished she were more like Layla. If Layla wanted something, she left the earth scorched to get it.

Layla! She could sweet-talk Warner into anything.

She glanced at her watch. It wasn't too late in New York. If she were lucky, Layla would be home.

She got up, locked her door, and then punched in Layla's number.

The phone rang four . . . five times. After the sixth ring a voice said, 'Hello,' impatiently.

'Layla?'

'Yeah. Who's this?'

'It's me, Sloane.'

'Oh, hi, sweetheart,' Layla said, relaxing her tone. 'How are you, hon? I haven't heard from you. I spoke to Warner when he was in Washington. He says your classes with Stella are going swimmingly.'

'That's what I'm calling you about,' Sloane said. 'Did Warner mention I've been offered a part in a miniseries?'

There was a pause on the line as though Layla was trying to recall their conversation. 'No,' she said slowly. 'Have you?'

'Yes, Layla. A big one. For Volker Rhule.'

'Now, that's odd,' Layla said, sounding mildly surprised. 'That's the second time I've heard that man's name today.'

Sloane stiffened. She felt as though things were happening that concerned her that she knew nothing about 'Really?' she said.

'Yeah, his press agent rang Cole this morning. He wanted a story on some girl he'd cast for a miniseries based on *Madame Bovary*, was it? No . . . wait a sec, it will come to me.'

'*Anna Karenina?*' Sloane asked flatly.

'Yeah! That was it.'

Afraid to ask but knowing she had to, Sloane tried to sound offhand. 'Do you remember the name of the girl he cast?'

'Sure, I have it right here on the schedule because I assigned Melon to interview her. Hold on, let me look.'

Sloane's mouth suddenly felt as though the skin would peel away if she moved her tongue. She took a swallow of vodka so large it filled her mouth and began to trickle down her chin. She didn't even bother to wipe it away.

'Ah . . . here we go,' Layla said. 'Daniella Paresi? Paresa? I can't read my own handwriting. I've never heard of her. Must be someone new.'

'Must be,' Sloane said numbly.

There was no reason to ask Layla to intervene for her now. Something had happened. Someone had done something that took away the one thing she wanted. That's probably why she hadn't heard from Volker Rhule all week. Warner probably killed the deal before he even went to Washington. There was no need to ask Layla for anything. Not this time. Somehow, she felt, the day was coming when she would.

'The Rhule fella is a busy guy. What are you doing for him?'

'Oh . . . ah . . . it's nothing definite, Layla. I really shouldn't jinx it by talking about it yet,' she said with lame cheerfulness. 'So . . . ah, what's Melon up to besides interviewing starlets?'

Sloane heard little of Layla's tale of Melon's latest outrages. She knew she was missing a hysterical account as only Layla could convey it. It was as though suppressed tears had flooded the inside of her head, deafening her to anything but the faint rumble of stirring demons.

She knew their habits well now. They would be ravenous when they were fully awake.

21

Melon was fifteen minutes early for her lunch interview
with some airhead actress and her press agent. Actually
she was right on time, but in the New York power game
at which she was becoming expert, she knew one never
got to the table *first*.

The ladies' room at the Four Seasons was on the street
level below the main dining rooms. Melon figured some
genius who understood women put it there. It permitted
one to whip in unobserved for a final fluff before making
an entrance into the Grill Room at the top of the stairs.

Lately, Melon lunched frequently at the chic boîte.
No, that was the wrong word – anyway, it was one she
loathed. Did anyone actually say 'boîte'? Or was it one
of those words you see only in magazines, like 'upper-
crust' neighborhood? No one said 'upper-crust' either.

She thought a lot about words now. Words, her words,
were the reason she dined so fashionably. Words, and her
ability to string them together and get them into print,
were beginning to pay off. She had a way to go before she
really felt she had arrived, but after the attention her
interviews had been receiving, not to mention the furor
they caused, she was becoming a media star. Somewhere,
buried in the back of her mind as she drove herself harder
and harder, was the hope that Matty Chiga was noticing.
She knew she had pushed him too hard and thereby
chased him away. She had been too needy. Perhaps, if she

proved she could really make it into the big-time, someday she would get him back.

The aborted Sloane Taylor article had been her last and only failure. After that she had locked herself into a determined pattern of work, sleep, push, hound, and hustle that had produced a string of sensational personality profiles. Top magazines were now paying attention and competing for her byline.

She spent a rainy afternoon with the new Mrs Springsteen while the stereo blared her husband's songs. She sat on Princess Stephanie's kinglier than king-sized bed in the Waldorf and listened to her cry about her rough-and-tumble jet-set life.

She went to an opening with Merv Griffin and a closing with Donald Trump when he bought another skyscraper.

She danced a waltz with Mayor Koch and walked the halls of Bedford Hills prison with lover-killer Jean Harris. A Sunday magazine bought her interview with a senator she had made cry for more than they had ever paid a freelance writer.

The articles she wrote from her interviews sparkled with telling details and damning quotes authenticated by the little body mike tucked inside her bra. Every word, every sigh, every self-incriminating murmur poured into her B cup, down a thread-thin wire, and into the tape recorder no larger than a pack of cigarettes strapped at the small of her back.

The money she loved and the power she craved were the result, although nothing quite made up for the empty bed she returned to each night. Her subjects, on the other hand, received ridicule, social ostracism, and legal papers from the lawyers of the offended and defamed. One of her subjects took an overdose after Melon wrote her own incautious words about her famous first husband's lack of erectile tissue.

'She shouldn't have told me her husband couldn't get it up if she didn't want me to write it,' had been Melon's crisp reply when a *Times* reporter called to ask her if she regretted what she had done. The remark made its way around town as fast as the speed of digit dialling would allow and overnight elevated her to mythic stature. Melon Tuft was the girl who would out-Walters Barbara and keep Liz Smith awake nights contemplating her retirement.

Melon never looked back. After each new outrage she dusted her hands and walked away, leaving those she had humiliated lying about grasping for their lost reputations.

More than wanting to be loved, Melon wanted to be taken seriously. By trashing celebrities she finally was.

She studied herself in the pink light of the ladies' room mirror. What she saw would do for today's interview. She hated interviewing young actresses, particularly when they had no real track record. There would be no article from this one, just a few lines for the 'Who's New' column in *Realto*. The press agent was a friend of Layla's who represented bigger stars. Melon was well aware by now of another New York game – do a favor, for a favor, get a favor.

She stabbed a rattail comb into the crown of her high, freshly streaked hair. She was now going to Alan Wade, Layla's hairdresser, who had changed her from Arctic Lemon Mousse to a more subtle White Mink. The lighter colour made her roots show and she needed a touch-up. What the hell, she thought. Today didn't matter.

She lifted the comb an inch or so higher and spritzed it with a blast of free hairspray from the tray of goodies the Four Seasons left on the counter for customers. She started to place the can back on the tray, remembered she was running low at home, and dropped it into her bag.

'Miss Tuft,' the captain said when she reached the top of the stairs. He bowed slightly and with just enough of a grovel to warm Melon's heart. 'Your party is waiting. May I show you to your table?'

'Thank you,' Melon said gravely, raising her chin and pulling back her shoulders. She was about to march through a room that at the moment contained the major movers and shakers of the New York publishing world. A certain posture was required.

As the captain led her toward a table for four at the far end of the room, she had to pass a long banquette filled with diners. Just as she reached the end of the aisle, she heard a hissing sound. As she paused to let a waiter pass, she heard it again and turned to see Matty Chiga gazing up at her from the banquette. Seated next to him was an exotic-looking woman in her fifties wearing a lot of Indian Squash Blossom jewelry.

'Hiya, babe.' Matty smiled, turning up one corner of his mouth. His black eyes twinkled.

Melon felt a lump clog her throat. He looked terrific. Someone had taken him in hand. He was wearing a stylish Italian silk jacket and a silk ascot. Probably the work of Miss Squash Blossom. 'Why, ah . . . ah . . . Matty!' she said. She hoped it sounded as though she had trouble recalling his name.

'How ya doin', kiddo?' He grinned. 'I saw your piece on that senator. You did good.'

'Why, thank you, Matty.' Melon glanced at the end of the aisle, where the captain was patiently waiting for her.

'You're going great guns, kid,' Matty said again, not making a move to introduce her to his companion.

'Well, ah . . . yeah. Thanks some more,' Melon said. 'Look, I've got some people to meet. Ah, see you sometime.'

'Right. See you sometime,' he said, pointing at her pistol style. 'Sometime soon.'

Damn. Damn. Damn. She cursed to herself as she walked the rest of the distance to the table. *Why did I wear this grotty outfit? It makes me look fat. My roots show. I didn't bother with eye makeup this morning. Shit?*

By the time she had joined the press agent and the starlet, who, of course, was drop-dead gorgeous, she was near tears.

Somehow she made it through lunch. The waiter had seated her in such a way that Matty was directly in her line of sight. Each time she looked up from her notebook he was staring at her with that crooked smile on his face. At least he was seeing her working. Why couldn't she have been with a real celebrity? Why, after all these months, did she have to run into him today? And who the fuck was that Pocahontas who kept rubbing her liver-spotted hands up and down his thousand-dollar Italian Spun Baby's Butt sleeve?

By the time she got back to her apartment it was nearly six. She flung her coat over the back of the couch and flicked on her answering machine. Matty had called at three-thirty, four-ten, five-fifteen, and five-forty. The last and most recent call must have come in while she was getting out of the cab.

She collapsed into the desk chair in front of her word processor and buried her face in her hands. 'He's back,' she sighed aloud. 'Matty's back. Four calls since lunch.' One call would have been enough. He called four times. She knew what that meant. Matty got like that when he couldn't have something. Hell, *she* got like that when she couldn't have something.

She pushed out of the chair and began to pace, telling herself this was her second chance. 'Don't fuck this one up, Tuft,' she scolded herself, pounding a fist into her open hand. 'Think for a minute. When you go after something and it keeps moving away, what do you do? Try harder. Right? Right.

'He's been reading your work. I hope to God he read the Donald Trump article. He's such a power-fucker, that alone would drive him wild. He's seeing your name in the columns. Today he actually sees you working, power-lunching in *the* power restaurant. You're not hounding

389

him and hocking him or sitting outside his house all night or swinging from a fire escape like some neurotic chimpanzee. You are now hot stuff and he wants you again.'

She walked to the mirror by the door and stared at herself, hard. Next to the mirror was a cork bulletin board full of clips and phone numbers. Under a recipe for Brazilian black-bean soup was a calendar. She reached over and made a big black X on the day's date.

She felt suddenly very calm and in control.

She knew what she had to do.

For every day she didn't call him she would mark another X on the bulletin board calendar. 'One day at a time, Mel, ol' buddy,' she whispered. 'One fucking day at a time.'

Of course, the more she held out, the more crazed for her he became.

He sent Derby-winner-size flower arrangements, tickets to shows, goo-goo-eyed stuffed toys, and food baskets from Dean & DeLuca. All of it was delivered by his broken-nosed Neanderthal schleppers.

She accepted everything with Church Lady isn't-that-special prissiness as the only return message and kept her answering machine on.

The day she made the twentieth X the hardware began to arrive. First a thick gold bracelet, then a colour TV, a cordless blender, and an antique music box.

By X number thirty she got her first note along with a diamond tennis bracelet fastened around a foot-long salami. The note read, 'Hint. Hint. Hint.'

She sat for a long time with the salami on her lap, stroking it and thinking about him, remembering the bad old days when she hungered for him, clawing her pillow at night in frustration. Then she would picture him handing her brownies to that hooker.

The next morning she took an enormous bite off the tip of the salami, scribbled a note saying, 'Not thinking of you,' and sent it back to him by UPS. She kept the bracelet.

She was actually enjoying the game. It made her feel stronger by the day. She discovered that, like dieting, giving up cigarettes, or getting your nails to grow, stonewalling a man who had broken your heart can make one feel righteous and holier-than-goddamn-thou.

She took her coffee to her desk and turned on her machine, noticing how the sunlight caught in the diamond tennis bracelet.

Today she would finish a piece she was doing on a bag-lady heiress living under Grand Central with half a million dollars in negotiable bonds wrapped up in filthy layers of *Town and Country* magazine. Her lead described the face-lift scars behind the woman's ears. It was a nice touch and she wanted to finish and get it over to *Woman* magazine by messenger by late afternoon.

She typed a paragraph that juxtaposed the woman's running leg sores with a description of the French silk stocking she wore at her coming-out party at the Waldorf in 1957.

The phone rang as she checked the transcribed tape for the correct spelling of the woman's very prominent family's name, something she had sworn to the sobbing woman she would not print.

She was so absorbed she automatically reached out and whipped up Garfield's paw, forgetting her vow to let the machine answer all her calls.

'Hiya, dollface,' said a familiar voice.

Melon's breath caught.

'Come on, baby,' Matty said, his voice soft and pleading. 'Please talk to me. You're breaking my heart. I just want to hear your voice, see how you're doin', tell you how crazy I am about ya. That's all. I ain't gonna cramp your style. I swear I'm not.'

She thought about the way his face must look at that moment. The way he always looked at her when she got

391

on top. She hadn't had sex in so long she was forgetting where a guy put it. What the hell, she shrugged. It was only a phone call and he had sent her some pretty nice stuff. 'Hello, Matty,' she said. 'Howya doin'?'

'Hey! You *can* talk. Man, am I glad to hear you talk. Jeez, I miss you. I was sittin' here reading that piece you did a couple of months ago where you got that big macho movie-star guy to talk about his murdered wife and kids. That was some job you did, describing how he asked you not to use what he said and then ran out to throw up. Really great.'

'Thanks. His press agent and lawyer weren't real happy about it.'

'What'd the creeps do, threaten to sue you?'

'Yeah, but there was nothing they could do.' She laughed. 'I got it all on tape, even the part where he's barfing and gagging. I had to follow him into the john to get it, too. I was thinking about using it as the message on my answering machine.'

'Damn, you're somethin' else, little girl. I wish you were here with me now.'

'Why? Where are you?'

'I'm sitting here in the apartment looking at a Manganaro's sandwich left over from a poker game this afternoon. It's six feet long.'

Melon slumped in her chair remembering the tin of tuna she had for lunch. She was starving. 'Describe it to me, Matty,' she said, feeling her kick-butt attitude draining away through her taste buds.

'Well,' he said eagerly, 'like I said, it's six feet long. Real fresh Italian bread, see. Now, first you got a layer of real good prosciutto.'

'Ummmm.' Melon nodded.

'Then comes your mozzarella. Then there's red onions, and on top o'that, a layer of Genoa salami and Swiss. You got slices of those Italian plum tomatoes, really juicy.

A . . . let's see. There's sprinkles o' black olives sliced real thin. Oh, yeah. There's a layer of –'

'Matty?'

'– real crisp lettuce.'

'Matty?' she tried again.

'Then on top of all that they put an olive-oil-and-wine-vinegar dressing and –'

'Matty!' she shouted.

'Yeah, doll?'

'You got any beer to go with that?'

'Nah. I'm fresh out. The boys drank it all.'

'I've got a six-pack of long-neck Buds.'

'You do?' he said in his under-every-pile-of shit-there's-a-pony voice.

'Do you suppose you could manœuvre that sandwich in the back of a cab?'

There was a momentary silence while what she was suggesting sank in. 'You mean it?'

'I mean it,' she said, smiling.

'Oh, Baby! Baby. Baby. Baby. I'll get this mother over there if I have to have the limo brought around. See you in ten minutes.'

When she returned Garfield's left arm to his shoulder hook, she was still smiling.

She walked over to the bulletin board and tore off the sheet with all the X's. It was the start of a new month anyway.

It came as no surprise when Warner announced that Sloane's European tour had been indefinitely postponed. She suspected all along the tour had been a ploy to keep her from doing the miniseries. She feigned surprise for his sake. He seemed to believe her.

Perhaps after all those months of work with Stella Altman she was becoming such a good actress she could fool even him.

Warner tried to console her by saying they would go abroad anyway. There was plenty for him to do abroad and they would have some time together. London at Christmas is lovely, he assured her.

It wasn't.

They spent December at Warner's house in Mayfair. It was draughty and dark. Sloane spent most of the day trying to get warm and most of the night quietly drinking too much before, during, and after the several dinner parties Warner had arranged. At least the dinners gave her someplace to wear the emerald drop earrings Warner had given her.

Everyone thought the lovely young Mrs Warner Bromley was such a good listener. The truth was that she listened because she didn't have anything to say.

Since the *Anna Karenina* incident she had begun to think of herself as a nonperson, an object that came alive only when she was in acting class. The rest of the time she sleepwalked through her beautifully organized life disguising her emptiness with what passed for charm.

After London, she, Warner, Rose (of course), and an English couple named Atterly-Benz repaired to Sea Spray in Bermuda to try and bake the London winter out of their bones.

It was there that Sloane discovered that a thoroughly clean sun-lotion bottle made a perfect flask and took to carrying vodka around in her beach bag.

It helped. It helped fill the emptiness. She felt as though she were falling through space, that soon there wouldn't even be a 'me' anymore. She would just dissolve and there wouldn't even be a hole where she had been.

She was feeling that way upon their return to the mansion in Bel Air at the end of January, when she found a stack of Christmas presents waiting for her.

One of the servants had left the presents on the desk in Sloane's little office. They had dutifully been dusting them for weeks as their wrapping faded in the sun from the bay window.

Sloane fell upon them with a squeal of delight. They were from New York, from those who were part of what she increasingly thought of as the 'happy times' when people could actually see her, touch her, talk to and be with her.

She lifted each package tenderly, vowing to open them alone after Warner left the following morning. Then she could spend hours on the phone thanking everyone.

Kayzie had sent a boxed set of videos of old Garbo classics and a silk scarf with I LOVE NEW YORK splashed all over it. Cole sent a leather-bound collection of Tennessee Williams's plays. Alan, her darling Alan, had taken an old snapshot of the two of them in their high school cheerleading uniforms making monkey faces and had it blown up to poster size. Layla's present was a mystery and a surprise. A first-class open round-trip plane ticket to Acapulco. No note, no explanation. Just the ticket in a Mark Cross wallet.

Sloane sat among the crumpled paper and ribbon and stared out the window, awash in homesick longing for her friends.

As she sipped the rest of her wine, she watched the leaves of the trees move slightly in the light breeze. It reminded her that back east a tree in Central Park would be without leaves.

She pictured herself racing down Fifth Avenue to another shoot, wondering if she would make it to the top before she hit thirty and it was too late.

But hadn't she 'made' it? Wouldn't anyone who knew her or even read about her say that marrying one of the wealthiest men in the country was 'making it.' She lived in luxury by anyone's standards. Miraculously, despite the drinking she still looked as good as when she was modelling. Her body responded to the constant workouts and dance routines and remained lean and limber. Her wide-set grey eyes were clear, her skin still the color and smoothness of peaches, thanks to hats and cream against the relentless California sun.

She wondered if Warner saw beneath the physical beauty, if he would love her if she didn't look the way she did.

The buzzing of the desk phone jolted her back to reality. She caught it on the second buzz. At the sound of the voice her heart soared. 'Oh, Alan. I'm so glad you called. Would you believe I'm sitting here opening my Christmas presents?' she almost shouted. 'I love my poster. It's hilarious. I was just going to call you and Kayzie and Cole and . . .' She couldn't go on.

'Baby-cakes! Are you all right?' Alan asked with alarm. 'Why are you crying?'

Sloane made an effort to get herself under control. 'I'm sorry, darling,' she choked. 'I'm so lonely for all you guys. Hearing your voice just got to me. I miss all of you so much. I'd kill to see you.'

'Well,' he said, 'have you opened Layla's present?'

'Just now. It's a ticket to Acapulco. I don't understand. Do you know anything about it?'

'I do, but you've got to cross your heart and swear to die you won't tell.'

Sloane laughed. Alan loved secrets, particularly parting with them. 'Cross. Heart. Die,' she said.

'It's supposed to be a big-deal surprise. You're supposed to find out when Cole calls you later today, so don't let on. Cole has the use of a villa in Acapulco for the last week of this month. When Layla heard about it, she suggested he invite you down. He said Warner wouldn't be amused, but Layla had just talked to him and he was complaining about how he thought maybe you could use a giggle with your old friends, after London and all. So she set the whole thing up as a surprise.'

'Oh, my God, are you going, too?' Sloane asked excitedly.

'Does Nancy Reagan get her clothes for free?'

'So it would be me and you and Cole? Alan, I'm so excited I'm going to jump out of my skin.'

'Hang on, it gets better,' Alan said. 'Kayzie and Ryan are coming too. It will be a regular *Realto* Irregulars Reunion. You game?'

'Alan. Alan. Alan. I'm speechless. Of course I'll come! You don't know how thrilled I am,' she said. 'Where are we staying?'

'You've read about the Neithergoulds, right?'

'Who hasn't? Billionaires with press agents.'

'Well, they're friends of Cole's. It's their beach house. Layla even gave Kayzie and Cole a couple of days off. We'll have a ball.'

'And Warner knows and everything?' she asked, incredulous.

'Yup. Act surprised there, too,' Alan said, clearly delighted to be bringing her the news. 'Now, here's the plan. We'll fly down on Friday night. We plan to stay over in Mexico City Saturday. Cole has tickets for the bullfights. Then Sunday we'll leave for Acapulco. The house is fabulous. Look in this month's *Architectural Digest*. Unbelievable!'

Alan rattled on. His most ecstatic descriptions were reserved for the color and excitement of the bullfights and the famous matador they would see.

All Sloane could think about was how much she wanted to go, how lonely she was for them all. She couldn't remember the last time she had had a good laugh with friends her own age.

Alan was winding down on his hard sell. 'There's a new disco in Acapulco that we hear is wild. Wouldn't it be fun to get bombed and dance the night away?'

'Oh, Alan,' she sighed. 'I haven't danced since my wedding.'

'Now, that's a waste of beauty and talent.'

'Listen, Alan, I'm going to call everyone to thank them for my presents now. Don't tell them, okay?'

'And you don't tell either, kitten.'

'No, no. Our secret, our fun, our reunion in the sun,' she singsonged, feeling giddy and wild with anticipation.

She kissed the receiver good-bye, picked up the Mark Cross wallet, and looked at the ticket.

How would she find the words to thank Layla for what she had done? She certainly couldn't tell her she was saving her sanity, probably her life. Maybe tonight she would send Conchita to the movies and actually cook a meal for Warner when he got home.

How dear of him. How unutterably sweet he was to plan this wonderful time for her. And how like him to try to make it look as though it was Layla's idea.

She pushed the cork back into the wine bottle. She wanted to be bright eyed and loving when he got home. He had made her so happy.

She could hear mariachi music already.

22

The dust kicked up by thousands of boisterous, excited aficionados soon sifted through Sloane's hair and lashes, even her teeth. Nothing seemed to bother the others as they were carried along in the stream of humanity that moved toward the stadium. Their flights had all arrived late the night before and none of them had slept much. Now they were all a bit high on breakfast margaritas and the fun they were all having. Sloane felt light-headed from the drinks and the freedom of just being here with the friends she loved.

She sensed a kind of unexplainable lust in the air and recognized it as the anticipation of danger, that very sensation that had excited her so in times past. She was both excited and afraid. The crowd, the smells and sounds, the rising anticipation of a bloody spectacle, began to sweep over her as the crowd surged toward the arena.

She climbed through the stands on trembling legs, blinded by the sun, clinging to the sleeve of Alan's polo shirt to keep from falling on the rough cement. Kayzie climbed ahead and located their seats in the front row of a tier and waved them up. The seats were no more than worn cushions plopped down on the curved concrete steps.

Ryan had grandly asked the bartender at breakfast to fill a goatskin with more margaritas. He now offered a drink to Sloane after showing her how to squirt it into her mouth from a foot away. Not wanting to refuse and dampen their high spirits, she accepted. The liquid hit the back of her throat with the first try. It was still cold and tasted remarkably refreshing in the fetid air. She swallowed, giggled, and handed the goatskin on to Cole, who was rattling away about the pageantry, the beauty, and tradition of the centuries-old blood sport.

He was particularly pleased with himself for having secured tickets. This fight had been sold out for months to fans of Miguel Vellis, a bullfighter who, Cole assured them, was a legend.

As though on cue, the wind picked up. The people pressed around them seemed to gasp in unison as a fanfare of brass filled the air, heralding the *paseo*, the procession that began the fight.

Cole leaned closer to Sloane. 'Wait till you see this Vellis,' he said breathlessly.

'Who?' she asked, bridging her hand against her forehead in order to see out into the ring.

Cole didn't answer. The procession had started. From across the bullring she saw two men on horseback dressed in medieval costumes leading the long line of toreros, the men who fight the bulls, into the sunlit ring. Each man had his left arm wrapped in a cape. Following them were more men on horseback. At the head of the parade walked the three matadors who were to fight. Each wore a resplendent suit of lights. They moved with great poise and dignity as they strode across the ring.

Sloane found herself fascinated.

As the procession approached their side of the stadium, the horsemen turned and exited. Her view was now unobstructed, and her eyes were drawn to the matador walking on the right side of the procession. He was wearing a ruffled snow-white shirt with a red tie under a purple suit of lights. His waist-length jacket was covered with gold embroidery so intricately worked it seemed actually to move in the light.

He was taller than the others, and while he walked in the same easy, measured cadence, he seemed more confident, more sure of his mission.

When he was close enough for Sloane to make out his features, she plucked at Cole's sleeve. 'Look at his face,' she said in a loud whisper.

'Which one?'

'The one on the right. He's absolutely beautiful.'

'Ah . . . that's Vellis,' Cole said. 'I saw him fight last year.'

'I think he's the most beautiful man I've ever seen.'

'Me, too,' Cole agreed with a grin.

Sloane studied the man's face, trying to figure out what made it unique. His expression was a solemn mask, his dark, piercing eyes focused on some invisible horizon. Unlike the other fighters with their broad, somewhat flat features, Vellis's face seemed chiseled. He had a high, aristocratic forehead and a straight Roman nose, high cheekbones, and a square jaw. It was his mouth that most intrigued her. The lips were full and turned down at the edges, a look that was both erotic and cruel.

'Is that the Vellis guy you were going on about at breakfast?' Kayzie called to Cole across Ryan and Alan.

Cole nodded without turning.

'Krikees, Sloane, have you ever?' she said.

Sloane didn't answer. She was studying his taut, beautifully formed body, the long, muscular thighs and small, high buttocks, every muscle defined by the tight knee-length pants. His broad shoulders were further exaggerated by the embroidered epaulets of his jacket.

Suddenly the matador turned and looked straight at Sloane. Their eyes locked, unmoving. It lasted only for a millisecond. The shock of recognition created a silence in which the only sound she could hear was her beating heart.

He turned away and withdrew into himself.

Sloane was stunned. She could not believe what she

401

had just seen. Here, in this otherworldly place – unlike any place she had ever been or known – she had received *the look*. The secret weapon that she had thought was hers alone. Sometimes she thought it was all she had. She had stalked men with that look. She had conquered them with that look. It had taken all her strength to abandon it because, in seeking to fill a vacuum in her life, the emptiness in her heart, it had brought her such pain. Now, here it was, like a sudden, violent clap of thunder on a peaceful summer day, seeking her out. Her weapon, in the eyes of this mesmerizing stranger.

Cole and Alan turned to her, as breathless as sorority girls. 'Sloane, he looked straight at you!' Cole gasped. 'Alan, did you see that? He looked right at Sloane.'

'Oh, please. You two,' Sloane said, trying to diffuse a situation that left her face hot and red.

They were not the only ones who noticed. The entire gallery around them had followed the matador's riveted gaze and turned to see who was the recipient.

Alan couldn't leave it alone. 'She had the same effect on men in high school,' he said, laughing.

Sloane ignored him. Whatever else he was going to say was drowned out by the fanfare announcing that the fight was about to begin.

Vellis began walking across the ring, heading for the gate through which the first bull would enter. He carried a large stiff cape, pink on one side, yellow on the reverse. He knelt in front of the gate and arranged the cape.

Suddenly the atmosphere was charged with danger. Sloane couldn't breathe. A massive black bull with foot-long outwardly curved horns thundered toward the kneeling matador.

She tried to remember Cole's breakfast lesson on the ancient art of bullfighting. What he hadn't bothered to tell them was how truly terrifying it could be.

Her heart was in her mouth as the matador swung his cape to the left, averting the bull from his body. Quickly he turned and deftly moved the cape to the right, met another charge, teasing, daring, mocking the huge animal. Then, brazenly, he stood, turned his back, and walked away.

'Why is he doing that?' she asked Cole, who was just as intensely involved as she, but for different reasons.

'He's testing the bull, seeing how it moves. Now, hush. Watch his men play with the bull. They want to see how the bull is going to behave. I'll explain it all to you later . . . again,' he said, smiling reassuringly.

She turned back to the ring to see Vellis standing behind the protective partition to which he had repaired. He stood with an easy nonchalance, resting his weight on one leg, one hand on the partition.

Suddenly his body went taut. He was ready to enter the ring again. Now the fight would begin in earnest. Again he turned and looked directly at Sloane, then looked away with a hint of a smile.

'You know this guy?' Ryan boomed at Sloane from across the seats.

'Not yet,' Alan teased. 'If she wants to, she will.'

Sloane turned from the ring to reprimand Alan. 'Alan! Will you please shut up. He wasn't looking at me.' She knew he was. She could again feel a thousand eyes in the stands staring at her. She imagined them muttering among themselves, 'Who is this *gringa* our matador is staring at?'

In her distraction something important had happened. The tension in the crowd was almost palpable. Vellis was now striding into the centre of the ring carrying two thin, brightly decorated shafts with harpoonlike tips. He stood facing the bull, brooding in quiet fury not thirty paces from him.

'Why is the bull bleeding?' Sloane said to Cole in a high, frightened voice.

'The picadors.'

'The what?' she asked.

'Hush!'

Sloane sat silently, repulsed by the sight of gore that coated the animal's withers and oozed down the side of its jet-black coat. She felt a deep sense of sorrow for the poor doomed animal and closed her eyes.

When she opened them, Vellis had raised the long shafts, one in each hand, and pointed them at the bull. He walked toward the bull with slow, menacing steps. On the fourth step, the bull charged toward him. He raced away in a semicircle, drawing the bull from its straight path but toward him nonetheless.

With a fierce lunge Vellis imbedded the shafts into a spot at the top of the bull's neck. The crowd roared while men with capes drew the bull away from the unprotected matador. The front of his beautiful suit was smeared with the blood of the bull.

It was too much. Sloane buried her head against Cole's chest. 'The man's going to get killed. I can't look.'

'Don't wimp out on me now.' Cole laughed, putting his arm around her.

She cringed against Cole until she heard the roar of the crowd, this time so loud it vibrated the air. She looked up to see a sea of white handkerchiefs waving. Out in the ring, Vellis walked about acknowledging his victory.

As he passed in front of their seats, he did not look at her again. Oh, well, she thought as she settled back to watch the other fighters ready themselves for their own performances, at least he noticed me before. Or did he? Yes, she knew he had. As brief as the contact between them had been, she would never forget it.

She had suppressed any thought of playing the Game for so long. Now it all flooded back. If she were ever to do it again, it would be with a man like Vellis. That meant she was safe. There was no way that would happen. A man like that was just a fantasy anyway. And yet, deep in the back of her mind, she heard the demon voices very, very faintly calling, 'Oh yeah?'

*

At the end of the long day of bullfighting, as they made their way from the long, dark tunnel beneath the stands and into the still-blinding late-afternoon sun in the vast parking lot, Cole threw his arm out against Sloane's chest and roughly pushed her back. A long burgundy Cadillac had appeared from nowhere and brushed so close to them that surely she would have been struck without Cole's intervention. They stood for a moment and stared as the car braked to a halt in front of them. The tinted windows hid whoever was inside. A window in the back silently glided down and Sloane recognized the piercing black eyes.

He leaned out of the window and addressed Cole, whose face was no more than a few inches away. 'I compliment you on your taste in companions,' he said in Spanish.

Delighted by the scene, Alan pushed his way toward the window, 'Ah, Señor Vellis. You fought so beautifully. This is our friend, Sloane Bromley. She is a famous American.'

The matador's face did not change expression. 'My compliments again,' he said. The window rose slowly and the car moved off into the day.

'Alan, you idiot,' Sloane said hotly. 'How could you do that? I'm mortified.'

'Oh, lighten up, hon. You should be flattered to pieces. Any woman in Mexico would have fainted dead away.'

'Well, I'm not flattered,' she lied. 'I'm embarrassed.'

'I bet he finds out where you are and comes looking for you,' Cole said with a leer.

'Cole, don't be ridiculous. He probably saw me in an ad and thought he knew me. Besides, I'm a married lady.'

Cole had hired a limousine to take them to dinner, its bar

stocked with more margaritas and iced champagne. Ryan appointed himself traveling bartender. Balancing his lanky frame on the jump seat, he spilled more than he served.

After the incident in the stands, compounded by the parking-lot meeting with the Great One, as they called Vellis, Sloane was teased mercilessly. Each of them in turn endowed her with everything from supernatural sexual power, X-ray eyes, and telepathic energy to the ability to drive a demigod who could have any woman in the world wild with desire. They were having such hysterical fun teasing her she resigned herself to it, sat back, and sipped her champagne, floating in the euphoria of the moment.

She would have been deliriously happy even without the bullfighter's attention. She had missed her friends dearly and now she was among them, free and laughing, without a care in the world.

Suddenly she was filled with an overwhelming love for each of them. Cole was the closest to her. She turned and threw her arms around his neck and kissed him loudly on the cheek.

'What's that for?' He laughed, making an elaborate show of wiping off a trace of her lipstick on his face.

'That's for making all this happen,' she said, squeezing his shoulder. 'I'm so happy!'

Ryan lifted his paper cup of champagne. 'To Lady Brett Ashley! Our Lady of the Bullring!' he cried, hanging on to the edge of the jump seat as the limousine careened into a sharp turn.

'Who's Lady Brett Ashley?' Sloane asked.

Kayzie took a gulp of champagne and answered, 'A Hemingway heroine who was in love with a guy who couldn't do it so she ran off with a bullfighter.'

There was a silence the length of a heartbeat inside the car until Ryan loudly cleared his throat and said to Kayzie, 'Thumbnail Literature 101, sweetheart?'

Cole and Alan exchanged looks. Sloane could see they were all embarrassed that Kayzie's remark might somehow relate to her situation. Suddenly everyone began to talk at once and the awkward moment passed as though it hadn't happened.

The limousine pulled into the parking lot and discharged its raucous cargo. Kayzie danced around, her fingers hooked like horns at her forehead, playing bull to Ryan's raincoat 'cape' while their driver smiled and shook his head at the crazy gringos.

As they entered the crowded restaurant where Cole had booked a table for dinner, Ryan continued to play bullfighter with his raincoat and a butter knife snatched from a table near the door as a sword. The merry band danced conga-line style into the bar shouting 'Olé!' and laughing hysterically. They climbed onto the high stools at the bar with shouts of 'Drinks for the matador's lady!' and tortured Spanish commands like 'Habla much champagne, por favor, bartendo!' from Ryan. Although the restaurant was used to rich, rowdy Americans after a bullfight, the only thing that saved them from being asked to leave was Cole's extravagant and steady tipping of anyone who looked like an employee. After more champagne at the bar they made their way to a table in the corner. They were immediately surrounded by smiling waiters who vied for a position near Cole and his generous right hand.

Sloane, exhilarated and nearly numb from the experience of the afternoon, joined in the merriment, but her mind still held the picture of the matador's eyes.

People who knew Cole kept coming over to the table, mostly good-looking American men, who were introduced. They all seemed to know who Sloane was. The waiter at her side kept refilling her glass as they gathered around paying her compliments and making a fuss over her.

She loved it. She felt as though she had been in some

kind of dark sanatorium and had just been released into the blazing sunlight of attention and praise. She laughed and chattered and innocently flirted, awash in the sheer joy of just being able to be around people again. She was only a little embarrassed that her brief encounter with the bullfighter dominated the talk of the table.

They had just finished their meal and were contemplating coffee and dessert when a hush fell over the room. Everyone turned to watch the scene at the door.

A group of short, stocky, somewhat brutish-looking men had entered and stationed themselves around the entrance.

The maître d', captain, and waiters scurried to the front and stood at attention. The large room remained hushed for a moment or two, and then everyone began to mutter to one another.

A man, taller than the others and dressed completely in white — white trousers, shoes, and white silk shirt unbuttoned low enough to reveal several ropes of gold — stepped into the large room. A white jacket was draped over his broad shoulders. His black hair glistened as though wet.

Sloane's hand flew to her throat.

Suddenly everyone rose and faced the door. The room exploded in applause.

'My God,' Cole gasped. 'It's him!'

They watched as Miguel Vellis made his way down the centre aisle, bowing almost imperceptibly, nodding, occasionally reaching out to accept a proffered hand, a rose, a touch.

Alan leaned across to Sloane and whispered, 'Will you look at the way they're treating him.'

'I told you he's some kind of god here,' Cole said.

'Yeah, but look at the way he accepts it. It's like watching the Pope,' Alan said, shaking his head.

Sloane stared in awe. Half of her was afraid he would see her at the back table. The other half prayed he would see her. She swallowed hard to keep from making some kind of sign.

As he moved through the room, his entourage formed a line behind him. Within minutes the group had moved into a private room at the back of the restaurant.

'Well!' Cole breathed, sitting down and reaching for his glass. 'Wasn't *that* a show.'

Ryan leaned across the table, grinning. 'You can start breathing again, Sloane.'

'You might also want to close your mouth.' Kayzie giggled. 'It's been hanging open for five minutes.'

More waiters arrived at the table and began setting down bottles of every conceivable liqueur, bottles of Tía Maria, brandies, Strega, and something with coffee beans floating in it.

A smiling Maître d' bent toward Cole. 'Compliments of the house, Mr Latimer,' he said softly.

'Why, thank you, Roberto.' Cole smiled up at him. 'That's very nice.'

'And this is for you, sir,' Roberto said, placing a small white card on the tablecloth in front of Cole. He took one step back and waited for Cole to read it.

'What's this?' Cole asked, picking up the card. He squinted at it, looked surprised, and reached for his reading glasses. 'If this is what I think it is, I'd better check my Spanish.' He put on his glasses and signalled Roberto to help him read it. There was a mumbled conference as the card was translated. Everyone at the table watched as Cole nodded and put the card down on the table. He raised his hand for attention. 'Sloane,' he said with great solemnity, 'Señor Vellis requests that you join him at his table.'

Sloane blinked. 'What?'

Cole handed her the card. 'That's what this says,' he said.

Kayzie let out a little squeal of delight.

'Oh . . . lay!' Ryan said, deeply impressed.

Sloane studied the card. It was in Spanish and made no sense to her whatsoever. She glanced around the table. 'This is absolutely ridiculous,' she said, bewildered.

'What do you mean ridiculous?' Alan said excitedly. 'The Great One has summoned you.'

She held the card between two fingers and fanned herself with it. 'I'm not summonable,' she said. 'Besides, he didn't send me this card. He sent it to Cole.'

'That's very Latin, Sloane,' Kayzie volunteered. 'It's like Cole is the man in charge and he's asking his permission.'

Alan picked up the card and studied it. 'I think you should go,' he said.

'I think we *all* should go,' Ryan said, beaming. 'Wouldn't *that* refry his beans.'

'Oh, let's!' Kayzie said, clapping her hands. 'Let's all march back there and surround him.'

'Count me out,' Sloane said, not amused. She turned to Cole. 'I think you should send back a note saying that *Mrs* Bromley is not available. Emphasize the Mrs – I mean, who does he think he is?'

'He is the mighty matador,' Ryan said grandly with a snap of his fingers over his head. 'He can have anything he commands.'

'Wrong,' Sloane said, wiggling her index finger at the maître d', who was clearly enjoying the scene. 'Roberto, would you tell Señor Vellis the lady says "gracias but no gracias."'

Roberto put his hand to his heart as though shocked. He nodded and repeated, 'Gracias but no gracias, sí, señora.' He turned briskly and walked toward the back room.

'He's not going to like that,' Ryan said, delighted at the adventure of it all. 'I wonder what he does when someone turns him down.'

410

Kayzie stood up. 'I don't think we should wait around to find out. What if he comes over here with those gorillas of his?'

Cole waved his hand dismissively. 'He won't do that. He would never risk public rejection.'

'Well, I think Sloane and I should be elsewhere when he gets the word,' Kayzie said, looking across at Sloane. 'You game for the girls'?'

'You bet,' Sloane said gratefully as she gathered up her bag.

In the tiny ladies' room, Kayzie filled her cupped hands with cold water and splashed it over her face. 'He's after you,' she said, blindly reaching for a paper towel. 'Aren't you excited?'

'Sure,' Sloane acknowledged, stroking fresh mascara on her lashes. 'Who wouldn't be? I'm married, not dead.'

'But you wouldn't do anything about it?' Kayzie asked. It was more of a statement than a question.

'No,' Sloane said. 'I couldn't handle it.'

'Well, I think it's incredibly exciting. I mean, he actually picked you out in the ring today. There had to be thousands of people there, and he walked right over to you.'

'Kayz, I think I want to forget about it now. What I'd really like to do is go back to the hotel. I'm half-smashed from all this nonstop drinking. I'm bone tired and dusty. I want a hot shower and a good sleep.'

Kayzie disappeared into the booth while Sloane finished touching up her makeup. She stared at herself in the mirror. Could Kayzie tell she was putting up a front? Could her closest female friend see that her whole body was shaking with fear and desire?

It would have been disastrous to show any interest in front of Cole and Alan, particularly. And yet, given the same chance under less public circumstances, she knew she would not be able to control an entirely different response.

411

By the time they got back to the table Cole had already paid the bill and was waiting for the others to leave.

'How did it go?' Sloane asked, touching Cole's shoulder.

He shrugged. 'I don't know. Roberto disappeared and that was that.'

'I wonder if he knew we were here,' Sloane asked as they made their way to the door.

'He did,' Cole said, smiling over his shoulder at her.

'What?'

'Roberto told me one of Vellis's men asked our driver where we were going after the fight.'

'And he told him?' Sloane asked in disbelief.

'Are you kidding?' Cole smiled. 'There's not a driver, waiter, or sewer worker in Mexico City who wouldn't cooperate with the Great One.'

'Yikes! The man doesn't quit,' said Kayzie, who was walking right behind Sloane.

'I think he will now,' Cole said. He put his arm around Sloane's back and led her toward the limousine. 'Thank God,' he breathed.

They visited a club Cole knew about and then returned to the hotel. Cole had reserved rooms for all of them on the same floor of the Maria Isabella, a five-star high-rise hotel on the Plaza Reforma. Sloane had the corner suite. The night before she had arrived so late she hadn't even noticed what her accommodations were like. Now she glanced around the pleasant room, thrilled and exhausted. She couldn't wait to sink into a hot, bubbly tub and fall into the king-sized bed she could see through the archway to the bedroom.

She crossed the darkened living room and pulled open the door to the minibar in search of a Perrier. She found one in the back behind the miniatures of wine and of orange juice and pulled it out. As she looked around for a bottle opener, she heard a soft sound, a small cough perhaps, but a human sound.

She froze, then slowly turned.

Standing in the archway looking exactly as he had when he entered the restaurant was Miguel Vellis.

He was smiling.

23

Kayzie and Ryan sat nervously waiting for Cole on the big leather couch in the lobby of the Maria Isabella.

Alan paced. Their bags lay in a pile next to the huge glass coffee table. They had already missed their Sunday-morning flight to Acapulco, but that was no longer important. No one spoke.

Kayzie looked up to see Cole coming toward them from the bank of elevators. His face was grim. 'She's gone,' he said as he reached them.

Alan stopped pacing. Kayzie and Ryan stood up.

'Her bag is gone,' he said. His voice was tight, as though fighting an all-out panic. 'The bed is kind of mussed up, but it hasn't been slept in. The only sign that she was there is an empty Perrier bottle and these.' He held up a box of thin black cigarillos wrapped in his handkerchief.

'Those certainly aren't Sloane's,' Kayzie said, reaching for the box.

Cole pulled away. 'Don't touch them, dear. We may need to have the box fingerprinted.'

Kayzie's hand flew to her mouth. 'Fingerprinted?' she gasped. 'Cole, you don't think someone did something to her?'

Cole took a deep, steadying breath. 'I don't know what to think. There's no note. I called the house in Bel Air just in case she decided to go home. She's not there.'

Ryan shoved his hands deep into the pockets of his

414

slacks. 'Have you checked with the phone operators?' he asked Cole. 'Maybe she made a call during the night. That might tell us something.'

'I checked,' Cole said. 'I'm going to see the manager right now. I spoke to him from the room. He's questioning the night staff to see if anyone saw anything.'

As Cole turned to go, Kayzie looked past him to see a small man in a dark suit moving rapidly toward them across the marble lobby floor.

'Señor Latimer,' he called. As he got closer, he extended his hand. 'I'm Renaldo Estevez, the managing director of the hotel. I have some information that may be of help to you.'

Cole shook his hand and nodded eagerly.

'May I speak to you alone, sir?' Estevez asked.

'That's quite all right, Señor Estevez. These are Mrs Bromley's closest friends.' Cole nodded to each of them in turn. 'Miss Markham, Mr Wade, Mr McKenna.'

The managing director bowed slightly to each of them, looking suddenly ill at ease. 'I see . . . well, ah . . . in that case. Ah . . . Mr Latimer, my night desk clerk has informed me that he permitted Miguel Vellis a passkey to Mrs Bromley's suite last night about nine o'clock. Of course we have dismissed the man. Something like that is completely irregular. However, you must understand, Señor Vellis is a man of great influence in this country and it is difficult to refuse him.'

Cole looked as though he were going to hit the manager. His face flushed bright red and he clenched his fists against his side. 'You are telling me you permitted . . . that . . . man in Mrs Bromley's suite without her knowledge or permission? Mr Estevez, I will have you up on charges before sunset. This is outrageous! Do you know who Mrs Bromley is?'

Estevez held up his hands, palms out, as though to damp down Cole's building rage. 'Mr Latimer, please, you have to understand –'

Cole exploded. 'The only thing I have to understand is that you let that man into Mrs Bromley's suite without permission and Mrs Bromley has disappeared,' he shouted. 'For all I know she has met with some harm. Whether she has or not, I am holding you totally responsible for her welfare and am informing the police and the American ambassador immediately that she has been kidnapped.'

'I wouldn't do that, Mr Latimer,' Estevez said, a note of menace in his voice. 'If you will let me explain.'

'Go ahead,' Cole snapped.

'The doorman informs me that he saw Mrs Bromley leave the hotel of her own free will at approximately eleven o'clock last night. She was with Señor Vellis. They left together in his car. Before they did so, he asked the desk to call the airline and hold two seats on the midnight flight to Acapulco.'

'Oh, my God,' Kayzie said, sitting down with a thud. 'I knew it.'

Cole spun around and stared at her. 'What do you mean, Kayzie? Knew what?'

Kayzie looked up at the manager. She didn't want to say anything in front of a stranger. Cole sensed her reluctance and turned back to Estevez. 'Thank you, señor,' he said curtly. 'If you would excuse us, please.'

Estevez bowed and stepped smartly back in the direction from which he had come. Kayzie got the feeling that he may not know who Sloane Bromley was, but he sure as hell knew who Miguel Vellis was. He acted as if what had happened wasn't such a big deal or a surprise to him.

As soon as he was out of earshot, Cole turned back to Kayzie. 'What were you going to say, Kayzie?' he asked.

'Last night, when we went to the john? Remember? She was acting funny about the bullfighter stuff. Kinda shaky and undone. I guess I must have teased her about him some more because she admitted she was excited by the

416

attention. I got the feeling that something was happening to her. Call it female intuition if you want,' she said, smiling wanly at Ryan. 'But I got the feeling that under the right circumstances she wouldn't say no to that guy.'

'So you think she's run off with him?' Cole asked.

'Yes I do.'

Cole sat down on the edge of the couch. 'Jesus,' he said in a soft, urgent voice. 'What in God's name are we going to do now?'

'I say let's go find her,' Alan said. 'Acapulco can't be that big. He's so damn famous, someone will know where he hangs out.'

Cole thought for a moment, then agreed. 'Okay. But we don't have long to do it.'

'Why not?' Kayzie asked.

'When I called the house, Warner's butler said they expected him home Monday. If we haven't found her by then, we're going to have to tell him she's missing.'

Ryan lifted his raincoat from the couch and reached for their bags. 'What do you suppose he'll do if we don't find her?'

Cole slowly shook his head. 'That . . . I don't even want to think about.'

Sloane hardly remembered the drive through the frantic streets of Mexico City to the airport on Saturday night. She was barely conscious of the hordes of people rushing to catch their flights even at such a late hour. She didn't pay attention to what was going on around her, what she was doing, or where she was going. All she knew was that she wanted to be with this man.

Since the moment he mysteriously appeared in her hotel suite, she felt transported into a dream state.

For a long moment he had just stood staring at her in silence.

It was *the look* again.

This time there was no mistaking it. His mere presence in the room removed any doubt. She was unable to move, incapable of uttering a sound in protest as he moved toward her. His strong arms encircled her and gently pulled her into his body as his mouth sought hers. His increasingly passionate kisses sent a surge of excitement coursing through her body. He forced her mouth open, dissolving her uncertainty. She returned the ardour of his embrace, pressing herself into his muscular frame.

Wordlessly, he walked her backward to the bed, eased her down, and crouched over her, covering her with kisses — her eyes, her neck, her shoulders — while his hands caressed her body through her clothes. She could feel herself becoming wet and very impatient as she felt his hand rub her pubic bone through her skirt, refusing to satisfy the yearning hunger for touch just inches away. Her hand reached down to cover his, and with the slightest pressure she invited a more intimate caress. He resisted the invitation, stood, and walked toward the door. Had she done something wrong?

She raised herself and rested on her elbows, bewildered as he walked away from the bed. *My God*, she thought, *is he leaving?*

He stopped near the door and pulled her suitcase from the open closet. He must have packed it for her before she returned to the hotel. He looked across the darkened room at her. Slowly he extended his hand, palm down.

Despite the raging protest from her aroused body and her confusion at her retreat, she noticed that even with the simple hand gesture he expressed the same compelling authority he displayed in the ring. He was demanding that she follow him. But where did he want her to go?

She pushed herself up from the bed, straightened her clothes. and took his outstretched hand. Their destination no longer mattered.

He opened the door and stepped into the hall, nodding to a bellboy who had been waiting. The bellboy stepped into the room, picked up her suitcase, and headed down the corridor toward the elevator.

It was as if they had been together forever. They moved as one through the lobby and into his car waiting at the curb.

As they drove away, Sloane realized that not a word had passed between them.

Sloane assumed he would take her to wherever he lived in Mexico City. When she saw that they were headed for the Mexico City airport, she began to feel a little as though she were being kidnapped.

Two eager young men wearing Aeromexico uniforms were waiting for them at the curb. They greeted Vellis warmly and immediately led them through the terminal to the head of the line at the departure gate. Sloane noticed the flight was bound for Acapulco. His presence drew respectful acknowledgment and greetings from the other passengers waiting their turn to board.

'*Hola, Matador,*' a man called out.

'*Como esta, Maestro,*' a pretty woman said demurely.

Sloane watched, fascinated, as he received the attention with quiet humility. She was pleasantly surprised at his gentle demeanor among these people. She followed him through the jetway and onto the empty plane. As they boarded, they were greeted by two pretty flight attendants who greeted him by name.

They were ushered to the front of the first class section and seated. The flight attendants stood by, watching him, poised for an immediate response to any sign that he might need something.

Sloane basked in the spotlight of his celebrity. How different from the attention paid to her in public. People who recognized her reacted to her familiar face. They didn't know her. They just knew they had seen her in ads on television. When she travelled with Warner, it was in the isolated state created by private planes and cars with darkened windows. Even when Warner was recognized,

419

people fawned, reacting to his wealth and power. This was different. People reacted to Miguel Vellis with adulation and awe. He was their hero, a man of proven, fearless courage, and still one of them.

She could see the envy in the eyes of the stewardesses. He held up two fingers. Instantly a bottle of champagne and two glasses were placed in front of them. He filled her glass and then his own, looking deeply into her eyes. He raised his glass in a silent toast to her, placing his free hand over hers.

Sloane sipped her champagne and studied his hand. The skin was the color of burnished bronze, the fingers long and slender. This hand, she thought, had killed that magnificent animal only hours before. His hands were trained to kill and would kill again. Yet they were capable of such a gentle touch, such tender caresses. She fantasized how lovely the hand would look in contrast to the whiteness of her belly. The excitement she had felt in the hotel room returned anew. Still, neither of them spoke.

How could he know that erotic silence was part of the Game? She *owned* the Game! She had invented it. She controlled it. Now she knew how her prey had felt. Now she was the one who had been baited, stalked, and drawn into *his* Game. He wouldn't speak. They both knew that created the nearly unbearable erotic tension. She knew to speak was to risk shattering the magic of this silent, spontaneous adventure. To find herself on the receiving end of silence was most revealing. Remaining an enigma was what had provided the autonomy and confidence to play the Game over and over again.

From time to time during the thirty-minute flight he looked at her with eyes that smouldered with an indefinable obsession, the promise of unspeakable acts of passion and abandon. She remembered how quickly he had been able to arouse her and yet retain the self-control he had displayed in the hotel room. More than once, she had felt a shiver run down her spine. Something about that look was as eerie and chilling as it was exciting. Quite unexpectedly, she found herself thinking about those eyes from the bull's point of view. She was delivering herself into the range of his sword. This time there would be no escape.

The Game had come full circle.

When they landed in Acapulco the airport was deserted. Theirs was the last flight of the night to arrive. He held her hand as he walked a pace in front of her, leading her through the terminal. She felt the protection and possession in the way he led her. The few people they encountered greeted him with the now familiar. 'Hola, Matador!' He acknowledged them as before, with quiet dignity.

They stepped out into the parking area into the warm, balmy night. It was a refreshing change from the cool, damp air of Mexico City. The parking lot was empty, except for one car. They headed toward it. When they reached it, he opened the passenger door of the low black Ferrari and helped her in.

He drove fast, with total control. From time to time he glanced over at her and smiled as though they shared a secret.

They passed the Acapulco Princess Hotel and began the incline through a slightly mountainous area. The road was narrow and they clung to the side nearest the mountain. As they climbed, she looked out toward the bay, awash in moonlight. Soon they were looking down at the twinkling lights extending from the curve of the bay to the homes reaching toward the mountains.

Looking down from this height at the scene below, she was suddenly filled with nostalgia. How long ago it seemed that she had looked down from the hills above Cap Ferrat with Warner by her side. How different her feelings were now with this exotic man whose very touch sent her blood coursing through her veins.

The combination of the hum of the engine, the silence of the night, and the headiness of all the alcohol she had consumed that day made her wonder if this was really happening. Had she really left Los Angeles only a day ago?

She was about to be with a stranger unlike any stranger she had ever known. Unlike her other encounters she felt no sense of being the predator. He had come for her. He had followed her and found her and taken her away. Knowing that filled her with deep desire, even lust. Fate had sent her the ultimate dangerous man. A man who faced death. A man who drew blood and killed as an art form.

She sensed that he had driven this road many times before as he turned right off the main road and proceeded up a narrow, winding drive. As they reached what appeared to be the entrance to a private area, a guard came toward the car. When he saw who it was, he tapped his cap and retreated to raise the arm of the gate protecting the entrance.

Vellis manœuvred the powerful little car up a cobble-stone street and turned into a secluded drive. The vegetation was so thick that the villa only a few yards away could barely be seen. He pulled to a stop in front of lighted tile steps that led to the house.

Each step held an enormous clay pot of flowers. When they reached the top of the steps, he opened a wide wooden door and led her into what seemed to be one sweeping, all-white room. The shiny black tile floor extended out toward the night sky. The house seemed to be suspended out over a cliff, floating in air. There were long, low white couches sitting at angles about the room and candles everywhere — clusters of low, fat ones along ledges and on glass tabletops, high tapers in black wrought-iron holders arranged around the edge of the terrace. Whoever had readied the house for his arrival had been told to arrange the room in such a way.

She followed him out onto a wide terrace. All Acapulco

stretched out at their feet. She could hear faint sounds of music from the streets below and the soft swish of the ocean rolling onto the beach. The night air was scented with the smell of a thousand flowers and the salt of the sea.

They stood silently for a moment, drinking in the sight and the hush of the night. The air felt wonderful on her bare arms and neck. She felt as though she could breathe the moonlight. She closed her eyes for a moment and thought: *Whatever happens to me, however I may have damaged my life by coming here, I will have had this — this is mine and no one will ever be able to take it away from me. This extraordinary man has singled me out of thousands and spirited me away.*

The distractions of the trip to this place were over. Now, as she finally stood alone in his presence, she felt a confusing mixture of intoxications, anticipation, awkwardness, and fear. She looked out over the moonlit ocean as much to hide her uneasiness as to savour its beauty. He took her by the hand and led her toward the pool, where someone had placed a bottle of champagne and chilled flutes on a small table. He filled both glasses and offered her one. They touched glasses and drank their wine in the silence that had become a part of their being together.

Slowly, he set his glass down and turned toward her. He reached out and touched her face, caressing her forehead, running his hand down her cheek, letting it come to rest on her shoulder. With his other hand he pushed a strand of her hair behind her ear and ran a finger over her eyebrow, following the lines of her face and neck until this arm, too, rested on her shoulder. He pulled her toward him, brushing his lips across her mouth, her cheek, and kissing her just below the ear. He raised his head and once more gazed into her eyes. Gently, he lifted her glass from her hands and set it next to his on the table.

For Sloane, the waiting had become an agony. When she

played the Game, she drew her victim in, toyed with them only long enough so they would succumb to her desires, and then consummated the exchange and escaped. He had drawn out this encounter for nearly half a day, over several hundred miles and four locations, and still he had not delivered the promise she had first seen in his eyes in the arena. Had he not made the first move, that look, she would probably have played her Game, with her rules. But thousands of people had seen his overture. Her Game was compromised before she could begin. It was his move, his game, his playing field, and there was no changing the scenario. She would just have to wait.

Once more he held her shoulders and began to kiss her. Feather-light kisses descended on her eyes, cheeks, and lips. His tongue teased her lips, refusing to enter her open mouth. Warm kisses explored her neck and ears. She wanted to be held, to be crushed against his strong, slender body, but his arms on her shoulders kept them apart.

She could hear his breathing change. Her own breath grew shallow and feverish. Still, he held her off. He studied her face again. Staring into her eyes, his lips joined hers with the faintest pressure, their breath intermingling. Slowly, the tension in his arms relaxed. His kisses grew more impassioned. Sloane drew his tongue into her open mouth, hungry to taste him, eager to encourage him.

This was the ultimate Game. She had, at long last, found a partner whose skill at seduction matched her own. A man who, as she had, with each encounter, pushed the envelope of risk, excitement, danger. The simple fulfilment of physical desire was not enough. Here was the man with whom she could play the Game and not flee.

She pulled away, still holding him. She studied his face, caressing his skin, his sensual lips. She could feel her own longing and desire reflected in his eyes. She wrapped her

424

arms around his neck and pressed her body into his, shaking with desire.

'*Porqué tu tiemblas, mi amor?*' he asked, breaking the silence between them, softly, gently, as though trying not to scare her with the sound of his voice.

She looked at him with wide eyes, not understanding.

'Why do you tremble, my love?' he translated, enfolding her in his arms as if to warm her in the cool night air. 'Only the bulls should have fear of me.'

She pulled away again. The bulls! The very mention reminded her that here was a man comfortable with death, skilled at killing. The image of the massive black bull falling to its knees in slow motion chilled her. Would he hurt her? Perhaps things were moving too fast. Part of his attraction was the implicit controlled violence of him.

He noticed the look of fear cross her face. He smiled and withdrew to refill their glasses.

She sipped her wine, relieved to have a prop of some kind. Something to defuse her tension.

As they toasted each other with their eyes, she saw a look, a shadow cross his face. It was not the look of love but of desire.

He led her up a double flight of wide stone stairs to the master bedroom flooded with moonlight. A king-sized bed covered with white satin sheets and piles of oversized pillows faced the wide-open window and the view. The room was filled with more candles, unlighted, and dozens of red roses sitting about in huge black clay pots. Someone had scattered rose petals on the white bed covering and pillows. There was another bottle of iced champagne on the night table. He poured them both a fresh glass.

He began to light each of the candles while she sat and sipped her champagne, watching him move about the room. She loved the look of his body, the utterly flat stomach, his wide shoulders, high, taut rear end, and, muscled arms. He moved as a dancer might, lithe, graceful. Dancer or panther? she suddenly thought, watching him, for there was an implied violence in his movements as well.

Her nerves began to calm with each sip of champagne. Still she was apprehensive about what would happen next.

Would she be the kind of woman he was expecting? Surely a man who had his bed dressed in satin sheets and had rose petals strewn about must not often sleep alone. Perhaps he would be too sexually sophisticated to be pleased with her.

The room shimmered in the glow of the candles flickering in a light breeze from the window. The air was perfumed with a mixture of roses and sandalwood.

In the unsteady light, he walked toward the bed, refilled her glass, and sat down beside her.

'Do you go to the bullfights often?' he asked incongruously. She smiled inwardly. Now *he* wanted to talk.

Could it be that he was nervous, too? But she had come too far for conversation. It would break the spell. Her hunger would be satisfied now only by wild, abandoned sex with him. What if, in talking to him, she discovered that he was stupid or coarse? That would truly ruin the mood.

He persisted. 'Why were you at the fight today?'

When she began to answer, she found herself stuttering, searching for simple words because she didn't know how much English he really spoke or understood. 'F-f-friends of mine . . . from New York . . . ah . . . invited me,' she managed to get out. She wanted to say the right things about appreciating his performance, his skill, her reaction to the beauty and terror of the ring, but she wasn't sure exactly how to say it in a way that wouldn't make her sound hopelessly ignorant of his work, if he called it that. How could she explain her appreciation of a man who is cheered and idolized wherever he goes

426

without sounding like a groupie or some crazed fan? 'You are fascinating to watch,' she finally said, hoping that would do.

The last round of champagne began to take effect, building on the intoxication and light-headedness she had felt since midmorning in Mexico City. She took another sip and leaned back into the softness of the pillows.

Smiling the same down-turned smile she had seen the second he looked at her in the ring, he lifted her glass from her hands and set it next to the silver bucket.

He held her face, kissing her deeply as her arms opened, pulling his body into hers. She could feel his breath in her ears, his tongue tracing a line toward the hollow of her throat. His hands wandered down her body, following the curves of her breasts. She leaned farther back, her hands resting on the back of his neck as his mouth sought the valley between her breasts. She could feel the heat of his breath on her nipples through the fabric of her blouse. His hands moved down her body until they reached her mound. Gently, he stroked her, moving in little circles, dipping down between her legs just far enough to tantalize but not close enough to satisfy. His mouth continued to linger at the base of her breasts. Once again, he seemed content to tease her unmercifully through her clothes. She could feel the passion rising in her and wished he would just tear her clothes away. She was desperate to feel his skin on hers. Any obstruction to total nakedness was unbearable.

She reached to unbutton her blouse. She couldn't move her hands. They were held in his painful, vicelike grip.

'There is time,' he said softly as she struggled to free her hands.

Then, mercifully but with agonizing slowness, he began to undress her. He removed her blouse and bra, sitting back to examine what his action had revealed. She lay against the pillows as he kissed her nipples.

He rose from the bed and extended his hand, easing her to his feet. He released the fastening of her skirt. It slithered to the floor. He slid his hands under her panties and cupped her cheeks. Then, falling to his knees, he lowered her last shred of covering. He remained on his knees looking up at her, letting his eyes roam over her naked body.

The hunger she saw in his eyes was so intense it was like a penetration. She held out her arms, begging him to come to her. Now his attention was focused on the dark triangle below her naval between her legs as she dissolved, clinging to him, legs vibrating, every touch and thrust of his tongue an unbearable joy until she reached the top of a cresting wave that sent a fluttering spasm through her legs, building until she vibrated from her head to her feet, approaching a crescendo that left her body in a catatonic stiffness. For a heartbeat she stood there immobile, her arched body tensed and poised. The centre of her universe had become the little place between the glistening wings of her sex. As the wave crested, a searing white light exploded behind her closed eyelids. She fell back toward the bed, struck down by the intensity of her orgasm, her joyous cries rising into the moonlit night.

He waited until her contractions faded and then began again. He was gentler now, kissing her between the legs, slowly firing her blood until she could feel her hunger to have him inside her. When she felt the waves building again, she reached down and pulled him up, kissing him deeply, tasting herself in his mouth. She reached for the buttons of his shirt. She didn't try to undo them but looked in his eyes with a silent plea.

As she watched him rise and undress, she felt a twinge of jealous possessiveness. She thought of the other women who had been in this room and found she could not bear the idea of anyone in her place. She could and would make him forget that there had ever been anyone but her.

He undressed with a deliberation and grace that verged on being ritualistic. When he removed his shirt, she noticed the scars, thin silver streaks across his flat stomach. They might have been repulsive on any other man, but on him they were sensuous badges of his defiance and courage, the physical proof of how closely and bravely he courted death.

It was not until he pulled off his pants that she could see how close he brought the bulls. Long, jagged scars, like lightning bolts, slashed the muscles of his inner thighs.

He turned to face her in the candlelight, proudly erect, showing himself to her, taunting her, knowing he was making her crazy with desire. It was now that he would truly take control. It was now, just as in the bullfight he would demonstrate his dominance.

It was her turn to admire his beauty. He looked totally at ease naked. He had a natural athlete's body, trim, taut, and well defined. But her eyes were drawn to the centre of his body, for there was the only nourishment that would appease the aching hunger in her own body.

He returned to the bed, bending to kiss her mouth while his hand first sought her breasts, then disappeared into the valley between her hips. Her body was immediately aflame. She reached between his legs to hold and caress him. She pulled him on top of her, desperate to have him inside her. He held himself and teased her, playing at the gates of her body, refusing to enter. She was growing wanton, her hips arching toward him, trying to achieve the union he withheld. She could feel the heat and fury of his breathing in her face and knew that he was as eager as she was. She felt him leave again as he moved down to kiss her, his fingers dancing inside her, the heat consuming her again. She could feel the gathering storm and pulled at him to enter her. Finally, mercifully, as she reached the edge of madness, he relented. Within seconds they reached orgasm simultaneously.

Through the night there was not an opening in her

body that he did not caress, fondle, kiss or probe with his tongue, his fingers, or the hard manhood spared by the bulls as though they knew and respected what rapture he was capable of giving her.

He paused in their lovemaking only to offer more champagne. When he tired of pouring it into her glass, he slowly dripped it over her body and drank from her skin.

Finally, as dawn broke over the bay beyond the window, he slept, his coal-black hair brushing against her shoulder, his beautiful mouth at her breast. Too exhilarated to join him in sleep and too exhausted to leave his side, she cradled him in her arms and tried to sort out the tangled skeins of feelings, sensations, and thoughts that now imprisoned her very soul.

Sloane had never taken drugs. She knew many people who did and never really understood how they chose to destroy their lives, or why so many kept going back to them when they vowed to stop. Her own struggle had been with the Game. Every episode before had held the promise of ultimate fulfilment and provided ultimate shame.

She knew a Game was temporary, a fleeting release of the pressure value of her own self-doubt. She had always held out the hope that one day she would meet someone who would fill the emptiness in her heart, a man whose passion, power, and daring could match and tame her own.

Miguel had transported her to a paradise within herself she knew existed but could never reach. He had taken her hand and led her there. She knew now she could not go on living if she could not return to that secret place. A wonderful sense of peace suffused her, mingling with the fatigue. She looked over at the man curled asleep beside her. 'Miguel,' she whispered, speaking his name for the first time in his presence, 'Miguel Vellis.' How beautiful it sounded. How beautiful was the man she had been searching for. Now she had found him. 'Miguel,' she repeated as she drifted off to sleep.

She was aware of a presence standing over her and opened her eyes. The light in the room was neither night or day. He was standing over her completely dressed, with a brandy snifter of orange juice and ice in one hand. He wore a fully cut pullover white cotton shirt, the low V collar of which revealed gold chains. The sleeves were wide and full. One cuff was encircled by an exquisite gold watch with a black onyx face. His trousers were black silk and his shoes the softest black Italian leather. He looked as if he had just stepped of a page of *Gentlemen's Quarterly*.

'You are so beautiful when you sleep.' He smiled, handing her the glass.

She struggled onto the pillows, pulling the sheet up under her arms as she accepted it.

'Don't,' he said, pulling the sheet away. 'I want to look at you.'

Before, she would have been embarrassed to sit completely naked in front of a man. Even with Warren she usually came to bed in a nightgown. But after the night they had spent, it felt absolutely normal.

As she sipped the cool, sweet juice, she could feel a slight bruise on her lip. She glanced down and saw what appeared to be a string of tiny bite marks on her inner thigh.

He saw her notice them and bent to kiss each one. The minute his mouth touched her, unbelievably, she was aflame again. She leaned farther back into the pillows and placed her hand on the back of his neck, pulling his head and mouth into her. She felt his tongue flickering deeper and deeper between her legs.

When he began, she thought she could lie back and sip her juice and let him play with her. She found that impossible. The fact that he had shaved, showered, and dressed while she slept was exciting. She would make him undress and make love to her again.

'Take your clothes off,' she gasped, trying to keep from thrashing about as he sent repeated sensual convulsions through her body.

He said nothing, merely shook his head and continued his delightful work.

'Please, darling,' she whimpered. 'Make love to me.'

He shook his head again.

The contest of wills was driving her wild with desire. She could contain herself no longer and gave into the approaching wave of frenzied joy, riding its crest to completion, dizzy, ecstatic, and happier than she had ever been in her life.

When she was finished, he rose, smiling with an expression of devilish, self-satisfied victory on his face. 'Now, get up. I am taking you to my favourite restaurant for dinner. I want people to see what a lucky man I am,' he said. 'Then I will take you out into the bay on my new boat.'

'Dinner?' she said, shocked. 'What time is it?'

'Nearly seven.'

'Seven at night?'

'Yes, Sloane Taylor. Seven at night. We have known each other for one full day.'

'So, Miguel the Matador,' Sloane said, smiling, 'how do you know who I am?'

'I have seen you in the magazines,' he said. 'From the moment I saw you in the stands, I knew that we were fated to be together. After last night, I have no doubts, *mi amor*. You have already stolen my heart. Now, if you don't get ready, you will steal my chance to have dinner.'

She pulled herself out of bed. Her legs felt like cooked spaghetti as she made her way to the bathroom. It, too, was an oversized room with the same view as the bedroom. The walls and counters were done in shiny black tiles like the floor. A mountain of black bath sheets was piled on a low chrome table beside a Jacuzzi next to the window.

432

On a clothes rack by the door hung the contents of her bag, freshly pressed. Her cosmetics were neatly lined across the black marble sink counter.

As she lowered herself into the swirling water, she realized her body, though sore and aching, felt like butter. Her skin felt thin and aflame as though buffed raw by rough hands. Every inch of flesh throbbed with a mixture of dull pain and sexual arousal. She felt absolutely, deliriously wonderful.

She drew a big black sponge bubbling with soapsuds that smelled like roses over her arms, aware that he was standing in the door watching her. She looked up and smiled.

'If you like, when you are finished, I will kiss you that way again.' He grinned. 'You seem to like it so.'

'Out!' She laughed, throwing the sponge at him. It narrowly missed the front of his immaculate shirt and bounced to the floor. He hadn't even flinched.

She wrapped herself in a black bath sheet and checked her face in the mirror. Her skin was glowing, her eyes clear and bright despite the quantities of champagne she'd consumed. The colour in her cheeks was more vivid than any blusher could enhance. She settled for a flick of mascara and a touch of lipstick. It was less makeup than she had appeared in public wearing since she was fourteen years old.

As he dressed in black and white, she chose a pair of white wide-legged linen slacks and a black cashmere T-shirt. She also chose a wide black enamel and diamond-stripped cuff bracelet and matching earrings and she slipped her feet into a pair of black thong sandals. Her freshly washed hair hung loose and curly around her face, free of any mousse or fuss.

When she reached for her handbag, she noticed her wallet was in a different compartment from where she usually kept it. Curious, she pulled it out and checked the fold where she had put her cash.

Five new one-hundred-dollar bills were missing. She tried to remember if she could have spent it in the last day.

Impossible. The bag had been with her constantly. Perhaps a pickpocket? Cole had warned her about them here. No, she decided, the only plausible explanation was that whoever had pressed her things must have taken it.

While having her money stolen was disconcerting, she decided to say nothing. Why spoil what had been the most incredible hours of her life with a sordid accusation? Surely she could arrange to get cash when she needed to. She pushed all unpleasant thoughts out of her head and walked quickly down the stone steps to the first floor.

He was waiting for her on the terrace, where it had all started the night before. A manservant, dressed entirely in white, appeared from nowhere as she stepped onto the terrace. He was carrying a silver tray holding a vodka bottle frozen into a block of ice, and thin frosted glasses filled with the icy liquid.

They raised their glasses to each other again.

'What do I call you?' she asked, smiling. 'Other than "darling."'

'Miguel,' he said simply. 'Aficionados have other names for me. All much too grand.'

'Miguel,' she said, savouring the name.

'It sounds beautiful when you say it.' He stepped toward her, brushing her lips with his. 'Say it again, softly,' he breathed.

'Miguel,' she sighed between kisses.

24

Their trip from Mexico City to his villa in the mountains above Acapulco was to be the last time they would travel alone.

As they walked down the stone steps in front of the house, she could see men leaning against the fenders of two cars parked behind his Ferrari. He seemed to give them a silent signal.

As he turned the car around to head back down the hill, she saw the men getting into their cars. She looked back to see that they were being followed. This was his entourage, he explained, and he was seldom without these dark, somewhat sinister companions.

The minute they pulled into the parking lot of a one-story, chic-looking restaurant, two attendants dashed for the car as though in competition to park the Great One's car.

The men who had been following them strode ahead and entered the restaurant as though checking it out. As they entered, Sloane saw them all milling around near the bar waiting for their orders. Miguel nodded at one of them and flicked his hand. Instantly, they all disappeared into the bar.

The entrance of El Matador created the same scene that she had witnessed in the restaurant in Mexico City, a hushed reverence and then applause from the other diners.

The maître d' greeted Miguel effusively. There was

much back pounding and laughter as they moved through the room. They were shown to what apparently was 'his' table, along the back wall. As soon as they were seated, a waiter brought a frozen bottle of vodka without being asked.

Their meal was interrupted constantly. It was impossible for them to make any real conversation. He introduced her to everyone. Each in turn treated her with great deference – after all, she was the lady of Miguel Vellis and entitled to the same respect they showed him.

He accepted everyone's compliments graciously but kept it brief, and asked no one to join them.

'Forgive me if I do not share you quite yet, *mi amor*,' he said softly, turning to stare into her eyes. 'There will be time. Soon you will know all my friends.'

They were on their second brandy when she heard someone calling her name. She stared out into the room to see Kayzie heading for their table. Her skin was the colour of boiled lobster. She seemed a bit tipsy, bumping into the backs of other customers' chairs.

Seeing Kazyie's familiar face in her own newfound paradise jolted Sloane back to reality. Before she could say anything to explain to Miguel, Kayzie was standing in front of them, her lips set in an angry straight line. 'Where the hell have you been?' she demanded. 'We're half out of our minds trying to find you!' Kazyie ignored Miguel, something he clearly was not accustomed to.

'Is this a friend of yours?' he asked Sloane, frowning up at Kayzie.

'Miguel, I'm sorry,' Sloane said, flustered. She fought through the fog of vodka, red wine, and brandy to make sense of what was happening. 'This is my friend Kayzie Markham from New York. We were at the bullfight together. Kayzie, this is Miguel Vellis.'

Miguel stood. He took Kayzie's hand and bowed toward it without actually touching it with his lips. 'My pleasure,' he said, and released her hand.

Kayzie smiled gamely and rattled off a stream of Spanish. Sloane was surprised that she spoke the language. Whatever she said to Miguel seemed to please him immensely. He smiled and asked her to sit down.

'What did you just say?' Sloane asked, feeling left out.

'I told him he fought magnificently,' Kayzie answered. 'And that I enjoyed watching him. I told him he was the first bullfigher I'd ever met.'

'I'm impressed,' Sloane said, trying somehow to make it up to Kayzie for the trouble she knew she was causing.

Kayzie took one of the extra chairs at the table for four. 'I can only stay for a minute. The others are in the bar,' she said. She was sitting directly opposite Sloane. She leaned across the tablecloth and stared into her eyes. 'Are you all right, kiddo?'

'May I get you a drink?' Miguel interrupted, obviously wanting to control the situation. This was his table, his hangout, his town, and he seemed determined to let whoever this bright-red Anglo was know that Sloane was his, too.

Kayzie shook her head at his offer and got right down to business. 'You know you had us scared to death?' she said, continuing to address Sloane. 'Cole is beside himself. He wanted to go to the embassy and the police. I can't tell you what we've been through. The only reason we all came to Acapulco instead of going to the authorities was to try and find you first ourselves. When we figured out who you were with, Cole tried to call Señor Vellis's villa, but the phone was off. We all drove up there this morning. Cole talked himself past the guard, but when we got to the house, some man shooed us away. He said no one was home.'

'Well,' Sloane said. 'Now you've found me and I'm fine. I'm sorry I ran off. I'll explain later.'

Kayzie shot a look at Miguel, who was listening intently.

Sloane wished he weren't smiling. Kayzie had every

437

right to be upset. There was no way she could explain, here, what a state she was in when she saw him standing in her hotel room. If Miguel weren't at the table, she would try to tell Kayzie what had happened, but she didn't want to embarrass him. 'I got carried away,' she said lamely, smiling at Miguel, who was gripping her thigh under the tablecloth.

'So? When are you coming to the Neithergould's villa? It's fabulous. We're all there baking around the pool worrying about you.'

'Please, Kayzie. I'm truly sorry. Try to understand.'

'Oh, I understand,' she said hotly. 'But I don't think Cole understands. Now that I've found you perhaps you can calm him down.'

Sloane felt Miguel tighten his grip on her leg. 'She's not going back to your villa tonight, Miss Markham. She is with me.'

'Excuse me?' Kayzie said sharply.

'Your friend is staying with me,' he said.

Until that moment Sloane had lived only in the present. Now he was talking about her future, and his saying she was staying with him excited her.

Kayzie squared her shoulders and peered at him. 'Señor Vellis,' she said theatrically, 'I'm sure you are one terrific fella, but perhaps Sloane hasn't filled you in on a little detail about her life back in the States.'

Sloane quickly looked from Kayzie to Miguel. The expression on his face told her instantly that he was not accustomed to being addressed in such a way by anyone, particularly not a woman – an American woman – and one who had now positioned herself as a threat to something he wanted. She knew what was coming and was desperate to stop Kayzie from saying more or angering Miguel. 'Kayz, would you like to come to the ladies' room with me for a minute?' she said sweetly.

Kayzie got the message and pushed back her chair.

'Right. That's one heck of an idea,' she said. 'Excuse us, señor,' she said. 'We won't be long.'

Miguel let go of Sloane's thigh and stood, bowing stiffly.

As soon as Kayzie and Sloane got to the ladies' room, Kayzie closed the door and said, 'Okay, Sloane, what the fuck is going on?'

'Kayzie!' Sloane said, hurt. 'You don't have to talk to me like that.'

'Well, I'm sorry about the language, Sloane, but I'm so angry at you,' she snapped. 'Let me rephrase that so as not to offend a married lady who has just scared her best friend to death by shacking up with a bullfighter! How's this?' She brought her face very close to Sloane's. 'Have you ef-ing word lost your ef-ing-word mind?'

Sloane folded her arms and leaned against the wall. 'Yes, I probably have,' she said quietly.

'Have you thought about Warner? What about your career and reputation, for God's sake?'

'No one knows . . . except you and the others.'

'Sloane,' Kayzie moaned. 'How long do you think that's going to last? You don't even know who might be out there having dinner right this minute. This place is full of jet-setters and for all we know some damn stringer for the *National Enquirer*. He could be on the phone right now. It takes just one sighting of the Bromley Woman playing licky-face in the corner with the greatest bullfighter in all May-hee-ko for this to be on the UPI wire. Gutenberg couldn't invent type large enough to justify the headline *that* would get!'

'Kayzie,' Sloane said, finally raising her voice, 'you are acting like I borrowed your sweater and returned it with sweat marks. It was rude of me to do this, I know that, but this is my life here and for once I'm going to follow my heart.'

'Follow your heart? Follow your heart!' Kayzie was nearly screaming. 'May I suggest, as an old pal and

439

someone who cares about you, that you are following a different part of your anatomy.'

'I don't have to take this, Kayzie,' Sloane said, newly emboldened by the events of the last twenty-four hours. 'I am wild about this man. I want him. He wants me, and I'm not leaving.'

Kayzie softened at Sloane's outburst. 'I'm sorry, Sloane. I've had a lot of margaritas and an ocean of beer. For all we know I'm probably a little jealous. He is gorgeous, but truly, hon, you've got to stop now and come back with us. We'll all pretend it never happened and you won't risk destroying your entire life. Not to mention Warner's.'

Sloane stared at the floor, speechless.

'Ooooh, shit,' Kayzie whispered. 'You haven't told him about Warner, have you?'

'No,' Sloane said.

Kayzie sighed and shook her head. 'Maybe it's just as well.' She shrugged. 'This guy, does he have any idea who you are?'

'Not really. He saw my picture in a magazine, that's all.'

'Good. You can just walk away and chalk it up to a holiday fling. Now,' she said as though everything had been settled, 'I'm going back to the bar and tell them I saw you and that you'll be over later this evening. Okay?'

Sloane looked squarely into Kayzie's eyes. 'No,' she said. 'I can't.'

'What do you *mean* you can't?' Kayzie shrieked. 'What are you, his *slave* Just say thanks for the swell visit and save your goddamned life!'

'I can't,' she repeated. 'I can't leave him.'

'Now, that is just plain nuts, Sloane. What were you two doing up there? Magic mushrooms or something? I think your brain's gone.'

'I'm as sane as I've ever been, Kayzie. I'm staying with Miguel as long as he will have me.'

440

Kayzie violently shook her head as though to clear it of an invisible swarm of gnats. 'You know, I've never wanted to be a man in my life until now.'

'What difference would that make?'

'If I were a man, I'd punch your lights out, tell the animal stabber out there you passed out, and throw you on the next flight to L.A.'

'I'd get right back on another plane and come back.' Her voice was calm and determined. 'Kayzie, I'm not leaving.'

'Jesus!' Kayzie swore, pressing her temples with the heels of her hands. 'I can't believe I'm hearing this. What are we supposed to tell people when we get back? Everyone knows we were meeting you down here.'

'Just say I liked Acapulco and decided to stay.'

'And Warner? The fellow who made you rich and famous and married you to boot. What about him?'

'I'll handle Warner. Don't you worry about him.'

'Man, oh, man,' Kayzie said, shaking her head some more. 'This has to be bigger than sex, this whole thing. There has to be something going on here that Helen Gurley Brown doesn't know about or she would have told us.'

'I can't help myself, Kayzie,' Sloane said softly, 'He does something to me that I've been looking for all my life.'

Kayzie looked very sad. 'He can't be good for you, Sloane. A man like that, well, they're a romantic cliché like racing car drivers or rock stars. Plus, this one is Latin. He'll just use you. He won't lose a thing and you'll lose it all.'

'Can't you understand?' Sloane said, her voice quavering. 'I want him to use me!'

Sloane could tell by the crestfallen expression on Kayzie's face that she had given up arguing with her.

'Okay,' Kayzie said, raising her arms and then dropping them limply at her sides in a gesture of total

441

defeat. 'I can see I'm not going to change your mind. I sure hope you know what you're doing about Warner. He'll have an L.A. SWAT team down here if he gets wind of this.'

'Don't worry. I know how to handle it.'

'You know I'm going to have to tell Cole and the others that I saw you.'

'Please, Kayzie. Tell them after you leave. I don't want a scene back at the table. Promise me?'

Kayzie pulled open the door and started to leave. 'All right . . . But you've got to do something for *me*, too.'

'If I can.'

'Keep out of sight as much as possible. And for all our sake's . . . be careful.'

Sloane nodded halfheartedly. The last thing in the world she was capable of now was being careful.

How could she make Kayzie understand that for all of her life she had been told she was beautiful. Now, at long last, she truly believed she was.

When she returned to the table, he was standing in front of it talking to two men. As she approached, they turned and moved on.

She noticed that the table had been cleared of everything but the bill, onto which was what appeared to be a crisp new one-hundred-dollar bill.

He smiled at her and cupped her elbow. 'Come, *mi reina*,' he said, turning her toward the door. She could see the men in his entourage waiting around the captain's stand.

She glanced back at the table. 'Don't you want your change?'

'I have my change. That's the tip,' he said, taking her hand and leading her toward the door.

After leaving the restaurant, Miguel said he felt like a boat ride. When he mentioned his boat, she pictured some sort of sail craft, quiet, peaceful, something that would glide over the moonlit bay.

Within twenty minutes of leaving the restaurant she was streaking across the blue-black water at over one hundred miles an hour, clinging to a railing with one arm and encircling his waist for dear life with the other. Far behind them, two men from his entourage kept their distance in a smaller boat.

The boat was a long, low, powerful black fibreglass monster. It slashed through water with the roar of a jet plane. Miguel handled the boat the way he drove, deftly, with total confidence, and at a terrifying speed. They thundered across the bay, side by side, the wind ripping at their hair and skin for nearly an hour. Conversation was impossible. She abandoned herself to the thrill of being close to him and the exhilarating danger of the boat's power.

Suddenly he throttled back and cut the engine. The boat drifted slowly for a few more yards and then came to rest in the still water.

They were in a little cove with high rocks rising up off the beach and yawning caves above. He turned and waved off the boat following them. She watched as it turned and headed back across the bay.

He reached under the dashboard and pulled out a plastic hamper. 'Now,' he said, 'we will have a little rest.'

'Where?' she asked with a delighted laugh. 'We're yards from the beach.'

He did not answer. He slipped off his Italian loafers and swung over the side, the hamper on his shoulder. He landed with a splash in water up to his knees and held his arms up to her. 'Come to me,' he said.

She slipped over the side and into his arms. Effortlessly he carried her through the water and up onto the beach. He bent to unzip the hamper and took out a blanket, a bottle of champagne, and two glasses.

She stood listening to the night sounds, watching him make a place for them on the powdery, moonlit sand.

He sat down first and offered her his hand. She sat down next to him as he opened the champagne and poured them their drinks.

Again, they toasted each other with their eyes. *Now*, she thought, *now I have to tell him*. 'Miguel?' she said tentatively after the first sip.

'*Sí mi amor*,' he said, running his hand up under her shirt and stroking her back.

'Did you mean it when you told my friend that I would be staying with you?'

'Of course. I do not say things I do not mean,' he said firmly. 'Why do you ask?'

'Well, there is someone in Los Angeles where I live. Someone who is going to want to know, very soon, where I am.'

'Tell them,' he said nonchalantly, deftly working on the hooks of her bra.

'That's the problem. They won't be happy about it.'

'This person in Los Angeles, is he your husband?'

'Yes,' she answered softly, afraid of his reaction.

'I see.'

'That doesn't bother you?'

'Not if it doesn't bother you.' He smiled. 'I am used to women who have husbands.'

She felt a twinge of jealousy she couldn't suppress. 'Oh? You do this a lot with married women?'

His hand cupped her left breast. He stroked the nipple gently with his thumb. 'Do *what* a lot with married women?' he teased, forcing her back onto the blanket. He half-rolled on top of her and brought his lips within a millimetre of her own.

'This,' she giggled, kissing him.

'I was not even alive until yesterday when I saw you. So, don't ask questions that have meaningless answers.' He bent to kiss her again but she pulled away and sat up.

444

'What am I going to tell my husband, Miguel?'

'What do you want to tell him?'

'I don't know, I'm so confused.' She hugged her knees and stared up at the moon. 'I'll have to go home sometime.'

'Why?'

'Darling,' she said. 'Be reasonable. Life doesn't work like that.'

'My life does.' He sounded hurt. Surely he didn't expect her to tell Warner the truth?

'I need time to think, Miguel,' she said.

He got to his feet and held out his hand.

'Are we going?' she asked, looking up at his silhouette against the stars in the sky.

'Not yet,' he said as she stood. He pulled her shirt over her head. Quickly he helped her to undress completely.

'What are you doing?' she asked, laughing again with delight.

'I'm going to show you something that will help you make up your mind,' he said. He pulled off his shirt and stepped out of his pants. He wore no underwear and was already fully erect. His skin looked like mahogany silk in the moonlight. He reached for her and lifted her nearly over his head. The only way she could steady herself was to put her legs around his waist. Instantly he inserted himself, impaling her. She gasped as a sharp, delicious, near-pain engulfed her body.

Coupled and moaning with desire for each other, he walked them to the edge of the soft, warm water and lay down on top of her, resting on his elbows on the sandy bottom in the shallow water. He lay perfectly still, huge inside. 'Now,' he said, 'does this help you think about what you are going to tell your husband?'

'Darling, don't talk,' she gasped. 'Not now.' She tried to thrust her hips against him. She couldn't move.

'Not until you give me an answer I like.'

'Oh, please, Miguel! You're *driving me crazy*.'

'I can stay like this for a very long time, you know,' he said, pinning her arms under the water.

'Now, darling, now,' she whispered, raising her head and sinking her teeth into his shoulder.

'Now what?'

She moaned.

'Say it,' he growled.

She leaned her head back into the water. Her eyes were wide and her breath was coming in little panting gasps as she looked up at him.

'Say it!' he repeated, almost shouting.

She hesitated. She knew what he wanted to hear. She had never said it to a man. But the only thing that was real to her was the feeling of him inside her. 'Fuck me,' she moaned, almost weeping. 'Please, Miguel, fuck me!' Now she was screaming and the words she had never before brought herself to speak echoed back from the caves high above them.

With three violent thrusts he brought her to orgasm. He stayed inside her until she lay spent and calm in the shallow water. Then he withdrew.

He stood and helped her up, then swung her into his arms and carried her back to the beach.

He lay down beside her again, on the blanket. 'Tell him you are staying at El Camino.'

She turned and looked at him. 'What?'

'Tell him you are staying at El Camino. It's a very famous spa about ten miles from here. I know the people who own it. I will take care of it first thing in the morning.' That solved, he rolled over and entered her again.

They made love until the champagne was gone and the moon had disappeared from the sky.

When they finally rose to go, he once again pulled her into his arms. '*Te amo con toda mi alma*,' he whispered against her neck. 'Do you know what that means?'

She shook her head.

'I love you with all of my soul.'

The next morning, the houseman served them breakfast beside the pool. Sloane wore a bright red French bikini, grateful for her daily workouts.

Miguel was fully dressed. He sat opposite her, sipping his coffee behind black Porsche sunglasses that covered half his face. She studied the hands holding the white clay coffee mug. They were large masculine hands that showed evidence of having been broken many times. The short sleeves of his powder-blue polo shirt exposed the scars on the inside of each arm that ran from his wrists to his elbows, like the result of an exaggerated suicide attempt. He had explained to her that they had actually been caused by the horns of the bulls. Miraculously, his face was unmarked.

Seeing the scars before by candlelight had filled her with wild excitement. Now, seeing them in daylight, she was acutely aware of the courage he had to possess to make his living in such a way. The scars proved his bravery in the face of death, and yet they showed his vulnerability as well. She reached over and gently ran her thumb along the edge of the scar on his right arm.

He stopped her by taking her hand and bringing it to his lips. 'I must leave you for a while. I have business in town this morning,' he said against her palm.

He must have seen the look of apprehension in her eyes, 'Don't worry, my darling. I'll be back for a late lunch and a swim. Besides, I know you have some phone calls to make.'

She watched him as he walked across the sun-bright terrace, longing for him before he had even left. His houseman handed him a leather briefcase. She wondered what sort of business he had to transact. She knew so little about him, really. Only the way he made her feel. That was all that mattered.

He turned at the entrance to the house, removed his sunglasses, and glanced back at her. The look in his eyes seemed to be daring her not to give in when she called Warner. As soon as he was gone, the houseman brought her a cordless phone. He placed it on the table in front of her and inquired if she would care for some more coffee. She accepted his offer and sat for a long time staring at the phone. *Oh, God*, she thought. *I've got to get my wits about me. Let me see, I'll say, 'Hello, Warner, darling, do you miss me?'* She whispered the words out loud, rehearsing as though for a big scene.

Maybe she could tell him she was having plastic surgery. That could take weeks. But he would never believe that. *'Hello, darling. I've found this wonderful spa and . . .'* What if he said he'd just hop down and join her? *'It's all women,'* she could say.

The worst scenario of all, of course, would be if he flatly refused to let her stay, demanding that she come home. What would she do then?

The houseman returned, poured more coffee, and left as quietly as he came.

She reached for the phone and punched in the office number at the Bel Air estate. While she waited for the call to go through, she nervously drilled her long red nails on the tabletop. Far out over the bay, a tourist dangled from a speedboat-drawn parachute.

She turned her gaze toward the house and saw the houseman returning. He was carrying a silver tray with an ice-block bottle of vodka on it. She glanced at her watch. It was nearly noon. She held up one finger and nodded. A good swig of icy vodka was exactly what she needed to make the call.

On the fourth ring, Rose answered in her usual frigid tone.

'Oh . . . Rose. It's Sloane. How was your vacation?'

'Very pleasant, thank you,' she said crisply. 'Mr Bromley is here. Did you want to speak to him?'

Sloane was a bit taken aback; Rose was being even brisker than usual. Was Warner furious and pacing, complaining to her when he had returned to an empty house the night before?

'Hello, my sweet,' Warner said cheerfully when he came on the line. 'Out adventuring, are we?'

She was so surprised at his chipper attitude, she inadvertently began to laugh. 'Hello, darling!'

'It sounds like you're having a wonderful time. Layla said you would.'

'Layla?'

'I had to stop in New York on the way back to close with the banks on the Japanese deal. Layla and I had a quick drink. She told me your merry band of New York cronies were having a great time. I'm so glad the trip is turning out well for you.'

She couldn't believe her luck. Without knowing it, Layla had covered for her. She began to relax a little.

'Do you need anything, darling?' Warner asked.

Suddenly she remembered the missing five hundred dollars. She *would* need more. He was giving her the perfect opening. 'Actually, I do. Some people we met here took me out to see El Camino and —'

He interrupted almost as if he wasn't fully listening.

'And you loved it, right? I hear it's a fabulous place.'

'Well, yes . . . I thought I might stay out there for a while, get some rest, exercise — whatever.'

'Listen, darling,' he said. 'You can't miss their mint-mud baths. They cover you from head to toe in some secret slime and steam it off with hot water. Sounds grim, but they are famous for the damn things. It's supposed to make you feel marvellous. Binky and Dierdre Carmichael — you remember them from the wedding, he's with the Fed — they swear by those baths. They go every year after Gstaad to work out the ski kinks.'

She couldn't believe her ears. He was dithering and gossiping away as though nothing were out of the ordinary about her talking about not coming back. He was being so nice she was beginning to feel guilty. 'Can you manage there for a while, darling?' she asked.

'Well, actually, I'm off again at the end of the week. I've got to meet with the Bank of England about the Japanese deal. I'll be in London for at least ten days.'

A small, dark cloud drifted across her mind. She did some quick arithmetic. The second vodka in the hot sun wasn't making it any easier. London . . . end of the week . . . there for another. That meant two weeks with Miguel! 'I'd love to stay down here and really soak up the sun while you're gone,' she said.

'Of course, darling. You deserve the rest,' he said offhandedly. 'Should I wire some funds to the Neithergoulds or the spa?'

Her head spun. She hated lying. Hated, hated, hated it. If she weren't in such a state of sexual euphoria, she could never pull this off. 'Ah . . . the spa I think. The others will be going back to New York. I'll pick it up there.' Miguel said he knew the owners, she remembered; he could arrange everything.

'Grand,' Warner said. 'I'll put Rose on it, right away. Two thousand sound about right? If you need more, call Rose in New York.'

'My goodness, yes, Warner. *Thank* you.'

'Enjoy yourself, my darling girl. I'll call from London. Or perhaps you'd rather call me. You might be up to your lovely neck in hot water,' he said, chuckling at his unwittingly ironic joke.

'I'll call,' she said, perhaps too eagerly.

'I love you, sweetheart. And miss you, too.'

'Me, too, Warner . . . me, too,' she said softly.

She sat holding the phone for a long while after he'd hung up, trying to sort out what she had just done. She was delirious that she would have so much time with Miguel; then again, Warner had been so sweet. If she started feeling guilty now, everything would be ruined.

She reached for the bottle of vodka, in its rapidly melting block of ice under the high, hot sun. One more drink would steady her nerves.

She was lying on her stomach on the lowered chaise when she felt the base of her spine being kissed. Her whole body tingled as she rolled over to see Miguel standing over her. He was holding an enormous bouquet of red roses, perhaps four dozen in all.

He put the roses on the table and sat down on the edge of the chaise. 'Did you make your call, *mi amor?*' he asked, running his thumb under the thin gold chain she wore around her waist.

She was suddenly overwhelmed with such hunger for him that she threw her arms around his neck, 'I'm staying,' she said ecstatically.

He held her close, speaking into the curve of her neck. 'Wonderful! Friday I fight in Mexico City. You will come. Before the fight I want you to see something women are forbidden to see.'

'What?' she asked, intrigued.

'The dressing ceremony.'

'Really? But why can't a woman see that?'

'They say that if a woman is present, the bull can smell her on the matador and it enrages him,' he said.

'Then perhaps I shouldn't.'

'No. I want you to see everything, to know everything. I will arrange it.'

'I'm so excited,' she said, giving him a quick squeeze before pulling away. 'Now, Señor Arranger, can you arrange to have a swim with me before lunch?'

He stood up, smiling at her. He had a look in his eye she was beginning to recognize. 'Of course,' he said as he began pulling off his clothes.

'Aren't you going to put on a suit?'

He was naked almost before she'd finished asking the question. He stood in front of her, smiling, and jumped into the pool. 'Come on,' he called, flicking water up at her.

'You're terrible,' she giggled, sliding in at the shallow end.

When he reached her, he shoved his hand down her bikini panties. He yanked them off with one hand and with the other gripped her tightly between the legs, rotating a finger up inside her. 'Not so terrible you didn't beg me last night. Remember?' he asked fiercely, withdrawing his finger and pushing her up against the circular steps. He thrust himself into her. She clung to him, riding his slow, rhythmic movements in the cool, turquoise water under a wide, bright-blue sky.

'You like it, don't you?' he said into her open mouth. 'You're always ready for me, aren't you?' He moved his tongue in and out of her mouth in a rhythm that matched the movement of his hips.

Over his shoulder she saw the houseman stroll out on the terrace with their lunch under a domed net. He placed the tray on the table only a yard or two from the edge of the pool. As he turned to leave, he glanced quickly toward the pool, smiled, and returned to the house.

The excitement of having someone actually see them together, naked and making love in the water, where his great, broken, and scarred hands held tight to her bottom, was so excruciatingly exciting she began to move in a corkscrew motion that plunged him even higher. 'Darling – your houseman . . . he saw us,' she gasped.

'Is he still watching?' he asked, smiling down at her.

She managed to shake her head no.

'Too bad. He missed seeing something beautiful.'

'What?' she asked, not breaking the rhythm. She looked down and watched her thighs moving on either side of his.

'Your beautiful face when you come. You're going to come now, aren't you, *mi amor?* I can feel it.' The large muscles on either side of his neck strained against the skin as he took charge, thrusting himself in, withdrawing

452

almost entirely, and then plunging into her again until he was as far as he could go.

'Yes,' she gasped. 'Oh, darling, yes!'

He held himself very still as her whole body burst and melted over the hardness of him. 'Look at me,' he commanded suddenly. 'Look into my eyes when you come. I want to see your soul give itself to me.'

He left her there. He had arrangements to make regarding the upcoming flight. She climbed aboard an inflated canvas mattress and still naked, rolled over on her stomach to float in her own Garden of Eden. She felt suspended in a gold and blue world, drenched with sun and vodka and sex, her heart pounded with what was becoming a terrible, terrible need for this fierce, passionate man.

Her addiction to him was now complete.

25

In the days that followed, Sloane realized that she was living in a completely male world. Except for unseen female servants who cooked, cleaned, and washed the clothes, there were only men.

All day, all night, they were there, in the house and along the road in front of the house. Men came and went. They lounged about the house and slouched around the pool, speaking in quiet tones as though they were at the court of a modern Sun King.

Miguel's every wish was anticipated. Everyone did his bidding as if by second nature. For all she knew, the order and pace of each day had been going on unchanged for years, only now she was a part of it. Or had she simply replaced someone?

She had no way of knowing who was on a payroll or who was just some kind of bullfighter groupie. Sometimes women came, but they were always accompanied by the men. Most of the time they sat around silently smiling or whispering among themselves in Spanish. Sloane had no way to communicate with them except to smile sweetly.

A constant presence among the men was a small, wiry man who seldom smiled. He was Miguel's manager. He saw to scheduling the fights, selling tickets, advertising the next venue, and handling the money. There was also Vellis's dresser, called the *mozo de espada*. There were men who were in charge of selecting the bulls in whatever city or town he was to fight in, and others who handled all the equipment that had to be transported from place to place, the swords and capes and heaven knew what else. She could have landed on Pluto and not been more out of her element.

Two men with gold incisors that glinted when they smiled seemed to have been assigned to protect her. Their names were Chico and Beto. They permitted no one to approach her in a restaurant or anywhere in public as they moved around Acapulco in a kind of royal caravan, from chic restaurants to the 'in' clubs and discos.

If a man approached her, and they did, they were quickly bumped away by Beto's basketball-shaped stomach or Chico's thick, tattooed arms.

She assumed the two were assigned to her because they spoke English. Beto had been in the U.S. Marines and Chico was raised in San Antonio, where his family owned a big Mexican restaurant. They were both Indians with straight black hair and low foreheads. Their noses were broad with extra large dark nostrils.

Of the two, she liked Beto best. He had a sense of humor and a braying Eddie Murphy laugh. He knew a lot about American pop culture, rock and roll, and popular American television characters.

Chico had a scar that ran the length of his chest. It started at his Adam's apple and didn't stop until it disappeared down the waistband of his bathing suit. He said he had once been a matador. Beto told her the scar was the result of a knife fight in which the other guy died. Whatever the case, the two of them took their job of protecting her very seriously.

Like many of the men, the two wore a lot of gold chains that dangled crucifixes and St Christopher medals. When Beto referred to his chains as his 'Mr T starter kit,' he made Sloane laugh and it sealed their friendship.

As polite as all the men were, Sloane knew most of them were not thrilled about her presence. Some were jealous and sullen. They knew they had to treat her differently than they would a Mexican woman. She was an American and they could tell from the way she dressed and the jewelry she owned that she was rich. They successfully hid their feelings about her until they learned that she would not only accompany the entourage to the next fight but that Miguel was going to permit her to be in the suite at the hotel during the dressing ceremony.

The news got out when Miguel told his dresser at drinks one evening beside the pool. There were eight or ten of his men standing and sitting round. Their faces froze and their black eyes became mean-spirited slits.

Later that evening as they all walked across the parking lot to yet another restaurant, Sloane turned to Beto and asked him why everybody seemed so upset.

'It's not allowed,' he said, sounding as if he agreed with the others. 'It's bad luck. A woman weakens the matador. She distracts him. During the dressing ceremony he must concentrate. It's like going into a deep hypnotic state to prepare to meet the bull. During the dressing ceremony he is supposed to be making his peace with God in case he's killed or hurt. A woman around gives off bad vibes. Besides, the bull will know.'

'Oh, Beto,' she said, laughing, 'you don't really believe that, do you?' The minute she said it she knew she shouldn't have. He might joke with her and know all the lyrics to 'Thriller', but he would not tolerate a woman's doubting laughter at the rituals of the ring – she had mocked death. She wanted to disappear down a big black hole.

'It would be best if you don't ask questions, señorita,' Beto said tightly. 'This is very serious business. Man's business.'

She should have seen then that she was in over her head, that she had let herself be led into a life far more constricted and controlled than her life with Warner. What she perceived as abandon and freedom was, had she recognized reality at the time, more of an invisible prison governed by secrecy and ritual, rules within rules and no explanation given, particularly not to her, a woman, an American woman. She was shown respect only because of her relationship to Miguel. If that had not existed, she would have been merely an object to be admired, a sought-after ornament.

She lived in a world that was layer after layer of absolutes. No sooner would she examine and question why something was done than she would find another enigma underneath.

There she was in the ultimate Game, the price for which was the abandonment of control. She controlled nothing, only Miguel's love, and at that point in time that was everything to her. As each day passed, she gave another part of herself away until the only thing that mattered was that Miguel approved of what she said and did. Making him happy was the only thing she had left.

As the day of the fight approached, she watched a subtle change come over Miguel. It was as though he had turned in on himself. He was still protective of her, holding her hand at dinner and caressing her in public, kissing her. Their lovemaking was just as fierce and constant, but now it was accomplished in silence, without his beautiful compliments and vows of eternal love. His body was with her but not his mind.

They arrived in Mexico City the day before the fight. On the flight from Acapulco, their group took up the entire front of the plane.

When they arrived, they were met by still more dark men who helped off-load their tons of custom-made leather luggage. The trunks contained their *charros*, the huge spangled hats, and the heavy capes, thickly embroidered by nuns who thought it an honour to do the intricate labour. There were heavy cases, especially made for the swords, that required two strong men even to lift them off the ground.

The *mozo*, Ricardo Mejias, was in charge of Vellis's personal clothes, his suits of light, and all the attendant equipment — special stockings, shoes, hats, his hairpieces, which were pinned to the back of a bullfighter's head.

Then there were the trunks and valises of religious paraphernalia for the altar that the dresser would reverently prepare in one corner of the hotel suite. Every item, every piece of regalia, every bit of fabric, was handled with great respect. Each was symbolic, considered almost holy in the bullfighter's world.

There were rituals within rituals and superstitions that were never defied regardless of the fact that their origins were lost in history. Sloane learned that there were general superstitions surrounding the ritual before, during, and after the fight, and specific superstitions held by each individual bullfighter.

She found the whole arcane business both unnerving and inexplicably exciting.

The morning they were to leave, the atmosphere at the villa was one of preparing for war. She tried to stay out of the way, pretending to read on one of the couches in the living room. But she could sense the anticipation of pain and blood and the ominous possibility of death.

She could see why these men idolized Miguel. To face death by choice was the ultimate manly act to them, and any part they played in strengthening him for the fight made them more manly in turn.

A line of big American cars and a van for the equipment were waiting outside the airport terminal. She sat back in the lead car for the drive to the hotel holding Vellis's hand. Looking down at their ringless fingers, she was reminded of an incident the afternoon before.

Even though she had overpacked for the trip from L.A., she had still brought only a weekend's worth of clothes and needed a few things. When one of Vellis's men returned from the spa with the money Warner had wired, she asked Miguel if he would drive her down to the smart shops that lined the avenue along the beach. The shops primarily catered to tourists, but they would have anything she might need.

It occurred to her that Latin men don't sit around dress shops watching their ladies try on clothes. She took pains to tell him just to drop her and pick her up in an hour.

The second shop she entered was run by an exotic-looking American woman who recognized her right away. Sloane smiled as the woman approached and called her Miss Taylor.

'What brings you to Acapulco?' she asked pleasantly. 'Are you on a modeling assignment?'

'Just a short vacation,' Sloane said. 'How nice to meet someone from home.'

'And how can I help you? We just got in some wonderful cottons by a local designer.'

'That sounds perfect,' Sloane said. 'I just need a few light dresses and perhaps another pair of slacks.' She followed the owner to a rack of clothes by a mirrored wall. 'Perhaps you can tell me. I've been invited to a bullfight in Mexico City but it's at night. Will it be cool?'

'Oh, a bit at this time of year. Why don't you look through the rack. Several of these dresses come with matching jackets. They'd work fine.'

Sloane selected half a dozen outfits from the rack and took them into the dressing room. The one she liked was bright yellow with a waist-length lined jacket. She slipped it on and stepped out to check it in the wall mirror.

'Oh! Miss Taylor. No. No. No. Not that one.' The American woman was walking toward her from the front of the shop shaking her head, greatly agitated. 'Please, that's all wrong!'

Sloane frowned at her in the mirror. 'I don't understand. What's the problem?'

'Yellow. That's the colour of bad luck. It means death!

No one would ever wear that colour to the bullfights. You'd panic the aficionados and God help you if you came anywhere near the actual bullfighter in that colour.'

'Good heavens!' Sloane said. 'I had no idea.'

'I'm sorry. I don't mean to get so excited,' the owner said. 'It's just that people here take that sort of thing very seriously and I wouldn't want your evening to be ruined.'

'That's all right.' Sloane smiled, grateful for the woman's concern. 'I appreciate your telling me. Wouldn't it be terrible if you hadn't?'

'Here, try this one,' the owner said, holding out the identical dress in bright pink. 'They love hot pink.'

Within an hour Sloane had everything she needed. The total bill far exceeded her available cash. Reluctantly, she produced her American Express card and watched the shop owner crunch it through the charge machine. For an instant she pictured Rose frowning at the morning mail and smugly walking the bill into Warner's office. She pushed the thought from her head and signed the bill.

'Oh?'

'I nearly bought a yellow dress to wear to the fight.'

His reaction startled her. 'That would have been a disaster,' he said, his face dark. His eyes fell to her hands in her lap. He reached over and lifted her hand. 'And you must not wear this,' he said, touching his thumb to a Victorian ring she had slipped on her little finger that morning. It was a gold snake with a diamond eye she had seen in a shop in the Village when she first came to New York.

'Why ever not?' she asked.

'Just take it off. Now!'

She slipped it from her finger and dropped it into her handbag. 'All right,' she said. 'But why?'

'Snakes,' he said angrily. 'Very bad.'

He pulled back into the stream of traffic. She sat back

in the seat and stared straight ahead. She had so much to learn, so much to understand.

And yet, here she was headed toward the hotel, where tomorrow she would witness a forbidden ceremony with his permission. She wondered if the strange discipline of his life wasn't determined by what he alone permitted. She knew the only way she could learn how to live in this ritualistic atmosphere was never to question why something was done. She knew further that she could do that, as long as he permitted her to love him.

Sloane awoke the morning of the fight, hung over and starving. The night before they had gone to a beautiful restaurant where Miguel was surrounded by fans. Somehow, in all the confusion and excitement of being there with Miguel, she drank too much and never got around to eating. All evening long their table had been surrounded by adoring fans, aficionados who only wanted to touch his hand or say a few words to wish him luck.

There were beautiful women. They hung back more than the men, but it was clear to Sloane that they would be available to him, or failing that, any one of his men.

Now, she looked over at Miguel, sound asleep in the other bed. He had laughed when he saw two beds instead of one big one and told her that it was the doing of the hotel manager. Matadors were not supposed to be with a woman before a fight. 'As though that would stop me,' he said, smiling, as he pulled her to one of the beds and promptly made love to her before dinner. Or rather, before the dinner she never ate.

Someone was rapping on the living room door. She opened it to find a room service waiter standing behind a covered table. She stood to one side as he pushed it into the room.

Wonderful, she thought. *If I don't eat, I'll faint.*

When the waiter left, she lifted the cloth to see a huge

bowl of fruit and a pitcher of ice water. She didn't understand. One of the things she knew about Miguel was that he loved his breakfasts; eggs, tortillas, bacon *and* ham, refried beans, and gallons of coffee. Even a bottle of beer or two. She wondered why he had left an order for fruit and water. She walked back to the bedroom to tell him his breakfast had arrived.

He was holding his arms up to her with that look on his face. She raced to the bed and snuggled in next to him. 'Breakfast is here, darling,' she said, kissing his neck. 'I'm afraid it's just fruit. Is that what you ordered?'

'Of course,' he said.

'But you love your big breakfasts.'

'Not on the day I fight.'

'Ummm,' she hummed, running her hands down his inner thigh. 'Why is that, darling?'

'If I am disembowelled, there is less mess for the doctors to clean up at the hospital.'

She stopped stroking him. A sudden, suffocating wave of fear and nausea swept into her stomach and up to her throat. She knew she was going to be sick. She threw back the covers and bolted for the bathroom.

After it was over she sat on the closed toilet seat and tried to catch her breath, mortified that he might have heard her being sick, but still weak at the mental picture of his being gored by a bull. Were these the last hours he would be alive? Was she about to lose him just when she had found the only man she could ever love?

She was washing her face with cool water when she heard him shout her name. It was more of an anguished scream. She jumped up and flung open the bathroom door.

He was standing in front of the closet staring down at the little shelf where she had stored her extra handbag and shoes. 'Get them out!' he shouted. 'Get them out of sight! How could you do this to me?'

She forgot her throbbing head and rushed to his side.

462

What in God's name was he talking about? 'That's just my bag and shoes, Miguel,' she said. 'What's the matter?'

He started to back away from the closet. He turned to her. The look of fear and rage in his eyes frightened her.

'Can't you see? They are made of *snake!*' he screamed.

She looked back at the closet floor. 'But darling, these are brand-new! I bought these at I. Magnin's just before I left –' She stopped herself. How dumb, she thought, he didn't care where she had bought them. The man was in mortal terror of her snakeskin handbag and shoes. She remembered Beto's words: 'This is very serious business, señorita. Man's business.' .

She bent and whisked the items from the closet floor, ran across the room to the open balcony door, and threw them over the railing. Some lucky Mexican lady would be wearing a thousand dollars' worth of snakeskin accessories very shortly.

She returned to the room to find him already back in bed. She sat on the edge of the bed trying to think of something to say. All she could think of was, 'I'm sorry, Miguel, I didn't know.'

'Come to me,' he said, pulling back the covers. He took her in his arms and went right back to sleep.

He woke at noon and had a mango and a piece of melon and went back to bed. The *mozo* was due to arrive in the late afternoon. Then the men who would assist him would come. She didn't want to be in the way.

At three she rose to dress and find an unobtrusive place to watch what was about to come.

She dressed in the pink outfit she had bought. She thought wistfully how nice the beige snakeskin shoes would have looked. But if she *had* worn them and something had happened to him in the ring, she wouldn't have been able to live with the guilt.

She pulled a desk chair out onto the little balcony, hoping to be as inconspicuous as possible, and settled in

463

to wait. Drapes covered half of the bedroom where he would dress.

Promptly at four, Ricardo Mejias, his *mozo de espada*, arrived to prepare the bedroom for the solemn ritual of the dressing ceremony. His assistants carried a trunk and a canvas cover bag of clothes into the room. Miguel usually traveled with three or four suits of light, knowing from past experience that they would be bloodied and torn in the bullfight. He had decided to wear a black suit tonight.

With an efficiency born of years of practice, Ricardo set to work transforming the ordinary hotel room into a private shrine. It was here that Miguel would begin the final stage of both the physical and spiritual preparation for the battle ahead. Here he would pray for courage and strength and humbly ask for victory. If things went badly in the ring tonight, this ceremony would be his last opportunity to enjoy the quiet company of his friends, the respectful presence of aficionados he had honoured by his invitation to be present, and perhaps, the last chance to make peace with his God before he died. It was more than the ritual of dressing; it could very well be his last rites.

Sloane watched from the balcony, praying she wouldn't cough or sneeze or cause the chair to scrape against the cement floor. She knew she wasn't supposed to be anywhere around, and her inclusion was both frightening and exciting. She knew how unhappy the men were about her witnessing the dressing ceremony, and she hoped it might help a little if she stayed out of sight on the balcony.

Without warning, Ricardo walked to the large picture window and pulled the drapes closed. Unwittingly, he left a three-inch opening through which she could watch.

He turned off the overhead lights and switched on two sconces on either side of the large mirror on the wall. He picked up a low table and set it under the mirror. Carefully, he wiped the table clean of dust. He laid a

464

small suitcase on the bed just behind him and with slow deliberation began to set up a little altar. Solemnly, he went about placing items on the table in a prescribed order. Each article had a special significance and meaning for Miguel. Each carried the promise, perhaps the proof, of good luck and grace. They had been accumulated over the years and had become powerful totems. It was as though they helped him to feel a sense of continuity and comfort as he faced the very real possibility of death.

First, Ricardo took out an old, travel-worn crucifix that Sloane knew had come from Miguel's parents' home. It had travelled with him since he began to fight. Reverently, Ricardo stood it against the wall in back of the table. Next came three leather-covered photo albums, each of which opened into three leaves. Ricardo placed two of the open binders against the wall on either side of the crucifix. The third he leaned against its base. Each leaf was filled with religious cards and family photos. The most important cards represented the Virgin of Guadalupe, the patron saint of bullfighters. Next, Ricardo tenderly placed the *montera*, Miguel's bull-fighting hat, on the right. To complete the altar, he placed a single votive candle in the centre of the table. He prayed as he lit the candle, which would burn until Miguel returned from the fight.

Sloane's heart skipped a beat as she saw Miguel walking out of the bathroom, his hair still wet from the shower, his lean, muscular body covered from the waist down with a towel. He walked to the foot of the bed, where Ricardo had laid a towel for him to stand on. For a few moments he stood drying himself, oblivious to the presence of people in the room.

Sloane hoped he wouldn't see her. Even though he knew she was there, actually seeing her might break some arcane, mystic thing that was going on in his head. If something happened to him tonight, she would forever blame herself for breaking the spell and jinxing him.

He turned and faced the altar. The look on his face was one Sloane had never seen, so intense and concentrated, it was as though he had located a place deep within himself from which he drew some mystical strength to face the bulls.

Ricardo knelt in front of him on one knee. He had draped three pairs of stockings across the knee that was bent. Miguel extended his legs and Ricardo eased on the first, light pair. Then he put on the second pair, which were not unlike a supportive Ace bandage. The last pair were bright pink.

Naked except for the stockings, Miguel stood and was helped into a pleated white cotton shirt. It had a small, pointed collar and a pleat that hid the buttons down the front. The tails of the shirt were designed to fasten between the legs. As Ricardo reached down to secure the shirt, Miguel made some remark to the people gathered in the room. It was the first time he had spoken. As soft laughter passed through the spectators, Sloane wished for what must have been the thousandth time that she could understand Spanish.

One of Ricardo's assistants stepped forward and helped Miguel into a pair of very tight knee-length pants. They reached six inches above the waist and fastened on the side with heavy metal hooks. Next came white suspenders, a tight black silk vest, and a soft red satin necktie to which Miguel pinned a tiny crucifix. He walked to the mirror, his face a solemn mask, and brushed his long black hair into place. Ricardo stood behind him and attached a doughnut-shaped tail of hair onto the back of his head with an incongruous bobby pin.

Another assistant removed the jacket of the suit of lights from under its protective canvas cover as Miguel stepped into the shoes Ricardo held out for him. They were soft black leather, like ballet slippers, with no heel or sole. Ricardo now held the very stiff jacket for the suit of lights. Large ovals were cut at the armpit under the sleeve to permit freedom of movement in the ring. Miguel slipped into the jacket and spent several moments pulling and tugging it into place.

The sight of him, completely dressed, the magnificently embroidered jacket sparkling even in the dim light of the hotel room, made Sloane nearly dizzy with desire. It was one thing to see him, as she usually did, in beautifully cut sports clothes and Italian loafers. But looking at him now, dressed in virtual battle gear, overwhelmed her with conflicting feelings of arousal and fear.

Miguel walked to the suitcase and retrieved a small zippered case from which he took religious medals on thin gold chains: a diamond-studded cross and a St Christopher's medal set with emeralds. The medals were small and very delicate. As he lifted each one, he made the sign of the cross and placed them around his neck, tucking them out of the way under his shirt.

The ceremony now complete, he stood before the altar reading prayers to the Virgin aloud from a little leather-bound book. When he finished, he turned in silence to the assembled group. His stance indicated that it was time to go. An assistant opened the door and the group slowly moved out to accompany Miguel to his fate.

Sloane had no idea what was expected of her now. Would someone come to get her? How would she get to the bull ring?

She stepped into the room with trepidation to see Beto standing in the doorway motioning to her to follow.

The men made a path for her in the hall, both sides of which were lined with eager fans who burst into applause as Miguel stepped out.

'Can I speak to him?' Sloane whispered to Beto.

'Of course. You must,' Beto whispered back. 'You must say *muchas suerte*. That means "good luck."'

'Is it okay to kiss him?'

Beto smiled. 'I think he would like that.'

Sloane walked up to Miguel and kissed him lightly on the lips. '*Muchas suerte*, darling,' she whispered.

He smiled and offered her his shimmering, spangled arm. 'Walk with me to the car,' he said softly.

As she moved down the hall, trailed by his entourage, she was vaguely aware of the smiling, adoring faces around them. She felt as though she were sending him off to war.

It occurred to her that she might never see him alive again. Or that he might live but lie, bloody and torn to bits, in the mud of the bullring. She fought back the tears. She was sure a crying woman was bad luck.

They moved through the lobby to more applause and cries that sounded like '*Mi-guel! Mi-guel!*' '*Hola! Matador!*' and '*Muchas suerte, Matador!*'

Her feelings of apprehension and fear were overcome by her bursting pride in him, in being with him, and the intoxication of being stared at herself with such envy and awe.

They were met at the curb by his *banderilleros*. Each wore suits similar to Miguel's but without any gold or elaborate decorations.

It wasn't until he bent to kiss her good-bye that she realized she would not be riding with him. Beto, who was standing by the door of another car, gestured for her to join him.

As she watched him walk to the lead car for his solemn ride to the bullring, she felt faint with terror. Beto sensed her anguish and took her elbow to guide her to their car and driver. He helped her into the backseat and joined her.

'Easy, Sloane, easy,' he said reassuringly. 'Don't show your fear. It will make him look weak for his lady not to have courage.'

'It's just that I didn't realize how vulnerable he is until I watched him getting dressed,' she said.

'His armor is his courage. Miguel Vellis is famous for his bravery.'

'That's all very well, but I've seen him fight only once. I don't have a real sense of his skill.'

Beto smiled. 'Ah, skill can be learned. What people admire Miguel for is the fire in his belly, his fearlessness. It is in his blood. I've seen him fight hundreds of times. My faith in his skill is based on the fact that he is still alive.'

'With battle scars to prove it,' she said, craning her neck to catch a glimpse of Vellis's car ahead of them as they waited for the other cars to move into place. 'Can I ask you a very indelicate question, Beto?'

'Please,' he answered with a warm laugh. 'I love indelicate questions from beautiful women.'

'Well . . . when they were dressing him, when the *mozo* was putting on his pants. It's just that, I was surprised. He wasn't wearing . . .' She paused, feeling shy about discussing the subject with Beto.

'Any underwear? Is that what's bothering you?'

'Well . . . yes. He's so . . . exposed!'

'Ah, but that's the point. The crowd loves that look. It's considered macho and shows that he is not afraid.'

The driver eased the car forward, pulling into their place in the procession.

Sloane held out her hand. 'Well, I am afraid, Beto. Look how I'm shaking,' she said.

'Get ahold of yourself before we get to the ring,' he cautioned. 'It's dangerous. If he looks up and sees that you're upset, he can get hurt. Also, let me warn you, if anyone approaches you while he is in the ring – say, to offer you a beer or just to chat – you look the other way. Several of us will be surrounding you to keep people away, but sometimes they get through.'

'Who are they?' Sloane asked, confused. 'Why would anybody approach *me*. I don't know anyone.'

'The managers for the other bullfighters will send people over hoping he will see it and go berserk.'

Sloane slumped back in the seat. 'God, Beto. Is he going to be all right? I'm so worried.'

469

Beto reached over and patted her arm. 'He'll be fine. You're the one I worry about.'

'Where will he go once he gets to the ring?'

'First he goes to the chapel. Then he will go with his men to his place. Ricardo will bandage part of his hands, for support. When his time comes, he will be handed his sword and cape. That's when you will see him again. When he steps into the ring.'

'I'm just worried about seeing him after the fight.'

Beto looked over at her and started to say something. He seemed to think better of it and stared straight ahead.

'What, Beto?'

'I shouldn't.'

'Beto? What? I want to know,' she said angrily. She knew it had to be something about Miguel.

'Look, Sloane,' he said, taking a deep breath. 'I like you. I like you a whole lot. You're a real lady and frankly the best thing that could happen to a man like Miguel. But there are a lot of things you don't understand. Perhaps you'd be better off if you never do.'

'What things?' she asked. She was beginning to panic at what he might be trying to tell her.

He hesitated and then plunged on. 'Sometimes – not every time, mind you – but sometimes after he fights, a bullfighter will –'

'Will what?' she said impatiently. 'Beto, just say it! I can take it.'

'Well . . . they disappear. They just go off. When you face death and win, your mind is in a strange place.'

'Where do they go, for heaven's sake?'

He didn't answer.

'Beto! Where?' His silence frightened her. 'Oh, God! You're talking about those women, aren't you? Those women who hang around all the time. I saw some of them in the corridor of the hotel. There were a couple of hang-up calls at the hotel last night. You're trying to tell me he goes off with a woman, aren't you?' She fought to keep her voice down. She wasn't sure whether the driver understood them or not.

Beto sighed. Then he nodded.

She couldn't hold back the tears now. 'Oh, God,' she said again. 'If he does that, I'll just die.'

'No, you won't!' Beto said sharply. 'If he does that, you will go back to the hotel and say nothing. Do you understand? If you want this man, you will not say a word. He lives his own life and if you complain about something, like this, you'll lose him. You don't want that, do you?'

She picked through her bag for a tissue, found one and her compact, and tried to repair the damage the tears were doing to her perfect eye makeup. 'No, Beto,' she said forlornly. 'I don't want that.'

They drove the rest of the way to the stadium in uneasy silence. Live without Miguel or accept his faithlessness! What a bitter choice. Her heart was breaking into little shards, each cutting her more deeply than the last. Why was this happening to her? The headiness, the thrill of finding him, seemed worthless in the face of such pain. She had never experienced infidelity before, and the shock of even the hint of it was overwhelming. There was no place to run, no place to escape from the searing disappointment. The thought of Warner flickered guiltily through her mind. Was this the way he would feel if he knew what was keeping her in Mexico? Impossible, she concluded, pushing the thought away. He couldn't possibly love her the way she loved Miguel. His love was a quiet, mature thing. What she felt for Miguel was a divine passion like none other.

How was she to behave with Miguel now? Should she confront him or should she throw herself at his feet and beg him not to hurt her by sharing his infinite passion with someone else? Her mind spun with the image of the two of them together, the moments when their souls had touched. How could he experience that with another woman? How could he betray what they had together?

If she lost Miguel, she would have nothing to live for. *Please God*, she prayed, her eyes closed against hot tears. *Punish me some other way. Not like this. It hurts too much.*

Outside the stadium, the usual gaiety, music, noise, and excitement seemed more charged with an undercurrent of violence than Sloane remembered. There was an irritability and tension in the air that led to scattered pushing-and-shoving matches. Perhaps because it was a night fight, people were more animated, more volatile, more intoxicated. Then again, her own mood might be all there was she thought she sensed around her. For the first time since Miguel had appeared in her life, being at a bullfight made her uncomfortable.

Posters of Miguel Vellis were plastered on every flat surface. They showed him wearing his lavender suit of lights executing a *valentia suerte*, the graceful movement that led the bull past him as he unfurled the cape over himself like a Japanese fan. She remembered seeing posters of bullfighters in childhood friends' bedrooms, in seedy bars and Mexican restaurants, never imagining that one day the real thing would come to life.

Beto led her into La Plaza Corrida. They passed through a special door some distance from the noisy hordes at the main entrance. Inside, four burly men were waiting for them. They were their chaperons, who would prevent anyone from approaching her and disturbing Miguel's concentration during the fight.

The entourage made its way through the dark tunnel under the stands for several hundred feet before they reached the floodlit arena. She was escorted to a front row adjacent to the special section of the stands reserved for VIPs.

The blazing floodlights forced her to squint as she looked out into the ring hoping to see Miguel. Dust and little bugs hung in the humid air and stuck in her hair. She knew he would be standing in the *patio de cuadrillas*, which was the name for the place where the matadors prepare themselves for entry into the ring. She knew he would be there, praying for courage. She waved away the gnats and scanned the corridor where the matadors entered the arena, wishing he would come out, feeling terribly alone even though she was surrounded by thousands of people.

When Beto passed her a flask of vodka, she accepted it gladly. She craved the fire in the fluid and the sweet numbness it would bring. She took a long swig, feeling the alcohol sear its way down into her belly.

The screaming in the arena was gathering force as the procession began to form in the dim corridor across the sandy ring. She could see several horsemen and could just make out three matadors in their twinkling suits of light. The one standing closest to the right wall turned to speak to another man. Was it Miguel?

For the second time in one day she found herself praying again. *Dear God, don't let anything happen to him.* It was one thing to have gone to a bullfight with friends as a lark, to sit and watch this spectacle dispassionately, as foreigners looking at some bizarre, even quaint, third-world pageant, feeling superior to the barbarity of it all. It was something quite different to love someone involved. Now she knew the real dangers. She had seen and touched the scars on his body. Was she about to watch this man she nearly worshiped die before her eyes?

'Beto, I'm scared,' she said in a small voice. 'I'm scared for him.'

Beto smiled at her and patted her hand. 'That's natural. But he lives for this. Out there' — he nodded toward the ring — 'is everything he wants as a man.'

Sloane could hear the near adulation in Beto's voice, but right now she wanted nothing more than to have Miguel walk away from this forever. *She* wanted to be everything he wanted as a man; why did he prefer injury

473

and pain and death? Why couldn't her love be everything to him? Why couldn't loving her be enough of a challenge? Why did he need this hideous and repeated tempting of fate?

As he walked toward her, his head held high, his right arm swinging freely, his stride loose and confident, she was blind to anything or anyone except him. The skintight suit of lights she had watched him so carefully arrange exposed the finely carved contours of his body. Mentally she undressed him, knowing every part of him, every inch of flesh.

She fixated on the sensuous mouth, now expressing a haughty, almost defiant half-smile. That mouth had enclosed her breasts, tasted her essences, whispered words of love to her. The hand, swinging freely at his side, had brought her to a place she had never been before, and those muscular thighs had quivered uncontrollably as she caressed him. She dared not look between his legs at what was pressing against the thin fabric of his pants.

The procession approached the stands only yards from where she sat. Each matador removed his *montera*, the peculiar traditional hat they wore to offer greetings to the mayor of Mexico City and *el presidente*, the official judge of the bullfight. The three then replaced their hats and strode toward the wooden inner ring that separated the stands from the sand floor of the arena. Miguel would be the first to fight. The rest of the matadors and their assistants would wait in the wings, entering only if they were needed.

Miguel walked to the protection of the wooden wall with great dignity. He assumed a casual stance as he withdrew into an intense private preparation for what was to come. His assistants spread out into the arena and awaited the bull's entry. When the gate opened, a magnificent brown bull thundered into the ring.

How Sloane loved him at that moment. But her love was not stronger than her fear. She had to look away.

Beto leaned close to her, his mouth nearly touching her ear. 'Don't do that,' he ordered. 'You must look out into the ring. If he sees you are afraid for him, it will be distracting.'

Sloane cringed inwardly. 'Beto, I *can't*.'

'You must,' he hissed. 'Close your eyes if you can't stand it, but he must think you are watching.'

She reached into her handbag and found her sunglasses. She slipped them on and faced back toward the ring, raising her chin to appear as though what was going on had her complete attention. Then she closed her eyes.

She sensed how well he was doing by the roar of the crowd. The sound rose in waves, then died away as the crowd seemed collectively to hold its breath.

When the crowd grew quiet, she chanced a look. The bull, its massive shoulder muscles glistening with blood from the wounds inflicted to infuriate the poor beast, continued to paw the ground. Long threads of mucus streamed from his flaring, snorting nostrils and gaping mouth. His horns gleamed, lethal and obscene. His bloodshot eyes glared at Miguel who was now standing perfectly still looking arrogantly over his shoulder at his potential killer.

In agony, Sloane watched him make the first two passes, then closed her eyes again, this time to quell the nausea welling up in her stomach.

Beto was sitting so close she knew he could feel her thigh shaking. He handed her a piece of bread. 'Put this between your teeth and breathe around it,' he said. '*You will not be sick*. Not here. Now now.'

She took the bread and held it in her trembling hands. 'I'll try, Beto,' she whimpered.

She watched Miguel from time to time as though underwater. Finally, it was time for the third and final act, the death of the bull. She took off her dark glasses and saw Miguel walking directly toward her. Only a few feet away he stopped and removed his *montera*. He raised it above his head as the great crowd grew silent. Looking straight at Sloane, he began to speak. She could not understand and turned to Beto, who frowned, and slowly shook his head.

He leaned close and whispered, 'He's dedicating the bull, this fight, to you.'

Miguel then turned and threw his hat over his shoulder directly at her. She caught it and clutched it to her breast.

'Put it on the railing,' Beto hissed. 'There, on the railing in front of you. He may call for you to return it.'

Embarrassed, Sloane did as she was told. The crowd cheered.

Miguel executed a half-bow and walked toward his *mozo de espada*, who stood holding a sword. She looked down at Miguel as he took up the sword and the small red cape used in the final act. Then he strode back into the centre of the ring for the final battle with death.

The thrill of his very public acknowledgement faded quickly. The arena swam before her eyes as he drew the bull into a series of close, short, and murderous charges. The hoarse screams of the crowd faded in her ears. She could no longer absorb the sight. A thunderous ovation tore her from her stupor as she saw Miguel standing over the dying bull. A sword hilt protruded from its withers. Another man approached the bull with the *descabello*, a short killing sword. With one thrust, he severed the spinal cord and put the bull out of its misery.

Miguel walked toward her again. Her legs felt rubbery with gratitude and relief. He bowed slightly and gestured for her to return his hat. She threw it down to him. He bowed again, put it on, and then strode toward the mayor and judge of the bullfight, bowing as he received thundering applause.

The plaza became a madhouse. A snowstorm of handkerchiefs waved in every part of the stands. He was awarded an ear but the handkerchiefs continued to wave. Then he was given another ear. He made his celebratory walk around the arena. Hats, cigars, *botas*, even women's undergarments rained down from the stands.

In a daze Sloane looked down to see Miguel standing in front of her again. He was offering her something. Not thinking, she reached down and took it from his hand. For a moment their eyes locked. As he turned and walked away, continuing to acknowledge the crowd's adulation, she looked down at her hands. Blood dripped between her fingers. Little mites were still crawling through the severed ear.

If she lived to be a thousand, she would never forget the look in his eyes. It had told her he had seen death, defied it, and wanted to share what he was capable of with her.

26

After the bullfight, Beto returned Sloane to the hotel suite. It was empty.

Seeing how agitated she was, he offered to stay with her. 'You want to go down to the bar for a drink?' he asked gently.

'No. Thank you, Beto,' she said, trying to keep her tone light. 'There's a fully stocked bar right here. Fix me a vodka and tonic, would you?' If Miguel did not return in an hour, she would need some moral support.

Beto walked to the wet bar and made them both stiff drinks. He passed one to her and raised his own. '*El matador número uno,*' he said. His two gold teeth winked at her.

She raised her glass but said nothing.

'Stop it,' he said. 'It won't help.'

'What?' she asked, looking up at him from the couch.

'Making yourself miserable. He'll be back, sooner or later.'

'You're trying to tell me – later, right?'

'I warned you, Sloane,' he said, easing into the chair next to her. 'This is part of the life.'

She looked down into her drink. 'Beto, if he goes with a woman, I'll go mad.'

'If he goes with a woman, you'll never know. Besides, after a fight they all go out and get drunk. They hang out, they talk to the press, sign autographs. Just because he isn't here doesn't mean he's being unfaithful to you.'

She shot him a look that told him she didn't believe him.

When it became apparent that Miguel would not be coming, Beto invited her out for a late dinner. She refused. She had had at least four drinks and wasn't hungry.

After Beto left she poured herself yet another vodka. She had been mixing it with tonic up until then, but now she drank it straight, with no ice, in order to blot out the obscene images that raced through her mind.

As she waited, she ran the gamut of emotions from rage to tears of pain to prayers of pleading to soul-stripping begging to be permitted to have him return and take her in his arms and convince her he had only been drinking with his friends. Thinking of him with another woman made her want to pull her hair out just to provide some distraction from the wild pain in her heart and mind.

The more she paced, the more she drank, the more she convinced herself that when – if – he ever returned, she was going to show him that there was no sexual act known to man or beast that she couldn't provide. She would seduce him, ravage him, torture and torment him sexually until he begged her the way she had begged him that night in the shallow water of the lagoon. If the only way to keep him from other women was to become a sexual machine capable of every excess, that's what she was determined to do.

She was just coming out of the shower when she heard his men arrive in the other room with the equipment, the sword boxes and capes, and his bloodied suit of lights. His dresser must have taken street clothes for him to change into.

The sight of the bloodied suit filled her with guilt. How could she be such a bitch? As Beto had warned her, he led his own life. He deserved a night 'with the boys.' She had to pull herself together and stop being jealous or she

479

would drive him away. No man wanted to come home to a screaming virago accusing him of being unfaithful.

She took her time in the bathroom, powdering and plucking, smoothing cream over every exposed inch of her body. She brushed her hair until it shone and applied fresh makeup.

She was just slipping into her grey silk robe when she heard the door. She tossed off the rest of the vodka in the glass on the edge of the sink and glided into the living room as though nothing had happened.

He had changed into a black silk shirt with full sleeves and beautifully cut Italian silk slacks with a thin alligator belt. He wore black patent leather loafers and a white linen Armani jacket.

She rushed to him and threw her arms around his neck. Without a word she began to kiss him, long, deep, lingering kisses that he fervently returned. She started pulling him toward the couch, her mouth still locked on his. He struggled a bit but not for long.

As soon as he sat down, she pushed him back against the pullows and, still kissing him, began to unzip his pants.

When he realized what she was doing, he began to moan. 'Yes, darling, yes,' he said, frantically trying to help her with the zipper. She pushed his hand away. She reached inside his pants and freed his huge erection.

She held him in both hands for a moment. Then she moved down his body and slipped him into her mouth. She could tell she was driving him crazy as he continued to moan her name and ran his hands through her hair and down her back.

She worked slowly, teasing him with her tongue, flicking and sucking the tip. She slipped him in a little farther each time until he was pressing against the back of her throat. Now she inhaled him, tightening her cheeks against him and then sliding up to flick the tip again.

He clawed at her robe, trying to pull it over her

shoulders, but she resisted and pulled it back. 'Let me love you,' he gasped. 'Now!'

'No,' she said, her words muffled, and she slipped her hand under him and fondled his testicles.

'My darling, please. Come to bed,' he pleaded, trying to pull out of her mouth.

'No,' she said, forcing him in again, against the back of her throat, sucking him hard.

He shoved his hips against her, one hand pressed hard against the back of her head, the other trying to rip off his shirt and pants.

He was just on the edge of orgasm when she lifted her head and smiled at him. 'Would you like a drink, darling?' she said sweetly, pleased at the expression of raw lust on his beautiful face.

'No,' he said hoarsely. 'I want only you. Now!'

'I don't think so. You had me terribly worried staying out so long. I thought something had happened to you.' She made a pretty pout and lowered her eyes.

She had to admit it amused her to see him looking so vulnerable, sitting there fully clothed with a throbbing erection sticking straight up out of his expensive silk trousers.

With a lunge he pulled himself up and stood over her as she knelt on the carpeting. She let her robe fall open, exposing her breasts. She cupped one of them in her hands and gazed up into his eyes, rubbing her thumb across the nipple. 'I think we should get some sleep now, don't you?'

With one violent motion he tore off his pants and then his shirt. When he was naked, he grabbed for her, but she rolled to one side and stood up. She ran into the bedroom and locked the door.

She stood with her back against the door, catching her breath.

'Move away from the door, Sloane,' he called from the other side.

'No,' she shouted back. 'Call up one of your whores if you need some place to sleep.'

'Move away from the door!' he repeated. Something in his voice made her move to one side just as the centre panel of the door splintered with a sickening crash. Foot-long pieces of wood flew about the room like toothpicks.

'My God!' she screamed. 'Are you out of your mind?'

'I do what I please,' he said, stepping through the shattered door.

She tried to make it to the bathroom, but he was too fast. He trapped her against the wall, grabbed her hair, and sharply yanked back her head.

Holding her by the hair, he pulled her toward the bed. He lay down on his back and pulled her like a rag doll until she was kneeling on the bed with her legs on either side of his head. Roughly he forced her hips down and locked his mouth between her legs. He put both great hands around her waist and moved her body in a circular motion against his tongue and teeth until she wanted to scream.

'You want it now, don't you?' he said, shoving three fingers into her. He pulled them out and shoved them in again.

'Yes!' she yelled. 'Take me. Now, Miguel!'

He flipped her over, jammed a pillow under her hips, and entered her from behind. Both hands were on her breasts, pinching, twisting her nipples as he plunged into her again and again. She was just on the edge of orgasm when he flipped her on her back, withdrew, and pinned both her arms to the bed with his knees.

Without warning he slapped her across the face. It was a sharp slap. 'I'll do it harder if you ever say no to me again,' he snarled.

'I'll say no as much as I want,' she taunted him.

He moved up until his erection was a few inches from her lips and slapped her again. This time it hurt.

She felt a hot urge of desire. 'I'm not saying no now,' she said, struggling to get free and force him into her. It took all her strength to roll him over and position herself astride him. She grabbed his erection and lowered herself onto it.

Slowly she began to rotate her body. She arched her back and stared down at him, moving her hips faster and faster. She was going wild, shivering, gyrating like someone possessed, unable to get enough of him.

'You won't say no again, will you?' he growled at her.

She couldn't speak. She was lost somewhere in her frenzy to reach orgasm.

As she began to come, he reached up and slapped her again, harder still than the last two times.

'Say you crave my cock. Say you'll do anything to get my cock inside you,' he demanded. He kept slapping her and shouting, 'Say you'll suck me whenever I say so. Say you love it!'

'I love it!' she screamed, her head thrown back, gasping the words as she drowned in wave after wave of pain and joy. 'I crave it! I'll do anything to get your cock inside me.'

He pulled her forward and bit her breasts, hard enough to draw blood, thrusting himself higher and higher until an overwhelming, shuddering convulsion racked her body.

She was still coming as he rolled over and got on top of her again. She knew he wasn't anywhere near stopping.

She must have blacked out from time to time during the night. Whenever she came to, he was either hard inside her again or had his mouth between her legs, biting, sucking, twisting his tongue and fingers inside her, demanding that she come again and again.

As daylight began to filter through the drapes, he finally withdrew. From all she knew he had not had an orgasm yet and was still fully erect. She reached across the twisted sheets and placed her hand on him. He was so large, two encircling fingers barely touched.

Sure that he was finally asleep, she moved one leg over the side of the bed. There was blood on the insides of her arms and on her stomach. She desperately wanted to get to the bathroom and see where it was coming from.

As she tried to stand, one great arm swept out and yanked her back into bed. He flattened her on her back and shoved his cock into her mouth. 'Now you can finish what you started,' he told her angrily. 'You said you loved it. Now finish it.'

She looked up at him. Sweat was pouring down his face and chest as he thrust himself into her throat. If she had been able to speak, she would have told him that she *did* love it.

When he finally came, it was with an animal roar that seemed to shake the bed beneath them.

She lay next to him so weak she could not move. He had subdued her as totally as he had subdued the bull.

How long would it be, she wondered, now that she knew he was capable of unlimited violence, before he left her bloodied and broken for others to dispose of?

She looked at the long, black lashes lying against his smooth bronze cheeks and knew she could not bear life without the violence of his love.

The long, golden days and indigo nights of Sloane's love affair flowed into each other, an endless ribbon of sensuality. She began to lose all sense of time.

They made their base in Miguel's villa in Acapulco, travelling out to various big cities and dusty little towns where he fought the bulls. Sometimes they flew. If there was no airport where they were going, they would travel out in a caravan of cars. Often, if Beto was not along, there was no one except Miguel who spoke English, which only served to heighten her feeling of isolation and dependence on him. Oddly, she rather liked giving herself over to being treated like one of the *mozo*'s altar objects, a precious thing to be lifted and carried and revered.

They lived as the central characters in a nonstop party. People came and went at the villa. Some stayed a day or two, left, and were replaced by others. At the centre of everything was Miguel; all action revolved around what he wanted to do. If he wanted to take the boat out, everyone went to the beach. If he wanted to race his car along the road past Las Brisas at one hundred miles an hour, they all piled into their cars. If he partied, they partied; if he was angry or tired, everyone skulked away to their bedrooms or nearby bars until word reached them that the Great One was in the mood for daiquiris and oysters at his favorite restaurant. The world revolved around his moods, his health, and his whims.

They never got to sleep before three or four in the morning. Miguel thought nothing of going out to dinner at midnight and then on to a disco to drink and dance, sometimes with as many as twenty-five or thirty people tagging along.

No one seemed to do any work, except the servants at the villa. Bills were presented in the clubs and restaurants, yet she never noticed how they got paid. The details of living were handled by others. She was an extension of Miguel and her only function was to please him. Most of the time, she did.

At the villa, one constant, besides the wide blue sky and the soft-scented nights, was Franco, the houseman who never seemed to be without a silver tray with a bottle of frozen vodka during the day and champagne at night. He poured drinks without asking at all times. When they traveled, it always seemed to be with alcohol, beer, wine, tequila, and brandy in portable bars, goatskins, or ice chests.

Sloane caught sleep when and where she could. Sometimes it was after Miguel left the king-sized bed in the morning to meet with his men, other times it was on one of the comfortable chaise longues around the pool.

Her skin was turning a honey brown. Her dark hair was streaked with strands of beige and gold. The vigor and frequency of her sex life and constant swimming tightened and toned her body to a better shape than years of exercise and dancing had achieved. Outwardly, she was the picture of a beautiful, contented woman in the prime of her youth.

Inside, something strange was happening.

She misplaced things, forgot them, or lost them altogether. Her emerald earrings, which she usually kept in a small leather pouch in her makeup case, disappeared. She had worn them to go dancing a few nights before because they matched her emerald satin pyjamas so perfectly. She couldn't remember dropping them or taking them off, but they were gone when she went to look for them again. A pair of custom-made sunglasses vanished, as did her camera. Any of the items could have been mislaid, considering the fog she was in most of the time. She chalked their loss up to being careless and forgot about them.

Her mind no longer worked the way it had. Although she knew as each day passed that time was running out, she refused to come to grips with what she would do when Warner returned from London and started trying to find her. It was as though she were having an out-of-body experience. The Sloane that was her physical self would plan on getting on a plane and flying back to Warner as though none of this had happened to her. The emotional Sloane would simply roll over on the chaise, take another sip of vodka, and continue to wait for Miguel to return to lead her up to the bedroom.

As disjointed as her thinking had become, she *was* aware that she was not reacting to things the way she had in the past. She had always been naturally observant and interested in her surroundings, alert to others' feelings and quick to sense when there was something she should do to make people more comfortable. At first she thought her disconnection from everything and everyone except Miguel was simply the euphoria of the affair, her constant need to melt into him, please him, touch him, make love and be loved. She was so besotted that she hardly noticed the little things – his short temper or the increasing violence of their lovemaking, even the little dark-blue marks that mysteriously appeared on the inside of her legs, on her throat, the backs of her arms. She would briefly notice the marks and shrug off their existence, figuring that between her tan and a little touch of darker makeup no one would notice. As for Miguel's quick changes of mood, she rationalized that someone had displeased him. His rage couldn't have anything to do with her. She lived to please him, to satisfy his every wish.

One afternoon Miguel suggested they pick up their bathing suits and go to a restaurant on the beach, where they could swim and get some sun. They had, as usual, been drinking all day. But Miguel was feeling attentive, which left Sloane's senses in an electrified state. He couldn't stop staring at her, touching her, making whispered, obscene references to the sex they had enjoyed the night before.

That afternoon they swam far out past the surf line and fondled each other under the water.

Exhausted and dizzy with desire, they returned to the thatched-roof restaurant on the sand. As he helped her into her chair, he momentarily reached over her shoulder and slipped one hand down her bra, the other down her bikini bottom and between her legs.

His playful assault lasted for only an instant. She laughed, knowing he had to be drunk or he wouldn't have done something like that in public. But she had matched him drink for drink, so she knew she must be drunk as well. If she hadn't been, she might have seen the

man in the window of the hotel just a few yards up the
beach taking pictures of them with a very long lens.

27

The day after Rose Motherwell returned to Sans Souci from London and what had proved to be a very successful trip for Warner and his new Japanese endeavor, she faced the usual stack of mail.

Her office in the Bel Air mansion was just down the hall from Warner's. Her habit was to open and sort the mail, then walk whatever he should see immediately into his office for them to discuss and dispense with.

This morning was different. She had received an envelope by overnight courier from her sister in Lantana, Florida, the contents of which she wanted to savor for just a bit longer before showing it to Warner.

Rose's sister, a retired New York City schoolteacher, worked in the billing department of the *National Enquirer*. One of the perks of her otherwise tedious occupation was an advance copy of the paper some considered a scandal sheet. The issue she had sent to Rose's attention would be out on the stands nationwide the next day.

Rose couldn't wait.

It had never been her nature to be upbeat. She supposed she was born with a somewhat cynical attitude toward life. Certainly the years of working and yearning for the embrace of a man who barely knew she was female had not lightened her soul. But after Rose had opened her sister's package, she actually laughed out loud.

489

For there, on the front page of the lurid tabloid, was a picture of Warner's totally unsuitable wife with most of her left breast exposed. She was wearing a red bikini top and seated at a table of an outdoor restaurant with what appeared to be a thatched roof. Her hair was tied back with a white scarf, and huge sunglasses covered half her face.

The reason so much of her left breast was showing was that a slick, dark-haired man was standing behind her plunging his hand down inside her bra.

As Rose studied the picture, to her great delight, she noticed that his other hand disappeared up to the wrist under the top of her bikini panties. The picture had been taken from an angle above the table and left no doubt as to what the hand under her bikini bottom was doing.

'Fingers at play in places far away,' she hummed happily, surprising herself by remembering a dirty ditty from her days at Holy Name Academy so many years before.

The picture would have been less pornographic if it had not been touched up so vividly that every hair and blemish were visible – including a dark blush of shadow just above Sloane's bikini pants.

The headline read: *Billion-Dollar Bromley Woman With Her Macho Matador.*

The story inside wasn't much more than a piece of fluff dreamed up by the editors to justify using the picture. But it was enough, more than enough to send a rush of excitement coursing through Rose's veins. She hadn't felt that way since Richard Burton leaned over to kiss Elizabeth Taylor on a yacht deck during the filming of *Cleopatra*. In this case, her excitement even surpassed that. It was nearly sexual in nature. This one photograph could accomplish what she could never have done on her own: the destruction of Warner's ridiculous marriage to Sloane Taylor.

It mattered not at all to Rose whether Sloane had found

this dark man at the spa she was supposed to be visiting or in some sleazy waterfront bar. She liked her facts presented with nuance. And a man didn't feel free to shove his hand down one's bra and panties unless permission had willingly been granted. Sloane Taylor was having an affair and lying to her husband! The knowledge made Rose want to dance down the hall and fling the photo under Warner's nose with a shout of joy for revenge realized.

Years of proper demeanor and the belief that she was a lady prevented any such behavior. She would include it among the morning's correspondence and display it for him as the first order of business. The sooner he knew the better he could move to cut Sloane off from the extraordinary life he had provided the ungrateful, deceitful — she hesitated in her thoughts, then plunged ahead — bitch! She permitted herself to think the word. She tried thinking of other words. *Whore* sprang to mind. *Gold digger?* She dismissed the phrase as too old-fashioned. How about . . . she giggled and pressed her fingers to her lips. How about . . . did she dare? Oh, what the hell, she felt so good she'd chance it . . . *cunt!*

She threw herself back in her high leather chair and laughed, a dry, crackling sound that must have carried down the hall because, immediately, her intercom buzzed.

'Rose? Was that you?' Warner's voice penetrated the silence of the office.

She cleared her throat and answered. 'Yes, sir, I'm just coming in with the mail.'

She stood and composed herself, throwing back her shoulders and smoothing her skirt. She would have to handle this with the greatest of decorum. She couldn't be sure what his reaction would be to this outrage, but she did not want him to think that she in any way enjoyed what would certainly be his greatest humiliation.

Warner was seated behind his desk as she entered the

room. She placed the mail tray in its usual spot on the front of his desk and took a seat in the chair to one side. The envelope from her sister lay in her lap.

Warner continued to study the report he was reading for a moment and then looked up at her and smiled. 'What's on the agenda, Rose?' he asked pleasantly. 'Nothing much, I hope. I want to get a ride in this afternoon.'

Rose took a deep, head-clearing breath of air and began, 'My sister sent me something I think you should take care of right away.'

'Your sister?' he said. 'The one in Florida?'

'Correct.' Rose nodded. 'You might remember, she works for the *National Enquirer*.'

'Ah, yes,' he said lightly, tenting his fingers. 'I always thought that was the perfect job for a retired lady. Keeps her on her toes, I'll bet.'

'Quite,' Rose said crisply. She lifted the Federal Express envelope and pulled out the paper. She unfolded it and placed it directly in front of Warner.

He studied it for a very long time before he spoke. 'Jesus H. Christ, Rose,' he said, his face forming what she would well remember for years as a look of murderous rage. In the past he had reserved it only for the few times he had been bested in a deal or had a company raided out from under him.

'Something must be done,' she said primly. 'I'll do anything I can to help.'

Warner folded the paper and threw it across the desk. 'Get me Layla Bronz in New York,' he said grimly. 'I don't know who this grease ball is, but his days are numbered, that's for sure.'

'And Mrs Bromley?' Rose dared to inquire. 'What about her? Shall I try to reach her at her spa?' She said the word 'spa' with an infinitesimal edge to it, as if a word could have an unpleasant odor.

'One thing at a time, Rose. I'll deal with that shortly.'

He stared down at the top of his desk for a long moment and then swiveled his chair so that the back was to her and she couldn't see his face. 'If you could let me have a few minutes alone, Rose, I'd appreciate it,' he said. His voice sounded very fragile, as though he was holding back tears.

Rose stood up and gathered the rest of the mail. 'Certainly, Warner,' she said. 'I'll go place that call.'

It took every bit of self-restraint Rose could muster not to whistle as she walked down the hall.

Warner sat alone in his office waiting for Rose to reach Layla in New York and tried to get himself under control.

It had happened. Had there been a day since he married Sloane that he truly believed it wouldn't?

The picture in the *Enquirer* confirmed the suspicions he had harboured since Sloane's departure for the little holiday he thought he had so cleverly arranged.

He reached across the desk for the tortoiseshell-framed picture of Sloane. Of the thousands taken of her, he loved this one the most. It captured what he felt was her real spirit. It was a candid shot taken by a photographer accompanying her to a job in New York shortly before they were married. She was striding down Fifth Avenue on a winter's day, her head thrown back, her thick, dark hair blown away from her exquisite face, save for one thick strand that fell across her forehead. She was wearing a long black mink. It was unbuttoned, held away from her body by the pace of her stride, exposing the outline of her remarkable figure in a simple black sweater and miniskirt. Her beautiful long legs were encased in knee-high boots. She was laughing at the camera lens, at the world because she was young and beautiful and carefree. She was also talented. What a fool he had been to stifle that in her, caging her up, deluding himself that the wealth and comforts he provided were enough.

He ran his thumb along the smooth surface of the frame. The most telling thing in the picture was the least noticeable. In the background, over her shoulder, three men had turned to stare as she passed. The expressions on their faces were of astonishment and awe.

That happened everywhere she went. People stopped what they were doing and stared.

Sloane had not come home.

Had she passed someone in Mexico who did more than pause? Had she met a man who could give her something he could not?

He replaced the picture and returned his gaze to the grotesquely colored photograph on the front page of the *Enquirer*.

Apparently she had. This man, this bullfighter, who was he? Why had Sloane betrayed him with this Miguel Vellis?

He loved Sloane too much to blame her. This man had to have done something to her, hypnotized her, tricked her in some insidious way. The more he studied the face of his tormentor, the more he focused his rage.

Rage had always served him well. Rage was more powerful than tears. Tears only fueled self-pity and made one weak and vulnerable. Hadn't he seen the targets of his rage crumble over the years? Wasn't his entire success in life based on his ability to remain cool and marshal his forces to win, or in this case, win back, what he wanted?

Tears were for the defeated, the defenceless. Tears were for those who had not properly protected their hearts.

Warner crumbled the obscene tabloid and threw it across the room, then sat staring into space.

By the time Layla came on the line he was in control of himself. The pain had turned to numbness. But his white-hot rage remained sharp and real.

494

'I'm so sorry, Warner. How dreadful for you,' were Layla's first words. 'This picture is obscene.'

'You've seen it?'

'Rose faxed me a Xerox copy just now. It's kind of fuzzy, but the message is certainly loud and clear,' Layla said.

Warner sighed. Dear Rose, always one jump ahead of him. 'Layla, what the hell do you think is going on?'

'Do you want me to say it?'

'No,' he said. 'Damn it, Layla, I don't know how to handle this. I'm not a violent man, but if I had a gun I'd . . .'

'No, you wouldn't. Let's think this through. Maybe this isn't what it looks like. Maybe she —'

'Don't patronize me, Layla,' Warner barked. 'I want to know who this bastard is and what he's doing with his greasy hands all over *my wife*. I want to know why she looks like she's enjoying it and I want to know now!'

'I'll help any way I can, Warner. What do you want?'

'I want information, Layla,' he said tightly. 'I want someone down there. I want this man checked out and I want Sloane back.'

'All right, Warner. Let me see who's available. It won't be easy on such short notice.'

Warner rifled through the stack of *Realto* magazines he kept on the table behind his desk. His eye fell on a cover strip announcing an interview with a heretofore inaccessible movie star. He pulled the magazine from the pile and studied it. 'What about this woman Melon Tuft? She seems to be able to get to people.'

'She's expensive, my dear.'

Warner slammed the magazine down on the desktop. 'Screw the expense! This is my life we're dealing with here. I want this *bullfighter*, or whatever he is, put out of business. Between us we know how that's done. Don't we, Layla?'

'Let me talk to Cole and Kayzie. They were down there

when this happened. Maybe they can give us a few leads so we don't have to start from ground zero.'

'You'll put Melon on it, right away?'

'Right away, Warner. I'll call her now and see if she's free for lunch tomorrow.'

'Fine,' he said. 'And Layla?'

'Yes, darling?'

'Did you know anything about this?' There was a long pause on the line. He could hear Layla exhaling smoke.

Layla cleared her throat and said, 'No, Warner. I didn't.'

Funny, Warner mused after he hung up. He had known Layla most of his life. He still couldn't tell if she was lying.

Life in Miguel's hazy, surreal world permitted Sloane to absorb the shock that Beto presented to her one blazing morning on the terrace.

She was sipping an orange blossom. The sweet, cool drink had become a breakfast staple. The juice and the triple sec covered the taste of the vodka. She looked up from the chaise as Beto's bulk blocked out the sun. He was holding what looked like a folded magazine printed on newsprint.

'Good morning,' he said with a smile that flashed his big gold teeth at her. 'I hope you're feeling mellow this morning, Sloane.'

She raised her arm to shade her face. 'Ummm, "mellow" is the word. Would you like an orange blossom, Beto?'

He shook his head. Only then did she see his expression. He was frowning, his lips thin and drawn down.

'Is there something wrong?' she asked, swinging her bare legs to the ground and sitting up.

Beto swung a lawn chair around from the table and sat down facing her. 'I think you'd better look at this,' he said, handing her the paper. 'You might be in some trouble.'

As he folded it open, she saw the big logo on the top of the front page and moaned. 'Oh, dear, Beto. You don't read that trash, do you?'

'Not usually,' he said. 'I was in a newsstand at El Presidente this morning getting cigarettes and this was staring out at me.'

Sloane took off her sunglasses to get a better look. 'My word,' she said lightly. 'That's me.'

'Umm, damn near *all* of you.'

'It's not a very good picture,' she said, giggling. 'And look at Miguel. He looks drunk.' She looked at it more closely. 'Good heavens, what's he doing with his hands?'

Beto continued to stare at her with a puzzled look on his face.

'Oh, Beto,' she said, laying it aside. 'This is kind of embarrassing, isn't it?'

Beto shook his head slowly from side to side. 'I don't get you at all, Sloane. That doesn't upset you?'

Sloane scratched her right temple and reached for her drink. 'Well . . . no . . . I mean, ah . . . yeah, sure. It's kind of a raunchy picture. Ah . . .'

'Sloane, are you all right?' Beto asked, staring into her eyes. 'How many of those things have you had this morning?' He gestured to the nearly empty glass in her hand.

'A couple, I guess,' she said airily. Actually, she thought it was more like four or five.

'Look,' he said, pushing his chair back. 'It's none of my business, that's for sure. But that rag is seen all over the U.S. Doesn't it bother you that your old man will see it? I hear he's a pretty heavy hitter in the States.'

Something clicked in the back of her head that, despite her groggy sun-and-vodka-drenched state, cleared her head. 'My *old man?* How do you know about him, Beto? I never told you anything about my life in the States.'

Beto lowered his eyes sheepishly and cleared his throat. 'Promise you won't say anything?'

'Beto?'

'Well, ah, Miguel's sent me to the spa at El Camino several times to check for messages for you. The people up there told me who your husband is. They were very impressed.'

Sloane flopped back against the cushion of the chaise. 'Damn it. That makes me angry.' She *was* angry, but in a dulled, annoyed way.

'Please don't tell him I discussed any of this, will you? He likes to keep his private life private and –'

'And so do I!' Sloane said, cutting him short.

'I'm sorry, Sloane,' he said.

She had to clear her head. It was all too confusing. After only two weeks of living in the euphoria of the moment, this sudden intrusion of her other life frightened her. She had to do something to clear her head so she could sort it out.

'Forget it,' she snapped. She got up and quickly walked to the edge of the pool and dove into the cool, clear water.

After a few bracing laps the layers of vodka fog began to peel away. She pulled herself out, wrapped a bath sheet around her body, and headed toward the house. Beto was still sitting on the lawn chair watching her. As she crossed the terrace, he waved the *National Enquirer* at her. 'Here, do you want this?' he called.

She paused for a moment, then walked toward him. 'I'll take it,' she said, holding out her hand. 'Only because I don't want anyone else to see it.'

Upstairs, she turned the water jets in the Jacuzzi as high as they would go and eased herself into the bubbling water. As the water spouts on all sides began to pummel her body, what was happening to her life began to come into focus.

That picture in the tabloid *was* trouble. And yet, in an odd way she welcomed the exposure. Now she would not have to face the Warner situation. It had been done for her by some sneaky paparazzo at the beach. Of course Warner would see it. There were people who wouldn't be able to wait to get it to him. He probably already had. Why then, she wondered, hadn't he tried to reach her at the spa by now? Beto said nothing about there being any messages.

As she lay back and let the powerful jets lift her body, she turned to see the bathroom door opening.

'So there you are,' Miguel said, smiling at her.

Sloane pulled up her knees and leaned on the side of the tub. 'Darling! You're back!'

'I'm back and I'm hot. It's sweltering in town.' He turned his back and began taking off his clothes.

'What are you doing?' she asked, laughing.

He tossed his shirt and trousers onto the back of the chair by the door. 'I'm joining you,' he said. As he spoke, he turned toward her, fully erect.

She held her arms wide as he stepped into the pulsating water. He sat facing her, his back against the side of the huge tub. He pulled her toward him, separated her legs, and eased her onto his lap. As he entered, she was seized by the fever she always felt when they began to make love, hot and cold simultaneously the way any addict must feel the first rush of excitement foretold the ecstasy to come.

Later, he carried her, dripping wet, to the satin-covered bed. Someone had pulled the heavy drapes against the high morning sun, and the room was cool and dark.

He lay flat on his back and pulled her toward him. As she took him into her mouth, she wondered why she even bothered to get upset about Warner's finding out about them. Why should she be upset about any twist of fate that would let her remain with Miguel?

Later she would ask him to call the spa. If anyone tried to reach her, they were to say she had checked out and left no forwarding address.

Miguel's head began to thrash about on the pillow. He grabbed a handful of her hair. 'Faster!' he demanded. 'Go ahead, bite it! Harder!'

Now, she thought feverishly as she felt him begin to throb inside her mouth, *now no one can make me leave. I have officially entered paradise.*

28

Melon sat at the desk in her apartment staring into the green glow of her word processor and smiled. It was eleven-fifty on a Sunday morning and Layla wanted her to drop everything and meet her for lunch on Monday. Even before she hung up the phone Melon knew this would be something very, very good. And she had her suspicions as to what it was all about, particularly after Layla said, enigmatically, that she wanted to discuss a 'very sensitive assignment.'

Melon would bet her new white fox chubby it had something to do with Sloane Taylor. Melon knew about Sloane and the bullfighter one hour and twenty minutes after Kayzie's plane touched down from the little holiday in Acapulco. It took that long for Kayzie and Cole to get to the *Realto* building, go directly into Layla's office, and shut the door. Randy was asked to sit at Kayzie's desk and answer the phone.

As soon as Randy took the empty iced-tea glass, his archaic but effective listening device, off the wall, he had phoned Melon with the news. Sloane had remained behind in Acapulco, crazy in love with some Mexican bullfighter. According to Randy, who employed romantic license in relaying any tale, the bullfighter had almost kidnapped her.

Randy heard Layla swearing Cole and Kayzie to secrecy, saying they should wait it out. Perhaps it would come to nothing and Sloane would be home safe and sound before anyone – meaning Warner – was the wiser.

Melon thought it interesting that the publisher was protecting the woman who had run off with the man she loved, and she wondered why Layla was doing it. No doubt she would find out at lunch.

For days Melon had pestered Kayzie to tell her what happened in Mexico. No amount of whining and wheedling and guilt-making I-thought-you-were-my-friend pouts would get Kayzie to say anything more direct than that Sloane had decided to stay on at a spa.

If a story about it was going to be done, Melon wanted to be the one to do it. She fairly drooled at the thought. The Model and the Matador! she thought as she stepped into the shower. Her pulse quickened at the thought of the commotion it would cause.

From across the dim expanse of the Four Seasons Grill Room, Melon could see Layla holding court at her regular table. She was wearing a white wool suit, a three-strand choker of black pearls, and a huge black mink beret that drooped dramatically down to one shoulder. Her black-pearl and diamond earrings glittered as she moved her head first to the man standing to the left of the table, then to the other standing to the right.

She stopped talking when she saw Melon approaching the table. The men scurried away obediently like kitchen roaches when the lights go on.

Melon was becoming accustomed to having people suddenly fall silent or flee when she appeared. She liked that. It meant they had secrets they wanted to keep.

'Melon!' Layla said, smiling up at her. 'You look absolutely smashing.'

Good sign. Melon thought. Women told her she looked smashing only when they wanted something. 'Hi,

Layla.' Melon grinned, sliding onto the banquette beside her. 'Umm, don't you smell good.'

'Why, thank you,' Layla said, crooking her finger at a passing waiter. 'What are you drinking? I'm having Perrier, but don't let that stop you.'

'Chablis,' Melon said to the waiter. He nodded and disappeared. She turned to Layla. 'So? How have you been?'

'Not too shiny,' Layla said crisply.

'You want to talk business before we eat?' Melon asked. 'They'll drum us out of the Ladies Who Lunch Society. We're supposed to gossip for at least a half-hour.'

'Can you be on a plane to Acapulco by tonight?' Layla asked.

Melon drew back in surprise. 'Wow! What's up?'

The waiter arrived with Melon's wine, covered Layla's loaded ashtray with another, whisked them away, and left a clean one. 'I'll tell you,' Layla said, pawing around in her bag, 'as soon as I can find my lighter.'

Melon took a sip of her wine and quickly cased the room for celebrities. Bill Blass sat opposite them at a banquette beside a skinny woman with legs that would shame a heron. Rupert Murdoch was at a table to the right with three other men probably buying Bolivia. Cleveland Amory sat at a table at the top of the stairs so he could hiss at any woman wearing a fur.

She didn't bother to look up at the balcony. That was Outer Mongolia. No one who was anyone ever sat up there. There were stories about nobodies who thought they were somebodies being dragged, kicking and screaming their resumes, up the balcony stairs by the maître d'.

Layla located her lighter. It had been in her lap all along. 'Sloane is in trouble,' she said without preamble as she put her cigarette in her mouth and a busboy's arm shot forward, beating her to lighting her cigarette.

'*Aha!* Melon thought, *I knew it. Play dumb*, she cautioned herself. Randy might have been shy of the facts. 'I take it she's in Acapulco,' she said calmly.

'We think so. Wherever she is, we know she's with a man.'

'We? Who's we?'

'Warner. He knows,' Layla said.

'Uh-oh. How come? What happened?'

'He got an advance copy of this,' she said, reaching into her bag and withdrawing a piece of paper.

It was a bad fax of an even worse Xerox copy, but Sloane's face – and figure – were unmistakable. With her was an extremely handsome Latin man with his hands all over her body. Melon studied the picture. 'Oh . . . my,' she breathed. 'Warner has seen this? He must be wild.'

'Beyond wild. I've never heard him so angry.'

'Layla! He's not going to divorce her, is he?'

Layla fixed her dark eyes on Melon and arched one eyebrow. 'Are you asking that as a reporter or as a concerned friend?'

Knowing full well what juicy information a possible Bromley divorce was, Melon weighed the possibilities of whatever Layla was about to propose and answered, 'A concerned friend.'

'Okay. Then the answer is no. He's not angry at Sloane. He's hurt. The one he's gunning for is this Vellis character. That's where you come in.'

Melon's eyes grew wide. 'Hot damn!' she said. 'You want a piece on him? A piece on the affair? What? I'm yours.' She threw up her hands in a gesture of complete submission.

Layla shook her head. The edge of her big mink beret swung ponderously against her cheek. 'I don't want you to write anything this time, Melon. I want you to do some investigative work. We . . . I will make it well worth your time.'

'In Acapulco,' Melon said.

504

'Correct,' Layla said, signaling for a waiter.

'What do you know about him?' Melon asked. 'I can't just go cold. It would take me weeks.'

The waiter materialized in front of them.

'I'm having the grilled salmon,' Layla said, then turned to Melon. 'That okay with you?'

Melon nodded. For once, she wasn't interested in food.

'Okay,' Layla said, relaxing a little. 'Most of my information comes from Kayzie and Cole. The rest I got from a call to a friend at the embassy and a pal who strings in Mexico City for the *Miami Herald*. Sloane is in this guy's villa. She travels with him when he fights. He's considered some kind of God down there and people are protective of him. He surrounds himself with layers of people and answers to no one. For all I know Sloane could be a prisoner. But to hear Kayzie tell it, she's completely besotted with the guy. Kayzie saw them together in a restaurant and tried to talk her out of staying. She said Sloane was positively glassy-eyed. She flatly refused to leave. There's something very dark about this whole thing. This guy clearly touched something in Sloane that relieved her of her senses.'

Their lunch arrived as Layla was filling in the next details of Melon's mission.

Melon sat very still, savoring what Layla was telling her. 'Damn!' she finally exclaimed. 'What a story!'

Layla had started to pick at her salmon. She deliberately placed her fork on the side of her plate and turned to Melon. 'No, Melon. You have to get this straight. This is *not* a story. This is an investigation. I know you are a good reporter, but this time out you are simply to get the facts and deliver them. No story. Not for the magazine. Not for anyone. Warner wants this thing wrapped up and Sloane home without a scandal. Do you understand?'

Melon couldn't believe her ears. 'Do you mean that?'

'Don't test me. Here,' Layla said, opening her handbag and sliding a white envelope across the table. 'Take this!'

505

'What is it?' Melon asked, eyeing the envelope.

Layla tapped it with her nail. 'In here is a round-trip ticket to Acapulco. You'll have to change planes in Mexico City, but that shouldn't be a problem. There's also two thousand in cash for out-of-pocket expenses and possible schmears. Mexican officials accept them as a way of life. You'll also find a platinum American Express card billable to the magazine and a ten-thousand-dollar cheque in your name. Deposit it before you go.'

Melon looked at the envelope and then back at Layla. 'What exactly do you want other than confirmation that he's having an affair with her?'

'Everything,' Layla said. 'We want to know where he came from, who he is, his financial situation, women, police record if he has one. Residences, entangling alliances, the works. But' – she paused, holding up one finger for emphasis – 'most important of all, we want to know how the hell he got his hands on Sloane and what he's doing with her and to her.'

Melon leaned back in her seat. 'Phew! How long do I have to do all that? I don't even speak Spanish.'

'As long as it takes. As soon as you get any information, get back to me no matter where I am. Don't worry about the language. We have embassy contacts who will help you.'

'What is Warner going to say to the press? This issue of the *Enquirer* is on the stands, isn't it?' Melon asked.

'Well, he's very clever. He issued a statement this morning through his PR firm saying the picture is misleading, that he and Sēnor Vellis are good friends, that Warner and Sloane were visiting him at his villa. Vellis was drinking and things got out of hand. That should virtually kill a follow-up.'

'Well . . .' Melon said, fascinated. 'Well . . . well . . . well. It looks like our Sloaney girl has gone looking for Mr Darkness once too often.'

'Will you do it, Melon?' Layla asked. 'I have to know right now.'

Melon hesitated, pressing her lips together. One of the many things Matty had taught her was to get a little extra on the 'if-come,' as he called it, when you do a favor for someone who has their back to the wall. 'Okay,' she said. 'I'll do it on one condition.'

'Don't tell me you want more money,' Layla said, exasperated.

'No, no. Ten grand is fine. What I want, Layla, is your promise that if what I find out is really delicious and no one has the story but me, you'll let me do a piece on the whole thing when I get back.'

Layla didn't look happy. She played with the ice in her Perrier. 'I've already said no, Melon. I won't hurt Sloane.'

'Excuse me?' Melon said, confused. 'A year ago you were ready to destroy Sloane Taylor with dirty pictures. Now you're protecting her like a mother hen. I don't understand why you don't want this for *Realto*. This story is the biggest Role-Model-Drops-the-Ball since *Penthouse* ran those pictures of Vanessa Williams muff-diving. Even better!'

Several heads turned toward them. 'Keep your voice down, Melon, please,' Layla said behind her hand.

Melon lowered the volume but didn't change her tone. 'Layla, this story reeks of sex, damn it. I mean, a *bullfighter*, for God's sake. Swords, horns, bulls, horses, blood, death, and love in the afternoon with the beautiful wife of a billionaire . . . Jesus! It's one long phallic festival. There would be fistfights at the newsstands to get copies of it. There can't be a woman in America not attached to a colostomy bag that doesn't want to fuck a bullfighter.'

'Don't be vulgar, Melon,' Layla said primly. 'You don't have to sell me on the story. I've been in this business since you were a virgin, and I'm telling you I will not hurt Sloane.'

'Then you can take your tickets back,' Melon said, tossing the envelope to Layla's side of the table. 'I'm not going to snoop for you unless I have some guarantee that I'll get a story out of it. I'm a journalist, not a spy.'

Layla threw her head back. 'Ha! You're both, Melon. And you're good. I need you so I'm going to take a chance and tell you something I've told no one except Cole. Maybe then you'll change your mind.'

Melon leaned closer. 'Yes?'

'There was a time when Warner was threatening to sell the magazine. I killed your story on Sloane because she said she would talk him out of it. The girl delivered. Those things I don't forget. *Realto* is my life.'

'I thought Warner was your life.'

'I thought so, too. For many years. I can't deny that when he married Sloane I didn't think I could survive without him. I discovered that losing him in no way compared to the possibility of losing my work, my dignity, my position in the working world. *That* is my life. I needed Warner's approval and applause to keep from failing, which all of us, even you, Melon, are secretly afraid of.'

Melon thought for a moment. She remembered her own obsession with Matty when he didn't want her and the neurotic lengths she had gone to in order to get his attention. She needed him to see her succeed. She succeeded without him and that's what brought him back.

'The irony here,' Layla continued, 'is that along with my pride and my power I still have Warner. Oh, I can't sleep with him anymore, but that was just an obsession. Obsessions are an excuse for not facing what you *really* need to be happy.'

A virtual carillon of little bells was going off in Melon's mind. So that's what happened to her story on Sloane! 'Boy,' she said, 'I sure was furious when you killed my story.'

'I'm sure you were, Melon,' Layla said softly. 'But how much did it matter? Look at you now.'

'And what about Sloane?' Melon asked. 'Why is she in this awful mess?'

'Because she was cursed with a beautiful face and body. She succeeded on other people's terms. Underneath all that is a little girl screaming at the world, "Look at me inside! Can't anyone see me in here, where I hurt?" '

'So she becomes obsessed with dangerous situations and men?'

'I think that's just the form her low self-esteem assumed. If she abused herself, if she felt enough pain, she at least had the control everyone denied her. She could cause something so shocking, so dreadful and threatening, the world would be forced to stop and examine the person behind the beautiful face. Those pictures of her? This bullfighter? I don't think any of this is about sex. It's about self.'

Melon picked at her salmon in silence and stared across the room. She knew what it must have taken for Layla to tell her this. A vain, proud woman's admission of her vulnerability could not come easily. Melon was flattered and to her surprise, touched that Layla would level with her. She reached over, retrieved the envelope, and dropped it into her bag. 'I'll call you from Acapulco. Where will you be?'

'Beside the phone.' Layla smiled. 'Thank you, Melon. I won't forget this.'

Melon stared back across the room. 'I don't think any of us will,' she said.

Melon arrived in Mexico City late Monday and spent all day Tuesday digging around. The contact at the embassy was useless, but Layla's friend from the *Miami Herald* was a gold mine. Not only was he cute, but he knew everything and everybody, including the chief of police in every town of any size in the country. Layla had been right about needing to backhand cash for information. By the time she left for Acapulco Tuesday night, half her bribe money was gone.

The next two days in Acapulco filled her little notebook completely. She was ready to make her first call to Layla. She knew what she had learned would blow the publisher's mind.

Kayzie informed her that Layla was taking her calls upstairs and put her through immediately.

'Hello? Melon?' Layla shouted into the phone. 'Where the hell are you?'

'Listen!' Melon shouted back. 'I only have a sec. I'm at the Acapulco Princess. I got a lot of stuff. This guy Vellis is some kinda sicko. He's been in trouble with the police, but all the files were trashed since the murder.'

Layla gasped. 'Murder! What murder?'

'No one we know,' Melon shot back. 'Don't interrupt. Anyway, whenever he gets in some kind of trouble, as soon as they realize who he is, they let him go.'

'What kind of trouble?'

'Bar brawls, drunk driving, car wrecks – minor sleaze for our purposes. His big scam is stalking beautiful, rich women. Americans preferably. He likes to smack them around. A year ago he smacked one a tad too hard and killed her. They say there may have been others, but he's such a big enchilada down here he gets it covered up. Even so, the women are crazy for him, follow him around, throw themselves in front of his car. Crazy shit like that. The word is he takes their money. If they don't give it to him, he gets it some other way.'

'Jesus!' Layla shouted. 'How did you get all this? Cole's friend at the embassy?'

'Yeah,' Melon said sarcastically. 'Thanks a bunch for that one. That guy was a big waste of time. He's a burned-out bureaucrat with absolutely no contact with the Euro-weenies and jet trash who hang around bullfighters. Those were the people I needed. I finally just got on a plane and came down here. This town is small enough and people are bored. All I had to do was find where Sloane and Vellis hang out and plant myself at the bar.'

'I hope you've got this right, Melon,' Layla said in a low, menacing voice. 'We don't want bartender and beach-boy gossip.'

'You know me better than that, Layla,' Melon said sharply. 'Cut me some slack.'

'Sorry. It's just that we've got to have everything absolutely airtight. Who are your sources?'

'Source,' Melon corrected her. 'This one was a jewel. She's a regular at the place that's kind of his headquarters when he's in town. A watering hole up in the hills where rich Americans and Europeans hang out. Sloane and Vellis are in there with their entourage almost every night when he's not slaughtering cows.'

'Bulls,' Layla corrected.

'Whatever. Look, do you want to hear this or not?'

'Of course I want to hear it. Just tell me how reliable your source is.'

'Okay,' Melon continued. 'She's an American, quite beautiful, and likes to be slapped around herself, according to the bartender who tipped me that she knew a lot about Vellis. I got chummy with her right away. When I started asking about the bullfighter, she gets hysterical. Seems they had a hot affair a couple of months ago. Like all the other women, she went berserk for him. She says he's the best lover she ever had. Keep in mind, this lady was into pain. So you figure out what kind of lover he really is. Anyway, she liked it so much she let him take her for over half a million bucks, a Ferrari, and VCRs for every relative from here to Tampico. And you know what?'

'What?' Layla asked.

'She's still hot for the guy. She follows him, phones him

511

in the middle of the night. She even sees him occasionally during the day, I guess when Sloane is sleeping. She says she'll give me the names of at least five other women he's taken. That's where I'm heading right now. She's bringing this other woman with her. I told her I'd meet her at the bar at five. So, I gotta run.'

'Wait! Melon, don't hang up. Did you see Sloane? How is she?'

'Yeah, I saw her. Last night at the restaurant.'

'Did she see you?'

'Layla, she couldn't have seen Too Tall Jones. She was sitting at a back table with the bullfighter and a gang of creatures right out of the bar scene in *Star Wars*. When they all left, they were holding her up. She was smashed out of her mind. And get this — they left in the Ferrari this lady I'm sitting in the bar with bought him. Yuck. Yuck. Yuck.'

'Oh, Lord,' Layla sighed. 'How am I going to break this to Warner.'

'Don't do it yet. Let me get the rest of the story. Then I'm getting the hell out of here. There's a real kinky atmosphere in this town. It's hot, it's decadent, everybody is stoned on something, doing weird things to themselves and their friends just so they can locate their numb nerve endings. I'm going to drive up to his villa and see what the situation is there. Then you and Warner can figure out how to get her out of here. But I can tell you one thing. You better do it fast.'

'Why?' Layla asked, alarmed.

'Because my barfly friend is stone jealous. Last night she looked straight across the room at Sloane and said, "If the bullfighter doesn't kill her soon, I'll do it myself." '

Kayzie stayed late at the office. She didn't want to leave until Layla came back downstairs.

At half past five she heard the little elevator door hum

512

open and looked up to see Layla emerge in a voluminous silk kimono. Her face was ashen and her hands trembled as she closed the elevator door.

'See if you can get me Warner, would you please,' she said. 'I need to talk to him right away.'

'Hey,' Kayzie said, studying Layla's face. 'Are you okay?'

'Yeah, yeah, I guess. That call from Melon was a real shocker.'

'Has she found Sloane?' Kayzie asked, deeply worried.

Layla nodded. 'Yes. She's found Sloane, but she hasn't talked to her. She checked out the bullfighter. Whew! Is he bad news.'

Kayzie followed Layla into her office and sat on the edge of the couch. 'Oh, Layla. You've got to tell me. I'm having nightmares about all this.'

Layla sat behind her desk. She pinched the bridge of her nose with two fingers as though to ward off a raging headache. 'He's into rough sex. He lives off women, beats them up. He may have killed one. All the police files have disappeared. There's no doubt that he's beating Sloane. Melon says I should wait to tell Warner but I can't do that. He's half out of his mind from waiting as it is.'

'Oh, my God,' Kayzie said. 'Here comes another attack of the guilts.'

'We've all got the guilts, Kayzie,' Layla said, lighting a cigarette, signaling that she was ready to get on the phone.

'We should have done something. Told Warner. Sent Cole back down there to get her. I don't know. We should have called the marines, damn it.'

'Nothing would have changed it. This was something Sloane had to live through.'

Kayzie nodded slowly and turned to leave. 'I'll place that call for you, right now.' She closed Layla's door and walked to her desk. Suddenly she felt tired and old, the way she always felt when she saw something very lovely broken or destroyed.

She placed the call to California, gathered up her bag and coat, and turned off the desk light. As she walked down the hall, she could hear Layla's muffled voice talking to Warner, giving him Melon's terrible bulletin from the heart of darkness Sloane had so recklessly chosen.

Poor man, she thought, poor rich, important, powerful man. She remembered the wedding, the candles, music, the way the light caught in Sloane's gown and jewels as she shimmered down the aisle. She had seemed luminous from within then, as if some special light shone out of her.

It occurred to Kayzie, as she stepped out into the dark street and hurried toward the West Side, that the only person she knew who did not connect with Sloane's special inner light was Sloane herself.

Kayzie would never forget the look in her friend's eyes as Cole had lifted her hand from the curve of his elbow and gently passed her to Warner. It was the look of gratitude and relief you see in the eyes of a small animal rescued from a trap. Warner had done the best he could, she supposed. But all he had really done was put her in a larger, more beautifully furnished trap than she'd been in before, right along with her demons.

Cole had been so sad after the wedding. He must have had similar feelings. Now she understood his remark when they got back to the Neithergoulds' villa the night she had seen Sloane with the bullfighter. When she told him about the conversation in the ladies' room after they'd left and explained that Sloane wasn't coming home, she expected him to be furious. Instead he simply sighed and said, 'She can't help it.'

She pushed through the door at Sardi's. As she handed her coat to the checkroom lady, she could see Ryan sitting at the bar. His great blond head was thrown back as he laughed at one of the bartender's silly jokes.

For the last few months she had steadfastly refused his constant pleas for her to move into his apartment. As much as she loved him, she would not do it. They had reached an impasse and the arguments were beginning. Finally, afraid of losing him, she had decided the night before that she would move in. Tonight was a summit meeting of sorts, after a week of self-imposed separation. She was going to tell him she had decided to do it.

She tiptoed up behind him and encircled his waist. She didn't move for a moment, resting her head against his tweed-covered back, feeling his warmth, smelling his cinnamon smell, knowing that no matter how heavy her compromise weighed on her heart, she couldn't bear life without him.

He turned and cupped her face in both hands and kissed her. 'Hello, sweetness,' he said against her mouth. 'Yum, you taste like cold raspberries.'

They were now a fixture at the bar. The bartender wordlessly placed her usual Jack Daniel's mist on a napkin before her. He had become sort of a friendly witness of their love affair and could see in Kayzie's solemn expression that tonight's was a serious meeting. He stepped away and left them alone on their favorite corner stools.

Ryan put his big hand over Kayzie's cold one. 'Have you decided?' he asked softly.

She nodded.

'You don't look happy.'

She took a deep breath. 'I'm happy,' she said. She knew she didn't sound it. 'Do you want to know what I decided?'

Ryan squeezed her hand. 'No.'

Kayzie threw her shoulders back and stared at him. 'No? You don't want to know?'

'No. Because it won't make any difference now.'

'Ryan . . .' She frowned at him. 'What do you mean?'

'Because *I've* decided.'

Oh God, she thought, *here it comes. He wants to be the one to do the breaking up. He's so sure I'm going to tell him I won't move in with him, he's going to save his pride. Okay, damn it. Let him have his pride.* 'And what have you decided, Mr McKenna?' she said grandly, hoping it would lighten the mood and slow the progress of the crack that had started in her heart.

'I've decided that I'm a fool. That I love you with all my heart, and if we live together, we should be married. But I can't do it if you don't agree. So,' he said, straightening himself on the stool so he faced her directly. He took both her hands and placed them on his knees. 'Will you marry me, Kayzie Markham? Please. Please. Please. Please. Please. I'll kill myself if you don't. I'll go out in the garden and eat worms. I'll wait until it snows and take off my clothes and lie down and die. I'll think bad thoughts about Mother Teresa and pussycats and the Democratic Party, and God will strike me down.'

Kayzie started to laugh. 'Oh, shut up, you nut,' she said, putting her hand over his mouth. 'Order another drink. I have to think for a minute.'

She didn't have to think for a second.

This . . . was what she wanted. This was her dream.

The bartender, his smile broader than usual, handed Ryan a fresh drink.

'Done thinking?' Ryan asked, turning to face her.

'Yes,' she said.

'Good. What's your answer?'

'That's it.'

'It?' he said, puzzled.

'That's my answer. Yes.'

He stood up and threw his arms around her. With one lift she was off the floor, spinning around. 'Oh, Kayzie, I love you. I really, really do love you,' he said, unashamedly letting her see the tears in his eyes. He lowered her back to the floor and rocked her back and forth in his arms.

516

29

Sloane awoke alone in the bedroom of Miguel's villa very late in the afternoon. Her head throbbed and her mouth tasted terrible. She lay very still with her eyes closed, trying to gather her senses. Lying on her back she could tell she was losing weight by her jutting rib cage and hip bones. When she tried to remember the last time she had eaten a full meal, her mind went blank, like a television screen that had lost its signal. That had been happening more and more lately, the blank white screen, the loss of memory. More and more she was seeing the world through a haze of disconnected happenings.

Every day when she awoke she lay like this, still and quiet, gathering the strength for her inevitable next move.

When she could stand the suspense no longer, she tentatively swept her hand across the other side of the bed to see if Miguel was there.

When he wasn't there, she died another tiny death.

It always began when they were partying. He had to be on the go all the time, rushing off to the best restaurant or bar in whichever town they found themselves. The drinking and dancing and general rowdiness lasted all night. Often she would lose sight of him in the crowd and not even know if he had left or not. Sometimes he would reappear and push away the men who had gathered around her to keep her entertained.

The nightmare for her was when he didn't return.

Someone always saw that she was taken care of. He

would reappear at the villa or hotel the next morning, shower, and slip into bed next to her without a word. He acted as though it was perfectly natural for him to stay out all night and not explain.

Even though these disappearances tore her apart, she could not bring herself to ask where he had gone or to complain.

Her need for him transcended her pain. If she did not please him, he would be angry with her. If he was angry with her, he would stop loving her. If he stopped loving her, life was over.

One night she had been alone and frantic in a hotel in a city she had never been to before or since because he hadn't returned. She had no one to turn to for help, no one to talk to. In desperation she decided to call Kayzie in New York. He wouldn't like it when the long-distance charges showed up on the hotel bill. She would chance his rage. She had to talk to someone.

She had mixed another drink and sat down on the edge of the bed. She didn't care if she woke Kayzie up; she would understand her despair. As she reached for the phone, it rang. Startled, hoping it was Miguel – although he had never called before – she snatched up the phone.

'Hello,' she said tentatively.

'Sloane Bromley?' asked a woman's rough, slurred voice. 'You better get away from that man fast. He's bad. Real bad. He ruined my life and he's going to ruin yours.'

Sloane was terrified. 'Who is this?' she managed to ask. 'How dare you call here!'

'I'm nobody. He made me a nobody. He'll do the same to you. You better get out. *Now*.' The line went dead.

Sloane slammed down the phone, shaking. Instantly she picked it up again and called the desk.

A sleepy clerk answered, '*Si . . .*'

'This is . . .' she began. Who was she? 'This is Señora Vellis in suite . . . ah . . .' She paused. Where was she?

'Suite *cinco uno. Sí, señora.* How can I help you?' he said in very clear English.

'That call you put through a minute ago . . Please, don't put through any more calls. We do not wish to be disturbed. Do you understand?'

'*Sí, señora. Por favor*, I did not put a call through tonight.'

'But I just took a call,' she insisted angrily. 'A very unpleasant call. Just now.'

'I'm sorry, señora. If you received a call, it did not come through the desk. Señor Vellis left orders not to ring the suite.'

'Then how could it happen?'

'The only way you could have received a call would be from someone in the hotel dialling you directly.'

Sloane sat thinking about what he had said. Suddenly she was very frightened. 'Thank you. Sorry to bother you.'

'*De nada, señora.*'

She would not call Kayzie. If she heard the sound of a friendly voice, she would become hysterical. What if he came back to find her in a state? He would be angry with her. More than anything she didn't want him to be angry with her.

There were to be more calls in other hotels and often at the villa in the middle of the night. Sloane never again answered the phone.

Now she finally dared to move her hand slowly across the sheet.

She was alone.

She sat up and listened. Muted voices were coming from the pool terrace below the window. She walked to the window and hid behind the gauzy drapes. She saw Miguel, dressed in white, sitting in a circle of men. They were drinking and talking around the edge of the pool. His hand and lower left arm were bandaged, and she knew his chest was encased in gauze and adhesive tape as well.

Faint with relief, she went back to bed. Perhaps with another hour's sleep her head would clear.

The afternoon before, Miguel had fought six bulls in a row. The bull in the third fight had tossed him into the air, bruised him in the ribs, and sliced his back, arm, and hand. As he lay in the bloody dust, his men had run into the ring, frantically waving their capes to distract the bull.

Miguel, covered with blood, had fought on. For the next fight he changed into a new, clean suit of lights. The crowd went absolutely mad, cheering, screaming his name in a rising chant that vibrated the stadium seats. Sloane stared, glassy-eyed, out into the ring, nibbling on the crust of bread Beto had handed her when Miguel was lifted off the ground. She washed it down with warm vodka from a goatskin.

If he had been injured earlier in their love affair, Sloane would have been too stunned and sick to remain in the stands. Her responses now were muted by her out-of-body state of mind.

It had been a wild celebration before, during, and after the fights. On the way back to Acapulco, their group alone took up every seat on the flight.

A mariachi band was waiting on the tarmac when the plane taxied to a halt at the Acapulco airport. She remembered everyone's leaving the plane with drinks in their hands, singing, laughing, stumbling about in a frenzied euphoria that had something to do with Miguel's spectacular feat that afternoon and the condition of a new group of people who had joined them somewhere en route. They were rich Americans from Texas who kept disappearing into the bathroom on the plane and returning to the nonstop party in the aisle even louder and more boisterous than before.

Sloane stayed in her seat next to Miguel. His rib cage and hand were bandaged. He groggily washed down painkillers with champagne, making light of his wounds and planning where they would go to continue the party.

They moved in a caravan of cars to his favorite haunt and then on to yet another new club for dancing until the sun came up.

It was all too much. She was beginning to run out of the energy it took to keep up with him. Somehow she had to find a way to get more sleep.

She sat up and reached for her robe at the foot of the bed. In retrieving it she noticed her nails.

She couldn't believe what she saw. The polish was chipped, the tips broken and torn. Little spikes of hard skin jutted from the cuticles. There was *dirt* under the broken tips.

She sat up, revolted. Never in her life had she let her nails get like this. One thing Noreen had always harped on, among the many, was that one could tell how a woman felt about herself by her grooming. First and foremost were her nails.

How could she not have noticed? She couldn't bear it another minute. She rushed to the bathroom feeling as though the only thing that mattered in the world was getting a nail clipper. After she got rid of the horrid hangnails, she would get her manicure things and set to work repairing the damage.

She began slamming around the bathroom, frantic to find some clippers. There were none in the mirrored cabinet over the sink. None on the shelves. Nothing in her makeup case or the drawers of the long bench beside the Jacuzzi.

If she had to, she would call one of the maids and somehow pantomime her problem. Even if she knew more than a smattering of Spanish words by now, the word for 'nail clipper' surely wasn't among them. When she thought about it, her Spanish vocabulary consisted mainly of the words of lovemaking.

She started back to the bedroom, agitated, biting and tearing at a particularly nasty hangnail on her thumb until it bled.

As she headed out of the bathroom, she saw Miguel's little briefcase sitting on the floor in front of the closet. There was a chance he might have some sort of a grooming kit in the case; after all, it travelled with him all the time.

The double-flanged catches popped open at her first touch. She was a little surprised that he didn't keep it locked, but then, she had never given him any reason to think she would ever touch his things.

She tilted back the lid and peered into the case. There were several documents in Spanish that looked like fight contracts of some kind. She lifted the packet of papers and found a Ziploc plastic bag half-filled with white powder. Curious, she opened it, put a touch on a wet finger, and tasted it. It was bitter and gritty and made her teeth and gums numb. Cocaine! She had been in enough discos in New York and Acapulco to know. She had even tried it once and hated the way it made her feel. Was this the reason he could stay up all night, making love for hours, and still fight six bulls in an afternoon? She wished she hadn't found it and was about to drop it back into the case when she froze. There, glittering up at her, were her emerald earrings! Next to them, carelessly wrapped in a tissue, was a diamond bar pin she hadn't even missed, and – she felt sick – her little Victorian snake ring with the diamond eye. Next to that, to her horror, her passport. Why would he steal her passport? To keep her from leaving the country? She gathered up her things and sat down on the floor, her head swimming, her stomach reeling.

It all came whirling back, pushing through the blank screen and white sound that her mind had become. She remembered the five one-hundred-dollar bills and the 'tip' lying on the table that first night. Her camera? *Please, God, not a crummy camera that can be bought at any tourist shop in town. Please don't let him be that low.*

A white-hot rage of betrayal swept over her.

She ran down the stairs, her robe flying behind her, bare feet slapping on the cold tile floor.

Blind with fury, she raced through the house and out onto the terrace. The men turned to look at her. She ran directly to Miguel, screaming so loudly her throat ached. *'You bastard! You lousy son-of-a-bitch dirty thieving bastard!'*

Miguel jumped to his feet. The expression on his face was one of confused amusement. He reached out and tried to grab her arms as she pummeled his bandaged chest with her fists, screaming, her hair falling over her eyes. She wanted to kick him but sensed, rather than knew, she wasn't wearing shoes. She was dimly aware of the men laughing nervously and shouting things in Spanish as though to encourage Miguel, egging him on as she flailed at him. She was amazed at her own strength as she wrenched free of Miguel's grip long enough to land a few more blows. She reached for his eyes with her nails and managed to gouge a long red streak into the skin of his cheek.

He smiled at her. Many times he had told her he liked women who were emotional. An occasional outburst excited him. He liked the challenge of subduing a woman who showed a little fire. She had tried to tease him occasionally, pretending to be angry or annoyed just to see him get aroused. Later, when they made up, he would be that much more passionate. They both knew they were playing. It was one thing to have a battle of wills in the privacy of their bedroom, but even as she was attacking him, it dawned on her that for her to behave like this in front of others was a serious breach.

Suddenly, from nowhere, something exploded in her face. The pain stunned her for a moment so she could not see. She lurched backward. She tasted salty blood flooding her mouth and knew he had struck her full in the face with his closed fist.

She seemed to be flying through the air. One of the men

caught her roughly, like a rag doll, before she hit the ground, and held her tightly. She pushed back her hair to see Miguel advancing toward her. The look in his eyes was one of sheer madness.

'Bitch!' he shouted. 'What is the matter with you?'

She tried to free her arms from the man holding them to her sides, but he was too strong. 'You know!' she screamed. 'You know! You stole from me. You stole my money and my jewellery. You lying, filthy —' Before she could search her seared mind for a word that would totally outrage his manhood, he pulled back and slapped her. The force twisted her upper body sideways. Her gown fell open. She was naked underneath.

'Get over there!' he commanded, pushing her roughly toward the chaise.

The men began to back away from the scene as she fell onto the chaise clutching her robe.

Miguel was advancing toward her pulling the belt out of the loops of his pants. He unzipped them and kicked them to one side. He stood, naked and erect, and smiled down at her. He raised the belt and with great force slapped her across her breasts. 'You like that, don't you?' he growled.

She fought back the tears and turned her head to one side so she wouldn't see the expression on his face.

He stood close to her head. His erection was bobbing, red and obscene as he yanked her head back by the hair. 'Call me a thief again, bitch,' he dared her. 'Call me some more names!' With his free hand he grabbed one breast and sunk his fingers in it, twisting and tearing at the flesh.

As he threw one leg over the chaise and straddled her, she realized what he was going to do. 'Miguel . . . please,' she whimpered, 'the *men*.'

'Oh, you want them to come back and watch? Is that it?' he snarled into her face. 'Shall I call them back?'

Over her shoulders she could see the last of the men moving quickly into the house, away from her screaming.

524

When she came to, there was no one around. The only sound was the wind in the thick tropical foliage around the pool. Somewhere far down the hill a radio was playing an old Frank Sinatra song.

She felt someone touch her shoulder and she cringed in fear. 'Don't please . . .' she sobbed.

'Sloane,' she heard a familiar voice say. '*Nombre de Dios!* What happened here? You're covered with blood.'

Painfully, she lifted her head. Beto was kneeling on the ground next to the chaise.

She was too numb to move. She felt him putting some kind of cloth over her – a towel, her robe – she couldn't tell. Gently, he lifted her in his arms and walked toward the darkened house.

'Where is he?' she whispered against his shoulder. 'Don't let him . . .'

'Shh . . . shh . . . shhh,' Beto hushed her, his lips against the top of her head. 'Everyone's gone. Don't worry.'

'My God, I must have blacked out.'

'Only for a moment,' he said. 'Let's get you cleaned up, fast. We've got to get out of here.'

He lay her on Miguel's bed and brought warm water in a basin with a washcloth, some cotton, and a brown bottle of something from the bathroom. Softly, deftly, as though she were a child, he made feathery strokes across every inch of her ravaged body. Whimpering in pain like a wounded animal, she submitted to his touch, caring nothing about her nakedness.

When he got to her breasts, he whispered. 'Do you mind? These marks are pretty bad. They have to be cleaned or they will get infected.'

She looked down for the first time and couldn't believe what she saw. 'What are they?' she asked.

'Bite marks, Sloane,' he said softly.

There were tears in his big black eyes.

He continued to clean away the blood, moving

525

quickly. 'All right now. Put something on. We've got to hurry.'

'Where are we going, Beto?' she asked. 'I'm so frightened.'

'I'll take you to my sister's house. Then we can decide.'

She tried to roll to one side but it was too painful. 'I can't go back to L.A. Not like this.'

'Where do you want to go? Where do you have friends who can care for you? You should see a doctor.'

She thought for a moment. She first thought of Alan or Kayzie, but she couldn't. She was too ashamed. She felt the same about Cole. She couldn't do that to him, either. She needed to be someplace where she could hide until she healed both her body and her mind. She had to be with someone who would understand. 'I have a friend who lives in New York,' she said finally. 'She has a big brownstone. I can stay there.'

Beto pushed himself up off his knees and dropped the bloody washcloth and cotton into the basin. 'Good. There's a flight to Mexico City first thing in the morning that connects to a New York flight. You can stay at my sister's until it's time to go. She'll make you a nice hot meal. You're skin and bones.' Beto went to call Layla with the number Sloane gave her. Sloane painfully made her way to the closet and grabbed her bag from the floor. A grey linen suit, freshly pressed, hung above it. She threw it and a few more things into the bag and pulled on a pair of slacks and a T-shirt. 'Oh, Beto,' she said. 'Don't take me anywhere where people will see me like this.'

'You don't have to worry about my sister. She used to cook here. She knows what goes on in this house.'

Sloane reached up and placed her hand on his massive arm. 'Beto, I'm so scared,' she said. 'What if he comes back? What will we do?'

Beto picked up the basin and looked down at her, his wide, dark face grim, his eyes flat. 'I will kill him,' he said calmly.

The little white Chrysler convertible with an Avis sticker on the windshield was pulled as far to the side of the road in front of the villa as it could park without falling into the ditch. Anyone sitting behind the wheel had a clear view through the low plantings that surrounded the terrace and pool of Miguel Vellis's sprawling house.

It had taken some manœuvring to get the car in a position where one could not only see, but not be seen. Melon was a good driver and accomplished the parking job just in time to see Sloane run screaming across the terrace and pound away at the matador's chest. In stunned disbelief she watched something she hoped never again to witness: someone she knew being savagely beaten and brutally raped.

When she had started up into the hills in the rented car, she had been feeling sassy, on top of her game. The hour spent at the bar with her original source had been fruitful. Yesterday after Melon's call to Layla, her source had arrived at the bar again as promised with yet another American woman whom Vellis had abused. Melon had come out of the villa today with the intention of confronting Vellis with what she knew in front of Sloane. She hoped that then Sloane would realize what he was and let Melon get her out of there.

But what she had instead ended up seeing made her sick. In disgust, she turned the car around and headed back to the hotel. There were few places Melon was afraid to go, but she'd be damned if she'd walk into that situation. There had to be another way.

Her mind raced as she tried to hold the little car to the winding mountain road in the growing twilight. She cursed Layla for making her promise not to write a short story on Sloane and the bullfighter. She cursed herself for not having the guts to do it anyway.

Her fury and frustration grew as she roared toward the

527

hotel. She pulled up into the driveway and slammed on the brakes so hard her neck snapped back against the rest. 'That bastard!' she snarled, pounding the steering wheel. 'That goddamn bastard.'

Melon tossed her keys to the doorman and rushed up to her room. There, she immediately put a call through to Layla. As soon as they were connected, Melon started talking.

'Layla? It's Melon. Don't talk, listen,' she demanded. She proceeded to tell Layla everything she had seen at the villa. Just as she started to describe the rape itself, Layla finally managed to interrupt.

'Melon! Melon, I know. Some friend of Sloane's just called me here, and I've been trying to call you. He's putting Sloane on the next flight out to New York tomorrow morning.'

Melon paused to catch her breath, then let it out in a whoosh. 'Layla, are you sure you won't change your mind about my doing a story? This changes everything. If Warner really wants to destroy the man, I've got the goods.'

'I'm in shock right now. I don't know what to do,' Layla said. 'Let me see what kind of shape Sloane is in when she arrives. She doesn't know how much I know about all this. After I see her, I'll talk to Warner.'

'All right, but I want to get this story done just in case you give me the go-ahead.'

'That's a good idea. Get it written up, and check all your sources. Somebody has to back your story up. In fact, why don't you call this guy Beto? He left his number with me so that I could call him about Sloane, and he sounded like he'd be more than happy to spill the beans on Vellis.'

Melon took the number from Layla and said, 'Okay, I'll get right on it. You can reach me here at the Princess.'

'The Acapulco Princess?'

'Why not? I've got your credit card.'

528

Layla sighed. 'I'll get back to you, Melon. And thanks. Thanks for everything.'

An hour after speaking with Layla, Melon had rented a word processor, a fax machine, a case of computer paper, and a printer. She called the American consulate and asked if they had anything about bullfighting in their library. 'In English!' she shouted into the phone. Then she called the *Herald* stringer in Mexico City and told him to stand by for random questions day or night. She pulled on her favorite working outfit, an oversized T-shirt with DIE YUPPIE SCUM stenciled on the front, called room service for two six-packs of Diet Coke and five one-pound bars of Toblerone chocolate, with almonds. Then she turned on the machine and began to reconstruct her memories of Sloane Taylor Bromley, a beautiful young model who found fame and pain.

Layla did not call all day Monday. Melon didn't care; she was too absorbed in her work. The fury at what she had witnessed at Vellis's villa sustained her. Layla would call when she had something to say.

It was after five o'clock Tuesday morning and Melon was just putting the finishing touches on her story when the phone rang.

'Layla?' she answered.

'I just spoke to Warner. Go ahead with the story. Do you want me to sell it up here for you? I can call the *Times*.' Layla sounded dead tired. Her voice was shaking. Clearly things were not going well.

Melon was too elated to inquire. 'Ah . . . no. No, thanks, Layla. I have a publication in mind I think everyone will be satisfied with. I'll take it from here.'

Melon grabbed a Toblerone bar and walked back to her bed, slowly peeling off the wrapper. In her heart she had always known this day would come. It might have taken her a lifetime. It didn't matter. As Matty would say,

'If you sit by the river long enough, you'll see all your enemies float by.'

She took a big bite of chocolate and let it melt against the roof of her mouth. She'd been sitting by the river long enough.

She had never forgotten how the executives at the *Los Angeles Tribune* had treated her the day she showed up with Crystal Kincaid's manuscript. She vowed that someday, somehow, she would show them she wasn't just a piece of fluff. Now – and Matty would forgive her for even thinking the phrase – she was about to make them an offer they couldn't refuse.

30

Dick Breslauer, the night managing editor of the *Los Angeles Tribune*, liked the early shift. It was quiet until around seven A.M. when the city room came alive with staff getting the afternoon edition set for press. But at 3 A.M. he and Julie, his assistant, had their little corner of the city room to themselves. She didn't mind if he smoked his beloved cigars. Later, there was no chance. If he lit up, people threw themselves around gagging and retching as if they were being gassed.

He poured himself a mug of coffee – light, no sugar – from the thermos Yvonne always put up before she went to bed and left on the kitchen table.

Just as he took his first sip, the phone rang.

'Damn,' he muttered. 'What the fuck is this?' He reached for the phone and yanked up the receiver. 'Breslauer,' he barked. 'Who zit?'

'Well, hello, big fella,' drawled a syrupy female voice. 'What are you doing working the graveyard shift?'

Oh shit, he thought, some insomniac was playing games. 'Yeah,' he responded. He'd let her say two sentences and then hang up.

'Dick? It's Melon Tuft.'

Something libidinous wiggled in the back of his brain as Melon's perky face and breasts swam into his consciousness. 'Well, I'll be damned,' he said, wiping his mouth with the back of his hand. He leaned back in his chair and put his feet up. 'How the hell are ya, gal? I've

531

been seeing your byline in the magazines. You've come a long way, baby.'

He tried to clear his mind of the image of Melon's breasts swinging in concentric circles as she bounced away those hot afternoons at the Day's Inn Motel.

'You got a minute?' she asked.

'For you? Sure.'

'I've got the whole rundown on Sloane Taylor Bromley and her bullfighter. I'm in Acapulco writing it right now. Are you familiar with the story?'

Dick Breslauer's feet crashed to the floor. 'Of course! It's a big rumor up here, but I have a feeling old man Bromley's been pulling strings to keep it under wraps. What have you got?'

She began to tell him what she had learned about the affair of a billionaire's beautiful wife and Mexico's leading matador. When she got to the part about the rape she had witnessed Sunday afternoon, the fine hairs on the back of his neck stood on end.

As Melon read him excerpts of what she had written, he looked up to see Julie sitting sleepily at her desk, raising a jelly doughnut to her mouth. He waved frantically for her to get on the extension.

When Melon got to a description of the matador's villa, he put his hand over the phone and mouthed, 'How much page-one room we got for today?'

Julie shrugged. 'Beats me. I just checked the wires. Nothing earth-shattering is going on. Yet.'

Breslauer nodded and went back to listening to Melon's description of the rape. 'Whoa, whoa, whoa, gal,' he said, interrupting her. 'This is pretty heavy stuff. You mean to tell me you've got an exclusive on this?'

'Well, shit yes, Dick!' Melon yelled.

'You want me to put a dictationist on?' He looked over at Julie, who was making a please-don't-make-me-do-it face from behind her jelly doughnut.

'No problem,' Melon said. 'I gotta fax right here. I can start moving stuff to you right this minute.'

'How much is this going to cost me?' Dick asked, bracing himself for a figure that would mean he would lose the story.

'Five hundred and it's yours,' Melon shrugged. 'But only if I get my picture over my byline. You must still have a picture of me in the personnel files. Use it.'

The editor was stunned. 'Five hundred? Melon, that's chicken feed.'

'That's okay. I'm settling a score with this one.'

'I'll pay you more if you want,' he said good-naturedly.

'Nah, that's okay,' she said. 'Five is cool. Just be sure I'm in the afternoon's edition.'

'You got it,' he said, delighted with the deal. 'We'll put a rewrite man on it as soon as one shows up.'

'You won't need to rewrite me, Dick,' Melon said. Her voice had lost its purring tone. 'You'll see.'

'Go to it, kid.' He hung up and let out a whoop that swiveled Julie's head. 'Julie!' he yelled. 'Throw Warner Bromley, Sloane Taylor Bromley, and Miguel Vellis into the computer. I want everything you get. Break up the poker game down in photo and see what kind of pictures we have.'

His assistant furiously made notes. 'Anything else?' she said.

'Yeah. As soon as someone shows up in personnel, get a picture of Melon Tuft up here. She worked here for a while. You remember.'

Julie rolled her eyes and made a face. 'Yeah. I remember. Jiggle, jiggle, click-click-click.'

'Yeah, well, she just jiggled her way into one hot scoop,' he said, easing his feet up on the desk and reaching for a cigar.

31

Aeromexico's nine A.M. flight to Mexico City sat immobile on the outer runway at JFK. The engines and air-conditioning had been turned off, and the passengers in the packed wide-body jet were beginning to get surly.

By ten-thirty, several people, trapped in their seats by the command that they keep their seat belts fastened, began to yell at the harried flight attendants, demanding to know the reason for the delay.

The rank, fetid air rang with the whining of irritable babies as mothers tried to calm them in English and Spanish.

The only seat available to Sloane at such short notice had been in the smoking section of tourist class. She was wedged between a young marine and a pregnant woman with a squirming toddler on her lap. Beads of sweat were visible on the marine's shaved head. The heavy fabric of his uniform had begun to give off a degree of funkiness that was truly memorable. The sugar doughnut Sloane had choked down at the airport coffee counter now sat like a cement ball in the pit of her stomach.

The window was smeared with the same jellylike substance that had formed a crusted ring around the little girl's mouth and coated her hands. Her mother's vain attempts to clean her up with a wadded tissue only infuriated the child.

Sloane knew if she acknowledged the baby's existence, she would be stuck entertaining her. The only thing she wanted, next to being offered a quick, painless way to kill herself, was to become invisible, to disappear.

She leaned back against the seat and closed her eyes. Her blouse was already sticking to her back and underarms. She ached all over and it felt as though her fever was coming back. The eternity of sleep she had stored up in Layla's guest room had done nothing to relieve her fatigue.

Behind her eyes she saw herself sitting in the upholstered club chair on Warner's plane, wearing white linen and pearls. One of the handsome stewards had just handed her a tall, iced glass of champagne from a silver tray. There was a strawberry floating in the frosted glass. Mozart filled the pure, cool air. She was beautiful and loved and on her way to some extraordinary place filled with flowers and servants where her every wish had been anticipated.

Her reverie was interrupted by the voices around her. Filtering through the cabin came jagged bits of information. 'Bomb scare,' someone near her said.

'They're taking the luggage off,' the woman across the aisle said, leaning out over the armrest to get a better look.

Sloane turned and looked out the window. There, lined up on the tarmac, were hundreds of pieces of luggage. Handlers drove carts from under the plane's wing carrying still more.

Sloane closed her eyes and returned to the beautiful life she had once led. She was swimming in the pool at Warner's Bermuda house. The pool was built out over the rocks, suspended in air. Down below, the azure sea lay glistening in the sun. Alabaster gulls swooped and glided above her.

Without warning, the little girl to her right threw up.

Sloane sat up in mute revulsion. Her armrest and the edge of her seat cushion were splattered. As both mother and child shrieked, Sloane looked down to see that the edge of her skirt and the side of her shoe were soiled. The smell was overwhelming, and for a moment she thought she was going to be sick herself.

Nombre de Dios, she said under her breath. *In the name of God, why am I doing this?* One call from him. One call tearing her out of her feverish sleep, telling her to come back, that he couldn't live without her – and here she was in the steaming metal tube rushing back to Mexico. For what?

Her career, her marriage, her friendships, her life, lay in shambles at her feet, and she was sitting on this putrid plane covered with sweat and vomit, her body racked with bite marks and pain, her liver screaming from too much alcohol and not enough food. And her brain! What had she done to her brain? Would she ever be able to think straight again?

She felt it coming. Trembling, she pulled a Hermès scarf from her bag and buried her face into it just as the first sob struck her body like a giant's fist. It tore up from her rib cage, squeezing her last breath out in a sound closer to a moan of pain than a sob.

'Don't be scared, lady,' the man next to her said. 'It's okay. They're putting the bags back now. See?'

He must have been pointing out the window. She couldn't see. She leaned forward and put her head on her knees, wrapping the scarf around her head to hide. She felt now as she had long ago when Noreen's emotional stranglehold would cut into her like a wire around her neck. Then, she could run to her room and bury her face into the pillows, pulling another over her head and tucking it in until the silent darkness shut out the anger, shut out the force against which she had no weapons. She would lie there for hours, hiding in plain sight from the pain and confusion, dreaming about her daddy and pretending she was running along the beach with him chasing butterflies.

Back then she had discovered, deep inside, there was a

comforting constant. Not so much an inner voice as a rock-solid peaceful place, a stillness that did not criticize or judge, a space that must have been where she kept the love she felt for herself.

Alan knew about the centre core. It was Alan who told her that having that still place deep inside was what made her so good at detaching from her unbearable surroundings.

Was the still place there now? Or had she managed to destroy it chasing the fantasy of love that met her obsessive need for beauty and danger. A love she could abandon herself to completely.

Something was terribly wrong. Maybe realizing that meant the still place was trying to tell her not to go back to Miguel.

Until that night in her hotel room in Mexico City, when Miguel had beckoned to her to come with him, her life had been on an even track. She had come to realize the Bad Girl Games were dangerous detours and had valiantly tried to stop. She *had* stopped until that night when the ultimate Bad Girl Game presented itself in the form of Miguel Vellis.

Had he loved her? Perhaps. Had he made her feel more wanted, more desirable, more beautiful than she had ever felt? Yes. *Yes.* Just thinking about it ripped at her heart. Then why was she sick to the very marrow of her bones? He had given her excitement, danger, romance, and passion beyond defining. But he had sacrificed nothing. In turn, she had given him everything she had – her beautiful life, her security, her career, and from the way she looked in Layla's bathroom mirror this morning, her looks. If she went back to him, how long would it be before she gave him the only thing she had left – her self-respect, her life.

She had seen a madness in his eyes when he beat her. He had enjoyed hurting her. How long before he would beat her to death?

Suddenly she felt the still place stir.

Don't go away with Fletcher Walker, Mary Sloane. He just wants to sleep with you, you are better than that.

Go with Fernando, Mary Sloane. You deserve the experience but be prepared for the consequences.

Go to New York, Mary Sloane, start living your own life and not Noreen's. You're never going to please her no matter what you do.

Marry Warner, Mary Sloane, he loves you. Who knows? It might work out.

Go to Mexico, Mary Sloane. Go play with your friends.

Why had the still place gone mute when she looked out across the bullring and into the black, bottomless eyes of Miguel Vellis? Perhaps it hadn't. Perhaps it had been crying out as it was now. Maybe she had just been too overcome to hear. Then.

You are better than this, Mary Sloane. Don't throw yourself away. I love you, Mary Sloane. Don't go back, Mary Sloane. He is your doom and your damnation.

Her head flew back. 'I've got to get off this plane!' she screamed.

Puzzled faces stared at her.

Immediately, a flight attendant with a concerned expression was at her side.

'It's all right, miss,' the flight attendant said, leaning forward, studying Sloane's face to see if she had a serious lunatic on her hands in a closed one-hundred-degree plane.

'I want to get off!' Sloane said, groping for her bag. Her sunglasses had fallen to the floor, and she realized people were staring at her half-mutilated face. 'Can I get off, please?' she whimpered, her eyes beseeching the harried flight attendant.

'I'm afraid not, ma'am,' she said. 'The luggage has been put back aboard. We're cleared for takeoff.'

'But you don't understand! I can't go. I can't . . .'

'I'm sorry.' The woman sounded sympathetic and, Sloane thought, grateful, now that she saw the lunatic wasn't going to incite the already seething crowd. 'It's just not possible. Are you ill?'

'Yes,' Sloane said. 'I mean . . . no. It's just that I can't leave New York. I live here. This is my home. I . . .' She saw the flight attendant shoot a look at the marine. *I'm babbling*, she thought. *They think I'm some nut case.* She leaned back in her seat. It was no use. 'I'm sorry,' she muttered.

Her words were drowned by the whine of the jets. The plane began to taxi and the flight attendant left to take a seat. The plane quickly picked up speed and the weary passengers broke into applause as the nose lifted skyward.

Sloane took a long, deep breath and held it until the plane cleared the runway, then exhaled. She was heading for Mexico City whether she liked it or not.

By the time the flight touched down in Mexico City, Sloane felt as though she had been flying for days. They had to make an unscheduled stop in Atlanta, where they sat, again, for an hour on the runway. It was nearly three in the afternoon local time when the plane was finally taxiing to the gate.

But her feelings had not abated. In fact, she had gone from being aghast at her own behavior to being angry – at Miguel for his use of her and at herself for allowing it. All her life she'd let other people tell her what to do, control her destiny for good or evil. She hated herself for never standing up for herself, but more than that hate she felt a solid determination to never let it happen again. She would start taking care of herself, and she would do a good job.

As she stepped into the terminal, her thoughts were obliterated by an explosion of light and the sound of a dozen voices calling, 'There she is! That's her!'

A wooden barrier holding back a pushing mob of people crashed to the tile floor as they poured toward her screaming, 'Ms Bromley! Miss Taylor! Sloane!'

She threw her arms over her face in a defensive gesture. Someone had turned on a blinding television light. Her dark glasses were little defence against it.

A hulking man in a baseball jacket pushed a television Minicam lens into her face. Beside him was a woman with a microphone shouting, 'Why are you back in Mexico, Sloane?' A man shoved a tape recorder at her and boomed, 'Are you going back to Miguel Vellis?' Another voice behind him called, 'Will you divorce Warner Bromley?'

Airport police tried to make a path so she could pass. It was hopeless. The crowd pushed forward until they were only inches away from her.

'I don't understand,' she said, stunned. 'What's going on? Why are you here?'

The woman with the microphone elbowed closer. 'Is it true that Miguel Vellis tried to kill you?'

'What are you saying? Where did you hear that!' Sloane said, recoiling in shock.

A man to her left shoved a fax copy of the afternoon edition of the *Los Angeles Tribune* in front of her. It was grainy and smeared but she could read it. Splashed across the width of the front page a headline roared: *Bromley Woman in Sadistic Love Tryst With Mexican Matador*. A line in smaller type below that read: *Eyewitness to Rape and Attempted Murder Tells All. Exclusive! by Tribune Special Correspondent Melon Tuft*.

A man with a tape recorder and an angry look on his face pushed forward. 'Miss Taylor, I'm Pablo Munez from *El Diario*. The wire services and CNN International are carrying a story from the *L.A. Tribune*. They are making some very serious charges concerning Señor Vellis. Are they true? Do you have any comment?'

540

Everyone pushed forward, straining to hear her response.

'I can't comment,' she said as calmly as she could. 'I haven't read this story.'

'What is your relationship with Miguel Vellis?'

'Why don't you ask him?' Sloane's words were only slightly louder than her pounding heart.

'The *Tribune* did.'

'When?' Sloane asked.

'This morning. It's at the end of the story.' The Mexican reporter folded his copy of the paper to the second page. 'Here, I'll read it. "I deny this incident ever took place. Unfortunately, someone in my profession attracts many followers and hangers-on who, in some cases, are unstable individuals."'

So there it was, she thought. That was all she had meant to him. Well, he wasn't going to get off scot-free.

She stepped back a pace or two and the mob instantly quieted. 'Excuse me!' she called. 'If you will all quiet down . . . There is something I want you to know. You won't need your notebooks, just your cameras.'

With that she put both hands to the neckline of her linen blouse and ripped it open. Buttons flew off in all directions. There was a collective gasp, accompanied by the sound of a dozen clicking, whirring cameras.

Sloane stood before them, naked from the waist up.

For a moment there was silence. Shock and revulsion seemed to hang in the air. Some of the men looked away, shamefaced. The woman reporter standing nearest to Sloane put her hand over her mouth.

Sloane removed her sunglasses to reveal her half-closed and swollen eyes and looked straight into the cameras. Somehow she found the level, clear voice she had perfected in Stella Altman's class. 'Miguel Vellis did this to my breasts,' she said. 'Miguel Vellis did this to my face. I have other injuries, but modesty prevents me from showing you those.' She held up one finger. 'This was done *after* he was caught stealing my money and jewelry.'

She stuffed her torn blouse into her bag, pulled out a large Hermès scarf, and tied it around her nakedness. 'Now, if you will excuse me. I have no further comment.'

The crowd that moments before seemed ready to lynch her for defaming their national hero now parted like a pasture of docile cows.

One man tried to follow her, shouting. 'Will you press charges?' She turned and stared him down. He held up his hands in a gesture of 'no offence' and scurried away to do whatever he planned to do with the pictures of her battered body.

She no longer cared *what* they did. No one could do anything worse to her than had already been done. No press, no man, no force, would ever treat her as badly as she had treated herself.

Head high, she walked to the nearest pay phone. She fumbled in her bag for her telephone credit card and the phone number she had always carried with her. When the line was picked up, Sloane said, 'Hello, is this the office of Dr Vincent Rollo?'

Epilogue

The *Realto* Ball was held every spring in the grand ballroom of the Plaza Hotel. Each year this gala event had a different theme. In 1988 it was planned as a black-and-white masked ball to celebrate Layla's new ownership of the magazine. Warner had given her *Realto* in gratitude for all she had done for Sloane during her long recovery. Layla was determined that the 1988 ball would be the most spectacular of them all.

Instructions were attached to invitations messengered to anyone prominently mentioned in the magazine the previous year. Guests were told to wear only black or white, and masks, the more fanciful the merrier. They would dine incognito and reveal themselves at the stroke of midnight. The competition among guests to outdo each other was stiff. Designer workshops around New York had worked feverishly for weeks to satisfy the demand.

Elegant little cocktail parties preceding the ten-o'clock dinner had been arranged. Warner was hosting his table of tycoons and their wives at his suite in the Carlyle. It was an opportunity for him to introduce them to his new assistant, Inga. Rose had retired to live with her sister in Florida, and Warner had replaced her with a long-legged blonde fresh out of the Wharton School of Economics. The week after she met Inga, Layla left for a private clinic in Brazil. She returned only days before the ball with a younger, tighter face and a handsome young plastic surgeon, both to be presented for the first time at the ball. To keep her new look a surprise she had spent the week before alone in her quarters at the top of the town house seeing to the details by phone.

Cole had planned to attend several of the predinner parties with Alan, who had done several cover celebrities' hair after his 'retirement.' In gratitude, Layla always saw that he was mentioned in her 'Letter From the Editor' column. Alan had begged for extra time to finish the work he was doing on their new apartment, saying he would meet Cole at the ball. Somehow Cole let himself get roped into escorting Melon, so he was obligated to go to the cocktail party she had put together.

He was curious to see the duplex Matty Chiga had bought her. It was over an Italian restaurant on Second Avenue. Rumor had it that Chiga had a dumbwaiter instaled to connect her kitchen to the restaurant's for round-the-clock service.

Melon was now the hostess of a talk show called *Hot!* The point of the show was that guests were invited only if they disliked a well-known person and were willing to say why on national television. Thanks to Melon's driving energy and ability to bring out the worst in people, *Hot!* had become just that.

Cole had hoped Kayzie would be at Melon's that night, but Ryan's announcement for the congressional primary rendered an appearance at a Chiga party unwise. Kayzie was looking forward to the birth of twins and hoped they would arrive in time for them all to be in the campaign photos.

Cole would have to settle for seeing her later at the ball. He missed her. When she had quit the magazine last year to plan her wedding, she left a void around the office.

Kayzie and Ryan had been married on a picture-perfect June afternoon in a little Episcopal church in her hometown. Melon, in pale apricot, had sobbed softly at Kayzie's side as her maid of honor.

Cole had not been able to go to the wedding. Alan's mother died in Los Angeles the week before, and Cole felt Alan needed him there to help settle her affairs.

Layla had gone, motoring up in the Rolls with Yitzak at the wheel. Her arrival in an electric-blue plumed D'Artagnan hat and cape caused as much of a stir as the news that she had gotten Warner to loan the newlyweds his house in Bermuda for the honeymoon.

Cole had met Kayzie at Des Artistes for a late lunch the afternoon of the ball. From there it would be just a quick walk over to the Plaza for a last-minute check of the room. Then Cole would run home to change and get to Melon's.

Kayzie had arrived, loaded with shopping bags, looking radiantly pregnant and hungry for news. She saved her questions about Sloane for last, knowing only that Layla had been in touch with her since that terrible day at the airport in Mexico City. Sloane had collapsed into a complete breakdown and gone into seclusion. Since then, Kayzie had gotten only secondhand reports from Cole.

'If it's secret, we can change the subject,' she said apologetically.

'You're family, Kayzie. I'm sure Layla would want me to fill you in,' Cole answered, waiting for his espresso to cool. 'I know it hurt when she never got in touch. She just couldn't.'

'I understand. All I care about is that she's getting better.'

'She is. After the divorce, she wouldn't take anything from Warner. The only thing she would let him do was buy out her Bromley Woman contract. Thank God the divorce was so amiable! She and Warner are friends now, you know. Anyway, so now she's in a little house in Malibu. She drives down to Palm Springs every so often for follow-up sessions at the Betty Ford Clinic. She's been able to cut her appointments with Dr Rollo back to twice a week. Her only friends are the people she met through

545

AA, and Layla, of course. The two of them speak several times a week, mostly in the middle of the night. Otherwise, Sloane spends most of her time alone, walking on the beach, reading, learning how to come to grips with her need to please people.'

Kayzie sipped the last of her wine. 'Is that what was at the bottom of all the self-destructive behavior?'

'Oh, I'm sure it's far more complicated than that. When you go into such deep therapy, you have to crawl all the way back to your beginning. As they say, the bleeding is worse closer to the heart. Apparently, she never permitted herself to grieve for her father. She told Layla she cried for two days when Dr Rollo pushed that button. Then there was the controlling mother to work through. Sloane took some of the money from the Bromley Woman contract and bought her mother a condo in Palm Springs and a new car.'

'Did she accept them?' Kayzie asked.

'Like a shot!'

'It sounds like Sloane's conquered the drinking, but what about all the sexual acting out?'

'I think the sex business was a desperate reaching out for something she could control. Everyone in her life told her what to do. She just wanted a piece of it that was all hers.'

'Did she ever go back to her acting class?'

'Just recently. She's working very hard. She told Layla just last week that she's up for a part in a new Stanley Markowitz play.'

'And the bullfighter?' asked Kayzie. 'I remember the day Melon's story broke and Layla called the ambassador to get Sloane flown back to the hospital in L.A. She worked the phones for over an hour. You know how she gets. Afterward she came into my office and said, "That bastard has fought his last bull." What in the world did she do to him?'

'He disappeared. More than that I don't know.'

'Good.' Kayzie smiled. 'He treated her so badly.'

'He did,' Cole agreed. 'Maybe a big part of Sloane's healing has been figuring out why she let him.'

As Cole walked over to the Plaza after his lunch with Kayzie, he detoured to look up at the windows of the co-op he and Alan now owned in the venerable Alwyn Court at the corner of Seventh Avenue and West Fifty-eighth Street. When he had left that morning, Alan had been hard at work on repairing the houndstooth mouldings in the dining room. When Alan's mother died last June, she left Alan a considerable sum from insurance. Alan quit the salon and agreed to do part-time work for Layla's cover photos so he could devote the rest of his time to remodeling the new apartment.

Cole stepped into the Plaza ballroom and gasped. He had only seen the decorating plans on paper. Not only had Layla's seemingly impossible scheme worked – it was spectacular.

Workmen had stretched a net over the entire ceiling of the baroque room and laboriously attached over it overlapping black and white ostrich feathers from wall to wall. Fifty round tables for ten were draped with black velvet drops to the floor, topped with a shorter white linen cloth edged in thick Belgian lace. The centerpieces were Baccarat crystal bowls, each crowded with dozens of white roses surrounded by high black tapers. The floor had been covered with a black laminate, and the walls were draped and festooned with several miles of white tulle that made the room feel as though it were suspended in a sea of cumulus clouds. The favors at each place setting were black lacquer Paloma Picasso evening bags for the women and black leather Mark Cross agenda holders for the men.

The back of each chair had been tied with a huge black blow cinched with white satin streamers. Even the wood banisters around the balcony had been wrapped in white leather. There was not another speck of color in the vast hall.

'Mind-boggling,' Cole said to a passing waiter. 'Ted Turner, eat your heart out.'

The waiter rushed away, too busy to respond.

As the Brazilian doctor was to escort Layla, she had dispatched Yitzak across town to pick up Cole at his apartment to take him to Melon's and then back across town to the ball.

As the huge old Rolls inched its way toward Melon's party, Cole checked the list of who was to be at the office table. The others would include Ryan and Kayzie, as well as Layla's trophy, the Brazilian doctor. Layla hardly ever sat down at her parties, preferring instead to flit around from table to table. This year she'd asked Cole to hold a chair for her at the staff table next to the doctor so she could check in from time to time. Then there was Dedrick Holly, the company lawyer, and his wife, Susan, a humorless seventies feminist. He would seat Alan next to her to keep her from boring everyone with her rhetoric. He had placed Caramia Dell'Aqua, who now worked full-time for the magazine as staff photographer, to Alan's right.

The crosstown traffic was dreadful, and Cole arrived at Melon's duplex later than he had planned. The apartment was jammed. As he handed his coat to a bulky individual wearing a waiter's tux, he heard Melon shouting from the living room.

'Cole! Damn it! Where have you been?' She came bearing down on him before he could get out of the hallway. She was wearing an antebellum black silk gown over a hoop skirt. The dress was very low cut with enormous puffed sleeves that ended in little fingerless fishnet mitts. 'Come,' she commanded, looping her arm through his.

He let himself be led into the living room, which had been done in early puffball. Bulging, pink balloon shades hung at the windows. Pink satin couches and club chairs stuffed the room and seemed to be slowly sinking into the long shag of the white carpeting. The most appalling touch were the matching four-foot blackamoor lamps with gold-fringed shades on either side of one of the couches. The lamps had to be a gift from Matty Chiga, Cole speculated. Even Melon's taste wasn't that outré.

Melon propelled him toward a glass-brick bar against the wall of the pink and gold dining room. 'Honey,' she said to a stocky man in a silver sharkskin suit standing at the bar, 'you remember Cole Latimer.'

'Sure. How ya doin'?' Matty said, offering a beefy hand. 'You gonna take good care of my girl tonight, aren't ya?'

'Absolutely,' Cole said, taking the glass of champagne the bartender held out to him. 'I'm sorry you're not going, Mr Chiga.'

'Can't,' Matty said. 'You know the rules. I didn't get mentioned in *Realto* this year.'

'But you went last year, didn't you, Boo-Boo?' Melon said around the meatball she had just snagged from a passing waiter's tray.

Cole remembered. Last year's dinner dance had been a costume ball, and Matty had gone as Gorbachev, wearing a regular suit and a Magic Marker red blotch smeared into his receding hairline. Cole had been amused, even though Chiga hadn't actually been mentioned in the magazine. When philanthropist Helene Bagdikian died, Layla commissioned a long article on the woman's good works. Mrs Bagdikian was described as having been a longtime resident of 'the Chiga-owned Galaxy Towers.' Kaysie had been in charge of the guest list then. How like her to put Chiga on the list to make Melon happy.

Cole looked around at the other guests. Most were

wearing elaborate headdresses. There was a bear in a tux in the corner talking to a ram with curled horns. The ram's companion wore white with a silver chain-mail helmet that left only her mouth and nose visible.

'Did you get our masks?' he asked Melon.

'Oh!' she said with a little jump. 'I almost forgot.'

She disappeared into the bedroom and returned wearing a black cat face. It had silver whiskers. 'Here's yours,' she said, handing Cole a plain black paper mask like those found at Woolworth's at Halloween. 'I figured most people won't know who you are, so you don't need anything fancy.'

'How kind,' Cole said, accepting the mask.

Yitzak inched the Rolls closer to the main entrance of the hotel. Melon and Cole gawked at the arriving guests. Each seemed to have outdone the next with the inventiveness of their headgear.

'It's really quite a clever idea,' Cole said, spotting an elephant escorting a lady in black wearing a hangman's hood. 'You really don't know who these people are. The elephant could be Douglas Fairbanks for all we know.'

'What's Layla wearing?' Melon asked, her silver whiskers twitching as she spoke.

'Big surprise. The only thing I know for sure is that she's the only one who won't be wearing a mask. Her dressmaker and two workmen arrived with a great bulky garment bag and several boxes as I was leaving the office.'

'Have you seen her since she got back from Brazil?'

'Uh-uh,' he said, shaking his head. 'No one has except Nina, and she was sworn to secrecy.' He put on his mask and turned to face Melon. 'How do I look?'

'Like the famous Cole Latimer wearing a mask,' she snickered.

Yitzak finally found room at the curb. He moved around the car to help them as Melon temporarily disappeared in a sea of fabric. Her hoop skirt did not accommodate being seated too well. After some struggle, Ytizak managed to extricate her and help her to the curb.

They joined the crush of other guests moving slowly through the lobby toward the ballroom. As they approached the double doors, Cole spotted a head arrangement so remarkable he wanted to get a good look at it, but to do so he had to stand on tiptoe to clear the feathers of the headdress on the woman in front of him.

'Oh, my God,' he said, clutching Melon's arm. 'You are not going to believe this!'

Melon pushed past a man wearing a mask and a burnoose. 'Cole! It's Layla!'

Layla stood just inside the ballroom doors greeting her guests, a living reincarnation of Marie Antoinette. Her gown was white damask. The bodice fit tightly and was laced to expose a great deal of cleavage. The skirt was, if possible, more voluminous than Melon's and covered with what appeared to be a ton of seed pearls worked into a lattice design. But it was her head that was causing such a commotion. She wore a shimmering white wig four feet high. Into the mass of curls had been imbedded little silver objects: birds, small animals, bells, hearts, and musical instruments. Sitting high atop the gigantic confection perched a replica of a two-masted brigantine with all sails flying. Tiny sailors wearing black-and-white-striped T-shirts stood at attention through the rigging. Whatever magic her Dr Dominici had performed in Brazil had whisked ten years from her face.

When they reached Layla, all Cole could say was, 'To die, darling,' and shake his head in wonderment.

'Thank you Cole, dear,' she said, offering an air kiss. 'Isn't this all too grand for words? Hello, Melon, how cute you look!'

'Layla, you look spectacular,' Melon said, intently studying Layla's face.

'Yes, nose, chin, neck, and slight implants in the

cheeks, darling. You can stuff your eyes back in your pussy . . . cat, now,' said Layla. She was looking over Melon's shoulder to see who was next in line. She turned back to Melon. 'You could do me a great favour. My friend Eduardo Dominici is already at the table. Would you take care of him for me? I don't know when I'll get there.'

'Sure,' Melon said, moving away. 'Does he speak English?'

Layla didn't answer. She was already receiving compliments from a harlequin and a sphinx.

'Damn, she looks great!' Melon said as they elbowed their way to the table. 'I wonder if it's the plastic or the surgeon.'

'Probably both,' Cole said.

Melon didn't hear him. She had spotted Kayzie sitting at their table 'Kaaaay-zeeeee!' she squealed.

Kayzie threw both arms straight up in the air as Melon flung herself at her. After a vigorous hug, Melon stepped back and examined Kayzie's stomach. 'You look great! What a perfect dress!'

Kayzie rested her palms on her stomach. 'It used to be the curtain at the Broadhurst Theater,' she said, laughing.

'Oooooh!' Melon cooed, wiggling her fingers at the bulge in Kayzie's black brocade tent. 'Babies! I can't wait.'

'Me, neither,' Kayzie said, rolling her eyes.

Melon turned to Ryan, who was standing beside Kayzie. 'Hiya, handsome.' She grinned.

'What's new pussycat?' Ryan said, tweaking her whiskers. 'Loved the show last week. When are you going to have me on? I do card tricks and the deficit.'

'Well, you know the deal, Ryan,' Melon said, slapping at her skirt so she could sit down. 'You've got to dish some important person. You're running for Congress. There must be someone you can't stand.'

'My opponent?' Ryan asked, helping Kayzie into her chair.

Cole introduced himself to Layla's doctor. He was tall and distinguished looking with a beautiful smile and a firm handshake. Behind his mask, his dark eyes danced with amusement at the scene.

'I just saw Layla,' Cole said, signaling a waiter for drinks. 'That wig is extraordinary. How did you manage to get her here?'

'I had to hire a horse and carriage from the park,' the doctor answered with a laugh.

'Inspired,' Cole said. He glanced out onto the dance floor. Layla and Warner had just stepped out to dance.

'How's she going to dance with forty blocks of Cleveland on her head?' Melon asked no one in particular.

They all turned to watch as Layla and Warner waltzed sedately around the floor to gathering applause.

The Hollys, Alan, and Caramia arrived simultaneously with the first course (vichyssoise with black truffles). Susan Holly wore a black-and-white checkerboard affair and dark Gloria Steinem aviator glasses. Her husband's mask appeared to be from the same source as Cole's.

Caramia excused herself and disappeared to take pictures for the next issue of the magazine.

'How can you see?' Melon asked, squinting across the table at Alan. His mask was a white satin bandeau onto which he had painted huge Carol Channing eyes.

'There are little pinholes where the pupils are,' he answered. 'It's great. You càn stare all you want and people don't even know it. I got a real close-up look at Warner's Ice Princess over at the tycoon table. Yi! Yi! Yi! I can see why Layla went roaring off to Brazil.'

'Keep it down,' Cole muttered behind his hand. Then he pointedly raised his voice and said, 'Alan, I'd like you to meet Layla's *doctor*, Eduardo Dominici. Dr Dominici is from *Brazil*. Doctor, this is Layla's former hairstylist, Alan Wade.'

The handsome doctor rose again, greeted Alan

warmly, and returned to his conversation with Ryan and Kayzie.

Cole reached over and snipped a fleck of plaster from the sleeve of Alan's tuxedo. 'Thanks for coming,' he whispered. 'Your mask is a scream.'

'So is the dining room moulding,' Alan said sarcastically. 'It looks like flung spaghetti. I should have stayed and finished it before it all dries.'

'I know, I know' — Cole nodded — 'but Layla said it was important that you be here.'

Alan rolled his eyes and turned to Susan Holly, 'Susan, how marvelous you look,' he said, beaming. 'Black and white are *your* colours!'

Cole moved back to his seat smiling to himself. Putting Alan next to Susan was the perfect solution.

As dinner progressed (black pasta with baby veal and white asparagus), Cole danced a trundling rumba with Kayzie, which ended in them both leaving the floor in hysterics over their efforts to look graceful.

As designated host, Cole was obliged to dance with Susan Holly. Thankfully, Melon was absorbed in an intense interrogation of Dr Dominici in which she repeatedly lifted her mask and pulled at the skin around her eyes.

The doctor was liberated from Melon's grilling when Layla slipped into the seat next to him. She squeezed his arm and apologized.

The band struck up 'Bad, Bad Leroy Brown' and Melon leapt from her chair. 'Come on, Cole. I love this song!' she said, grabbing his hand.

'Probably the line about the junkyard dog,' Alan said as Cole brushed past.

Cole knew from last year's ball that dancing with Melon meant merely moving in place while she flung herself wildly around the floor, often in time to the music.

It was close to midnight by the time Cole got a chance to dance with Layla. As the band played 'Someday My

Prince Will Come,' he located her standing in a circle beside Dustin Hoffman's table. 'They are playing my song,' he said, taking her hand and leading her toward the floor.

She moved into his arms, in perfect step. 'Ah, but your prince *has* come,' she said into his right ear.

'As has yours, apparently,' Cole said. 'He's awfully attractive.'

'Umm,' Layla hummed. 'Some people come back from the Amazon with human heads.'

Cole pulled back to look at her. 'Leave it to you to bring back the rest of the body.'

'That's the best part.' She grinned lasciviously.

The music stopped in midwaltz. The band blared a fanfare.

'It's midnight,' the bandleader shouted into the microphone. 'Remove your masks and reveal yourselves!'

There followed a hubbub and shrieks of recognition as people saw celebrities all around them. Cole didn't even see Layla leaving the floor. Nodding to George Plimpton, carrying an elephant's head on his arm, Cole wove his way back to the table.

Just as he was sitting down, the houselights dimmed to near darkness. A baby spotlight pierced the feathered ceiling. It swept around the room to rest on Layla, standing behind the bandleader's microphone. The music died and the room fell silent as all heads turned toward her.

'Ladies and gentlemen,' she began in a strong, firm voice. 'Now that we all know who we are, I want to introduce you to my guest of honor for this year's ball.'

'Guest of honor?' Melon asked Cole.

Cole shrugged. 'I'm as bewildered as you are. We've never had a guest of honor.'

'Sh!' Kayzie hissed across the table.

'As you know,' Layla continued, 'you are all here because you have reached the pinnacle of success, a mention in *Realto* magazine. My special guest tonight

555

has not only been mentioned but has appeared on the cover. Granted it was more than a year ago, but I make the rules. Right?'

Everyone laughed.

Melon leaned close to Cole. 'You don't suppose she got some big star, do you?' she asked. 'Layla's supposed to be the star. What's the point?'

The spotlight left Layla's face and moved across the room toward the ballroom entrance. Sweeping through the door was a startlingly beautiful woman in a brilliant scarlet taffeta gown. Her dark hair was swept high and studded with sparkling jewels.

'May I present,' Layla intoned, 'a most courageous lady, soon to make her Broadway debut in Stanley Markowitz's new drama. Dear friends, please welcome Miss Sloane Taylor.'

Everyone was on their feet. Sloane's walk into the room was quickly slowed as she was surrounded by admirers.

'God! This is so neat!' Kayzie said, joining in the thundering applause.

'I *love* it!' said Alan, jumping up and applauding furiously. 'God, it's good to see her.'

'Shit!' said Melon, who remained in her chair.

'What's the matter?' asked Holly.

'How come *she* gets to wear *red*,' Melon said, jabbing her spoon into her second helping of dessert (white chocolate mousse with black-cherry brandy sauce).

Cole could not speak right away. Not until the lump in his throat cleared. He watched as Sloane slowly made her way toward their table. She had never looked more beautiful. There was a new composure to her face, an assurance to the set of her shoulders that she had never had before. She made it, he thought to himself.

Kayzie looked over her shoulder at Alan. Their eyes caught and held. Kayzie nodded and smiled; they both had tears in their eyes.

Cole swallowed hard, seeing Kayzie's and Alan's reactions to the return of their dearest friend.

From the corner of his eye he saw the head of Orion Pictures excuse himself from his wife and guests at the next table. He straightened his tie and sucked in his stomach as he headed toward Sloane.

As he introduced himself and offered her his hand, the band struck up 'Isn't She Lovely'. Sloane nodded and excused herself from the group around her. She effortlessly slipped into his arm and whirled out onto the dance floor to more applause.

She was the only spot of color in the room.

Cole was still watching when Layla leaned over his shoulder.

'Cole, dear,' she said softly. 'If you'll excuse us, I want to take Eduardo over to meet Warner and his guests.'

'You devil,' Cole said, kissing her cheek.

'You angel,' she said, her eyes circling the eclectic mix of guests Cole was entertaining, then slipped away with her handsome surgeon.

Melon, still pouting, leaned over to Cole and said in a stage whisper, 'Isn't that a bit much, parading him around like that?'

'Wouldn't you?' Cole grinned.

Melon ignored him. Her attention was riveted on the dance floor. Sloane had stopped dancing and was now deep in conversation with the movie mogul.

'Look at her!' Melon said, clutching Cole's arm. 'You wanna bet she's cutting a deal for herself this very minute?'

'Life goes on, Melon, darling,' Cole said, gently removing her fingers so he could reach a fresh bottle of champagne. 'Life goes on.'

Bestselling General Fiction